LYING WITH STRANGERS

OTHER FIVE STAR BOOKS BY JONNIE JACOBS

Paradise Falls

LYING WITH STRANGERS

JONNIE JACOBS

FIVE STAR
A part of Gale, Cengage Learning

GALE
CENGAGE Learning®

Detroit • New York • San Francisco • New Haven, Conn • Waterville, Maine • London

GALE
CENGAGE Learning

Copyright © 2013 by Jonnie Jacobs.
Five Star™ Publishing, a part of Gale, Cengage Learning.

LIBRARY OF CONGRESS CATALOGING-IN-PUBLICATION DATA

Jacobs, Jonnie.
   Lying with strangers / Jonnie Jacobs. — First Edition.
      pages cm
   ISBN-13: 978-1-4328-2731-1 (hardcover)
   ISBN-10: 1-4328-2731-6 (hardcover)
   1. Robbery—Fiction. 2. Accomplices—Fiction. 3. Accidents—Fiction. I. Title.
   PS3560.A2543L95 2013
   813'.54—dc23   2013021223

Find us on Facebook– https://www.facebook.com/FiveStarCengage
Visit our website– http://www.gale.cengage.com/fivestar/
Contact Five Star™ Publishing at FiveStar@cengage.com

Printed in Mexico
2 3 4 5 6 7 17 16 15 14

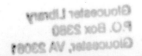

LYING WITH STRANGERS

CHAPTER 1

Chloe closed her eyes and swayed to the beat of the music blasting from the car's stereo. It was louder than she liked, but every time she turned the volume down, Trace turned it up again, higher than before. It was his car, he said, and he paid for the gas, so she didn't have any right to complain. Chloe wasn't in a complaining mood anyway. For the first time in her life—well, in a really long time—she felt almost happy.

The late September sun beat through the old Camaro's windows and warmed her skin. She stretched her legs out in front of her and tried to pretend she was at the beach, at a warm beach somewhere nice, like Hawaii or Tahiti. The only beach Chloe had ever been to was Ocean Beach in San Francisco and it was almost never warm there, even when the sun was out. Chloe's dream—one of her many dreams—was to someday lie in the sun on a tropical beach. White sand, blue water, gentle breezes, and maybe one of those fancy drinks they served with a teensy umbrella. Chloe went to movies and she read books. She knew there was a whole world out there waiting for her if her luck ever changed.

Trace slammed on the brakes and hit the horn. "Asshole," he screamed as he swerved around the car in front of him and gave the driver the finger.

Chloe gripped the armrest. "Slow down."

"Are you driving?" Trace shot back. He sped up.

"Please, Trace."

" 'Please, Trace,' " he mimicked. "Pretty please with sugar on top."

"For the baby." Chloe put her hand on her abdomen. There was a small rounded mound there that pleased her. Finally, she was beginning to show.

"Hell, he's gonna take after his old man and love going fast." But Trace slowed to a mere seventy-five.

"She," Chloe whispered under her breath. If the fates were listening, she wanted to keep the odds even, maybe even tilt them in favor of a girl.

Chloe closed her eyes again, but she'd left the beach behind. Just as well. No point wishing for what she'd never have. And she couldn't really complain. She'd been scared to death to tell Trace she was pregnant. She knew he wouldn't be happy about it, and he hadn't been, but at least he hadn't asked her to get rid of it. Well, once or twice, but only when he'd been drinking or was angry with her. And now he sometimes seemed almost tickled about having a kid. Chloe wasn't sure Trace had any idea what having a baby was actually like, but he sure liked to boast about it with his buddies. It made him feel like a man.

Not that Chloe knew any more about babies than Trace did. But one of her other dreams was of having a family of her own. A real family, not like the one she'd grown up in. A normal family with a normal life. And here she was now, expecting her own, sweet little girl. Okay, maybe it would be a boy. But they'd have a girl next.

Trace slowed further and pulled off the freeway.

"What are you doing?" Chloe asked, suddenly wrenched from the serenity of her dreams. They were nowhere near their apartment. They hadn't even crossed the bridge into Oakland.

"What I'm doing is driving the fucking car."

"I meant why are we getting off here? This isn't the right exit." It wasn't even a good part of town. Chloe could tell by

8

looking. A lot of the storefronts were boarded up and the rest had iron bars across the windows. The street reminded her of some of the pictures she'd seen from the Iraq war.

"We're just going to be a minute, okay? So shut up and sit tight."

"What's going on?"

Trace's muscled arms tensed as he gripped the wheel. Then he looked over at her and patted her knee. "Everything's cool."

He pulled into the QuickStop lot and parked. The storefront was covered in graffiti and the grimy windows were plastered with faded advertisements for booze and cigarettes.

"Don't go anywhere," he joked, getting out of the car.

As if, Chloe thought. Where would she go? She might have her dreams, but her realities were pretty limited.

A dark-haired man with a green gym bag slung over his shoulder came out of the store. He gave her a friendly nod, then got into the only other car in the lot, a shiny new Lexus. It seemed like an odd place for someone who could afford a Lexus to shop, but Chloe knew if she put her mind to it, she could come up with plenty of reasons why he might. If Trace was here they might have started a game of "Maybe." Maybe he needed cigarettes, or a soft drink. Maybe he was the landlord. Maybe he was scouting out locations for a movie. The explanations usually got so preposterous that Chloe would wind up with the giggles. Without Trace, the game wasn't the same.

She closed her eyes but the magic dreaminess was gone. The building blocked the sun, and besides, she felt uncomfortable sitting in a car alone in this neighborhood. It wasn't like their own block was so great, but it was a whole lot better than this.

Chloe was thirsty anyway. She grabbed her purse and headed into the store. The man in the Lexus was sitting in his car, looking at a map spread out against his steering wheel. He had to have been really lost to end up in this part of town.

The door triggered a little bell that jangled as she entered. Both Trace and the clerk jumped and turned toward her.

Trace glared. "I told you to stay in the car."

He hadn't, not really, but Chloe wasn't about to argue. "I'm thirsty." She spotted the refrigerator case across the store. "I'm going to get a soda."

"Get the hell out of here, Chloe."

She turned. She hadn't seen the gun in Trace's hand until now. Her body went cold. She hadn't even known he owned a gun.

"Go on," he ordered. "Get out."

She felt suddenly lightheaded and shaky. Her chest was pounding. Slowly, she began to back away.

Just then the door chime jangled again. The man Chloe had seen getting into the Lexus moments earlier entered the store, his gym bag still slung over his shoulder. Trace spun around just as the man reached to remove his sunglasses.

"Say, I can't find—"

The man's words were cut short by a sharp crack from Trace's gun. It wasn't a loud sound. In fact it took Chloe several seconds to figure out what had happened. The man, too, looked puzzled. Then he grabbed his chest and sank slowly to the floor. Blood pooled next to him, spreading in odd directions like a child's painting.

Chloe choked back a scream. "Oh God, you shot him!"

"It's his own fault." Trace was breathing hard. "He shouldn't have come back in."

"Oh my God, my God." Chloe's heart was beating so fast she thought it might fly right out of her chest.

"Hey, man," the clerk said in a tight, warbly voice. "That wasn't part of the plan."

Trace snapped, "You think I fucking don't know that?"

The clerk, a slender, young Hispanic guy, shook his head and fists. "I don't want no part—"

Trace raised the arm with the gun and pointed it at the clerk.

This time Chloe did scream. Trace glanced in her direction. "Shut up."

From somewhere under the counter, the clerk had found a gun of his own. It was in his hand before Chloe could see how it got there.

She screamed again, a shrill gasp of terror that was drowned out by more shots. The clerk's body fell forward over the counter, then slowly slid down onto the floor. It landed with a muffled thump.

Trace held his shoulder, his face drained of color.

"Get the man's wallet," he ordered between clenched teeth. "I'm going to clean out the cash register."

The clerk groaned and Trace went behind the counter and shot him again. Two sharp cracks that made Chloe's ears ring.

She circled her arms across her chest. Nausea rose in her throat. Slowly, she approached the man on the floor.

"Hurry up," Trace said. "We haven't got all day." Blood was beginning to seep through the fingers holding his injured shoulder.

Chloe took one more step toward the man. She swallowed hard, wiped her nose with the back of her hand. She couldn't do it. She couldn't step into that pool of blood and she couldn't reach her hand into the man's pocket. She just couldn't.

And then she saw one of his eyelids flutter.

The man was alive. Oh, God, what now?

Chloe knew if she told Trace he'd shoot the man again like he had the clerk. And she knew she should tell him. If the man lived, he might be able to identify them. But she couldn't do it. That would be as bad as pulling the trigger herself.

"Fucking cash register's locked," Trace yelled, pounding it with the butt of his gun. "Come on, get the guy's wallet and let's get out of here."

Half closing her eyes, the way she did when she watched a scary movie, Chloe stepped toward the man's body and grabbed his gym bag.

"I can't find a wallet, but I've got his gym bag. Let's go."

Chloe held the door for Trace and they raced to the car. He tossed her the keys. "You drive."

Chloe dumped the canvas bag into the back seat and started the engine. She was shaking so badly she didn't think she'd be able to steer in a straight line. Gripping the wheel, she pulled slowly out of the parking lot.

"Speed it up, Chloe. We got to get out of here."

She didn't drive much. Trace had taught her how but he hardly ever let her use the car. She pressed down on the accelerator, and the car lurched forward.

"You need a hospital," Chloe said, fighting a rising tide of anxiety that made it difficult to think. "I don't know where the closest one is."

"Yeah, right, hospital and then straight to jail. No fucking way."

She took her eyes off the road long enough to look over at Trace. He was leaning back in the seat, his eyes closed tight and his mouth clenched. The hand holding his left shoulder was now drenched in blood. It ran in rivulets down his shirt and onto his pants.

"Trace, please. You're hurt."

"Yeah, Sherlock, I'm aware of that. Just shut up and drive."

"To where?"

"Home, where else? You were maybe thinking an afternoon at the mall?"

"You don't have to be mean."

"My shoulder burns like hell, Chloe. I don't feel like making nice."

She bit her lip. Tears clouded her sight. Trace couldn't die. *Please don't let him die,* she prayed. Without Trace, she'd be all alone.

"Maybe a doctor," she suggested. "There's a clinic near—"

"Shut up, Chloe. You've caused enough trouble already."

"Me? What did I do?"

"I told you to stay in the fucking car!"

He hadn't. Not really. And she couldn't see that her being in the car would have made any difference. But she didn't argue.

She slid her arms from the new, peach-colored cardigan she wore and handed it to Trace. "Here, press this against your shoulder. We need to stop the bleeding."

And then she concentrated on driving them home.

CHAPTER 2

Diana Walker paced the perimeter of her desk. She rolled her shoulders, stretched, and took a deep breath. She wasn't used to feeling angry, especially at Roy. But he'd been wrong this morning, and it had been bothering her all day that she hadn't succeeded in making him understand that.

He was a good father, really. Truly devoted to Jeremy. But lately, he'd been so . . . so *off*. And Diana didn't know why.

When Roy came back home this evening, she'd try again. She'd probably been too quick to criticize, too sharp with her choice of words. Roy was a reasonable man, but even reasonable men bristled when they felt attacked.

That settled, Diana sat back down at the desk and again turned her attention to the computer screen. A simple twice-a-week column for the local paper. Nothing heavy or profound, just personal ramblings on a variety of life's lighter issues. How hard could it be?

Always harder than she thought.

The ideas and words that rolled so freely through her mind when she was busy with other things faded like skywriting in the wind once she sat down at the computer. Today, she was having a particularly difficult time.

She'd started with the intention of writing about friction in marriage but found herself veering off to the argument she'd had with Roy that morning—the incident which had given rise to the idea for the column. She was irritated that Roy had chosen golf over an afternoon with his son, and further annoyed by the fact that he couldn't understand why she was upset. The tone of what she'd written was wrong, though, and the slant much too personal.

Diana read the two short paragraphs over once again, then scooted her chair closer to the keyboard and hit delete. She took a breath and started fresh. A column on the marital balancing act could wait for another day.

Food shopping, she wrote instead, *is no feat for the timid. Variety may be the spice of life, but it can be a real stumbling block in the grocery aisle. Gone are the days of simple choices—Shredded Wheat or Cheerios? Tide or Cheer? White or wheat? Today there are enough combinations and permutations to make my head spin. I can't even buy canned tomatoes without digging my reading glasses out of my purse, where they've invariably found their way to the bottom.*

Yuck. Diana hit delete again and closed out of her word-processing program. Roy would be home soon, and she needed to start dinner. Maybe she'd find inspiration over a pot of pasta sauce.

She stood and wandered to the window overlooking the yard. Jeremy and Digger were playing a rough-and-tumble game of fetch. She wasn't sure which was harder on her garden, the seven-year-old boy or the terrier-mix puppy Roy had insisted on buying Jeremy for his last birthday. She cringed when her eye caught the clump of newly trampled salvia.

This was a phase, she reminded herself, a short segment of her life, and she'd been down this road before. A similar road, at any rate. She'd raised Emily alone for over half of her daughter's eighteen years. A time marked by financial constraints and struggle. And seemingly endless battles. Money was no longer an issue, not a day-to-day issue anyway, but her relationship with Emily was as prickly as ever. At least now that Emily was off to college and living six hundred miles to the south in

San Diego, her insults weren't thrown into Diana's face quite as often.

Diana looked around the comfortably furnished family room and then again out into the garden, which despite the assaults of boy and dog still shimmered with the vibrant colors of late summer. Eight years into her second marriage, Diana considered herself very lucky.

Not that Roy was always easy to live with. A person didn't advance in the district attorney's office the way Roy had by being accommodating. Still, she'd been surprised by the harshness in his tone this morning.

Jeremy tossed a ball that sent Digger scurrying into the impatiens. Then Jeremy raced for the house, throwing open the French doors with a *thunk*.

"I have to go to the bathroom," he exclaimed, tracking mud across the carpet.

"Take your shoes off first."

"I can't. I really need to go."

Diana sucked in a breath, equally amused and exasperated. She'd noticed this about herself lately. She seemed to be of two minds about a lot of things, like she was two different people occupying the same space.

The phone rang, She hoped it would be Emily but knew it wasn't. Calls from her daughter were as rare as summer snow.

"Mrs. Walker?"

"Yes." She waited impatiently for the anonymous "How are you today?" which seemed to be the greeting favored by telemarketers.

She was on the verge of hanging up when the caller said, "Roy Walker is your husband?"

"Yes." Diana's skin prickled. A reporter? Someone with a beef against the DA's office? The man didn't sound like he was selling anything.

"I'm Inspector Knowles from the San Francisco Police Department. I'm afraid I have some bad news about your husband."

Diana's vision dimmed, as though a cloud had passed over the sun. "Bad news?"

"He's been wounded," the detective explained. "A gunshot. He was taken to San Francisco General. He's alive but I'm afraid his condition is critical."

"What? What are you talking about?" Diana was having trouble processing what the man was saying. Why would they take Roy all the way to San Francisco? And how could he have been shot while playing golf?

"There must be some mistake," Diana said. "Roy is golfing in Oakland."

"No mistake, I'm afraid."

"But that makes no sense."

"I don't want to be rude, ma'am, but I think you should get here as soon as possible."

After a frantic, garbled call to her friend Allison Miller, Diana hustled Jeremy into the car.

"Daddy's had a little accident, honey, and I have to go check on him. You're going to stay with Allison for a bit, okay?"

"Is Daddy hurt?"

"That's what I need to find out." She worried she would need to reassure him, but Jeremy stayed with Allison often enough that he seemed to take it in stride.

Five minutes later, Diana was on her way to the city. She pushed the speed limit, which was something she rarely did. Thank goodness the traffic wasn't heavy. Sometimes the Bay Bridge was worse on weekends than on commute days. She tried not to think of anything but her driving. Tried to shut out the frightening visions that played in her mind. She worked on breathing and driving and saying *Please God* as a mantra.

And then she was in the lobby of the hospital and she was suddenly, horribly afraid.

Inspector Knowles was waiting for her. He was a tall, thin man with a face that looked as though it hadn't cracked a smile in years.

"Where's Roy?" Diana asked. She realized she sounded every bit as frantic as she felt. "I need to see him."

"In a minute. I've got a few questions first."

"Can't they wait?"

"Not really."

Diana glanced toward the elevators. Knowles didn't have the right to stop her. The hospital was a public building.

Except Diana had no idea where to go. And she had questions of her own. Maybe more questions than Knowles.

"He's in intensive care," the detective said. "His condition is critical but stable. One of our officers is standing guard." Maybe his mouth hadn't smiled in years, but his eyes were kind.

Diana let herself be led to a cluster of chairs at one side of the lobby. She hadn't taken time to comb her hair or apply lipstick, and she was still dressed in her Sunday sweats. She probably looked more like a bag lady than the wife of an assistant DA.

"Tell me what happened," she said, trying for a calm she didn't feel. "Who shot him? How did it happen?"

"We don't know who shot him. It appears he walked in on an armed robbery at a convenience store in the Bayview district."

"Bayview?" One of San Francisco's high-crime neighborhoods. "What was he doing there?"

"That's what we'd like to know."

"It doesn't make sense." Diana felt a new sense of urgency. Nothing this detective was telling her made any sense at all.

"When I called you earlier, you said your husband was playing golf."

She nodded. "Please, can't we do this later? I need to see my husband."

"The sooner we get some answers—"

"I don't *have* any answers," Diana said tearfully. "Please, let me see him."

Knowles ran a hand along his jaw. "Fine. Follow me."

They rode the elevator to the fourth floor in silence. All the while Diana was surrounded by a sense of the surreal. This couldn't really be happening. It had to be a bad dream. She just needed to hold on until she woke up.

But after they'd entered the wide double doors of the ICU and signed in at the nurse's station, and Diana finally saw her husband, she knew she wasn't dreaming.

Roy was a healthy, athletic man. A vibrant man. Yet here he was, still as a corpse. Lying in the narrow hospital bed with tubes and drips and beeping monitors, he looked frail and old. And half his normal size.

"I'll wait for you in the hallway," Knowles said quietly.

Diana stepped closer. A nurse was adjusting the flow of the IV into Roy's arm.

"How is he?" Diana asked.

"Hanging on."

The answer was hardly reassuring. "Is he going to be okay?"

"You'll have to ask the doctor." The nurse checked the flickering graph lines on the machine to Roy's right and wrote something on his chart. "I'll leave you alone for a few minutes."

"Alone" was a relative term in an ICU with twenty or so beds and almost as many nurses. Although no one was looking her way, Diana felt self-conscious when her eyes teared up. She brushed the tears away and touched Roy's arm above where the IV went into his vein.

"Hi, honey," she whispered.

Nothing, not even a change in the pattern of bleeps recorded by the bedside monitor.

"Oh, Roy. What happened?" Diana swallowed hard and took a deep breath. "I need you to be okay. You have to stay strong. You have to get better. You'll do that, won't you?"

She leaned over the bed and touched her lips to Roy's cool forehead, the only area of skin free of wires and tubes. "I love you, Roy. You're going to be fine, you hear me? Jeremy and I are counting on you."

The nurse reappeared. "Visits in the ICU are limited to a few minutes. I'm sorry."

"Yes, I understand."

"There's a family lounge down the hall, but it's a far cry from home. My advice is to make sure the front desk nurse has your contact numbers, then get some rest. You'll need it in the days ahead."

Inspector Knowles waited for her outside the ICU.

"I know you're upset," he said. "But I really need to ask you a few more questions. It's important to get some answers if we're going to catch whoever did this."

Diana pulled a tissue from her purse and blew her nose. "I don't think I know anything that can help you."

"You told me your husband was playing golf," Knowles said.

"That's what he told me, but he obviously wasn't, was he?" The inspector probably thought she was some pathetic, clueless housewife whose husband strung her along with lies. Maybe she was.

"What time was his game?" Knowles asked.

"He didn't have a scheduled tee time. He sometimes goes out to the club and either practices at the driving range or gets picked up as part of a foursome. He left the house about noon."

"And told you he was going to be playing in Oakland?"

"Yes. Redwood Heights Country Club in the Oakland hills. He has a membership there."

"So you have no idea what he was doing in San Francisco?"

"No idea whatsoever." And that troubled Diana more than she wanted to admit.

"Your husband's an Alameda County DA, right? Maybe his trip to San Francisco had something to do with his job?"

"If it was work related, he'd have told me. There was no need to lie about it."

Diana had worked in the DA's office at one time. Administrative assistant, a fancy word for secretary, but she was no stranger to the kind of work Roy did.

She gripped the wadded-up tissue in her fist. "Was anyone else hurt in the holdup?"

"The store clerk. He died at the scene."

Diana pressed her knuckles to her mouth. This was the sort of thing you read about in the paper. It didn't happen to people like her and Roy.

"If anything comes to you," Knowles said, handing her his card, "be sure to get in touch. That's got my direct line as well as my cell. You can get word to me any time."

Diana remained at the hospital for another hour. She found the doctor on duty. He explained that while they'd stabilized Roy's vital signs and stopped the bleeding, it was still too risky to go after the bullet. There was, he told her, quite a bit of internal damage.

"What does that mean?" she asked. "Is he going to get better?"

"I wish I had an answer for you, but I don't." The doctor looked down at his feet when he spoke, then raised his eyes to hers. "I'm sorry."

She returned to the ICU twice. Each time she was granted a short couple of minutes with her husband, who seemed less like the man she knew with each visit. He remained expressionless and unresponsive. Finally, Diana realized the nurse had been right. There was nothing she could do by staying there.

Nothing but pray and cry. She did plenty of both on the long drive home.

Chapter 3

It was close to ten when Diana pulled up in front of Allison Miller's compact, split-level home in the Oakland hills. She'd first met Allison when Emily and Allison's daughter, Becca, had become best friends in second grade. Their daughters' friendship had faded over the years, but Diana's and Allison's had grown deeper. Allison was not only Diana's best friend, she was her only real friend. The kind you could speak your heart to and know your confidences wouldn't be betrayed, or thrown back in your face at some later date.

Allison's fiancé, Len Phillips, answered the door when she rang. "How's Roy? Is he okay?"

"No, he's not okay. I mean, he's alive, but . . ." Diana's voice caught.

Len put an arm around her shoulder. "I'm so sorry."

Although he was a bit soft around the middle and the jowls, Len had the kind of sandy-haired good looks many women were attracted to. He'd moved in with Allison late last spring, after four months of dating, which Diana thought was way too soon. But Allison said she was tired of being alone, and besides, hadn't Diana done pretty much the same thing? In fact, Diana had known Roy for seven months before getting married, but Allison said she was splitting hairs.

Len worked for himself—something to do with property management that Diana never could quite understand. He was outgoing and amiable, if sometimes a bit too brash for her liking. Len was different in temperament and style from Roy, who tended to be more reserved and pensive. In fact, the two of them had taken an almost instant dislike to one another, an antipathy neither Allison nor Diana could understand. The men gamely made a show of putting feelings aside for the sake of the women, but the tension when they were all four together was palpable enough that those occasions were few and far between.

Allison came into the hallway and gave Diana a warm hug. "How is he? How are you?" She pulled Diana into the den. "Have you eaten? Do you want a drink?"

"Thanks but no. I just came to pick up Jeremy. How did he do?"

"A little subdued, but basically he did fine. He's upstairs now, asleep." Allison took a seat next to Len on their honey-colored leather sofa. "So tell us. What in the world happened?"

"Roy was shot," Diana said, dropping into the matching leather armchair.

"Shot?" Allison's eyes widened. "Oh, my God."

The color drained from Len's face. "How could he be shot?"

"He's in intensive care," Diana said, "connected to more monitors and medical stuff than I've ever seen." Her voice broke and she took a breath before continuing. "He's unconscious. He didn't respond at all to my being there."

Allison sucked in a breath. "How awful."

"What happened?" Len asked.

"He apparently walked in on an armed robbery at a convenience store in the Bayview district of San Francisco." Diana started crying in earnest. She'd kept it together most of the evening, but now it was all too much.

Allison reached over and squeezed Diana's hand. "I'm so sorry."

"What was he doing there?" Diana lamented. "He told me he was going to play golf. He lied to me."

"I'm sure there's a reason."

"Well, it can't have been another woman," Len said with a stab at levity. "Not in that part of town."

Allison shot him a nasty look.

"Hey," Len said, holding up his hands, "I was only trying to be helpful."

Allison turned her attention back to Diana. "Do they have any suspects? Any leads?"

"No. And the detective didn't sound particularly optimistic about it, either."

"Oh, Diana. I am so sorry. Something is bound to break. They'll find whoever did this. You shouldn't worry about that now. Roy needs all your attention."

Diana pulled a tissue from her purse and blew her nose. "You sure Jeremy was okay? He wasn't too upset?"

"I don't think he really understands what's happened. I fed him dinner and gave him a bath. He loves our Jacuzzi, if you remember. He fell asleep about half an hour ago while Len was reading to him."

"Thank you so much, both of you, for helping out on such short notice. I don't know what I would have done—"

"Don't think twice about it," Len said. "I just wish there was more—"

"I know."

"Any time," Allison said. "You know you can call us any time."

Diana carried Jeremy to the car, buckled him in and drove home, where she tucked him into bed. He stirred only once, opening his eyes to ask sleepily, "Is Daddy back yet?"

"Not yet, honey. He's sleeping at the hospital tonight."

Diana watched until Jeremy's eyes closed again. He curled into a ball, breathing peacefully. She wished she could crawl into bed and fall into an equally mind-numbing and innocent sleep. But that wasn't going to happen. Although her body ached with exhaustion, her mind was pounding a treadmill.

She poured herself a glass of wine and made a fried egg sandwich.

What was Roy doing at a convenience store in San Francisco? And why had he lied to her about his plans for the afternoon?

Not another woman, Len had said. As inappropriate as Allison seemed to feel the comment was, Diana had found herself thinking the same thing. But if Roy was having an affair, it would be with some slender, young, high-achiever. They certainly wouldn't rendezvous in a dangerous, violence-torn part of San Francisco.

She mentally reviewed the events of that morning. Roy had been casual and chipper. Almost too cheerful now that she thought of it, as if his sudden decision to find a game of golf had been rehearsed rather than spontaneous. Yet she hadn't made note of it at the time, so maybe she was imagining it now. He'd snarled at her only when she'd suggested he spend the afternoon with Jeremy instead of golfing. Of course, he hadn't planned to be golfing at all.

But Roy *had* been tenser than usual these past few weeks. She'd noticed that. Even mentioned the fact to Allison, who'd dismissed it as the fallout from a heavy workload and a high-pressure job. And just maybe the routine of an established marriage.

Allison didn't read much into nuance, but Diana did, and she was pretty well attuned to the shadows and overtones of her marriage. Something *had* been on Roy's mind. He'd been absorbed of late, snapping at her and even at Jeremy, which was something he almost never did. And their lovemaking had become infrequent and mechanical. These were observations Diana had made to herself over the weeks, but until now she hadn't really put them all together. In light of what had happened today, they painted a picture that left her feeling more than a little uneasy.

At midnight, Diana called the hospital once more to check on Roy, and then climbed into bed. She slept in her clothes so that she could leave on a moment's notice. Not that she expected to sleep. But she did.

And it wasn't until she awoke to go to the bathroom at four in morning that she remembered she hadn't called Emily.

CHAPTER 4

Trace moaned and took a series of rapid, shallow breaths. "Jesus fucking Christ. It feels like my arm is on fire."

Chloe wiped his forehead. "The Vicodin should kick in before long," she soothed. As soon as they'd struggled up the stairs to their tiny third-floor apartment, with Chloe acting like a living crutch and Trace dragging himself a step at a time, she'd given him one of the two remaining pills she'd been prescribed for an abscessed tooth last year.

"It better work soon," Trace said with a grimace. His skin was pale and clammy, his gaze unfocused. The bleeding had mostly stopped but Trace wouldn't let her look at the wound, much less clean it. Maybe later, he'd told her, when the drugs had taken the edge off.

"What's in the canvas bag?" he asked.

"Nothing valuable. Just some clothes and papers." She didn't mention the gun she'd found there.

"Shit. Stupid guy ruined everything."

Chloe thought of the dark-haired man lying in a pool of his own blood. She again felt the rise of nausea in her throat. What had been ruined, she thought, was his life. And theirs. Not to mention the clerk's.

"It was all worked out," Trace said. "Now we got nothing."

"What do you mean? What was all worked out?"

"Hector and me, we had a plan."

"Hector?"

"The guy behind the counter. It was all set. Him and me, we were going split the take."

An air bubble rose uncomfortably in Chloe's chest. "The clerk was in on it?"

Trace nodded and then winced as he shifted position. "Sunday's a big day. The whole weekend's worth of cash was in the till."

Chloe picked at her cuticles, a habit she'd broken years ago. "The clerk," she said softly. "You knew him?"

"Yeah. Well, sort of."

She clasped her hand to her mouth, afraid she really was going to be sick. "But you shot him! I think you killed him."

"I hope so."

"You hope so? How could you shoot a friend?"

"I didn't say he was a friend, I said I knew him."

"It's the same—"

"What? After the whole thing blew up you think he was going to keep his mouth shut? 'Oh, no, Mr. Cop, I don't have any idea who held me up and shot that dude who walked through the door. No, I can't describe the shooter. I didn't see nothing.' You think that's the way it would have gone down?"

"Maybe."

"Then you're dumber than I thought. Let me tell you something, Chloe. It was him or me. You trust someone in a situation like that and you might as well put the gun to your own head."

Chloe bit her lip, hard. She wanted desperately to rewind the day to that morning when Trace had gently spread his fingers over the swell of her abdomen and teased her about names for the baby. She'd felt so full of hope, so much at peace. All she felt now was a brittle, cold fear.

"We could have—"

"Could have what? We can barely make it as it is. Having a fucking baby costs money."

Chloe shook her head. "But look what happened. What are we going to do now?"

"Maybe if you'd stayed in the car like I told you, we wouldn't be in this mess."

"You didn't say—"

"Maybe if you hadn't gotten pregnant in the first place. Ever think about that, huh?"

Chloe felt the sting of tears. It wasn't the only time he'd said something like that, but it was the first time he sounded like he really meant it. "You dragged me into this, Trace. I could go to the cops right now and tell them what happened. I wasn't part of it."

"Like hell you weren't. You drove the getaway car. You're an accomplice, Chloe. The law says you're as much a part of this as I am."

"But I didn't know—"

"No one's going to believe that."

An angry fear gnawed at Chloe's gut. "How could you do this? How could—"

"You think I liked shooting two guys? You think that makes me feel good? 'Cuz it doesn't. It wasn't like I planned it that way."

"But you didn't have to shoot him."

"Leave me alone, Chloe. I've had enough of you."

Trace shut his eyes and laid his head against the tattered cushion of the sofa back. After a while, his breathing grew more regular. The Vicodin seemed to finally be taking effect.

Chloe eased herself off the sofa and went into their ugly green bathroom, where she put her face in her hands and cried silently. Trace didn't like her to cry. He said tears were girly and stupid. Sometimes Chloe couldn't help it, though. She tried to keep from crying when Trace could see her.

What would happen to them? It was all such a mess. Everything. And it wasn't her fault. It really wasn't. She hadn't shot anyone. She hadn't even known Trace planned to rob the store.

But she hadn't pulled out her cell phone and called 9-1-1 right away, either. She hadn't even tried to save the customer as he lay bleeding to death. Instinctively, she'd aligned herself with Trace. And as much as his words just now had hurt her, she loved him. Trace was all she had.

The pain was making him crazy. That was it. When he was better again, they'd come up with a plan.

After a while, she splashed her face with water and dried it with a towel. Her eyes were red, so she loaded them with eyeliner. In the mirror, she looked like a kid who'd gotten into her mother's makeup, but it was harder to tell she'd been crying.

She checked on Trace again. At first she thought he'd fallen asleep, but then she noticed he'd sort of drift off before jerking back into a vacant-eyed stupor. His skin was waxy and pale, his forehead hot. He breathed heavily and his shoulder had started to bleed again.

Trace needed help. Needed it badly.

If he saw a doctor, he'd end up in prison. If he didn't, he might die. She didn't want Trace to die. Even now, knowing what he'd done. He'd done it for her and the baby. He cared about her. He cared more for her than anyone had in her whole life.

Chloe couldn't let him die.

She thought of Janet, a woman who used to work at the Craft Connection with Chloe. Janet had a brother who'd been in trouble with the law, but he'd also been a medic in Iraq. Chloe had gone with Janet to the brother's a couple of times for parties. She hoped the guy still lived in the same ground floor apartment in the flatlands of Berkeley. And that he wouldn't shoot her for ringing his doorbell close to midnight.

She tiptoed into the bedroom and grabbed the money she'd hidden under the paper lining of her bureau drawer. She left Trace a note in case he woke up, then she got in the car and drove to the brother's apartment building. He was still awake. She could tell from the flickering light of the television through the drapes. Shaking, Chloe rang the bell. She couldn't even remember the guy's name.

"Yeah, who is it?"

"Chloe Henderson. We met at one of your parties. I used to work with your sister."

The door swept open. The scent of pot wafted from inside the darkened room.

Jerry, that was his name. Janet and Jerry.

"What do you want at this hour?" Jerry's large, partially clad frame loomed in the doorway. Either he'd forgotten he was wearing only his boxers or he didn't care.

"I . . ."

He took an unsteady step forward. "You looking for company?"

Chloe shook her head. "A doctor."

"A what?" Jerry laughed. "Does this look like a clinic to you?"

"You know people. And you were a medic in the war."

"Go to the hospital if you're sick."

"Please, my boyfriend needs help. He's been shot."

Jerry rubbed his eyes and belched. "Take him to emergency. They got to treat him, money or not."

"He was, uh, involved in something. Something that might get him in trouble if we go to the hospital."

"What'd he do—deal drugs? Jack a car?"

"Something like that."

Jerry narrowed his gaze. He seemed more alert than he had when he opened the door. "Why should I help you?"

Chloe felt tears threaten again. "Because I'm scared and I don't know what else to do."

"You got money?"

She reached into her purse for the hundred dollars that was her rainy-day stash. Food money for when things got really tight.

Jerry sneered. "A hundred? You've got to be kidding."

"Please. It's all I've got."

He tilted his head and gave her an appraising look. A slow smile spread across his face. "It's not all you've got, sweetheart. Not hardly."

"It is. Really."

But Jerry wasn't listening. He reached out a hand and began kneading her breast.

Chloe froze.

Jerry slid the hand down the front of her shirt and dipped into her pants, next to her skin. "You've got plenty to offer, sweetheart. And I just might be interested."

Chloe backed away, shaking. A sour taste rose in her mouth.

"Up to you. You want to help your boyfriend or not?"

Chloe swallowed. She could do it if she had to. She'd done it before when her stepfather used to slip into her bed. She'd done it many times. All she had to do was close her eyes and take her mind to that safe place far away.

But the words that came out of her mouth were, "I'm pregnant."

"You don't look pregnant."

"Four months."

Jerry shrugged. "Doesn't bother me."

But it bothered Chloe. It seemed a very wrong thing to do.

She bit her lip. "What about a blow job?"

"You want my help or not?"

"A blow job and the hundred dollars."

He seemed to think about it, then pulled her inside the apartment and reached for his zipper. "That'll work for a down payment."

Chloe saw the morning sky outside her bedroom window beginning to lighten. She listened to Trace's breathing, which was more regular now, and steady. Earlier, Jerry had dressed the wound and helped her move Trace onto the bed.

"Your boyfriend still ought to see a doctor," he said.

Before leaving, he'd handed her a fistful of pills. "Remember, all I got so far was the down payment. Don't think I won't be looking to collect the rest."

Chloe hadn't slept at all. But she'd crawled onto the bed next to Trace, pulled the blanket over them both, and tried not to think about Jerry. About what she'd done and what would happen when he came after her to collect.

Now, with the dawn, Chloe got up quietly. She went downstairs to grab the neighbor's newspaper. If she read it carefully she could put it back before the old woman went out to retrieve it.

Chloe found the headline she was looking for on the front page of the second section: "Store Robbery Leaves One Dead and One Critical."

So the customer had survived. The immediate relief Chloe felt was short-lived. What if he could identify them?

She began reading in a whisper. "An Alameda County Assistant District Attorney is in critical condition after being shot in a convenience store robbery that left the store clerk dead."

Her head began to spin.

Oh, God. A district attorney. Could things get any worse?

CHAPTER 5

In the morning, Diana showered and dressed, going through the motions by rote. She felt as though her body was made of spun glass. She moved stiffly and awkwardly, and when she looked in the mirror, her skin looked dull and blotchy, and there were dark circles under her eyes. She looked like a Halloween mask of her normal self.

She called the hospital again and spoke with the head nurse in ICU. Roy's condition was unchanged, and no, the nurse didn't have any other details. The doctor would be in later that morning and perhaps Diana could talk to him then.

No change. Was that good or bad? Diana tried not to dwell on the array of horrible outcomes that were possible, but they buzzed around her head like pesky flies at a summer picnic.

Roy had to pull through. He simply had to. He wouldn't let her down by dying. He'd always been someone she could count on. That was one of the things she loved about him. Roy was solid and responsible.

She woke Jeremy by kissing his cheek, as she did every morning, then sat down on his bed and stroked his forehead. "You were pretty sleepy last night," she said. "Do you remember my carrying you into the house?"

"Sort of." He rubbed his eyes. "Is Daddy home yet?"

"Daddy's had an accident," she told him, working to keep her voice even. "He's still in the hospital and I need to go there again this morning."

Jeremy propped himself up on an elbow. "Is he hurt bad?"

Diana had known she would need an answer to this question, but she'd yet to come up with one. How did you prepare a seven-year-old for the fact that his father might not live?

"Pretty bad," she said, smoothing the cowlick at his left temple. "I'll know more after I talk to the doctor. You're going to stay with Allison again, okay?"

"Today's a school day," Jeremy said. "Why can't I go to school?"

"Do you want to go to school?" That thought hadn't crossed Diana's mind.

"Shouldn't I go? It's what I'm supposed to do."

Her dear, sweet boy, Emily's polar opposite. Emily rebelled at everything; Jeremy followed the rules. Like his dad. And maybe it made sense to keep his day as normal as possible. "It's up to you," she told him.

"Can't I go to the hospital with you?"

"Not this morning, honey. But soon."

"I guess I'll go to school then. Tell Daddy I hope he feels better soon."

"I'll do that. Now get yourself dressed and I'll fix breakfast."

Later, after she'd taken Jeremy to school and spoken with both his teacher and the principal to make sure they understood the situation, she drove to the hospital in the thick of the morning commute. It took her well over an hour, including twenty minutes of virtual standstill at the Bay Bridge toll plaza.

Her cell phone rang as she pulled into the hospital's parking lot.

"How could you not call me?" Emily shrieked. "My stepfather is shot and I have to hear about it from my friends! How do you think that makes me look?"

It seemed to Diana the better question was, how did it make

her feel. But maybe that was what Emily meant. "I'm so sorry, Em. I was at the hospital until late last night and I'm on my way back there now. In fact, I just pulled into the lot here. I didn't want to wake you and I figured I'd have a better idea how things were going in a few hours."

"You had to know I'd hear about it."

"I wasn't thinking clearly. I should have called you. I really am sorry."

"You didn't think about me at all, did you? You forgot all about me. You always forget about me."

Diana had learned long ago that arguing with Emily was a no-win situation, and she truly did feel bad about not calling. Emily was understandably scared and upset. Roy might not be her real father, but he'd been more of a constant in her life than Garrick. Still, it irritated Diana that there wasn't a word of sympathy from Emily.

"I said I was sorry."

"What happened anyway?" Emily asked. "Why was he even in the Bayview? Isn't that a really dangerous part of the city?"

"I'm as confused as you."

"Is it bad? Is he going to die?"

"I don't know that either. He's in . . . pretty bad shape, though." Diana couldn't bring herself to say "critical." "I hope to talk to the doctor soon and I'll call you then. I promise."

"Yeah, well I won't hold my breath."

"Honey, I know you must feel—"

"I've got to go, I've got class." The phone clicked off.

"And I'm holding up pretty well," Diana remarked into the dead phone line. "Thanks for asking."

At the door to the ICU, Diana paused to take a breath, then she shut her mind to everything but her concern for Roy. She mentally bathed him in a healing white light and willed herself to think only positive thoughts.

After speaking briefly with the duty nurse, she went to Roy's bed.

She found the machinery surrounding Roy—with its beeps and bleeps and pulsing graphs—intimidating. She was afraid she'd inadvertently disturb something and set off alarms. She edged in next to the IV pole and touched Roy's shoulder.

"Hi, sweetheart. How are you feeling?"

She didn't expect a response, and she didn't get one. But she'd read somewhere that it was good to talk to patients even when you thought they couldn't hear you.

"Jeremy wanted to come visit," she continued, "but I told him not yet. Soon though. He says he hopes you feel better."

Diana smoothed the sheet under Roy's arm. "And Emily's worried, too. We all are. We love you. You can't leave us. You know that, don't you?"

And then she fell silent because she felt like an idiot talking to herself.

"I can't stay long," she told him finally. "That's the rule in ICU. But I call the hospital all the time to check on you. And I'm going now to find the doctor."

Roy's lips twitched slightly. Had Diana imagined it or had his mouth really moved?

"Roy? Can you hear me?" She put her hand in his. "Squeeze my hand if you can hear me."

Roy's hand was cold and limp. But after a moment, Diana felt a faint pressure on her hand. Did she imagine it?

"Roy, sweetheart. Are you there?"

Gently, she squeezed his hand and felt him squeeze back. A tremor of joy pulsed through her veins.

And then Roy's eyes fluttered open.

"Not . . ." His parched lips barely moved, but he was trying to talk.

"Not what?" she asked, leaning her ear close to Roy's mouth to hear.

"He . . ."

She waited a moment. "He? Who, Roy?"

"Not me."

He. Not me. Diana struggled to understand.

"You and who, honey?"

"Mia." His eyes had closed again, but Diana could see the movement beneath the lids. He was breathing more rapidly. "Mia," he said again.

"Who's Mia?" Len's tasteless comment from last night came instantly to Diana's mind. She hated that an affair would be the first thing she'd think of.

"Who's Mia?" she asked again.

But Roy's head had rolled to the side, and his breathing was once again regular. His moment of consciousness had passed.

Diana hung around the nursing station until she was able to corner the doctor on duty that morning. A different doctor this time but just as young. He wasn't particularly interested when Diana told him about Roy squeezing her hand and speaking.

"Nonresponsiveness is a funny thing," he told her. "A slight physical response doesn't necessarily mean anything."

"But it must mean he's getting better."

"It might. No two people in similar situations are alike. Your husband could wake up tomorrow, or six months from now, or never. It's fine to be hopeful, but I don't want you to have false expectations."

Diana wasn't someone who always saw the glass as half-full, but Roy's responsiveness, however fleeting, had given her renewed hope. The doctor's words rekindled her despair.

"But physically, he's doing better?"

39

"He's stable," the doctor said. "That's all we can say for now."

Diana held her tears until she was outside on the street. And she waited until they'd passed before she called Emily.

The phone rang straight to voicemail. Diana left a message saying Roy's condition was stable but that it was too soon to know what was going to happen. And she added, "Take care of yourself, honey. I love you."

It was the way she ended every message she left Emily. Diana had no way of knowing if her daughter even listened to her messages all the way to the end. Emily wasn't big on follow-through.

Diana wondered if there was anyone else she should notify. She'd already talked to Roy's boss, Alec Thurston. He'd assured her that his office was working with the SFPD to solve this "horrific crime" as quickly as possible. Diana doubted there was much they could do to help, but the fact that Roy was an assistant DA meant that the investigation wouldn't fall between the cracks.

Diana had no family to call, aside from a sister in England she rarely spoke to. And Roy had no family at all, at least none he was in touch with. He'd never known his father, and his mother had died when Roy was nineteen. As for Diana's friends and coworkers, they'd probably heard that Roy had been shot and would offer words of sympathy, but that was the last thing she wanted right now. Pulling herself together enough to respond was more than she could manage.

Except for Allison. Diana and Allison had shared so much over the years that Diana was as comfortable with her as she was with herself. Maybe more comfortable, because where Diana tended to be filled with self-doubt, Allison had a way of putting things in perspective.

As though Allison had read her mind, Diana's phone rang

and Allison said, "Are you at the hospital?"

"Just leaving."

"Is there any improvement in Roy's condition?"

"Nothing definitive. He squeezed my hand and mumbled a few words, but the doctor says it might not mean anything."

"How are you holding up? No, wait. Let's not do this over the phone. How about I meet you at your place in say, an hour."

"Thanks. I may need a shoulder to cry on."

"That's why you have me."

Later, when they were settled at Diana's kitchen table with mugs of coffee and a plate of blueberry scones Allison had brought, Diana recounted her morning's visit to the hospital.

"He said what?" Allison asked, breaking off a piece of scone and dunking it in her coffee.

" 'Mia.' At least I think that's what he said. He also said something like 'he, not me.' I have no idea what that means."

Allison frowned and plopped the bite of scone into her mouth. Allison believed in food as comfort, which was probably one of the reasons she was overweight or, as Len liked to say, "pleasantly rounded." Even though Diana thought Allison was rushing things with Len, she was happy Allison had finally met a man who could look past her weight and appreciate her quick smile and sparkly brown eyes. There was no doubt that Len was good for Allison.

"Mia must mean something to him," Diana said. "Why else would he call out her name?"

"She could be anyone from his high school sweetheart to . . . I don't know, his grandmother. What strikes me as more important, is the fact he was able to speak at all. That's a good sign."

"I thought so too, but the doctor wasn't impressed." Diana took a sip of coffee. It tasted bitter and sharp, although she suspected it was her taste that was off and not the coffee. "What will I do if he doesn't make it?"

Allison's expression clouded. She wrapped her shoulder-length curls around her hand, then let them fall loose again. "You'll cry a lot," she said after a moment, "and then you'll move on." Allison spoke from experience. She'd lost her husband in a boating accident when Becca was only three. "But chances are, he'll be fine. Try not to worry about the what-ifs."

"Easier said than done," Diana said with a wan smile.

"You have to be strong for Jeremy. Becca kept me going. I might have given up if not for her."

"It's not just that Roy was shot, but that he lied to me. Telling me he was going to play golf when he wasn't. Why would he lie if he didn't have something to hide?"

For once, Allison didn't have an answer.

CHAPTER 6

Chloe made sure the water running from the faucet was good and hot before she started on the dishes in the sink. When she was living in the group home, there'd been a couple of girls who never washed dishes properly. They'd just start in with the sponge the minute they turned on the faucet. Cold water and hardly any soap. Sometimes no soap at all. The dishes—especially glasses—were pretty disgusting when they'd finished. Ironically, these were the same girls who used all the hot water when they took a shower, and left their wet towels on the floor and their hairs in the sink. They didn't think about anybody but themselves.

She didn't miss the group home, but she really hadn't minded it all that much at the time—except for the few girls who got on her nerves, and the fact that the TV was always on, and there was no place to be alone. Whatever else the home had been, it was better than what Chloe had known before.

Chloe finished with the morning's breakfast dishes, then tackled yesterday's dishes, now caked with the remains of a bacon and cheese omelet. She didn't usually let the dishes pile up like that, but there hadn't been time before they took off for the concert Sunday morning, and by the time they'd returned home that afternoon, dirty dishes had been the last thing on her mind as she tended to Trace's wounds.

God, was that only yesterday? She felt a terrible weight in her chest. How could things have gone so wrong?

Trace worked a lot of weekends but he'd had yesterday off, and he hadn't even wanted to spend it hanging with his friends, drinking beer. It had been Trace's idea, in fact, to go to the local bands concert at the Shoreline Amphitheater. Just the two of them. Chloe didn't actually care where they went, she just enjoyed being with Trace. It made her feel whole, like a complete person in a way she didn't feel when she was alone.

And then he'd gone into that convenience store and everything had changed in an instant.

Chloe dried the breakfast dishes and put them away so the counter was clear. She liked having a tidy kitchen.

She thought about taking another shower. She'd taken one first thing, the minute she got up, even though she'd taken one last night after Jerry left. She still felt dirty, and all the scrubbing in the world wasn't going to make her feel clean.

She had to remind herself she'd done it for Trace.

All morning she'd been checking on him in his sleep. When he'd woken up complaining about the pain, she'd given him another of the pills Jerry had left and fixed him a piece of toast, which he ignored.

"I'm not hungry," he grumbled, folding the pillow over his face.

"You should eat. You haven't had any food for almost twenty-four hours."

"Lay off, Chloe. I said I wasn't hungry."

And she'd helped him into the bathroom several times. He would have stumbled if she hadn't had hold of him. And then he'd crawl back into bed, cursing.

Now he was once again sleeping, fitfully. He'd waken, moan and call out something she couldn't understand, and then slip back into sleep. Chloe decided the grogginess was *because* of the pills. At least she hoped it was the pills and not some raging infection.

Earlier, she'd called Trace's supervisor at Costco and her own at the Craft Connection, in both instances pleading the flu. She realized afterward that she should have come up with a different excuse for Trace, something that might account down the road for his injured shoulder. It was a mistake that would make Trace angry. He was always after her to use her brain and think things through instead of living in some fantasy world, an unfair criticism because her world was hardly a fantasy.

As if to prove to herself that she did think ahead, Chloe checked the fridge, which offered little in the way of dinner choices. After looking in on Trace one more time, she made a mad dash to the corner market, where she almost never shopped because the prices were so high.

She picked up canned soup and packaged macaroni and cheese—both foods she thought might appeal to someone who wasn't feeling well. And then, because Trace liked meat with his meals, she added a couple of frozen hearty-man dinners and a frozen beef burrito to her basket. Although there was beer at the apartment, she knew Trace would appreciate something stronger. She'd have liked to get it for him, but did she dare? She was barely eighteen, although she did have a fake ID. Feeling torn, she lingered in the alcohol aisle long enough that the clerk began watching her with suspicion. Finally, she picked out a package of the chocolate fudge cookies Trace liked. She didn't want to risk getting busted now, on top of everything.

The clerk was an older guy with a big belly and tufts of hair growing out of his ears. Her mind flashed to the young kid behind the counter at the convenience store. He couldn't have been more than a few years older than she was, and now he was dead. She felt a wave of nausea wash over her. It had happened so fast, so unexpectedly, she could almost convince herself she'd been watching a movie. But the brutal reality was, she had been there.

The big-bellied clerk had been yammering about problems with the cash register and Chloe hasn't really been listening, but now he said, "Did you read about the convenience store clerk and DA that got shot yesterday in the city?"

Chloe jumped. It was almost like he'd been reading her mind.

"Guess I shouldn't complain about a stupid machine," the clerk continued. "At least I'm not working in a neighborhood like that. We may be a little down at the heels and all, but that there's a whole different scene, know what I mean?"

Chloe nodded. She wanted to get her groceries and leave.

"Sad thing is, stuff like that happens all the time in bad neighborhoods. It only made the news 'cause of the DA. A big-time, important guy from the right part of town gets shot and it's hot news. The rest of the folks can shoot each other right and left and you don't hear much about it."

"Yeah, it's not fair," Chloe agreed, because she knew some response was called for. She handed over her money and began bagging her groceries herself. She wanted to get out of there.

"On the news they said there was a witness. Someone who got a description and partial plate. Maybe this time they'll actually find the creep that did it."

"A witness?" Chloe almost dropped the can of soup she was holding. "I hadn't heard that."

"Yup. The same guy who called nine-one-one."

"How good a description did he get?" Her heart raced. Would they be able to put together a police sketch? She had a sudden, horrible vision of turning on the TV and seeing a sketch of Trace's face plastered across the screen. Or her own.

The clerk shrugged. "Enough that they mentioned it on the news." He added the last items to her bag. "Here you go, miss. You have a nice day, now."

"You, too," Chloe mumbled. Her day was anything but nice, and had just gotten a whole lot worse.

The store was only two blocks from their apartment and Chloe walked quickly, conscious the entire time that her face was exposed to the public for anyone to recognize. Or had the witness only gotten a description of the car? She wished she'd thought to ask. Not that it mattered. A partial plate along with make, model, and color—wouldn't the cops be able to find them based on that?

For a moment she was furious with Trace for getting her into this mess. Getting *them* in this mess. Trace lived in a fantasy world, not her. And sometimes he was so stupid she wanted to throttle him. But mostly, Trace was the best thing that had ever happened to her. She didn't want to forget that.

They'd met at a movie theater. Well, just outside the theater really. She'd gone to a matinee with a couple of other girls from the group home. One of the girls started flirting with Trace in the popcorn line, and then after the movie, when they were all hanging around the plaza outside, he started talking to Chloe. Not to her friends, but her. Chloe was never the girl guys noticed. She wasn't slender and dainty, or stacked and curvy. She didn't have full lips or long lashes or straight, blond hair. She was just kind of there in a nondescript, mousy-brown way. And Trace had noticed her. He'd smiled at her and offered her a sip of his Coke.

Three months later she walked away from the group home and moved in with him. She was only seventeen and was still a few months short of graduation, which might not have happened anyway unless she brought up her grade in math, so she'd been worried the authorities would come after her. But they hadn't. Not the cops, not her social worker, not even the supervisor of the group home who claimed to care so much about Chloe's future. It had surprised Chloe to discover she was disappointed no one had made any effort to track her down. Not disappointed exactly, because she didn't want to go back, but hurt. It was frightening to realize that no one really cared.

No one but Trace, that is.

By evening, Trace had improved enough that he was able to get out of bed and sit at the table. He still looked tired and he held his shoulder at an odd angle. He ate a bowl of soup and one of the frozen dinners Chloe had picked up at the store. When she was washing dishes afterward, he came up behind her and stroked the back of her neck.

"You're the best, Chloe. I like having you take care of me."

"Good thing," she joked, " 'cuz that's what I'm going to keep doing." Inside, she glowed with the warmth of Trace's words. It felt so good when he was sweet to her.

"You taped up the wound really nice, too."

Chloe felt herself stiffen. She didn't like lying to Trace, but she couldn't tell him about Jerry. What she'd done made her feel dirty, and even though she'd done it for Trace, she knew he'd be angry. So she simply nodded.

"How's it look?" he asked. "Is it bad?"

"I still think you should see a doctor."

He managed a laugh. "I got you, babe. I don't need a doctor."

She dried her hands and turned to face him. "That man you shot, the customer who came into the store, he's a lawyer, a district attorney."

Trace sneered. "Guess he deserved what he got, then."

"He's somebody important," Chloe explained, not that she agreed he'd deserved being shot, either. "What happened is going to get a lot of attention."

"Did he die?"

She shook her head. "He's in critical condition."

Trace rubbed the stubble on his jaw. "Shit. I hope he won't be able to identify us."

"He may not have to." Chloe's voice was growing thinner, the fear inside her truly unleashed for the first time since yesterday. "They say there's a witness. Someone who saw the car and got part of the license number. He may have seen us, too."

"Fuck it." Trace kicked the cabinet door.

"We can't go out in public. We can't go anywhere. Somebody might see the car and turn us in. What are we going to do?"

"You're going to get us some new plates, as a start."

"Me? How?"

"Grow up, Chloe. You know how to use a screwdriver, don't you?"

She'd only be making things worse for herself if she went along with stealing plates. Digging herself in deeper. She hadn't shot anyone. She wasn't really part of what happened yesterday.

Except she was. Trace was right, she was an accessory. She'd watched enough TV to know that in the eyes of the law, she was as guilty as he was. She had to do what she could to keep them from being found out. For the baby's sake if nothing else.

"As soon as it's dark," she said. And even though he hadn't asked, she added, "I'll be careful."

CHAPTER 7

By eleven o'clock, Chloe had run out of excuses. It was as dark as it was going to get, and the neighborhood was quiet. That wasn't to say the streets were empty, but even if she waited until later, there was no guarantee someone wouldn't be coming home from a late date or out walking his dog. And she didn't really want to be out prowling the streets alone at three in the morning.

She pulled her hair into a ponytail and tucked it up under an old baseball cap. She'd dressed in black, including her shoes, and pulled the hood of her sweatshirt over her cap.

Outside, she checked the street for activity, then jammed her hands into her pockets and started walking. The area was a mix of small homes and apartment buildings. Most of the residents parked on the street, but a few of the larger complexes had parking lots, and Chloe figured that was her best option. She needed a place where she wouldn't be spotted removing the plate. She walked half a long block before she even started looking for a possible target. Every place she considered had some drawback. Too bright, too exposed, too many windows facing the parking area. Three blocks later, Chloe was getting desperate. She couldn't walk around all night. She chose an apartment building at random and headed for the parking lot. But just as she got to the farthest row of cars, a pair of headlights swung into the driveway. Keeping her back to the car that had just pulled in, Chloe walked toward the apartment entrance like she lived there, and then walked past the door onto the sidewalk away from the driveway.

Her heart pounded. She put her hand on her belly and patted it reassuringly. "It's okay, Carly. That wasn't even a close call."

No, not Carly. It sounded too much like Curly, and even though she knew Carly Simon was a famous singer, the name didn't sound right to Chloe once she'd said it aloud. She tried again. "We're doing fine, Abigail. We'll go home soon." Abigail or Abby? Definitely Abby. But she wasn't sure that was a keeper either.

She felt her eyes fill with tears. What did it matter? She wasn't doing fine, and she couldn't go home until she had a stupid license plate. A stupid, stolen license plate.

Chloe felt the sudden urge to throw herself onto her bed, pound her fists into the mattress, and kick like the devil, the way she'd done when she was a kid. Life was so unfair. But screaming hadn't solved any of her problems then, and it certainly wouldn't help her now. True, things were kind of a mess at present—no, not just kind of, they were a real stinking mess—but she had to remember they could be worse.

Chloe had never known her father, only the series of men her mother would bring home—some for a night or a week, some for months on end. Two of the men had stuck around long enough to become stepfathers, although Chloe didn't see that marriage made any difference. The only things her first stepfather cared about were booze and sex, but at least he'd confined the sex to her mother. That was more than Chloe could say for her second stepfather. Chloe was eleven when her mother married him, thirteen when he drove the car, with her mother in it, across the center line, killing them both, as well as the woman and child in the oncoming car. That was the beginning of foster homes, which, despite the glowing enthusiasm from a string of social workers, weren't the wonderful homes she'd been led to believe they were. They weren't all bad, they just weren't homes.

The group home had actually been the best of the lot, what Chloe imagined living in a college dorm might be like—only with more rules. Most of the girls likened it to living in a prison, but Chloe didn't mind rules. It was kind of nice to know what you could and couldn't do. Knowing the rules made it easier to stay out of trouble.

The hardest part for Chloe was that girls cycled through the house so often it was almost impossible to make friends. And at school, the other kids knew which girls lived in the home, and kept their distance. So she'd had no real friends, no parties or sleepovers, no one to go to the mall with except for the other girls in the house. But that was all behind her now.

Chloe put her hand on her belly. "You're pretty lucky, Abby. I'm going to take good care of you and make sure nothing bad happens to you. Ever."

Finally an apartment building across the road caught her eye. The parking spaces were beneath an overhang with shrubs growing between them and the street. And the main light at the center of the lot had burned out.

She walked to the end of the block and crossed, casually, as though she were out on an evening stroll. Then she walked toward the lot like she belonged there, and hid in the shadows near the fence separating the building from the one next door. She double-checked to make sure no one was coming, then crouched down and started to remove the front license plate on an older car. She worried the spot where the license had been would stand out as bare. She was sure the car's owner would notice it was missing, but Trace said most people hardly ever looked at the front bumper. She hoped that if the owner did notice, he'd think it had fallen off.

A sudden, loud crash broke the quiet. Chloe froze. More clatter, then footsteps near the rear of the building. From the apartments above the lot, someone opened a window.

Chloe could feel her heart racing. Should she run? Wouldn't that draw attention? But what if she was found here, holding a screwdriver and crouching in front of a car with a loose license plate? She should never have agreed to do this. It was a stupid idea. She experienced a swell of resentment toward Trace.

She heard the clatter of what sounded like bottles being dumped into the trash, and then the footsteps retreated into the building. A dog barked and a cat darted across the asphalt. Chloe let out the breath she hadn't known she was holding. She took out the last screw and pulled the plate free, tucking it under her jacket.

On the walk home, she saw a shadowed figure of a man coming toward her. She kept her head down and walked with a determined stride, then turned up the walkway to a nearby house. He wouldn't attack her there, would he? The house was dark, but if she screamed, surely someone would come running. Or at least look out the window.

Or maybe not. This was a neighborhood where people pretty much minded their own business. She reached into her pocket for the screwdriver. She'd go for his eyes. That was advice she'd read in one of those women's magazines near the checkout stand at the grocery. Go for his eyes and scream.

The man walked past, muttering to himself. He was old and frail and totally spaced out. He didn't even look at her as he passed by.

Chloe practically ran the rest of the way home. When she closed the door to her own apartment, relief rolled over her like an ocean swell and left her almost giddy.

Trace was already in bed. Two empty beer bottles were on the counter by the sink. Chloe put them in the recycling bag and wiped the sticky counter. Then she went into the bathroom, washed her face, and brushed her teeth. The apartment was cold and Chloe shivered. In bed she scooted closer to Trace. As she fit her body into the curl of his, he rolled over and away.

She fought an unwelcome wave of emptiness. She put her hand to her abdomen. "Good night, Melanie," she told the baby, testing yet another name. "Everything's going to be just fine. You wait and see."

CHAPTER 8

"I really appreciate the ride," Diana told Len as she buckled herself into the plush leather seat of his cream-colored BMW. "I would have taken BART to the city but the police impound lot is nowhere near a station."

"Don't be ridiculous. I'm happy to help."

Len was unfailingly gracious and accommodating—in large part, Diana thought, because she was Allison's friend. But being congenial was also in Len's nature. He rarely expressed opinions or voiced disapproval, and was quick to smooth over awkward moments with hearty banter. These were traits which irritated Roy, but Diana usually enjoyed Len's company. Today, though, she would have preferred the company, and support, of a best friend. But Allison taught graphic design at the community college on Tuesdays, and Diana didn't want to leave Roy's car in impound any longer than necessary. It was as if by bringing his car home, she'd be keeping Roy closer.

Len took his right hand from the wheel long enough to adjust the climate control in the dashboard. "Any news on Roy's condition?"

"I wasn't able to reach the doctor this morning, but the ICU nurse I spoke with said nothing's changed."

He grimaced. "So it's a matter of wait and see?"

"It seems so." Except that waiting seemed too mild a word. Waiting was what she did in grocery lines and at airports, in doctor's and dentist's offices. Waiting was a matter of biding her time. The frantic worry and fear that now lodged in her chest felt more akin to desperation.

The notion that Roy might die sent her into a blind, freefall panic. She couldn't imagine her life without him. The eight years they'd been together had healed thirty years of self-doubt. She'd blossomed into someone who felt deserving of love. And Roy's confidence in her had given her an inner strength she'd never known. The detective's phone call Sunday had shown her how fragile the construct of that security was.

And then there were the questions that swirled through her mind like a stalled twister. Why had Roy gone to San Francisco? Why had he lied about his plans? And who was Mia?

Diana had spent hours last night after Jeremy was in bed going through Roy's computer files, and had found no mention of a Mia. No indication of another woman at all. Only household records, family photos, and the travel itinerary for their most recent vacation to the Grand Canyon. Roy's web browsing history revealed nothing of interest, either. She tried to convince herself that Mia was just some random name Roy pulled from the mist of his groggy, sedated state. It meant nothing. Maybe it wasn't a name at all, but a word.

She wasn't buying that, though. She'd heard him clearly, and Roy hadn't been rambling, he'd been trying to tell her something specific. She felt sure of it.

"You okay?" Len asked. "You seem . . . well . . . distracted. Not that you don't have good reason to be."

"Sorry, I was thinking about Roy. It's hard to stay hopeful when there's still so much that can go wrong."

Len reached across the gear console and gave her forearm a reassuring squeeze. "It'll work out, Diana. Roy is a fighter."

She acknowledged his remark with a smile, but she was far from reassured.

"I'll wait here," he said when he dropped her at the impound lot, "and follow you home."

"There's no need for that."

"I insist." He reached to turn off the engine.

"No, really," she said firmly. "I've got a few errands to do on the way." Len was only trying to be helpful, but it irritated Diana the way he couldn't take no for an answer.

Len hesitated. "Well, if you're really sure."

"I am. Thanks again for the ride."

When he drove off, Diana rang the buzzer on the gate. It gave off a sharp and surprisingly shrill sound. She'd expected it to ring inside the small shed at the edge of the lot but when she looked more closely, she saw the shed wasn't manned. She rang again. A minute or so later, a gangly man with a cigarette dangling between his lips came out of the building next door.

"Hold your horses, I'm coming." He opened the gate and let her in. "You here to pick up your car?"

Diana nodded. "It's a silver Lexus registered to Roy Walker." She hoped she didn't need the license plate number because she suddenly realized she didn't know it.

"Who are you?"

"His wife."

"You got ID?"

Diana pulled her driver's license from her wallet and handed it to him.

The man ground out his cigarette on the pavement. "It's nice of you to do his dirty work for him. What'd he do, park in a tow-away zone or forget to pay his parking tickets?"

"He was shot," Diana said. She'd meant to leave it at that— she wasn't here to exchange life histories with this man—but the words sounded so abrupt, so stark, she plowed on. "He was a bystander to a holdup at a convenience store. The police had his car towed from the lot."

"Shot," the man muttered, shaking his head with no sign of

recognition. He obviously didn't keep up with the news. "We don't get many of them. Mostly it's parking violations."

Diana swallowed against the lump of sadness in her throat. "I was a little surprised they towed it. Roy was a victim. He hadn't done anything wrong." Nothing she knew about, anyway.

"Probably just as well," the attendant said. "Fancy new car like that would have been stolen or stripped otherwise."

Diana hadn't thought about that.

"Come on in," the man told her, heading to the shed. "We need to take care of the paperwork." He opened the door and pulled some forms from a desk drawer. "Name, address, and so forth. It's all pretty self-explanatory. If you give me the key, I'll get the car and bring it to the front while you do that. And I'll need five hundred dollars."

"Five hundred?" Diana gulped.

"Three hundred for towing, and hundred for each day it's left here. I should probably charge you for today, too, but seeing as how it's before noon, I'll let that one go."

"Thank you," Diana said in a tone which she hoped conveyed none of the sarcasm she heard in her head. At least she'd had the foresight to bring a car key. She pulled out her checkbook.

"Sorry, ma'am. Cash only."

"Cash? I don't have that much cash with me."

He shrugged. "Company policy."

"How about a credit card?"

"No can do."

"Why won't you take a check? There's more than enough in our account to cover it."

"Lady, you wouldn't believe the kinds of people we get and the stories I've heard." He cleared his throat. "Not that I'm doubting you, personally, of course."

What now? Diana was stuck in San Francisco with no car and not enough cash to retrieve Roy's Lexus. Reluctantly, she pulled out her cell phone and called Len. At least he wouldn't have gone far yet.

"Diana?" He'd clearly checked the readout before answering.

"I'm so sorry to bother you again, but this place won't take a check or credit card." Her voice was tight and she could feel tears of frustration threatening. She wasn't going to let *that* happen. Breathing deeply, she continued in a calmer voice. "I'm wondering if—"

"Sure thing," he said. "How much do you need?"

"The bill is five hundred. I have eighty-five in my wallet."

"I'll find an ATM and be there in short order."

"Thank you."

"No problemo."

Len might have some irritating quirks, Diana thought, but deep down he was a really decent guy, in spite of what Roy might think.

Half an hour later, Len had come, handed Diana a wad of cash, and then, at Diana's insistence, driven off again. When the attendant pulled Roy's car up to the gate, Diana experienced a moment's rockiness. Roy loved that car. He'd had a special sound system installed and some kind of shift and brake upgrade. And now, to her, it looked like an empty shell. *Oh, God, Roy, what happened?*

The attendant climbed out and Diana climbed in, pulling the seat forward and adjusting the mirrors. It looked as pristine inside as it did when Roy drove it. Despite the hefty towing fee, she was glad the police hadn't left it sitting in front of the store. The attendant was right, the car would be in pieces by now.

Eager as she was to look around the interior for some clue about Roy's mission on Sunday, she didn't want to do that in front of the attendant. She drove several blocks and found a parking spot at the curb in an area that appeared safe. Aside from a map of San Francisco on the passenger seat, the interior was as neat as always. She looked in the glove compartment. Nothing but the owner's manual for the car, a flashlight, and a bottle of Motrin.

Next, she looked in the trunk, empty except for the earthquake blanket and bottled water Roy always carried. No odd pieces of paper or scraps of mail under the seats, either. She experienced a ripple of disappointment. She'd so hoped for some answers.

Back in the driver's seat, she remembered the compartment under the armrest where Roy kept change for parking meters. Inside, she found the torn corner of a newspaper advertising supplement with an address scrawled in the margin in blue ink. No city, just 1162 Bayo Vista. The handwriting was neat and square. It wasn't Roy's.

She pulled away from the curb slowly. The slip of paper could have been there for months. It might have nothing at all to do with Roy's activities Sunday afternoon. But it was *something*. Something was more than nothing.

It would have to wait, however. She'd arranged to meet with Inspector Knowles and she was already late. She pulled away from the curb and headed for the Hall of Justice.

Diana took an elevator to the fourth floor, walked down the hallway, and pushed open the door marked HOMICIDE. The lettering gave her a moment's pause. Roy was alive. The store clerk was dead, though, so maybe that's why the case had been assigned to Knowles. Or maybe aggravated assault was lumped in with homicide.

Knowles saw her enter and came forward to greet her.

"How are you holding up?" he asked.

"I'm managing."

"It's never easy."

Diana wondered how many times he'd said the same words in the course of his career. His manner wasn't brusque, but there wasn't a lot of warmth in his tone. She'd guess he was in his late fifties. Experienced enough that he'd seen tragedy played out many times. It had to have grown almost routine for him.

"Any news on your husband's condition?" he asked.

"There's been no change. I get the impression that's not necessarily good."

Knowles nodded grimly. "I'm sorry to hear that." He led her to his desk, where he gestured for her to be seated in a straight-backed wooden chair facing his own. "I'm afraid your assessment applies to our investigation, as well."

"But the news reports said there was a witness."

"Right." Knowles cracked his knuckles. "A man who pulled into the lot just as another car was leaving. He didn't get a look at the driver, and his description of the car is fairly vague. Dark color, older model sedan."

"That's it?"

"Afraid so. He's backtracked some from his initial statement. Doesn't know cars, he says. He did get the last two digits on the license plate, or he thinks he did. He isn't really sure about that, either."

"But that's . . . that's not very helpful, is it?"

"It's not as helpful as we'd hoped." Knowles had eyes like an old basset hound, warm but sad. He regarded her now with kindness, and Diana realized his work wasn't routine to him at all. He simply needed to measure his emotional responses in order to continue doing what he did day after day.

"We're working with Alameda County authorities on this," Knowles continued. "On account of your husband's position with the DA's office. And we're bringing everything we've got to this investigation. Someone out there knows something, and sooner or later, we'll find that person."

"There's no guarantee of that," Diana said. She hated false promises.

Knowles sighed. "No. There's no guarantee." He rubbed the bags under his eyes. "You haven't learned any more about what your husband was doing in that area of the city, have you?"

She shook her head. "I picked his car up from impound this morning. I was hoping I'd find some clue there." She paused, recalling the slip of paper with the address. It might not be relevant. It might be—her thoughts drifted to Mia—personal. She'd see what she could learn first and then she'd tell Knowles about it.

"Don't most stores have some sort of surveillance camera?" she asked. "Especially in . . . uh, questionable neighborhoods. I should think the owners would want to protect against shoplifting."

"There's a camera, all right," Knowles replied, sucking on his cheek. "But the tape was missing."

"Oh." Disappointment rolled over her. "So you've really got nothing to go on."

"For the moment. Like I said, most of these cases get solved because someone talks. The guy who did it gets drunk and tells a friend, that sort of thing. We've also got contacts on the street. They know there might be some money in it for them if they can give us a name. There's a decent chance we'll find who did it."

A decent chance. Hardly a statement that evoked confidence.

Knowles stood. "I've got your husband's personal belongings for you. His keys, watch, wallet, and cell phone. If you come with me I'll release them to you."

Diana followed him down the hallway. "What about his gym bag?"

Knowles turned and looked at her. "Gym bag?"

"He took it with him. It's not in his car so I assumed the

police had taken it."

Knowles shook his head. "We didn't find a gym bag. Are you sure he had it with him?"

"Positive." Could Roy have actually gone to play golf and left it at the club? Maybe something happened during the game that caused him to drive to San Francisco.

"We don't have it." Knowles opened the door to a small room lined with cardboard boxes and pulled one down from the shelf. "Here you go. The hospital will have his clothes, but I don't imagine you'll want those, given the state they're in."

"No, I think not," Diana said, although part of her wanted every component of Roy she could get—bloodied clothes and all. "Did you check his phone for incoming or outgoing calls?"

Knowles nodded. "That's how I got your number. We were hoping maybe he'd called to report suspicious activity or something, but there were no calls at all that day, made or received. In fact, his phone wasn't even on."

"But Roy always kept his phone on. He needed to be available for people at work, and for his family."

"All I can say is that it was off when we found it." Knowles hesitated for a moment. "Did your husband always carry a lot of cash with him?"

"A hundred, maybe a bit more depending on how recently he'd been to the ATM."

"I meant more than a couple of hundred." Knowles cleared his throat. "His wallet has over five thousand dollars in it, mostly in hundred-dollar bills."

Diana swallowed, fighting a growing uneasiness. Five thousand dollars cash?

"Does your husband own a gun, Mrs. Walker?"

"Yes. Why? Roy didn't shoot himself."

"The clerk didn't shoot himself, either."

"What?" Diana's skin felt prickly. "You think Roy shot the clerk?"

Instead of responding right away, Knowles studied her for a few moments. When he finally spoke, he ignored her question. "You sure you don't have any idea what your husband was doing that day?"

"You don't believe me?"

"I want to believe you, Mrs. Walker. But we've got a missing surveillance tape, a rising assistant district attorney who lied to his wife about where he was going, and a wallet stuffed with hundred-dollar bills. You tell me that doesn't raise questions."

CHAPTER 9

Diana maneuvered Roy's Lexus through heavy midday traffic and onto the lower deck of the Bay Bridge. Because of ongoing construction, the lanes were narrow and poorly marked, and the roadbed was uneven. Still, drivers buzzed in and out of the lanes, twice swerving in front of her with what seemed like only inches to spare. She gripped the steering wheel and cursed under her breath. She needed to concentrate on the road, but her mind couldn't stop replaying her conversation with Inspector Knowles. Why had he asked about Roy's gun? Did he think Roy might have been something other than an innocent victim?

She played through possible scenarios in her head. She could easily imagine Roy trying to stop a robbery in progress—he sometimes took his commitment to serving justice a bit too much to heart. Perhaps he'd intervened, and the assailants had wrestled his gun from his grasp and then shot him.

Except that Roy didn't carry a gun. He kept it locked in a metal chest on the top shelf of their bedroom closet.

Maybe he'd been receiving threats? That might explain his edginess the last week or so. If he sensed potential danger, he might have taken his gun for protection. But if he'd sensed danger, why go at all? Roy wasn't stupid, and he wasn't reckless.

And why would he have been carrying so much cash?

Most troubling of all, he'd *lied* to her.

Ahead, a bus was stalled in the right-hand lane. Diana eased left to pass, and was almost mowed down by an SUV crossing three lanes of traffic to pull in front of her. She hit the horn and was rewarded with a three-finger salute.

"Ass," she yelled to the driver from the safe confines of her car. Her husband had been shot. He might die, and all these idiots could think about was shaving two minutes off their commute. She took a deep breath. No point wasting energy on jerks in cars.

She couldn't recall Roy ever lying to her. He was scrupulously honest—a trait she admired in theory but sometimes found annoying in practice. Unwillingly, her mind again jumped to the possibility of another woman.

No, not Roy. The idea was absurd.

Wasn't the wife always the last to know? An eddy of doubt caught Diana unaware. No, she couldn't believe she'd been that blind. There had to be another explanation. But she couldn't believe Roy would be involved in anything shady. Her husband was Mr. Integrity. A trait that earned him the begrudging respect of colleagues and adversaries alike.

Roy was modest about his professional achievements, but Diana knew how quickly he'd made a name for himself in a department brimming with ambitious, hardworking lawyers. His success had not been handed to him. He'd worked for it.

He had taken a couple of years off after high school—traveling, he'd told her when they first met; pulling his life together, he'd admitted later, without elaboration. Despite working to put himself through college, he'd managed to graduate in three years and then finish law school in the top ten percent of his class. What stood out, however, was his unwavering commitment to doing what was right. Roy didn't stretch the truth to make a case. He didn't play politics. He didn't make rash promises. And he avoided even the mere appearance of impropriety.

He led an equally upright personal life. He never exceeded the speed limit (although, thankfully, he'd stopped lecturing Diana when she did). He wouldn't drink at all if he'd be driving home after an evening out. He'd even confiscated Emily's illegally downloaded music files—a move that unleashed the wrath of both mother and daughter.

Roy could be annoying but he was never unscrupulous. So why the hell had he gone to the Bayview district of San Francisco with five thousand dollars in his wallet, and why had he lied to her about it?

The Alameda County district attorney's office was in the courthouse near Lake Merritt in Oakland. Parking was never easy, but Diana managed to find a spot only two blocks away.

She climbed the steps of the courthouse, then made her way through security and up to Roy's office. His secretary, Jan, jumped up from her desk when Diana entered. "I didn't expect you," Jan said, hurriedly enveloping Diana in a hug. "Is there news about Roy?"

Diana shook her head. "I'm afraid not."

Jan grabbed both of Diana's hands in her own. "We're all praying for him. The whole office."

"Thank you." Jan's hands were soft and plump, like the woman herself. Now in her late fifties, Jan had worked for Roy almost since his first days there. Diana had worked in a different division of the DA's office and hadn't known Jan until her marriage to Roy. She liked Jan, but she was always a little uncomfortable around the woman. Jan acted as though she was the ultimate authority on everything, including Roy.

"It doesn't seem possible," Jan continued, finally letting go of Diana's hands. "Roy is someone who comes across larger than life. Almost like he's invincible. You don't expect bad news where Roy's concerned."

"I know. I'm—"

Jan's phone rang and she picked it up only long enough to say, "Can I call you back? Thanks." She turned back to Diana. "I know you must have a lot of your mind. What can I help you with?"

Diana was unsure how to proceed and, in truth, a little afraid of overstepping some unspoken boundary. How did you discreetly pry into the life of your husband?

"I have some questions," she began. She really didn't want to be discussing her husband with Jan, but she didn't know how else to get answers.

Jan gave her a curious look.

"I'm trying to understand what happened," Diana explained.

"Of course you are. We all are." Jan checked her watch. "Do you have time for a quick cup of coffee? I was about to head over to Starbuck's for my afternoon latte. We can talk on the way."

"Good idea."

On their way there, they talked about Jan's grandson, and about Jeremy and Emily, and the weather—anything but the subject that was foremost in their minds. Finally, coffee in hand, Jan turned to Diana and asked, "Now then. What is it?"

"I was wondering if any of Roy's cases involve someone named Mia."

Jan frowned. "The name doesn't ring a bell."

They walked back toward the courthouse, sipping their coffee as they went. Diana welcomed the jolt of caffeine.

"What about someone named Mia in the DA's office?" she asked. "Or maybe a defense attorney Roy might have dealt with?"

"Sorry." Jan shook her head. "The only Mia that comes to mind is Mia Farrow. Why?"

Diana would gladly have fabricated some innocuous reason

for asking, except that she was unable to think of one fast enough. "It's a name Roy mumbled in the hospital," she explained.

"He's alert?" Jan stopped mid-step. "Why didn't you say so before this?"

"It was just for a minute, maybe less. He opened his eyes and looked right at me. And he said a few words. Then he slipped back into his coma."

"But that's a good sign, isn't it, that he could wake up enough to talk at all?"

"The doctor wasn't impressed." Diana wasn't sure he'd even believed her.

Jan removed the lid from her coffee cup and tossed it into the trash container at the curb. "Do you think Roy was trying to tell you who shot him?"

"Could be. But I was thinking it might explain what he was doing that afternoon. What about cases involving San Francisco residents? Is Roy dealing with anything like that?"

"I'm sure he must be, although I can't come up with a particular case right off the bat. You know the Bay Area, it's really one big city, in spite of local governments and local law enforcement."

The light changed and they crossed the street. Diana, who normally walked briskly, especially at crosswalks, slowed her pace to match Jan's. When they reached the far curb, she said, "The police seem to be considering the possibility that Roy wasn't simply a random victim."

"I know. They were here yesterday, asking questions."

"The police? What kind of questions?"

"Like what you're asking. Mostly about Roy's cases, possible enemies, strange calls, that sort of thing."

"Were there enemies or strange calls?"

"I'm sure the criminals he's put away are none too happy

with him, but nothing out of the ordinary." Jan hesitated a moment. "Except . . ."

"Except what?"

"There was a message on his answering machine when I came into work Monday morning. It must have come in over the weekend. A man's voice, but no name. He said, pardon my French, 'You'd better not be fucking with me.' It wasn't even so much what he said. It was his tone. Tense, kind of threatening."

"Did you tell the police?"

Jan bristled. "Of course I told them." She paused. "Do they think someone set out to kill Roy, is that it?"

"I don't know what they think," Diana said, not bothering to hide her annoyance at police protocol. "It doesn't make sense that someone would lure him over to San Francisco to kill him. Why not just shoot him on his way to work or something?"

"I guess they're covering all the bases. Roy's an important figure, someone they'll go the extra mile for." Jan's tone was condescending, as though Diana didn't know her own husband.

They'd reached the courthouse. Diana eyed the imposing front steps. "Would it be okay if I looked in his office?"

Jan raised an eyebrow. "I can't do that. Confidentiality, and all."

"You can trust me," Diana pleaded. "You know you can."

Jan shook her head. "I'd lose my job. Gotta follow protocol."

"But this is important. Somebody shot my husband." Diana was close to tears.

Jan looked at her apologetically. "Sorry. But maybe I can help. What are you looking for?"

"I don't know. Something that might tell me what's going on." Diana pressed her fingers against her eyelids. She wasn't going to cry. Not now. Not here. "Could Roy have come in to work on Sunday?"

"I doubt it. His desk looked untouched. I'm sure the police

checked the sign-in log, but I'll take a look and let you know."

"Thanks, I'd appreciate that. And keep your eye out for a green gym bag."

"That old thing? It's not in his office, I can tell you that. I've been after him forever to get a new one. Told him it did nothing for his image. Not that Roy gives a rat's ass about his image."

Diana's head hurt by the time she got home. The answering machine was full of condolence messages from friends and interview requests from the press. She ignored them all. She had ninety minutes before she had to pick up Jeremy, and she had a column to write.

But first, she called the country club and spoke with the assistant at the pro shop to confirm that Roy had not played there on Sunday. He hadn't.

"Oh, he could have slipped on without signing in, I suppose," the assistant told her. "But his name's not in the book."

And Diana knew Roy always signed in. Roy played by the rules.

So where was his gym bag? Diana distinctly remembered seeing him leave the house with it. She replayed the scene in her mind. Roy had come into the kitchen where she was putting away groceries.

"I'm off," he'd said.

"Fine. Suit yourself. You seem to be doing a lot of that lately."

Their argument from that morning was still fresh in Diana's mind, and Roy's plea to "just be patient and bear with me for a bit" had done nothing to soften her anger.

"Jeremy needs you," she had told him. "You're his father. A boy needs a father. Isn't he more important than some stupid golf game?" A golf game, she added silently, that he hadn't even scheduled.

There'd been a moment of silence and Diana wondered if

she'd managed to anger her ordinarily unflappable husband.

"Diana," he'd said finally, and then paused. He looked ready to say more, but then kissed her lightly and said, "Love you. I should be back by five."

I should be back by five, Diana repeated to herself. Would a man squeeze an assignation with his lover into such a narrow window of time?

Maybe, if he was desperate enough.

Roy had definitely had that ratty old gym bag over his shoulder. It wasn't something he usually took to the club, but Diana hadn't thought much about it at the time because she'd been focused on her anger. Maybe he'd packed the thing with the necessities for a romantic afternoon, whatever *they* might be. Sorrow and anger squeezed Diana's heart, even as she mentally tried to reassure herself. Roy was not the sort of man to have a secret affair.

She pushed the conflicting emotions aside and sat down at her computer.

Several days ago, she wrote, *my husband was shot in an armed robbery. Talk about putting things into perspective. We'd argued that morning. My last words to him were hurtful, spoken in anger.*

Diana's throat grew tight. Dear God, don't let them be my final words to Roy. Please let him be okay.

Difficult as it was to write, Diana finished the piece with ten minutes to spare. She wanted to close her eyes and regroup before she left to get Jeremy. Instead, she called Emily, who rarely answered Diana's calls, and left a message, adding, as always, "I love you."

Diana hadn't planned on getting pregnant with Emily. She and Garrick had been in college, and although they'd talked about marriage, it was something for the future. It was Garrick who pushed for marriage after the pregnancy test came back positive, but he never really saw being married as anything more than dating with full-time benefits. Diana agreed because it seemed the right thing to do. But from the moment she'd felt the first flutter of movement inside her, she had fallen under the spell of the tiny, magical creature who claimed her heart.

Diana wasn't sure just when—or why—her relationship with Emily began to show signs of strain, but by the time Garrick, who'd walked away from them when Emily was three, re-appeared in his daughter's life her freshman year in high school, Emily had shuttered herself from Diana in every way possible.

Hormones, said the doctor she talked to. Teenage growing pains, said the counselor. Give her time, said Roy. But none of them had to live with the pain of being rejected by your own child.

Diana felt drained. She went to the closet to get a sweater and remembered Roy's gun. She wasn't about to deliver the damn thing to the police. If they wanted it, they could come get it.

She pushed aside the stack of folded blankets and took down the metal safe. It was lighter than she remembered, and when she opened the combination lock, she knew why.

The gun was gone.

CHAPTER 10

Joel Richards had been born and raised in Littleton, Georgia, and while it was a perfectly fine place to grow up, and a popular spot for beachfront vacationing, he hadn't expected he'd still be living there at the age of twenty-five. He'd envisioned himself up north—New York, Boston, Chicago, or maybe out west in San Francisco or Los Angeles. Even Atlanta would be a step in the right direction. He was a journalist, after all, or at least that's what he hoped he was, and the stories he longed to write weren't to be found in Littleton.

The good thing about newspaper work in a small town was that he got to cover pretty much everything—town council meetings, school events, human interest pieces and the occasional accident or fire. The bad part was that *everything* in a small coastal town in Georgia wasn't really much at all.

Until now.

Joel still couldn't believe what Skeet Birnbaum, editor-in-chief of the *Littleton Post*, was telling him.

"You know those bones they found when they were clearing land for that new waterfront development?" Skeet asked, settling back in his office chair.

"Yeah, sure." The discovery ten days earlier had caused quite a stir. The developers, fearing they'd happened on some ancient Indian burial ground, had at first tried to keep the news from the press. When it had been determined the skeleton was more recent, the developers breathed more easily, but speculation among townsfolk had grown rampant.

"Well . . ." Skeet paused, and did his best imitation of a drum roll. "They've been identified as belonging to Miranda Saxton." He looked triumphantly at Joel, then sighed. "You've never heard of her, I take it."

Joel shook his head.

"You've heard of Harry Saxton, though?"

"Sure. U.S. senator from Virginia. One of the longest serving members of Congress."

"Miranda was his daughter."

Joel was suddenly curious. "What happened to her?"

Skeet steepled his fingers at his chin and looked over them at Joel. "Well now, that's what the cops tried to figure out twenty-some years ago when she disappeared."

"Disappeared? All that time her family didn't know if she was alive or dead?"

"Nope. Although I imagine as the years went by they more or less assumed the worst. She was vacationing with her family here in Littleton. They were guests of Walter St. John, another name you've probably never heard of. St. John used to own that whole stretch of coast south of town. Every summer he'd invite a handful of the rich and powerful to mingle at his compound for a couple of weeks."

"Rough life," Joel offered with a touch of sarcasm. Littleton still had its share of fancy condos and resorts, but Joel knew that the town's heyday as a mecca for the wealthy was before his time.

"The day before the family was scheduled to leave for home," Skeet continued, "Miranda disappeared. Caused quite a hullabaloo around here."

Joel shuddered. "How old was she?"

"Seventeen or eighteen, as I recall. She was set to attend Yale in the fall." Skeet said it in a tone that showed just what he thought of Yale, which wasn't much.

It wasn't that Skeet had anything against Yale; he simply didn't like Ivy League, period. The old guy had been impressed that Joel had stayed local and gone to a state school, although his regard for Joel's choice had been somewhat tempered when Joel explained that it was only because his father had been ill and needed Joel's help.

"They must have had some theories about what happened to her," Joel said.

"Oh, there were theories, all right. That she'd run off. That she'd committed suicide. Even some speculation early on that she'd been kidnapped for ransom. But the one theory that jelled involved a young man from town, the last known person to have seen her the night she disappeared. Pretty soon it was more or less accepted fact that he'd killed her."

Joel was intrigued. "Did they arrest him?"

"They did, but they couldn't hold him. Wasn't any evidence of an actual crime."

"Until now."

Skeet smiled. "So here's the thing. The big media guns are going to be all over this thing. But you're local. It's too bad you didn't know her—"

"How could I have known her?" Joel blurted. "I was only five years old when she disappeared."

Skeet brushed the air with his hands. "As I was saying, even if you didn't know her, you know the town and you know the people who were here then."

"I do?" Joel's father had worked as a fisherman. He doubted his father would know anything about the world of the St. Johns and the Saxtons, even if his mind was lucid enough to remember anything from twenty years ago.

"You know me," Skeet replied. "And Chief Holt—he was a detective then. I can put you in touch with others. This is your chance, kid. Your chance to make a mark. That's what you've been pining for, isn't it?"

Damn! Skeet had seen through him so easily. He'd tried to hide his impatience with small-town news. "You want me to cover the story?"

"More than that. Yes, of course, cover it for us. But you'll be in a position to coordinate for the other folks. You play this right, you might get national coverage."

Joel's heart was racing. He was both excited and afraid. And a little uneasy. "It doesn't seem right to build a name on the bones of a dead girl," he said after a moment.

"That's journalism, son. Get over it or learn to love selling insurance. You with me on this?"

"Yes."

Skeet handed him a thick folder. "Here's what I could pull together from the files. The coroner and Chief Holt are expecting your call. Don't make me doubt my confidence in you."

"No, sir. I'll do my best."

"That's the spirit." Skeet hooked his thumbs into the waistband of his slacks and grinned like a man who'd just bagged a five-point buck. "You absorb what's in those files, and anything else you can find, and we'll talk again."

Joel beat a hasty retreat back to his desk. What if he wasn't up to this? It was one thing to chase after a dream when you knew it was only a dream. It was something else entirely to be put to the test and come up short.

He was terrified he'd discover he'd been deluding himself all along. But he had to try, didn't he? If he failed, well, like Skeet said, he could learn to love selling insurance.

He wiped his sweaty palms on his pants legs as he recalled the words of his dear, deceased mother paraphrasing Yoda. *There is no try, there is only do.*

CHAPTER 11

When Chloe got home from work Tuesday evening, Trace was sprawled on the couch in front of the TV, watching a rerun of *The Simpsons*. Dirty dishes, potato chip crumbs, and three empty beer bottles littered the floor nearby. From the looks of things, he'd probably spent a good part of the day anchored to that same spot.

"How are you doing?" she asked, bending to kiss him.

"My shoulder hurts like hell when I move," he grumbled, "and like heck when I don't."

"You think it's infected?"

"How should I know? But don't start bugging me about seeing a doctor, okay? If my arm doesn't fall off, I'll probably live."

He did look better, even though he hadn't showered or shaved in two days. Or changed his clothes. Still, he seemed more alert, and the color had returned to his skin.

"Has there been any stuff in the news?" she asked. "About, you know, what happened?"

"There's not going to be anything more. You worry too much."

And Trace didn't worry enough.

"You didn't say anything to anyone at work, did you?" Trace asked sharply.

"No, of course not."

Chloe hadn't wanted to go to work that morning, but it wasn't like either of them had cushy jobs with sick leave and time off. If they didn't work, they didn't get paid. She'd been nervous the whole day, especially when she was working the register. Once, a guy in a dark blue uniform came into the shop and she just about bolted out the back door. Turned out he was parking enforcement looking to buy some poster paint, but she'd been sure he'd come to arrest her.

Her friend Velma, working the other register, remarked that Chloe seemed jumpy.

"I'm not totally over the flu," Chloe had explained.

"You should have stayed home then."

"I'm better, just not a hundred percent."

Velma had eyed Chloe with concern, her eyes very white against her dark skin. "You didn't take any meds, did you? It's not good for the baby, you know."

"I know, and I didn't take anything."

"You think it's hard being pregnant," her friend said with a laugh, "just wait till you've got a kid to take care of."

Chloe *was* waiting, eagerly. Or she had been until Sunday. Now she was worried she'd end up in prison and never see her baby.

With effort, Trace pushed himself to a sitting position on the couch. "You positive you didn't say anything about what happened? I know how girls get with one another sometimes. They don't know when to shut up."

"I would never say anything," Chloe protested.

"Maybe not on purpose, but you can't be too careful."

"I am careful." Just talking about it caused a flutter of panic in Chloe's chest. "They could still find us, you know. Cops have ways."

"You always go right to the worst case in everything." Trace aimed the remote at the TV. "I'm out of beer. Why don't you run down the store and get some more."

"No."

"What?"

She cringed inwardly. "I can't. What if I get caught? They might recognize me from something that witness said."

Trace threw the remote on the floor. "You're a goddamn black cloud of worst-case worry."

"I'm sorry, Trace, but we need to be careful."

"Yeah, yeah. That's why I told you not to yap to your friends about what happened. Oh, never mind. We have any pain pills left?"

"A couple."

"Get me one of those then." His eyes raked her flesh with their displeasure. "If you'll be so kind."

When Trace dozed off, Chloe went to the linen closet in the bathroom and retrieved the DA's gym bag from under the extra blanket where she'd hidden it. First thing, she wanted to get rid of the gun she'd found in the bag. Trace and guns were a bad combination.

Guns scared Chloe so she lifted it carefully with the barrel pointing to the floor, and stuck it in her purse. She would dump it in the trash somewhere on her way to work tomorrow. Then she went through the remaining contents of the bag. She knew there was nothing valuable there because she'd looked Sunday evening, but now she wanted to see what was in there.

She pulled out a wadded-up pair of grease-streaked khakis and an equally unkempt T-shirt. The DA wasn't much of a clotheshorse, although he'd looked decent enough on Sunday. She added some gum and stick deodorant to the pile, along with an Oakland Raiders baseball cap. She wondered if a cap with a *football* team logo on it was actually a *baseball* cap. But she'd never heard of a football cap.

At the bottom of the bag were a couple of photos and a key ring with five keys. She turned the bag inside out and shook it because she'd once read a mystery book where the main character did that and found secret papers. But there was nothing more in this gym bag except a quarter that clattered to the floor.

She held her breath, hoping Trace hadn't heard. His snoring continued, uninterrupted.

She turned to the photographs. One was a snapshot of four people—two men and two women. She thought the man on the left might be the DA who was shot but she couldn't be sure. One of the women was probably his wife and the other two, friends or relatives.

There was a second, smaller, photo—a woman and a young boy about twelve. The woman had her arm around the boy's shoulder and they were both squinting into the sun, grinning at the camera. Chloe imagined an adoring father behind the camera, laughing and pleading with the two of them to hold still. She patted her belly and mentally added *camera* to the list of things she needed to get before the baby arrived. Trace was right about one thing. They needed money.

She stuck the contents back into the bag and returned it to the closet. The gym bag was a real disappointment. There was nothing of value in it. Nothing of interest, even.

She lay on the bed with the library book she'd gotten last week. It was a best seller, which had to mean that a lot of people thought it was really good. But Chloe was finding it hard to care about any of the characters, even the main character who she was pretty sure she was supposed to be rooting for.

Chloe liked to read. She went to the library regularly and usually checked out several books at a time. She liked mystery and romance best, but she read what the librarian called serious stuff, too. Books about people in poor countries or with horrible childhoods. Chloe thought you could learn a lot about the world by reading.

She heard Trace call her from the other room.

"Hey, baby," he said when she came into the room. "I'm feeling so much better." He reached out his good arm and pulled her onto the sofa next to him, favoring her with one of his goofy smiles. She loved it when Trace smiled at her like that.

She laughed. "You're high from the medicine."

"Probably so, but it's better than being in pain. Soooo much better." He leaned closer and kissed her under her ear, a spot that always made her tingle with pleasure. "You're my gal and I love you."

"I love you, too."

"We're going to be okay, Chloe. I know things are a little rough now, but we'll work it out."

Trace's optimism soothed some of the worry she felt. "As long as we're together," she said, "you, me, and the baby. That's all I want."

Trace leaned his head against the back of the couch and lightly stroked Chloe's forearm with his fingers. "I've been thinking," he said after a few moments. "I'm going to have to quit my job."

She sat forward. "But we need the money."

"I know we need money but I can't load pallets with a bum shoulder. And how am I going to explain it, anyway? I take a couple of days off for the flu and come back with only one good arm? Doesn't make sense. People are bound to be suspicious."

"But what I make doesn't—"

"Cut the whining, okay? Things might be different if you'd gotten that DA's wallet like I told you to."

"I couldn't, Trace. It was under him. And there was blood . . . everywhere."

"You're pathetic, Chloe." Trace sounded almost amused.

It had to be the pills, but Chloe was glad he wasn't angry.

"It's getting late," she said. "Are you hungry? You want some dinner?"

"Nah, I made a can of soup earlier. But you go ahead and make something for yourself. Maybe I'll have a couple of bites."

Chloe hesitated. "About your job—"

"I can't go back. You see that, don't you?"

She supposed Trace was right. People would ask questions. But they needed Trace's income.

"I've got an idea, though," he added.

"What?" Chloe didn't trust Trace and his ideas. That's what had gotten them into the fix they were in.

The doorbell rang, followed by a loud knock. Chloe rose to answer it. She'd barely turned the knob when three tough-looking guys shoved past her and into the apartment.

Trace's face whitened. He struggled to his feet. "Go into the other room, Chloe!"

She didn't recognize the men but Trace must have known them. They weren't much bigger than Trace but they looked meaner. There were three of them and only one of him. And Trace was injured.

"Go on," Trace commanded. "For once, do what I tell you."

She glanced at the three men and then nervously back to Trace, but he didn't take his eyes off the three men.

Reluctantly, she retreated to the bedroom.

"Close the door," Trace called after her.

Chloe closed the door.

Only then did she remember the gun in her purse, still in the living room. If only she'd brought it with her.

But would she have used it? *Could* she have used it? Someone smart and brave, like women she read about in books, would have come up with a plan. But Chloe wasn't able to wrap her mind around anything but pure panic.

She heard them talking and leaned close to the door.

"It didn't work out," Trace was saying apologetically. "I couldn't get there the way we planned."

"Yeah? Why's that?"

"My girlfriend, she's pregnant, has to pee all the time. Stop here, stop there, and it takes her forever. We never made it to the store. Figured we'd just do it another day."

"You just figured, huh?"

Chloe didn't know which of the men was speaking, but she imagined it was the weasel-faced one with the shaved head and the skull tattoo.

"You think about *us* at all, asshole? You said you'd get the money."

"I will."

"Funny thing," said a second voice, low and menacing. "You didn't get there Sunday but someone just happened to hold up the store. What a coincidence."

"Weird, huh?" Trace muttered.

"You're not holding out on us, are you?"

"No, I swear. I'll get the money. I got other options."

Chloe was afraid her heart would race right out of her chest. What had Trace gotten involved in now?

"You're a piece of shit, Trace. You owe us. Just get the money."

"I will. I promise."

"And if it turns out you're pulling a fast one," added the third voice, "you're screwed. You got that?"

"Yeah. I hear you."

Chloe heard a series of loud clatters and she stifled a scream. The sound of shattering glass followed.

"Geez, Trace," said the weasel-face voice. "Looks like you've got a bit of a mess to clean up here."

The apartment door slammed shut.

Chloe slowly opened the bedroom door and peered out, afraid she might find Trace bleeding or knocked out on the floor. But he sat on the couch, breathing hard.

"You okay?" She rushed to his side.

"No, I'm not okay." He stood up and backhanded her across the face. "Why didn't you just stay in the fucking car like you were supposed to?"

CHAPTER 12

At six-thirty the next morning, Diana dragged herself out of bed after a mostly futile effort at sleep. Her body felt stiff and sore, as though she'd physically fought off every fear and doubt during the night.

She threw on her robe and called the hospital, even before she brushed her teeth. She knew she'd have heard if there'd been a change in Roy's condition. Still, the measured, dispassionate voice of the duty nurse confirming that there was no improvement sent Diana into a pit of unexpected despair. Roy was never going to get better, the shooter would never be caught, and she would never learn why Roy had lied to her.

Groggily, she downed a couple of ibuprofen and showered quickly, refusing to let her gaze linger on the haggard face she saw in the mirror. This was one of her days to volunteer in Jeremy's classroom—a twice-a-month commitment she always enjoyed. But today, her usual enthusiasm had deserted her.

She didn't *have* to go. It wouldn't be the first time a parent hadn't shown up. They probably didn't expect her anyway. Not with Roy in the hospital. But if Jeremy could go to school at a time like this, shouldn't she be as strong?

She dressed for a day in the classroom—an easily washable T-shirt and old jersey pants she wouldn't miss if they were ruined. Paint and dirt, and occasionally blood, were all part of a day spent with seven-year-olds.

Downstairs, she fed Digger and poured cereal into a bowl for

Jeremy. Diana knew she should eat something herself, but she had no appetite. Over breakfast, she told Jeremy that they'd visit Roy together that afternoon.

"What if he's still sleeping?" Jeremy asked, picking a single Cheerio from his bowl with his fingers.

"I'm pretty sure he will be, honey. But he'll know we're there, anyway."

Jeremy popped the Cheerio in his mouth and munched it slowly. "And that will make him feel better, right?"

"Absolutely."

It broke Diana's heart to see her little boy looking so sad. She wondered if she was doing the right thing taking him to the hospital. The visit would be hard on him, but it might be harder in the long run if she didn't take him, especially since he'd been asking repeatedly to go. And just maybe, Jeremy's visit might be the jump-start Roy needed to start healing.

Diana made it as far as the classroom door, where shrieks of laughter and a swarm of eager faces greeted her. Normal life abuzz, not ten feet in front of her. But the chasm was so great it stopped her cold. She couldn't cross it. She could no more go in there, bristling with good cheer and encouragement, than she could fly to the moon.

She put her hand on Jeremy's shoulder just as he was about to run off and greet his friends. "I'm sorry, honey, but I'm suddenly not feeling so well. I'm afraid I'm not going to be able to help in the classroom today."

Jeremy's face fell. "What about seeing Daddy? You promised."

"We'll do that. We will. This afternoon, just like I told you. But this morning I need to rest. You okay with that?"

With the visit to his dad still assured, Jeremy nodded, if somewhat reluctantly, and joined the throng of movement inside the classroom. Diana found the teacher and made her apologies.

"Oh, of course you don't need to be here. I never for a minute thought to expect you today. Don't think twice about it." She touched Diana's arm. "You and your family are in my prayers."

Diana wasn't convinced that all the prayers in the world would make a difference.

Back home, Diana called Emily. Normally, they didn't talk more than once a week at most, but life was hardly normal, and Diana, who always felt as though she walked on eggshells where Emily was concerned, was feeling especially anxious about not angering her daughter.

"I can't talk," Emily said, although she *had* answered the phone, which was unusual. "How's Roy? Any news?"

"No real change." As for news, Diana saw no point in telling Emily that Roy had mumbled a strange woman's name while unconscious or that the police seemed to suspect he might somehow be implicated in the robbery in which he was shot. Those were not the sort of suspicions a good mother shared with her daughter. And Diana tried desperately to be a good mother, even when she wasn't.

"Oh," Emily said, sounding somewhat perplexed. "Then why'd you call?"

"I wanted to see how you were doing." Diana was suddenly unsure why she'd thought calling Emily was a good idea.

"You know, same old stuff." Emily's words were muffled, either by bad cell phone reception or because she was distracted and not talking into the phone. "Roy's going to get better, isn't he?"

"I hope so."

"I do, too." Emily's voice broke. "He's got to."

"How are your classes?" Diana asked, priming the conversation pump. "Are you managing to keep up?" Emily had never been a strong student, and Diana worried that the rigors of college might be too much for her, even without a family tragedy.

"Sort of. Speaking of class, I need to get going."

"Okay, talk to you soon. Bye, honey. I love you."

A stretch of silence and then a muffled "Bye, Mom."

Diana sighed, made a second cup of coffee, and sat down with the morning's paper. Since Monday, when she'd combed the paper for everything she could find about the shooting, she hadn't done more than skim the front page headlines. She wasn't particularly interested in what was going on outside of her own unsettled world, but sipping coffee while reading the paper was a familiar ritual and she welcomed familiar wherever she could find it.

It wasn't until she reached the third page of the second section, the local news section, that she started reading in earnest. There she found a human interest piece about Hector Kimball, the clerk who'd been killed in the same botched robbery where Roy had been shot. Hector was the second of five children, the youngest of whom was only four years old. His father was a disabled shipyard worker and his mother worked nights for a commercial janitorial service. Hector's older brother, the first and only person in the family to have graduated from high school, had been killed last year in Iraq. Hector hadn't yet turned eighteen and his funeral was tomorrow.

For all her own pain, Diana was struck by the terrible losses the Kimball family had suffered. She'd pictured the clerk as some faceless entity, another cog in the blur of poverty. She was horrified now at her callousness. These were human beings whose anguish was as great as her own.

She studied the newspaper photo of Hector. It showed a serious young man, a boy really, with a thin face and deep-set eyes. Had Roy been shot helping him resist the robbery? Diana wanted to believe that was the case, but she was reminded again that she didn't have the slightest understanding of what Roy had been up to that afternoon.

Diana dumped what was left of her coffee into the sink. She couldn't live with so many open questions. She needed answers.

An address scribbled on a torn margin of an advertising supplement wasn't much to go on, but at the moment it was all she had. She grabbed her purse and car keys, then decided to drive Roy's Lexus instead of her own Volvo so she could take it to the car wash. Roy was meticulous about his car and he wouldn't be happy with the oily coat of grime that had accumulated during the two days in the impound lot. It depressed her to think this was one of the few things she could do for him.

As she pulled into a parking spot on Bayo Vista, Diana wondered if she should have asked Len to accompany her. It wasn't that the neighborhood seemed especially dangerous—in fact, on previous blocks she'd seen occasional pedestrians, including a mother and child, and there were workmen of some sort in the block ahead. But most of the houses were small and rundown, with bars on their first-floor windows. And in the bare dirt park across the street, two men were standing next to a smoking trash can and drinking from a container in a brown paper bag.

It didn't look like the sort of neighborhood where Roy might find a lover.

The address in question was toward the middle of the block. Diana's heart sank when she realized it was an apartment building with maybe twelve or fifteen units. The paper with the address hadn't listed an apartment number. She had no idea where to start.

She studied the faded pink, three-story stucco building, then sighed. It was all she had at the moment so she'd have to make the best of it. With Roy's photo tucked inside her purse, she got out of the car, stepped around a broken beer bottle on the sidewalk, and headed for the apartment building.

Out of the five apartments on the first floor, only one elderly resident answered her knock. He gave Roy's photo a cursory look, then shook his head.

"Never seen him," he said before closing the door in Diana's face.

Feeling uncomfortably out of her element, she climbed the open stairway to the second floor, where two doors opened for her. One was a young man who shot a torrent of Spanish at her without bothering to undo the security chain. The other was an overly thin, light-skinned black woman whose apartment reeked of cigarette smoke. She was probably only in her early thirties, but she had the hard, lined face of someone whom life had not treated well.

She took her time studying Roy's photo, then shook her head.

"He doesn't look familiar. Are you with the police? Is he dangerous?"

"No." Diana hadn't thought how to explain herself. "My brother," she said, going with the first thought that came to her. "We've lost touch and this is the last address I had for him."

"He's a good-looking guy."

"Yes, he is."

"Family is such a hassle, isn't it?" The woman laughed without humor. "Me, I'd be only too happy to lose touch with my brother."

"Well, sorry to have bothered you."

She handed the photo back to Diana. "Your brother, he's a nice guy?"

"Very."

She gave Diana a wistful look. "You're lucky. Mine's a bum. Good luck. Hope you find him." Another humorless laugh. "If you do and he's single, tell him Brenda Harris would like to meet him."

The third floor proved equally unhelpful. Dispirited, Diana started down the cracked cement stairs to the street. Her phone rang as she reached the second floor landing, reverberating loudly in the narrow stairwell.

"Hi," Allison said. "I expected voicemail. Isn't this your day to work at Jeremy's school?"

"I bailed, couldn't handle it."

"Not surprising. Where are you, anyway? You sound like you're talking from the bottom of a well."

"I am. A stairwell." She told Allison about checking out the address she'd found in Roy's car. "It's a down-at-the-heels apartment building in a similar sort of neighborhood, assuming the address on the paper even refers to San Francisco. There was no city, just a street and number."

"Shouldn't you leave that stuff to the police?"

"Probably. At least I can be reasonably sure it's not the address of a mistress."

"You can't honestly have thought it might be."

"The name 'Mia' has to mean something to him," Diana said. "And Roy's been different this last month or so. Distracted and detached."

"Whatever was on his mind," Allison insisted, "it must have been about work."

"In any case, today was a waste of time. That address has probably been sitting in his car for months." Diana reached the ground floor and crossed the street to her car. "Oh, my God."

"What is it?"

"My windshield. Roy's windshield. It's smashed." Diana's first reaction was one of disbelief, followed by anger. "I wasn't gone even half an hour."

"Is there anyone around?"

"No. There were a couple of guys hanging out in the park when I got here, but nobody now." Diana peered through the mosaic of shattered window glass. "And my leather jacket is gone from the front seat."

Normally, she'd have called Roy. He'd talk her through it, calm her down, and then make everything right. She wanted to cry.

"Call the police," Allison said, "and then Triple A. Where are you?"

"On Bayo Vista, across from something called Dewey Park, although it's not much of a park." The bleakness of the litter-strewn dirt park matched her mood.

"Do you want me to come get you?"

Diana looked at her watch. She had no idea how long it would take to get the car towed and deal with whatever reports needed to be filed. "It would be a big help if you'd pick up Jeremy for me. I hate to ask but—"

"Of course, no problem. Give Len a call and he'll come get you. I'll tell him to expect your call."

"What would I do without you two?"

"Luckily you don't have to find out."

Diana called AAA and gave them her location, reading the address from the scrap of newspaper ad she'd found in Roy's car. As she finished the call, she noticed the paper was dated the Sunday Roy had been shot.

Diana's pulse quickened. The scrap of paper hadn't been in Roy's car forever. It had to be connected in some way to what had happened.

CHAPTER 13

Chloe's shift would end in half an hour and she still didn't know what she was going to do when it was time to go home. At least Trace hadn't stormed into the Craft Connection today, as she'd been afraid he might. There was no telling what Trace would do when he got angry. And last night he'd been as angry as she'd ever seen him.

Reflexively, Chloe touched her cheek, which made the dull throbbing sharpen with knifelike intensity. Her eye was swollen and she knew the makeup she'd layered on that morning hadn't done a very good job of covering the bruise, even with repeated applications. She certainly hadn't fooled her friend Velma, who'd commented on it right off.

"That boyfriend of yours hit you?" Velma asked when they were unlocking their cash registers that morning.

"I ran into the bathroom door in the dark," Chloe told her.

"Honey, that doesn't look like a door kind of bruise to me."

When Chloe didn't respond, she added, "I been hit myself. I know what it's like. But pretending it didn't happen won't change anything. Abuse is abuse."

Chloe looked her friend in the eye. "I'm a big girl, Velma. I don't need you running my life for me."

It was the right thing to say, because Velma only gave her a long look, then turned away, shaking her head. But Chloe felt bad, because Velma was one of the only friends she had—although "friend" was probably stretching it, since Velma was twelve years older and they never saw each other outside of work. Chloe didn't know much about Velma's life except that she and her little boy lived with her sister and no one was happy with the arrangement.

So Velma had been hit in the past. Well, so had Chloe.

But abuse? That was pushing it. Trace had been angry was all, and short-tempered because he was in pain. No one was on their best behavior when they were hurting. He'd also been scared by the three guys who'd forced their way into the apartment. Scared and afraid to admit it.

She still didn't know what the men wanted and had been afraid to ask. After Trace hit her, she'd expected an apology. That's what usually happened. She'd do something to push him over the edge and he'd react. But he usually apologized right away and begged her to forgive him. So last night when he hit her a second time, Chloe hadn't seen it coming. When she tried to get away, he grabbed her by the hair until she twisted free, ran into the bedroom, and locked the door. Thankfully Trace hadn't tried to kick it in, because he easily could have. The whole building was so poorly constructed, it was a miracle it was still standing.

Chloe had been frightened. She might not admit it to Velma, but at the time, she'd been really scared of what Trace might do. She'd heard him in the living room swearing and kicking the wall, but he hadn't come after her. When she left for work this morning, he'd been sound asleep on the couch, and she felt guilty for having been afraid. Trace loved her. She should never think the worst of him.

She had tossed the DA's gun in a dumpster on her way to work. There'd been a moment last night when it had crossed her mind she might have to use it against Trace, and that frightened her most of all.

She wasn't eager to go home just yet. But what other options did she have? She'd have to go back sooner or later. Besides, Trace never stayed angry for very long.

She'd be really good to him. She'd stop by the store and buy one of those rotisserie chickens he liked. And the expensive brand of French fries. He had to be feeling bad about hitting her. If she was careful not to make a big deal out of it, they could put the whole thing behind them. Couples had arguments. That was normal. The important thing was not to hold a grudge. She had read that more than once in those women's magazines by the checkout stand.

When her shift ended, she gathered her jacket and her purse. Velma was working the cash register by the door, waiting on a customer. When Chloe walked by, Velma said, "You take care, honey. Remember, you got a baby to think about now."

Chloe wanted to give another sharp retort, but knew Velma meant well. Velma had a big heart and you couldn't fault someone for that. "I am thinking about the baby," Chloe told her. "And everything's going to be fine."

And as she headed for the bus stop, she put a hand on her belly. "It is, Jenny," she told the baby. "I promise. Daddy was just having a bad night, that's all."

Chloe entered the apartment carrying a bag of groceries and shaking with trepidation. She wasn't sure what to expect. Usually after a fight Trace was really sweet, but sometimes he was cool and distant. What she didn't expect was that Trace would simply not be there.

"Trace?" She put the groceries on the kitchen counter and peered into the small living-dining area. She checked the bedroom and bathroom. All empty. The apartment was still a mess of overturned furniture and broken glass, and there was no sign of Trace. Not even a note.

Chloe's heart sank. What if he'd walked out and left her for good? What would she do? She'd be all alone. Trace was her whole life. Good memories flooded her mind and brought tears to her eyes. She'd screwed up again. Driven him away. Why did she always make a mess of everything?

She raced back to the bedroom to the closet and was relieved to find it wasn't empty. Trace's pants and shirts were still there. His underwear and socks were in his drawer, his toothbrush in the bathroom. Wherever he was, he hadn't left her.

So where was he? And why hadn't he scribbled a note? He was wounded and weak. He wouldn't go out for no reason. Was he still mad at her?

She put away the groceries and debated what to do about dinner. She didn't want to heat the fries too early or they'd be cold by the time Trace came home. And the roasted chicken couldn't sit out forever. You could get sick that way. Chloe had had that lesson drummed into her at the group home.

Then another thought hit her. What if Weasel-face and his friends from last night had returned? The apartment was messed up—overturned tables and lamps, broken glass, and a big dent in the plaster where it looked like Trace had kicked it in anger. But was it any worse than when she'd left for work this morning? Hard to tell.

By now she'd worked herself into a state of panic. Trace might be in trouble. What if the thugs had beaten Trace and taken him captive? She couldn't very well call the police, could she? She walked around the apartment, growing more and more agitated. Finally she put the chicken in the fridge—better cold than deadly—and took the garbage downstairs to the dumpster.

Coming back into the lobby, she ran into the short-haired woman with the black Lab who'd moved in about a month earlier.

"Hi," the woman said, holding the door for Chloe. "I'm Ellie. I've seen you around."

Ellie looked to be a few years older than Chloe, and though they'd nodded to each other in passing, this was the first time they'd spoken.

"Hi." Chloe didn't offer up her own name. Her mind was consumed with worry about Trace.

"You live on the third floor, with a guy, right?" Ellie signaled to the Lab to sit. "Roommate or boyfriend?"

"Boyfriend," Chloe replied, noting that Ellie hadn't thought to include "husband" as an option.

Trace hadn't offered up that option either, even though she said with the baby coming they ought to get married. Not that being married would change the mess they were in now.

It dawned on her that Ellie might have seen Trace leaving. "You didn't by any chance see my boyfriend this afternoon, did you?"

Ellie shook her head. "What'd he do, go out and forget to tell you? Men can be so thoughtless sometimes."

"I guess maybe he went out with some friends. You didn't see any strangers around earlier, did you?"

"Sorry. I was at work and then I took Ranger here for a walk. Hey, since your boyfriend's not here, why don't you join me? I've got wine and a frozen pizza I was going to put in the oven. Nothing fancy, but I'm kind of tired of dinners alone."

"Oh, thanks. But I can't." Chloe wanted to blurt out everything that happened. She longed to talk to someone, because keeping the fear bottled inside her was making her ill. But she knew that would be a very bad idea.

"Sure you can. Leave a note and tell him to come on down when he gets home."

"No, really. But thanks." Chloe started up the stairs, then turned. "My name's Chloe, by the way."

"Nice to meet you, Chloe. Maybe another time, okay?"

"Yeah, maybe." Trace would have a cow if Chloe got friendly with one of their neighbors. He didn't like nosy neighbors.

When night settled in and Trace still hadn't come home, Chloe's panic grew.

Her mind raced. He'd been hurt. Or killed. Or kidnapped. Or—and she couldn't believe it hadn't crossed her mind until now—arrested. Would he give the cops her name? Tell them how she'd been the one to take the DA's gym bag and how she'd driven the getaway car?

They could be coming to arrest her any minute now.

How could she explain what she'd done? She hadn't known that Trace was going to rob a store, hadn't known he had a gun. But she hadn't called the cops, either.

She felt as though she were drowning. She was going under and there was nothing to grab on to. She felt her stomach rise up. She made it to the bathroom just in time. When she finished throwing up, she sank down on the floor and leaned against the toilet.

Her baby would be born in jail. What did they do with babies whose mothers and fathers were in prison? Tears filled her eyes and the vomit stung her throat. She put her hands to her belly but the words would not come. How could she promise her child anything?

CHAPTER 14

Joel Richards added the file he'd been reading to the stack at the side of his desk, then drained the remains of coffee from his cup. His fourth or fifth cup since breakfast. Definitely more than he was used to. He'd never be able to sleep tonight. Probably wouldn't have slept anyway. The Miranda Saxton murder had his mind racing, his nerves tingling, and his eyes seeing double. It intrigued him for reasons he didn't quite understand. Maybe because it happened locally, and Joel knew the geography and some of the folks who'd been involved in the investigation back then. Or maybe it was something about Miranda that captured Joel's imagination. And he didn't think it was just that she was Senator Saxton's daughter.

He'd spent last night and this morning poring over the files Skeet Birnbaum had given him—newspaper clippings mostly, but photos and court documents as well. It had taken a while to absorb it all, but Joel thought he had a pretty clear outline of what had happened that night twenty years ago.

Miranda had disappeared the Saturday night of Labor Day weekend. She'd been at a beach bonfire, an end-of-the-summer celebration attended by twenty or so of the college students who'd been working at the St. John compound and nearby resorts. It had been one of those hot, humid days, but by evening a breeze had come up and everyone was feeling newly energized.

She'd spent most of the evening dancing with one of the local boys, Brian Riley, son of the county sheriff. Nobody could recall if he'd actually been invited or simply shown up, but no one really cared. It was the end of the summer and they were out to have a good time. One person more or less didn't really matter.

Alcohol had flowed freely, and Miranda was as tipsy as anyone else, but not, according to others in attendance, drunk. None of them remembered seeing her leave, but an older couple vacationing at a neighboring beach house reported seeing a boy and girl sitting by the water's edge a little before midnight, arguing. Their description of the pair fit Miranda and Brian. No one remembered seeing Miranda after that, and no one saw Brian until he stumbled home at four the next morning, igniting the anger of his father.

Joel could easily imagine the scene. Even now, you could walk along the beach any warm weekend evening in summer and see bonfires and parties that were magnets for young people—mostly the tanned preppy types who took cushy summer jobs as lifeguards and tennis instructors at the upscale resorts, but sometimes locals as well, the kids who worked the less glamorous jobs bussing tables and cleaning rooms. Joel had not been part of that crowd, even when he was younger—he'd spent his vacations helping out on his father's fishing boat instead—but he'd spent many a lonely evening back when he was in high school watching the smooth, bronzed bodies, and wishing he could be one of them.

In the initial days after Miranda disappeared there was talk of a kidnapping or accidental drowning, but it wasn't long before suspicion focused on Brian Riley. His father recused himself from the investigation and Brian was arrested ten days later.

Brian claimed to have left Miranda on the beach around twelve-thirty. He explained that she'd wanted to stay and enjoy her last night of summer and had refused to leave. He offered no details about where he'd been or what had happened in the hours between then and his arrival home, except to say that he'd wandered around a bit and then fallen asleep on a bench near the town pier.

He was charged with murder, but despite pressure from the Saxton family, the charges were eventually dropped. The district attorney declined to pursue the case, explaining that the evidence was insufficient to go to trial. A few people close to Brian maintained he was innocent of any wrongdoing, but the general consensus was that his father had called in favors, and that Brian had gotten away with murder.

The case made headlines across the nation as well as locally. And people were angry. There were calls for an ethics investigation and for a grand jury inquiry, and a movement to recall the district attorney, but in the end none of it amounted to anything. The story faded from the headlines as other scandals and crimes emerged.

Joel studied the photos in the clippings. They were mostly of Miranda. Her high school graduation photo, snapshots of vacations and holidays from the family album, including one taken by her father the morning of the day she disappeared. Miranda had been a beauty, all right. Honey-blond hair that wisped around a flawless, heart-shaped face. Her skin was clear, her teeth straight and white, her eyes and smile as bright as an evening star. Why was it, Joel wondered, that people of privilege never had unattractive children?

There were only two photos of Brian Riley in the file. One was his high school graduation photo, which had run in the local paper and some of national papers. The other was his booking photo. Brian was dark-haired and intense, with deep-set eyes and an angular face. He wasn't a bad-looking kid, but certainly not the type you'd picture with a beauty like Miranda. Joel knew what that was like. He'd known since eighth grade that some girls were simply off limits to guys like him.

Brian had been eighteen that summer, Miranda seventeen, almost seven years younger than Joel was now. In the photos they were kids. It was strange to think they'd now be nearing forty. Had she lived, Miranda would still be lovely, Joel would bet on that. She'd have a handsome, successful husband and a couple of gorgeous kids. And Brian? What was he like now?

Maybe he had a frumpy wife and gangly kids. Or maybe he'd married someone like Miranda and was now a successful entrepreneur. Either way, his comfortable life was about to change. With the discovery of Miranda's remains, the authorities wanted to question him again.

Joel checked his watch. He'd attended the official press conference that morning along with probably twenty other media folks from all over the country—a conference during which nothing new was revealed. But thanks to Skeet Birnbaum, he also had an appointment at three o'clock with Chief Holt at police headquarters. If there was inside information to be had, Joel would get first crack.

It was now almost two and Joel hadn't eaten since breakfast. He put the file aside. He'd pick up a bite to eat and then go see what he could learn from Holt.

"So, Joel," Chief Holt said, gesturing for Joel to sit. "You've pulled the story of Miranda's bones. Ought to get you some front-page exposure."

Holt was married to Skeet Birnbaum's sister. In addition, both men had grown up locally, so they had an intertwined past that made Joel dizzy whenever Birnbaum made reference to it. A solidly built man who'd put on a few extra pounds around the middle over the years, Holt's gray hair was trimmed short and neat, his shirt pressed as though it had come directly from the cleaners.

Joel sat in the chair Holt indicated. "Yes, sir. It's bound to be a story that gets people's attention."

"You got that right. You were there this morning. That was the biggest damn crowd of media types I've seen at a press conference around here since the girl went missing twenty years ago."

"Not a lot happens in Littleton. In terms of news."

"Right. And that's the way I like it. So, what can I do for you? Skeet want you to pick my brain for stuff that's not public knowledge?"

Joel smiled. "Something like that."

"Wish I could oblige, son. But we got rules." Holt winked. "Though off the record, there isn't much I could tell you anyway. A skull and a few bones isn't a lot to go on."

"Could you determine how she died? Or where? I mean was it near where her, uh, remains were found?"

"Coroner hasn't issued a full report, but with a homicide this old, my guess is that he won't be able to learn more than he knows now. There's a depression in her skull like she fell or was hit with a blunt object, but that's not to say she wasn't strangled or stabbed or shot too. We've secured the area and have officers going over it with a fine-tooth comb. Maybe we'll find something that tells us more. But probably not. What's important is that we've been able to identify the skull as belonging to Miranda Saxton. I suppose that might bring closure for her family if you believe that sort of stuff. Personally, I find closure is an over-rated thing."

Despite Holt's insistence on rules, he'd already revealed a bit more than he had this morning at the press conference. Joel felt emboldened.

"What about her killer?" he asked. "You said this morning that you're taking a fresh look at all the evidence."

Holt nodded. "A crime twenty years old and no physical evidence to speak of doesn't hold out much promise, but the 'fresh look' stuff sounds nice. People like to hear that." Holt leaned back in his chair and steepled his fingers. "Back then I was sure Brian Riley was involved, and I'm just as sure now."

"Why? Because he was the last person seen with her?"

"That's part of it. Word was, he and the Saxton girl were going at it pretty hot and heavy. Way I figure it, she wouldn't put out and he got angry."

"Was he a known troublemaker?"

"Not officially, no. But everyone who knew him said he had a temper. I'd met him, of course—his dad was my boss back then—but I didn't really know the kid. It was kind of an uncomfortable position for me to be in, arresting my boss's son, but Sheriff Riley made it clear he wanted me to run a clean investigation with no special favors."

"Does that mean you'll arrest Brian Riley again?"

"We have to find him first."

Holt hadn't really answered the question about arrest, but Joel let it go. "Somebody must know where he is."

"You'd think so. But we haven't found that person."

"What about family?"

"No family left. Brian's mom died when he was a freshman in high school. His dad committed suicide less than a year after Miranda disappeared."

That was news to Joel, though hardly an inside scoop. "Why?"

Holt shook his head. "A sad, sad thing. He was the sheriff, remember. He wanted a clean investigation, but I know he was humiliated to have his son charged with murder. Even after Brian got off, everyone believed he was guilty, maybe even the old man. And the town turned on him. Accused him of using his clout to get his son off."

"Did he?"

"Not a chance. Sheriff Riley didn't have that kind of power. And the DA would never have bowed to it if he had. But people tend to believe the worst. They love a good scandal. Things got pretty ugly."

"Couldn't Sheriff Riley simply have moved out of town?"

"He could have but he wasn't that kind of man. He took his service revolver and shot himself."

Joel thought of his own father, now in the grips of dementia. But before his mind faded, he'd been so proud of Joel. Proud of every meaningless accomplishment Joel had achieved from kindergarten on through college graduation. He'd even claimed to be proud that Joel wanted to be journalist, although Joel knew his father had hoped for something grander. Joel hated to think how hurt his dad would have been if Joel had been in Brian's shoes. And if he'd killed himself because of it? How did a son live with that?

"How terrible," Joel said, feeling truly shaken.

"The boy, Brian, was the one who found him. I always wondered if the old man planned it that way."

Joel shuddered. "Any question about it being suicide?"

"You can bet we looked real closely at that one, but the evidence was clear. He also wrote out a note. Brian Riley left town not long after. He didn't keep in touch with anyone but a few friends, and gradually that faded, too."

"Maybe he'll turn himself in," Joel said hopefully. "Doesn't remorse catch up with people sometimes?"

"It's a possibility I guess. More likely, we'll have to track him down, and I suspect that will take a lot of time. Years maybe. This story of yours isn't going to have an ending any time soon."

CHAPTER 15

"The thing is," Diana said, "the address on Bayo Vista has to be important. It was written by someone other than Roy in the margin of a newspaper supplement dated the day he was shot."

"You're sure the supplement was from that Sunday?" Len asked.

"I double-checked the date."

Allison frowned. "So you think someone wrote down the address for Roy?"

Diana nodded. "And there was an open map of San Francisco in Roy's car."

They were sitting around the glass-topped table in Allison and Len's kitchen, finishing off the bottle of merlot they'd shared over Chinese takeout. Jeremy had devoured half the order of pot stickers and then gone into the den to watch *The Land before Time,* one of the numerous DVDs Allison kept on hand for such occasions. Over the hum of the refrigerator, Diana could hear muted sounds from the movie.

She felt vaguely guilty for not heading home immediately after picking up Jeremy, but by the time Roy's Lexus had been towed, the windshield replacement had been scheduled, and Len had driven her home to get her own car, she hadn't had the strength to endure one more challenge. She'd welcomed Allison's invitation to stay for dinner. Now, after a satisfying meal and several glasses of wine, Diana was finally able to focus on the underlying reason for her excursion that afternoon. Not that focusing brought her any closer to understanding what Roy had been doing at a convenience store in a bad part of San Francisco when he was supposed to be playing golf in Oakland.

Diana sighed. "If it was connected to something at work, he would have told me. So what was he doing there?"

"Could it have been about drugs?" Len's high, wide brow grew furrowed.

Allison looked at him like he was nuts. "Roy and drugs? Are you kidding?"

"Just trying to come up with ideas," Len said.

"I thought of that, too," Diana offered. "But Allison is right. Roy is the last person I'd suspect of being involved with drugs."

He *had* been carrying five thousand dollars and, apparently, his gun, so anything was possible. But Diana hadn't shared that information with anyone, and she couldn't bring herself to do so now.

"Yeah, I guess you're right." Len aligned his chopsticks on the edge of his plate. "Have you noticed anything unusual lately?"

"What do you mean?"

"About Roy. How has he been? More distracted? Worried?"

"Not really." Diana wasn't being completely honest but she didn't want to air their dirty laundry for Len, even though it was likely that Allison had privately relayed some of what Diana told her. Besides, what did being impatient and short-tempered have to do with an inexplicable trip to a crummy neighborhood? Or, for that matter, what would being involved with someone named Mia have to do with it?

"With luck, the police will figure it out," Allison said. "You've got more important things to deal with right now."

Diana knew she should tell Inspector Knowles about the address, but if Roy had been involved with another woman, or with some shady activity, did she really want that known?

She set the last of her wine aside. "I'd better head home. Poor Digger will wonder what happened to us. I appreciate the dinner, the ride, and the moral support. I don't know what I'd do without you guys."

"You want me to pick Jeremy up from school again?" Allison asked.

"No, thanks. He hasn't been to visit Roy yet. I told him I'd take him this afternoon but that obviously didn't work out. I figure we'll do it tomorrow."

Diana called Jeremy from the den, and Allison walked them to the door.

"I can't believe Len brought up drugs," Allison said. "Sometimes I think he just opens his mouth without thinking."

"Don't worry about it. He means well. If he makes you happy, that's what's important."

"He does make me happy," Allison said. "I'd sort of given up on love, and now, here I am, feeling like a teenager at times."

Diana gave her a hug. "Good for you. You deserve a man who appreciates you."

Digger greeted Diana and Jeremy with his usual wild enthusiasm, compounded by a long day alone. Diana turned on the back lights and sent Jeremy into the yard to toss the dog his favorite ball. While she filled his food dish and sorted through the day's mail, she considered how to best organize her day tomorrow.

The windshield repair people were scheduled to come at one o'clock. If she kept Jeremy out of school, they could visit Roy at the hospital in the morning and still be home in plenty of time for the window repair. That made more sense than waiting until the afternoon, when the repair might or might not be done, and then fighting commute traffic into and out of the city. With luck, she could then grab a couple of hours in the afternoon to write her column. Maybe between now and then she'd even think of something to write about.

By the time Diana tucked Jeremy into bed that night, she was half asleep herself.

"I'm really sorry you didn't get to see Daddy today," Diana told him, smoothing the cowlick at his left temple. "I know you must have been really disappointed." She'd apologized earlier, when she first got to Allison's, but she wanted to make sure he understood she hadn't reneged on purpose.

"Yeah." Jeremy flopped back against this pillows and frowned. "I drew him a picture, and everything."

"We'll go tomorrow, instead. Okay?"

Jeremy's face lit up. "Daddy's going to be so surprised, isn't he?"

Diana felt a tightness in her throat. Was she doing the right thing taking Jeremy to the hospital? Her own father had died of a heart attack when she was eleven. He was in the hospital for three days before, but her mother hadn't let Diana see him. Sick people, she told Diana, didn't need little children about. Diana had been close to her father, closer than she was to her mother, and the "little children" stung. Maybe that was what her mother intended. It was one of the many ways Diana had felt marginalized and slighted by her mother over the years.

Diana wasn't smart enough, except when she was "too smart for your own good." She chose the wrong friends, the wrong clothes, and ultimately, the wrong man when she married Emily's father.

Both her parents were gone now, but it was her father's death that could still bring tears to her eyes. If she was making a mistake taking Jeremy to see Roy, at least it wasn't the same mistake her mother had made.

Diana kissed Jeremy's forehead. "He will be very surprised," she told him. "And very happy to see you."

Chloe woke up with a pounding headache from crying herself to sleep. She knew her eyes and face would be puffy, and that would elicit some further comment from Velma about no man being worth that kind of grief. The dark thoughts that had sucked her into despair last night still spiraled through her head. Weren't people always saying things looked better in the morning? Well, they didn't.

Maybe things only looked better if they weren't really so bad to begin with. If the father of your unborn child wasn't in jail and if the police weren't coming any minute to arrest you.

She cradled her belly. "Don't worry, Sophie. I'll figure something out." But Chloe wasn't sure how.

She turned onto her back. The morning air had a chill to it. Fall was coming, and then winter. The thought depressed her even further. She wondered if jail cells were heated. She pulled the covers up under her chin and started counting. On ten, she told herself, she'd get out of bed. When she reached eleven, she told herself she'd get up on twenty-five.

And then she heard a noise coming from the kitchen—soft, like running water—and she leapt out of bed without thinking.

Cops or one of those apes who'd burst in two night ago?

Her heart raced. She couldn't hide in the bathroom. That was the worst place because you'd be trapped. She looked around the tiny bedroom with its platform bed and single closet. She was trapped in any case, unless she climbed out a window. That's what the smart, quick heroines she read about in books would do. Either that or they'd use their black-belt skills to overcome the intruder, which wasn't so smart if the person turned out to be a cop.

But Chloe didn't know karate, and she wasn't about to drop

three stories in the hopes of landing on a soft awning, especially since there were no awnings anywhere near the apartment.

She shivered, whether from fear or the cold she couldn't tell. All she could do was hope whoever it was found what he wanted and went away.

And then the familiar aroma of coffee wafted into the bedroom. Fresh-brewed coffee. Like Trace made each morning.

She tiptoed toward the kitchen, and when she saw Trace sitting there at the yellow Formica table with a mug of fresh coffee in front of him, she burst into tears.

"You're home," she managed. "Are you okay? I've been so worried."

"I'm fine. I didn't mean to worry you." Still seated, he wrapped an arm around Chloe's waist and nuzzled his head against her.

Trace didn't look so fine. He had dark circles under his eyes and a gash on his forehead she didn't think had been there yesterday. His clothes were rumpled and dirty, and his shirt had a rip in the sleeve.

"Didn't mean to worry me?" she asked in disbelief. "How could you think I wouldn't be worried? You didn't leave a note, or call, or"—her voice broke as she fought a second round of tears—"or anything."

"My phone died, okay? I'm sorry." He unwrapped his arm from her waist and put both elbows on the table. "Look, I've had a hard night. I'd like a little peace and quiet, if that's okay."

She sat at the table. Her relief at seeing Trace was giving way to anger.

"I had a hard night, too." She leaned forward to look him in the eye. "Where *were* you?"

"What? You my mama now? I don't have to answer to you, Chloe."

The words stung as much as if he'd slapped her again. She

sat up straight. "No, Trace. I'm not your mama. I'm the woman you say you're going to marry. The mother of your child. Someone who cares about you. You can't stay out all night, worry me half to death, and then come waltzing in here like it's none of my business. You've dragged me into some god-awful mess, and I deserve to know what's going on."

Trace said nothing. Wouldn't even look at her. Had she gone too far? Would he hit her again or just walk out the door for good?

"I was so scared," she said, trembling at the memory of the dark places her mind had taken her. "I thought you'd been hurt. Or arrested. I was afraid you might need help and I didn't know what to do."

"I'm sorry, baby. Really, I am. I guess I wasn't thinking clearly." He reached a hand across the table and linked his fingers with hers. "I didn't mean to upset you."

"How could I *not* be upset?"

"I said I was sorry, Chloe. I don't know what else to do."

"So where did you go?"

"I had a few things to take care of."

"Like what?"

He slid his hand free of Chloe's and reached for his mug. "You need to get going or you'll be late for work. I've got a plan. We'll talk about it tonight, okay?"

"You'll tell me what's going on?"

"Yeah, sure. I'm going to go to bed now, I'm exhausted. You have a good day."

Trace was home. Alive and safe. Chloe didn't care what the rest of the day was like. It was already a good day.

CHAPTER 16

Even with the heavy morning commute–traffic into the city, Diana and Jeremy arrived at the hospital a little after ten. Over the course of the morning, Jeremy had gone from jubilant to subdued to, now that they were in the hospital elevator, reluctant.

"What if he doesn't want to see me?" Jeremy asked.

"Oh, honey, of course he wants to see you. Just remember, he's in a special kind of sleep called a coma. That happens sometimes when people have been hurt really badly. He'll know we're there but he won't see us and he won't be able to talk to us."

Jeremy's brow furrowed, and his eyes grew somber. At times he looked so much like Roy it took Diana's breath way. "Is it like being blind or something?" Jeremy asked.

"No, more like . . ." She struggled to find a way to explain to a seven-year-old what she didn't really understand herself. "You know how it is when you're asleep and we carry you in from the car at night? You're sort of aware of what's going on but you don't really wake up? It's more like that."

"Oh." The answer seemed to mollify Jeremy some. But he reached for her hand and gripped it tightly as they walked down the long corridor toward Roy's room.

Roy had been moved from ICU and was now in what was referred to as "constant care," which meant that he was in a room with only one other bed (occupied at her last visit by a very elderly man who snored loudly), and that the nursing staff was spread more thinly than in ICU. Diana had the horrible feeling that constant care was where they moved the patients who were beyond help.

As she and Jeremy entered the room, she tried hard to hide her own distress at seeing Roy. With each visit he looked less and less like himself and more like a wax likeness of a gaunt old man. Shifting her gaze, she noted that the second bed in the room was now empty. She wondered if the former occupant had died.

Still holding Jeremy's hand, she strode with purpose to the side of Roy's bed that was free of monitors and drips. Jeremy pulled back.

"It looks scary," she whispered, urging him forward, "but the tubes are helping Daddy. They're giving him food and medicine."

Jeremy shuffled a few steps closer to the bed, but his eyes were still on the machinery.

"Hello, Roy," Diana said softly. "I brought someone very special to see you. Jeremy's here."

"Hi, Daddy." Jeremy's words were tentative, as though he were speaking into a microphone and didn't know quite what to say or how loudly to speak.

"How are you doing, honey?" Diana brushed Roy's forehead with a kiss. "They've moved you out of intensive care. You're getting better." Diana wasn't sure that was true, but her mind was scrambling for something to say.

Jeremy looked at her and whispered, "What do I do now?"

"Just talk to him. Tell him about what you've been doing." Diana pulled two chairs closer to the bed and they sat.

"I got a hundred percent on my spelling test," Jeremy said. "And we're going to start learning cursive in a couple of weeks."

The steady ping, ping of the IV drip and the low hum from

the chest monitor filled the empty silences. The scene before her was so wrong. In normal times, Roy would have given a whoop of pleasure and high-fived Jeremy in celebration. And he would have made some remark about his own terrible cursive and how Jeremy should pay attention to his teacher. Roy was fond of giving lessons based on his own perceived failings.

"And Billy Lawton shared his M&Ms with me at lunch the other day," Jeremy continued after a bit.

Diana desperately wanted to see some reaction in Roy. She'd been sure that Jeremy's presence would compel a response. Even a quickened breath or the slightest flutter of his eyelids. But nothing. They might as well be talking to a stone. Maybe her mother had been right in thinking children didn't belong at the hospital.

"Oh, and I drew a picture for you," Jeremy added. He pulled a drawing of the four of them from his backpack and held it out to Roy before hastily dropping his hand and looking to Diana for direction. She took the drawing and held it open for Roy, although she knew he couldn't see it.

"Isn't this beautiful, Roy?"

"It's our family," Jeremy explained. "So you won't forget us."

"That's Jeremy and Digger on your left," Diana told Roy. "And me and Emily on your right." Roy and Jeremy were twice the size of the other figures—something she knew would make Roy smile. But she didn't feel she should point that out in front of Jeremy.

"I miss you, Daddy. I want you to come home soon."

"Me, too," Diana said. "You're going to beat this, Roy. You're going to get well and come back to us." *Please*, she added silently.

On the way home they stopped at Fenton's and ordered ice cream sundaes. Jeremy had barely spoken a word during the drive back to the East Bay, and she worried that she'd made a mistake in taking him to the hospital.

"What will happen if Daddy dies?" Jeremy asked, mashing his chocolate chip ice cream with the back of his spoon, but not eating any.

"What do you mean?" Diana didn't want to have the whole *heaven* discussion because she wasn't sure it was what she believed. But a child needed assurance, didn't he? White lie or truth? She looked to Jeremy for guidance about how to proceed.

"When Nick's father died," he told her, "the whole family had to go live with his grandparents way far away in a different part of the country."

Nick was a classmate whose father had died of cancer in the middle of the last school year. Diana hadn't known the family well, but Nick was part of the group of boys Jeremy and his friends played with at school. She knew Nick kept in touch with at least one of that group.

"Nick has to share a bedroom with his two brothers," Jeremy continued. "And they don't have any money for toys and stuff. And he can't play after school because he has to help his grandmother around the house." Jeremy looked at her forlornly. "I don't even have grandparents."

Her son's plaintive tone was a knife in Diana's heart. Relieved as she was to be spared a philosophical discussion of death, this was worse. And it brought her up short to realize that Jeremy was worried about their future—something she, herself, hadn't considered.

"We won't have to move," Diana reassured him. She could get a real job. Something that paid more than the pittance she earned as a columnist. She'd managed to raise Emily on her own, hadn't she? Roy had life insurance, and she and Roy did have savings. Not a lot, but enough.

"Besides, Daddy's not going to die. It's just going to take him a little time to get better."

When Chloe got home from work, the house was so quiet she was afraid that Trace had gone away again. She was relieved to discover he was only napping on the sofa. She could tell from the bread crumbs on the carpet and the sticky ice cream bowl left on the coffee table that he'd spent the afternoon in front of the TV.

She kissed his forehead. "Trace, I'm home."

He groaned and pulled one of the loose decorative pillows over his head.

"Hey, get up. It's evening." Chloe turned on a light. All day at work she'd been on edge, wondering about Trace's plan.

Trace sat up sleepily. "Why'd you have to wake me? I was having a nice dream."

"Too bad. You promised to tell me what's going on."

He groaned again and rubbed his eyes. "Cut the attitude, Chloe. You're acting like you've got PMS or something."

"You know I hate it when you say that."

"And you know I hate it when you're always on my case."

"I'm not 'always on your case.'" Chloe walked into the kitchen area. "You want a Coke?"

"We got any beer?"

"Afraid not."

"Okay, a Coke is fine." Trace leaned back in the couch and finger-combed his hair. "How was work?"

"Same as always." Except today she'd caused a customer to yell at her, something that hadn't happened before.

She wasn't like Velma, who didn't hesitate to speak her mind, even with customers. Velma had been yelled at more than once, something she was actually proud of. "You don't let jerks push you around," she'd told Chloe the first time it happened. That's why Chloe had been so surprised at Velma's admission yesterday about having been hit. *Abused,* was what she'd said.

Chloe had almost worked up the nerve to ask her about it today, but then she'd had the run-in with the customer who called her "stupid trash" because she'd rung up thirteen yards of ribbon instead of three. "It's a sign of the times that stores are stuck with stupid trash like you," the woman had said loudly. Chloe had apologized for the error—the woman hadn't even paid for the merchandise yet so it wasn't really much of an inconvenience, except that Chloe had to ring her order up a second time—but the woman wasn't placated. She'd turned to her companion and gone on and on about dumb and lazy help, like Chloe wasn't standing there right in front of her bagging up purchases and fighting tears.

Velma said afterward when Chloe was pulling herself together in the restroom that it was just the hormones from being pregnant that made her cry. "Your whole system goes nuts when you're pregnant," she told Chloe. "You get emotional about everything." Maybe so, but Chloe thought it was probably more likely that everything in her life was so awful right now.

She didn't want to get into that with Trace though, especially because it was mostly his fault things were so awful.

She handed him his can of Coke and sat down at the other end of the couch. "So, where were you last night? And who were those guys who pushed their way in here?"

Trace took a long drink, then wiped his mouth with the back of his hand. "I owe them some money, okay? That's why I set the thing up with Hector. I needed money."

"I thought you said you were doing it for the baby."

"Yeah. But I got to pay these guys first."

Chloe wasn't really surprised—she'd pretty much heard what they'd said to Trace from her hiding place in the bedroom—but there was still a sick feeling starting up in her stomach as she listened to Trace explain.

"Why? What do you owe them money for? I thought we were doing okay."

"We were. We are. Or we will be."

Trace was talking nonsense. "We aren't doing okay if you owe money. Especially if you owe more than we've got. And you still haven't told me why you owe them."

"It's more like they think I took what was theirs," Trace said. He was breathing faster, not looking at her, squeezing the Coke can so it made little popping noises.

"Did you?" Chloe asked.

"It was mostly a misunderstanding. But the thing is, they aren't guys you argue with."

"A misunderstanding?" The sick feeling intensified. "What'd you do, Trace? What were you involved with?"

He shrugged. "It was a deal we did a couple of months back. A business deal, really. We had this truckload of merchandise—"

"Stolen merchandise?"

"Yeah, I guess. Wasn't like we actually stole it or anything, but we got it cheap."

She'd been about say *I can't believe you are so stupid,* but caught herself. She didn't want to sound like the customer who'd yelled at her that afternoon. "I don't understand why you'd do something like that, Trace. I thought you said you were going straight."

"I am. This is left over from before. I got to get right with these guys first."

"And what about shooting Hector? How are you going to get right with that?"

He made a dismissive gesture with his arm. "It was a deal gone bad. I didn't have a choice." He finished off his Coke and crushed the can with one hand. "I got a plan to get the money."

"What is it?" she asked, trying to keep the uncertainty out of her voice.

"That DA that messed up the robbery? He's got to have money, right? And you have his house key. It was in his bag."

"We don't know any of those keys are for his house."

"One of them has got to be. So what I'm thinking is, you go there, check it out, and get a feel for the wife's schedule. Then when we know it's safe, we'll let ourselves in and take what we can."

"No."

"I don't mean clean the place out. Just take enough to make us even."

"No, Trace. That woman's husband is in the hospital. He might die. I am not going to go rob her house."

"It'd be burglary, not robbery."

"I don't care what it is, I'm not doing it."

"Do it so we can make a clean start. You love me, don't you?"

"Of course I do."

"I need to get these guys off my back or they'll kill me. Please, Chloe. We don't have a choice."

There was always a choice. Even Chloe knew that.

"I'll make it up to you," Trace pleaded. "We'll start fresh— you, me, and the baby. Please, Chloe. I need you." His hand caressed the side of her face and traced the outline of her lips with the lightness of a feather. "I really, really need you."

She closed her eyes. It was hard to say no when Trace was being so nice to her. "I get off early tomorrow. I'll go have a look. But that's all I'm promising, just a look."

"That's my girl. I knew I could count on you."

He had it backward, Chloe thought. She should be the one who could count on him.

CHAPTER 17

Chloe stuck her hands in her pocket and wondered how she was supposed to watch a house without being watched herself. She couldn't believe she'd agreed to such a fool's errand. She wasn't going to be part of any burglary, no matter what Trace said. There had to be another way to get the money he needed.

She'd almost backed out at least a dozen times, but then she'd remember the desperation in Trace's eyes, the pleading fear in his voice. She didn't have the heart to straight-out refuse. Or the nerve. It was easier to appear to go along with this harebrained scheme and then find some reason the plan wouldn't work. That way Trace wouldn't be angry with her and she wouldn't feel she was letting him down.

But in truth, she *was* letting him down, wasn't she? Trace meant everything to her. How could she stand by and not help him?

Chloe felt confused, or as Rose, the supervisor of the group home, used to say, conflicted. Whatever the dilemma, Rose was able to cut through the confusion and lay things out in simple terms. "You may feel conflicted," she'd say, "but if you step back and think, it's pretty easy to separate right from wrong." Chloe had learned a lot from Rose, but she was finding that the differences between right and wrong weren't always as clear as Rose made it seem.

Chloe had agreed to check out the DA's house and neighborhood. But she'd left the ring of keys at home.

She'd taken the bus—several buses in fact—across town to the well-to-do neighborhood where the lawyer lived. And now she stood on a quiet, tree-lined street, across from a gabled two-story house that looked like something out of a children's storybook. There was even a rocker on the front porch, barely visible through the flowering vines that climbed the side of the house. Painted a soft blue-gray with charcoal trim, the house was at the same time elegant and welcoming. As was the whole neighborhood. It was the sort of home on the sort of street Chloe had always dreamed about, and known would never be hers. She experienced a pang of, well, of what she couldn't quite say. Nostalgia maybe. Nostalgia for what might have been in her life with a different roll of the dice.

A woman wearing designer jeans and pushing a fancy baby stroller walked by and smiled at Chloe.

"Glorious day, isn't it?" the woman said.

Chloe agreed, and took a surreptitious peek into the stroller. A sleeping bundle of pink—pink booties, pink blanket, pink cheeks. She felt a flutter in her chest like champagne bubbles rising to the surface. Instinctively, she placed her hand on the swell of her belly. Her own decidedly non-designer jeans were already so tight she couldn't fasten the top button. Five more months, and she'd have a pink bundle of her own.

But the similarities ended there. Chloe took a deep breath. How wonderful it would be to live in a nice neighborhood like this and take an afternoon walk with your baby, free of worries. It was a fantasy she found as captivating as it was impossible.

She shook herself free of her dream world and started walking in the opposite direction from the woman and her baby. She couldn't stand there and watch the lawyer's house all afternoon. What had Trace been thinking? Although to be fair, Chloe hadn't exactly seen that pitfall either. This was clearly the sort of neighborhood where a stranger would stand out.

She walked two blocks and then turned left. At the corner she passed a woman in a wide-brimmed hat deadheading flowers in her front yard, and farther on, an elderly gentleman walking his equally elderly beagle.

Chloe touched her belly. "What do you think, Cassidy? Pretty nice, huh? Don't get your hopes up, though. I'm afraid we're not this lucky."

Cassidy? The name had a nice ring, but kids might joke about Butch Cassidy and horses. Chloe couldn't give her daughter riches, but she could give her a name that didn't invite teasing.

She turned left again, circling back toward the lawyer's house. She liked to think of the man as "the lawyer" because it made him seem less real, but she knew his name—Roy Walker. She knew his wife's name too—Diana. It had been on the news.

Chloe again stood across the street and down a couple of houses from the Walkers'. A woman was out front now, watering plants, her little terrier sniffing the grass nearby. Chloe wasn't close enough to see if it was the same woman she'd seen in the photo in the lawyer's—in Roy Walker's—gym bag, but it had to be Diana. She wore jeans and a T-shirt and had her reddish, shoulder-length hair clipped back from her face.

The sharp reality of what had brought her here made Chloe's knees weak. Trace had shot this woman's husband. And she, Chloe, hadn't done a thing to help him. A wave of nausea washed over her. She felt suddenly flushed and lightheaded. Dear God, what had they done?

An older woman came from the house next to the Walkers' and started talking to Diana. She reached down and petted the terrier.

As Chloe watched, captivated by the simple charm of the scene, she debated what to do next. She couldn't stand here forever without raising suspicion. Suddenly a cat darted across the yard and into the street, and the terrier took off after it. Diana Walker called the dog, then looked in the direction Chloe was standing and yelled something else. Chloe turned just in time to see a boy on a bike flying down the sidewalk.

What happened next happened so fast Chloe didn't have time to register it all. The boy swerved to avoid the dog and instead crashed straight into Chloe.

She went down hard, landing on her left knee and then her cheek, before skidding across the cement. For a moment she lay without moving, without breathing. She saw flashes of dancing light before her eyes and then large, black spots.

Pain came slowly at first, then swiftly and fiercely. She tasted blood. She caught her breath and moaned between hard, quick gasps.

The boy had fallen, too, tangled in his bike, but he'd landed on the grassy parking strip and was already up and moving. Diana Walker and the neighbor woman rushed to Chloe.

"Oh my God," Diana said, "are you okay? No, of course you aren't." She turned to the boy. "Jeremy, haven't I told you a thousand times to slow down? What were you thinking? You have to watch out for people." And back to Chloe. "Oh dear God. Shall I call an ambulance?"

The terrier moved in and nosed Chloe's cheek, its tail wagging a mile a minute. The boy was in tears.

Chloe blinked at the worried faces hovering over her, wanting to assure them she was fine, or would be in a minute or two. But the effort was too great. Instead, she closed her eyes and imagined she could ride away on a puffy white cloud.

Diana had seen the teenaged girl with the ponytail walking down the street. Not someone she recognized from the neighborhood, and she wondered if the girl might be lost. It was unusual to see a girl her age simply strolling the street alone. More often, teenage girls strode with purpose and sure athletic steps, or walked in packs accompanied by high-pitched chatter. So the girl had caught Diana's eye, but she'd been immersed in conversation with Judy from next door and hadn't really paid much attention until she'd seen Jeremy riding unsteadily down the sidewalk. Diana had been about to call to him to slow down when Digger had unexpectedly taken off like a shot. The rest was a blur that had come to a crashing standstill with the moaning, bleeding girl on the sidewalk in front of her.

"Oh my God," Diana cried. "Are you okay?" As soon as the words were out of her mouth she realized how stupid the question sounded. Of course the girl wasn't okay.

She'd seemed alert in the first moments after the accident, but then her eyes had closed and Diana worried she'd lost consciousness. She held the girl's head, and stroked her forehead. "Can you hear me, honey? Talk to me."

The girl opened her eyes and regarded Diana blankly.

"I'll go call nine-one-one," Judy said.

"Yes, I think you'd better."

The girl grimaced. "No. No, please. I'll be fine." She struggled to sit up.

"Can you move your fingers and toes?" Diana asked, helping her to a sitting position.

The girl made a rippling movement with her long, delicate fingers, as though she were playing the scales of a piano.

"Jeremy, run into the house for some towels," Diana said. "And take Digger with you."

The girl tried to stand and would have fallen if Diana hadn't held her.

"What hurts most?" Diana asked.

"My knee."

"Can you walk on it?"

"I think so." With Diana and Judy supporting the girl on either side, they managed to get her to her feet. The girl tried putting weight on the leg and winced, but she managed a few shuffling steps.

"Come on," Diana said. "Let's get you inside and cleaned up."

It took all three of them to get the girl across the street and into Diana's kitchen. She sat silently in the straight-backed chair at the head of the long wooden table, while Diana took wet towels and gently mopped the girl's wounds. The flesh on her cheek was raw and scraped but luckily the damage was confined to the surface. It looked ugly and would hurt like the dickens for days to come, but Diana thought there'd be no permanent scarring. She felt less sure about the knee. She gave the girl an ice pack, but already the area looked swollen.

"Let me drive you to emergency," Diana said. "You really ought to get that knee looked at. They probably have some stronger salve for the scrapes, too."

The girl's eyes widened with trepidation. She shook her head. "No hospitals."

Standard response of the young or something more? Diana sensed something close to genuine terror in the girl's reaction. "If it's an insurance thing, I'll pay—"

"No," the girl said sharply. "I'll be fine, really."

"What's your name?" Diana asked. "Who should I call?"

"Please, there's no need to call anyone."

Jeremy was standing in the doorway, his head hung low, his expression contrite. Digger pushed past him and started sniffing the girl's feet.

"What's your name?" Diana asked again.

"Chloe."

"I'm Diana."

Chloe offered a tepid smile. She touched her belly for probably the third or fourth time.

"Do you feel sick?" Diana asked in alarm. She was already

envisioning internal bleeding or other major injury, and was more convinced than ever that Chloe ought to be checked out by a doctor.

Chloe's gaze swept Diana's kitchen, then circled back. "I don't feel sick. It's a nervous habit, that's all."

"Do you live nearby? Let me call someone for you."

"Really, I'll be just fine in a minute." Chloe held her hand out to Digger, and when he'd sniffed her fingers some, she reached behind his head and scratched his ears.

"I'm so sorry," Diana said. "My dog is usually very well behaved, and my son knows he's not supposed to go so fast."

"I'm sorry, too," Jeremy said, inching toward them. "I didn't mean to hit you. I didn't want you to be hurt." He looked at Chloe and then at Diana. His eyes filled with tears.

"Hey," Chloe said with a genuine smile this time. "It was an accident. I know you didn't mean to hit me."

"Do you want a cookie?" Jeremy asked.

"A cookie?"

"You know, to stop the hurt."

"Ah." The bewilderment that had been so apparent in Chloe's expression lifted. "That would be great. Maybe some milk, too."

Jeremy scampered to the cupboard for a cookie while Diana poured a glass of milk and set it on the table.

"I really think you should see a doctor," Diana said. "I can call my own doctor if you'd like."

Chloe gave a determined shake of her head. "Thanks, but I don't need a doctor."

Jeremy returned with a box of Chips Ahoy and another of frosted animal crackers—hardly the comfort food of teenage girls. But Chloe nibbled a cookie from each box, then finished off her glass of milk.

"You're sitting in my dad's chair," Jeremy said solemnly after a moment.

"Oh," Chloe said, and shifted as if to move to a different chair.

"It's fine," Diana assured her. "Roy wouldn't mind."

Chloe lowered her gaze, and again, Diana detected a flicker of something like fear in the girl's eyes.

"He's in the hospital," Jeremy continued. "I went to visit him but he couldn't see me because he's in a co—" He looked to Diana for help.

"A coma," she explained.,

"It's what happens," Jeremy said, "when someone is very, very sick."

Chloe studied her hands. "I'm sorry to hear that. It must be terrible for all of you." She finally looked up. "I think I feel strong enough to leave now."

"You ought to sit a bit longer."

"No, I really need to go."

"Where do you live?" Diana asked. "I'll drive you home."

"You don't have to do that. I can just—"

"Walk? Drive? I don't think you can. If you've got a car nearby you can come back for it another time."

A look of panic flashed on Chloe's face. "No, please, it's really not necessary."

Diana was both intrigued and disturbed by Chloe's reaction, but she wasn't about to let an injured young woman wander off alone.

Diana reached for her keys. "Come on," she said in a tone that brooked no argument. "Driving you home is the least I can do. I feel guilty enough already about what happened."

By the time Chloe had hobbled up the three flights of stairs to her apartment, her heart pounded as hard as her head. Her knee was swollen and stiff, and the scrapes on her cheek felt like they were on fire. All she wanted to do was climb into bed and be left alone, but she knew Trace would hound her with questions.

It had been hard enough explaining to Velma what had happened. Chloe had had Diana drop her off near the new condos a block from the Craft Connection, steadfastly refusing Diana's offer to see Chloe to her door. From there, Chloe had limped to the store to beg a ride from Velma, who clearly doubted Chloe's story about being hit by a boy on a bike. But while Velma been wise enough not to push the issue, Trace would be a different matter.

The sound of the TV greeted Chloe as she opened the front door to her apartment.

"Hey," Trace called out. "How'd it go?"

"Okay, I guess."

"What did you learn? Did you get in?" Trace took his eyes off the screen to glance at Chloe. "Holy shit, what happened to you?"

"I got knocked over by a bicycle."

"A bicycle? What'd'ya do, walk right in front of it?"

Chloe explained how she'd been watching the house the way she was supposed to when the boy on the bike came out of nowhere.

"Did you get his name? Maybe we can sue him."

"It was the lawyer's son."

Trace snapped his fingers. "Better yet."

"He's only seven. He didn't mean to hit me."

Trace looked at her like she was a dimwit. "So what?"

"I'm not suing a kid for riding a bike." *Especially not the kid of the man you shot*, she added silently. "If I'd been paying attention, I'd have gotten out of the way."

"You can't do anything without screwing up, can you?"

Chloe closed her eyes. She could have used a dose of Diana's sympathy about then. Diana had been so kind, even when

Chloe's dirty and torn jeans messed up the smooth leather seat in her car.

"The woman, the lawyer's wife, she felt really bad about it," Chloe said. "So did the boy."

"Or so they said. Don't think they weren't worried about a lawsuit."

"They were nice, both of them." Despite the pain and fear at being found out, Chloe had felt a sort of peace sitting in Diana's kitchen.

"What did you do, hang around and have tea with them?" The sarcasm in Trace's tone wasn't lost on Chloe.

"Milk and cookies," she told him.

"Oh, isn't that sweet. All chummy and feel good. But at least you got inside. Did you take a good look around?"

Trace was like a dog with a bone he wouldn't let go. "No, I didn't look around. I was hurt."

"I hope you didn't tell them your name."

"Only my first name," Chloe said. "They don't know where I live or who I am."

Trace tossed down the TV remote in disgust. "Still, it's not like you can go back there without drawing attention to yourself. We'll have to go in without casing the place first."

"I'm going to go to bed, Trace. My whole body hurts."

"Fine, whatever." He turned his attention back to the TV with a loud sigh. "I swear to God, Chloe, sometimes you're more trouble than you're worth."

She undressed with difficulty, discovering new sore spots with every twist and turn. She took the piece of paper Diana had given her with Diana's phone numbers on it—house and cell—and slipped it under the lining of her bureau drawer, then crawled into bed.

She thought about the little boy, Jeremy, whose father lay in a coma because of Trace. And about Diana whose world had been turned upside down.

She stroked her belly. "What are we going to do, Erin? How did this happen?" And then, tentatively, she tried it a second time. "What are we going to do, Aaron?" Chloe called up a picture of Jeremy and conceded that having a baby boy would be pretty nice, too.

CHAPTER 18

The call Diana had been dreading came at 2:46 a.m. Wednesday. She was aware of the precise time because she looked at the clock. Looked at the clock and then took her time answering, intentionally stalling the inevitable. Good news did not arrive at two in the morning.

It was a doctor she'd never met, probably one of the young residents nearing the end of a long shift. His words, no doubt scripted for just such occasions, were meant to convey compassion, but what Diana heard most clearly was the exhaustion in his voice and his aversion to the task.

He explained that Roy's heart had stopped, that they'd been unable to revive him despite intense efforts from the entire hospital team.

"No," Diana whispered. "That can't be."

"I'm very sorry, Mrs. Walker. We did everything we could."

"But his heart was strong," Diana insisted. "Dr. Peterson told me so the other day."

"I'm sorry," the doctor said. "Sometimes these things happen. In medicine, nothing is one hundred percent predictable."

Which pretty much echoed what every doctor she'd talked to had said. Diana wondered if they'd been taught that caveat in medical school or if they'd learned it in the trenches of patient care.

She sat on the edge of the bed for a long time after she'd hung up the phone. The window was open and the night air felt chilly. She thought about putting on a sweater or climbing back under the covers, but she did neither. Outside in the distance she heard the wail of an ambulance. Another death? Or a life saved?

She knew she was supposed to feel something, probably many things—sorrow, anger, despair, fear. But she felt nothing. She wasn't a screamer or a wailer or a fainter, although she wished for a moment she were. Surely something as momentous as the death of a husband deserved some discernible reaction.

She knew there'd be pockets, probably even oceans, of raw grief and agonizing loneliness in the weeks ahead. Long dark hours when she'd miss Roy so much the pain would cut like a knife.

But right now, at ground zero, the shock waves hadn't yet reached her.

The four days that followed were a blur of phone calls and arrangements and condolences, and Diana moved through them as though she were an automaton. It was, she supposed, a measure of self-preservation. Don't think, don't feel, just do what needed to be done. But there were moments she wished she could simply fall apart and let others carry on.

She'd dreaded breaking the news to her children, especially Jeremy, but she'd plowed through the ordeal with the same sense of detachment. She was both participant and observer, two people at once, and yet not entirely whole. She wondered briefly if she might be headed for the nut house.

Emily flew home from school Wednesday afternoon. After her initial accusatory outburst—"You didn't tell me he was going to die!"—she'd sunk into a sullen petulance that seemed intended, by some weird machinations of the mind, to punish Diana. Jeremy's moods were all over the map—demonstrably forlorn one minute, withdrawn the next, and then bouncing about with

Digger as though nothing had changed. Diana wasn't sure he fully understood that death was forever.

On Sunday, the three of them sat together in the front row of the community church for the funeral. Allison and Len sat to their left. They had been by Diana's side practically nonstop.

The church was full—friends and acquaintances of Diana's, and colleagues of Roy's, along with the mayor of Oakland and a host of county dignitaries. She knew Jan, Roy's secretary, and Alec Thurston, Roy's boss, and others from his office, but there were a lot of people she didn't recognize. She wondered how many of them were reporters. Members of the media had been leaving messages on her phone ever since Roy was shot, but the number of calls had doubled after he died.

And she wondered if one of the unfamiliar women could be Mia. It felt terribly wrong to be doubting her husband's fidelity at his funeral, but she couldn't help it.

She'd clung to the hope that someone from Roy's family would show up, or at least get in touch with her. She knew that Roy's parents were dead and that he was estranged from his extended family. They weren't part of his life anymore, Roy had explained before they were married, and in a tone that didn't invite questions. Diana gathered there'd been a blowup of some kind but she never did get the details. In the beginning of their relationship, it bothered her that Roy wouldn't elaborate, but she hadn't thought about it for quite some time. In truth, she found it easier not having to deal with in-laws and distant relatives. But with Roy's death, she felt a need to connect. His family deserved to know what had happened to him.

She had run a death notice in several of the newspapers around Grand Forks, North Dakota, where he'd grown up, and had hoped the news of his death might prompt a short note from someone in the family.

After the burial, during which Jeremy had stood stoically by

Diana on one side while Emily fidgeted on the other, a small group of friends gathered at Diana's for drinks and a light buffet. Diana couldn't eat. In fact she'd lost four pounds in the four days since Roy's death, but she reached eagerly for the glass of wine Len handed her.

"You look like you could use it," he told her.

"Most definitely. I could probably use the whole bottle, if truth be told."

Len had been a godsend at the funeral and burial, hovering by her side and fending off members of the media. And he'd stepped in to oversee the gathering at the house and make sure that people got food and drink.

"You're holding up remarkably well," he told her.

"I am?"

"From outward appearances, anyway."

Diana took several large sips of wine and felt its magic instantly smooth the rawness inside her. "I guess I'm good at coping, or seeming to."

"Roy's death is a tremendous upheaval in your life. You can't expect to jump right back into the swing of things."

She understood, but that didn't make her heart ache any less. "I wish you and Roy had gotten along better."

Len looked surprised. "We got along fine."

Diana's glass was half empty. She'd have to slow down or she *would* go through a whole bottle. "Been better friends, then. I never could understand what it was between you two."

Len rocked back on his heels. "What did Roy say?"

She shrugged. "That you're different sorts of people."

"That about sums it up." Len paused. "That doesn't mean I'm not terribly sorry he's dead. It's a tragedy what happened. And I feel awful for you and the kids. Anything I can do, you let me know."

Diana gave Len a warm hug. "I know that, and I appreciate it."

Allison swooped in to join them. She'd forgone the usual bright colors she favored in clothes, opting for black instead, and Diana thought she looked striking.

"The entire day seems surreal," Diana said.

"Of course it does. Funerals aren't supposed to feel normal."

Len excused himself and took the bottle of wine and headed into the room to refill glasses.

"Len's been a big help," Diana said.

Allison laughed half-heartedly. "Nice to know he cares about *someone*."

"Oh-oh, do I detect a note of bitterness in that comment?"

"It's no big deal. Just that the bloom has faded from the relationship, I guess."

It seemed like a big deal to Diana. "Since when?"

"The last couple of weeks. Or maybe I'm imagining things. We've all been pretty torn up about Roy. Anyway, I didn't mean to unload on you, especially today."

Diana felt a niggle of guilt. She'd been so involved with her own problems, she hadn't really been much of a friend. "Let's have lunch soon. Maybe we can figure out what's going on."

Out of the corner of her eye, she caught sight of Emily, backed into a corner by an overbearing woman who'd worked with Roy at the DA's office. "I'd better go rescue Emily," she told Allison. "But don't worry about Len. He adores you."

Allison snorted. "That remains to be seen. But go liberate your daughter and we'll talk later."

Emily gave her a grateful smile when Diana pulled her away, saying she needed some help.

"That woman never stops talking." Emily furtively pulled her cell phone from her pocket to quickly check for messages. At least she'd left the iPod in her bedroom for the afternoon.

"She thinks she's being nice."

Emily rolled her eyes, then looked around the room. "How long before people leave?"

"Soon, I'd think."

"Funerals are kind of ghoulish, aren't they? Kind of an orgy of public grief."

"I suppose you could look at it that way."

Emily twisted her watch band. "I wish I'd known Roy was going to die. I should have come home and gone to see him."

Diana put her arm around Emily's thin shoulders. The last thing she wanted was for her daughter to feel guilty. "He was in a coma, honey. It wouldn't have mattered."

Emily pulled away, flipping her straight, blond hair in a gesture of protest. "It would have mattered to *me*. And it might have mattered to Roy. You aren't the only one who misses him, you know."

When Emily walked off, Diana swallowed hard. Once again she'd managed to say the wrong thing to her daughter.

People had begun to leave. Diana said goodbye to Jan, promising to stay in touch, even though they both knew that wouldn't happen, and to Alec Thurston, who told her once again what a wonderful man Roy had been to work with. Diana's editor, Jack Saffire, gripped her hands in his and told her to call him if there was anything he could do to help.

"I know what it's like to lose a spouse," he said. "How difficult and lonely it is." His usually gruff demeanor softened when he spoke to her, and Diana was touched.

"Thank you," she said. "I appreciate it. And I appreciate your coming today."

Len was busy cleaning up, carrying glasses into the kitchen and wrapping the leftover food. Diana was ready for everyone to go, even Allison and Len. She suspected they were lingering because they thought she didn't want to be alone.

She poured herself another half glass of wine. When everyone was gone she'd spend some time with the kids. Just the three of them. They'd watch a movie, or maybe she'd read to Jeremy while Emily barricaded herself in her room with her iPod. Diana would have to make an effort to connect with Emily, too. She understood her daughter's outward coolness masked a well of sadness. What she didn't understand was how to comfort someone who kept her at arm's length.

Eventually, Diana could retire to her room and stop pretending to be strong. Her personal retreat, where she and Roy had made love, conceived their son, shared fears and hopes, and planned their future—sometimes in drifts and dribbles, other times with the energy of a full-out assault, but always presuming a future they'd both be part of.

The phone rang and Diana ignored it. Whoever it was could leave a message. It was probably someone from the media anyway. She had nothing to say to any of them. And she couldn't bear another condolence call.

"Mom," Emily called from the den. "It's for you."

"Take a message, honey. I don't really want to talk right now."

Emily stood at the doorway, phone in hand, looking a little dazed. She covered the mouthpiece. "I think you'd better take it. It's someone from North Dakota."

Diana grabbed the receiver and moved to a quiet corner in the hallway where she leaned against the wall.

"Are you the person who placed the death notice for Roy Walker in the *Grand Forks Star*?" a woman's voice asked. Thin but with a decided Dakota twang.

"Yes, I am," Diana replied eagerly. "Did you know him?"

"Is this your idea of some sick joke?"

"What?"

"Your notice. What are you trying to pull?"

"Who is this?"

"Barbara Walker, Roy Walker's mother." The woman's voice had grown stronger, and louder.

Mother? Roy had told her both his parents were dead.

"Mrs. Walker, I don't know what happened between you and your son, but—"

"What happened is that my son died."

"Yes, that's why—"

"He died twenty-two years ago when a drunk driver with four prior arrests crossed the double line going forty miles over the speed limit. He died a week before his eighteenth birthday. We buried him right here in Grand Forks. How dare you make a mockery of his death."

Stunned, Diana didn't know where to begin. "We must not be talking about the same person."

"Says right here when he was born. That's my son's birth date."

"There must be some mistake."

"I know when my son was born! Five-thirty-two in the morning right here in Grand Forks."

"But I married Roy—"

"I'm telling you right now, you better stop this harassment or I'm taking legal action." The call ended with a loud click.

Diana held the receiver in her hand and stared at it. Two Roy Walkers born on the same date in the same small town in North Dakota? How likely was that?

"What is it, Mom?"

Diana shook her head. Could Roy's differences with his family have been so great they'd figuratively killed him off? No. The woman's voice had been filled with pain, even now, twenty-two years after her son's death.

What did it mean? Was this something else that Roy had lied about?

For the first time since she'd gotten the phone call telling her that Roy had been shot, Diana lost it. She slid down the wall, curled into a ball on the floor, and wept.

CHAPTER 19

Diana's mind was a swirl of raging emotion. She felt as if she'd been sucked into the eye of a twister and, like Dorothy, whisked far away from all that was familiar. Roy was her anchor. The force through which she pulled together and processed the world. How could he have lied to her about so much? How was it that she hadn't known him at all?

She had known that marrying Garrick, her first husband, was a bad idea. She'd gone through with it because she was pregnant with Emily, because she couldn't bear her mother's smug "I knew you'd mess up," and somewhere deep in that bottomless well of eternal hope, she'd thought it might work out.

Despite her leap of faith, she wasn't at all surprised when Garrick walked away four years later. In retrospect, it surprised her he'd stayed as long as he had.

But Diana had felt from the first moment she met Roy that he was someone she could trust. It was in the softness of his blue-gray eyes, the quirky way the corners of his mouth lifted when he smiled, the way he listened for the meaning behind the words, and the way he looked into her eyes as though nothing else was important. And she'd known after their first date that she'd found Mr. Right.

She had been part of the secretarial pool in the DA's office, filling in for the secretary to one of the senior attorneys, when Roy came by to check on the status of a case. He told her later that he'd felt weak in the knees when he'd seen her. Like some dumb, love-struck teenager, he said.

Diana hadn't seen any of that, but then she'd been pretty weak-kneed herself.

He'd started to ask for the case file, then realized he couldn't remember the name of the case. "I sound like an idiot, don't I?" he said.

Diana was normally shy around the attorneys, especially the well-known ones, but Roy's quixotic grin seemed to inspire confidence. "Yes, you do," she replied lightly.

"Sometimes I *am* an idiot."

She laughed. "Me, too."

"Hey, that's something we have in common."

About the only thing they could have in common, Diana remembered thinking at the time. But she liked that Roy had said it.

He found reason to come back to her desk at least once a day after that. When the secretary she was filling in for returned, he sought out Diana's own station in the secretarial pool and, out of the blue, asked if she wanted to have dinner with him.

"I have a ten-year-old daughter," she blurted out without knowing why.

His eyes crinkled in bewilderment. "And?"

"I thought you should know that."

"Duly noted." He paused. "I love kids, I've just never had any myself." Then smiled. "Thought you should know that."

They'd gone out to dinner that Friday evening, and then to the San Francisco Zoo the next day with Emily. They were married seven months later. And Diana had never had a moment's doubt that he was the man she was meant to love.

She was thinking about this now as she lay propped up on the living room sofa with the green wool afghan Roy had given her last Christmas spread over her, surrounded by the anxious faces of her children and Allison.

Len had gone to get Diana a glass of water, while Allison had coaxed her from the floor to the couch.

Jeremy stood off to one side looking scared and confused.

Emily stared at Diana like her mother was some particularly obnoxious insect. "Get a grip, Mom. Geez."

Diana felt woozy, although she hadn't fainted. At least she didn't think she had. But a shadowy darkness had descended on her suddenly, sucking her breath from her lungs, and she'd found herself in a heap on the floor.

Allison stroked Diana's forehead, murmuring softly, "You're going to be okay, Diana. Really. You've held it together so well these last few days, it's not surprising the stress finally got to you."

A series of video clips flashed through Diana's mind. Roy at their wedding, promising to take care of her forever. Roy with Emily, patient and kind even during her difficult teenaged years. Roy holding his newborn son as though Jeremy were as fragile as a newly hatched butterfly. Roy, her life's partner, her friend, her confidant. How could this man who was Mr. Honesty himself have been hiding a secret as big as his own identity? Surely, there had to be some mistake.

"Was that a relative of Roy's on the phone?" Emily asked.

"No," Diana said hotly. "No, it wasn't."

Len returned and handed Diana a glass of water. She drank it like she hadn't had a drop in days.

"It was someone who knew him though, wasn't it?" Emily insisted. "From when he was growing up in North Dakota?"

"No," Diana said slowly. "It was a mix-up, is all. A mistake."

Emily sighed. "Well you certainly made a production out of it."

"Emily, let your mother be," Allison said. "It's been a tough couple of weeks for her."

"For me and Jeremy, too."

"Yes, of course, honey." Allison stroked Emily's long blond hair. "I know it's been hard for you two."

Jeremy looked upset still, and Diana beckoned him closer. She pulled him into her lap. "I'm fine, sweetie. I just needed to cry a little. There's nothing worry about. You understand that, don't you?"

Jeremy nodded mutely.

"I think I need to go upstairs and lie down for a bit," Diana said. "I'm sorry to have made such a scene."

"Do you have any sleeping pills?" Allison asked. "Maybe you ought to take one. I can stay here with the kids."

"No, I'll sleep just fine. It's just that I don't feel so well, suddenly." She got to her feet unsteadily and turned to her children. "Sorry to flake out on you two. You'll be okay?"

"Of course we'll be okay," Emily said.

Jeremy hugged Diana hard. "I love you, mommy."

"I love you, too, sweetie." She turned to Emily. "And you, too, Em."

"Why don't I come upstairs with you?" Allison said. "I want to make sure you're all right."

"I'm fine." Diana knew Allison would question her further about the phone call.

There were some secrets too awful to be shared, even with your best friend.

Chloe was lying on the bed with a romance novel she'd gotten from the library—a story about a handsome and wealthy landowner who'd hired a lovely young governess to care for the niece he was raising. Chloe was only on chapter five and she was already falling for the landowner, while the governess, who was something of a lightweight, found every opportunity to put him down. In fact, Chloe didn't like the governess at all. She was supposedly beautiful, but she wasn't nice.

The scrapes on Chloe's cheek and hands had scabbed over and hurt every time she moved. Her hip was still bruised and so sore she had trouble sitting. And when she walked, her knee occasionally sent daggers of red hot pain up her leg. She'd gone into work the Monday after the accident, but the manager had sent her home saying they couldn't have a cashier who looked like she'd been in a train wreck. So Chloe had spent most of the week hanging around the apartment, trying to stay out of Trace's way. It was one of the times Chloe really missed her mother.

As far back as a young child, Chloe had known her mother wasn't like other mothers. Her mother worked most days, and when she was home, she drank heavily and spent a lot of time sleeping. Sometimes she'd hide out in the bedroom with men Chloe had never seen before. Men who tried, with lollipops and bags of candy, to bribe Chloe to go play outside. Her mother was not, as the counselor at the group home had taken pains to point out to Chloe, an ideal mother. Not even close. But when Chloe was sick or hurt, her mother had usually come through. There weren't many such occasions—despite her haphazard home life, Chloe had been remarkably healthy as a child—but those stolen moments alone with her mother were among the few fond memories she had of growing up.

Once, when one of the men her mother brought home shoved Chloe so hard she fell and broke her arm, her mother stayed home from work and made Chloe chicken soup. Well, not made it exactly. She'd heated it from a can, but she'd sat with Chloe and fed her, spoonful by spoonful, even though it was Chloe's left arm that was broken.

That was what Chloe craved now. Someone to coddle and pamper her. Someone who cared about her.

Trace cared, of course. But he wasn't good at showing it. And he was angry she'd messed up when she'd gone to the lawyer's house. He'd been sleeping on the couch in front of the

TV and had barely spoken to her all week except to complain about needing to come up with the money he owed.

She felt a tear of self-pity roll down her cheek and she pushed it away. She wasn't a child anymore. She was almost a mother herself. She shouldn't expect anyone to kiss away her troubles.

Besides, it wasn't all bad. Her fall hadn't hurt the baby. She had worried about that more than anything. She'd waited for cramping or spotting or any of the signs that might spell trouble, and they hadn't happened. So she really didn't have anything to complain about.

There was a knock at the apartment door and she heard Trace talking to someone.

Her heart stopped when she left the bedroom and recognized the man in the doorway as one of the three Trace owed money to, the man with the face like a weasel. He was at least four inches taller than Trace and probably fifty pounds heavier. He pushed past Trace, into the room, and said, "Well, hotshot, did you get the money?"

"Not yet." Trace looked nervously around the room. "I'm working on it."

"Not good enough. Promises don't mean nothing."

Trace stepped back a couple of steps. "Look, can't we come up with some sort of payment plan?"

"Payment plan?" The man gave an icy chuckle.

"You know, installments. I can probably manage that."

The big man swung his arm and pushed Trace against the wall, pinning him there with a hand pressed hard against Trace's chest. Chloe wondered if she should call 9-1-1 and began to move toward the dresser where she'd left her phone.

"Uh-uh," the man said to her. "You stay where I can see you. Come here, in fact."

She moved hesitantly toward him. She didn't want to get too close.

"What do you think I should do about this no-good boyfriend of yours, huh? Asking nicely gets me nothing. Tell me the truth, is he holding out on me?"

Chloe shook her head. Her whole body was shaking too, so her head felt like one of those bobble-head toys you see on the dashboard of cars. "No," she said. "Really, we don't have the money."

"So what am I supposed to do?"

"Just give me a little more time," Trace pleaded.

"A little more time," the man mimicked. "I don't think so."

He socked Trace hard in the belly and Trace doubled over, holding his stomach and moaning. Chloe felt the fire of anger in her chest. She tried to get to the man but he yanked her by the wrist.

"Your boyfriend thought he was tough enough to play with the big guys. He doesn't look so tough now, does he, sweetheart?"

"Leave him alone," she cried as she tried to twist free. "We can't pay you if we don't have any money."

The man laughed. "What do you want with a wimp like this guy, anyway? Maybe we ought to get rid of him, huh? World would be a better place without the likes of him."

"Look man," Trace gasped. "I'm trying, I really am. You kill me and you'll never get your money. If you just cut me a little slack—"

"What do you think I've been doing, dickwad? Problem is, word gets around. We got to send a message, you know what I mean? We let you get away with shitting us, no one's going to take us seriously."

Still holding tight to Chloe's wrist, Weasel-face pulled her close enough that she could smell the garlic on his breath. "What happened to your eye? This no-good boyfriend of yours do that? You ought to get yourself a real man."

With his free hand, he yanked Chloe's shirt front open, sending buttons popping to the floor. Then he held her chin hard in a vice-like grip. "Take off your bra."

"No, please," she said, choking on her words. "Please don't." She looked to Trace for support.

He looked away. "Do it, Chloe. Just do what he wants."

She felt like she might be sick.

The man laughed and let go of her chin.

"You're a piece of work, Trace. A real piece of work. And here's a word of advice, you'd better start watching your back."

The man grabbed Trace's shirt front, kicked him in the shins, then slammed his head against the wall.

And then he left.

Chloe rushed to Trace. "Oh, God. Are you hurt?"

Trace writhed on the floor. "My shoulder. That bastard got me right where I was shot. Jesus Christ, it hurts. We got to get out of here, Chloe."

"Where would we go?"

"I don't know where." He moaned in pain. "But we've got to get away before there's real trouble."

"We don't have any money. I've got like, ten dollars. I get paid tomorrow. Can't we wait until then?"

Trace might not have agreed if hadn't been hurting so much. "Lock the door and don't open it no matter what. We'll talk about this later." He managed to sit up and brace himself against the wall. "Now get me some of those pain pills."

CHAPTER 20

Diana ended up taking a sleeping pill after all, but she still couldn't sleep. She didn't dare take a second one. Her mind twisted and turned, flooded with unbidden memories. How was it possible to love someone, miss them terribly, and be angry with them all at the same time? It was as though she'd lost Roy twice. Once to death and a second time to something worse.

A little after midnight, she went downstairs to the file cabinet in the den where she and Roy kept their important documents. She looked through the files until she found his birth certificate. In the soft light of the desk lamp, she examined it.

His mother's name was listed as Barbara Walker. Place of birth, Grand Forks, North Dakota. And the time of birth, 5:32 a.m.

The woman on the phone wasn't crazy. She was the mother of a dead boy whose identity Roy had stolen.

Diana's chest was tight, her mouth dry. A silent scream exploded in her head. Her beloved Roy, the man who connected all the disjointed parts of her and made her feel whole, was an imposter.

Shivering from the cold and the shock, she slowly climbed the stairs back to her bed. The truth was a heavy weight in her chest, too terrible to contemplate. Diana, who had always believed in facing her demons, found to her great surprise that she had something in common with Scarlett O'Hara. Tomorrow, she told herself. She'd think about it tomorrow.

Trace was still asleep, snoring loudly, when Chloe left for work Monday morning. She'd stayed up half the night quaking with fear at every sound from the outside, terrified Weasel-face would return and terrorize them further. Trace's idea of running made some sense, but where would they go? A motel? For how long? And how would they pay for it? Besides, driving around in a car with stolen plates was asking for trouble of a different sort.

The only real solution was to repay the money Trace owed. A couple of thousand, he'd said. She wasn't sure she believed him—it could be a lot more. To some people a couple of thousand might not seem like much. But Chloe had trouble even getting her mind around that much money.

She had packed up last night and had no regrets about leaving the ugly, soiled furniture that had come with the apartment, or the ratty linens and cracked plates they'd gotten at a thrift shop. She used her old suitcase—the one she'd carried into foster care—to pack clothes for both of them. She used the lawyer's gym bag for toiletries, a few kitchen basics, and bulkier items like her warm sweater. It surprised her to see how meager their possessions were. Everything they owned, practically, fit into a suitcase and a bag. She hid them, and the TV Trace refused to leave behind, in the storage room downstairs so that if Weasel-face returned and they had to leave in a hurry, they could come back and get their stuff later.

The more she thought about it, though, running away was a terrible idea. Trace would be able to work soon. He was strong, despite the injury to his shoulder, so he shouldn't have trouble finding a job. And her job didn't pay a lot, but it was something. Maybe if Trace began paying the men some money, they'd back off a bit.

Tomorrow Chloe would go to work, pick up her paycheck, and then head back to the apartment. Trace would try to figure out where they could go.

But the manager at the Craft Connection was late.

"Where's Mr. Black?" Chloe asked Velma, when it was almost noon and he still hadn't shown up.

"All I know is he called and said he'd be late."

"We're supposed to get paid today."

"I'm sure he knows that. He's never stiffed us yet, has he?"

He hadn't. But Chloe had never been desperate to get her check before closing, either. She bit her lower lip. "I was hoping to get to the bank today."

"You that short on cash? I could lend you twenty to tide you over until tomorrow."

Chloe shook her head, afraid she might burst into tears any moment.

Trace called twice. The first time Chloe explained that the manager was late.

"Christ, Chloe, we need to get going."

"What am I supposed to do," she whispered into the phone. "We need that paycheck."

"Shit." He hung up abruptly.

The second time he called, Chloe let the phone go to voicemail. It wasn't her fault that Mr. Black was late.

He arrived about four, but she didn't get her paycheck until the end of her shift at five. The bank would be closed by the time she got there, and they wouldn't be able to leave until the next morning. Trace would be angry.

Maybe she could convince him that running wasn't such a good idea, after all. She could cash her paycheck and give the whole thing to Trace to give to the men. She and Trace could get by somehow, even if she had to root through the trash at McDonald's to find food. It wouldn't be the first time she'd done it. Amazing the stuff people threw away!

Problem was, her paycheck didn't amount to much. Certainly not enough to give the men confidence that the rest of the money would be coming soon. It would be much better if she could sweeten the deal a little.

She didn't want to sue anybody, but Diana *had* urged her to visit the doctor about her knee, promising to cover the cost. Surely if Chloe asked for money for a doctor's visit, Diana would give it to her.

Chloe tried calling Trace to tell him she'd be late, but he didn't answer. She decided against leaving a message because she wanted to explain her plan in person. Besides, she wasn't sure she'd have the nerve to go through with it.

Without debating further, she climbed on the bus that would take her to Diana's neighborhood.

As she walked from the bus stop to Diana's street, she was enchanted once again by the majesty of the houses and the rich greenery of the surroundings. There was no freeway noise, no squeal of truck brakes. It was so quiet, in fact, you could actually hear birds chirping in the trees.

She stood on the corner, eyeing Diana's house, building her courage. She'd be doing it for Trace, she reminded herself. For Trace and the life they'd have together after the baby was born. Just as she approached the house, she saw Diana's car back down the long driveway. She caught sight of Jeremy in the back passenger seat as the car drove off.

Chloe's heart sank. She'd missed her chance. If only she hadn't wasted time admiring the neighborhood.

And then she remembered the ring of keys she'd stuck in her purse to keep Trace from finding it. The ring that might hold the key that would open the door to Diana's now-empty house.

Stealing was wrong. It was the very thing she'd told Trace she wouldn't do.

But she was desperate. She'd much rather have asked for money under the pretense of visiting a doctor, but fate had intervened and Diana had driven off.

One or two little things, was all. Items Diana might not even miss. Nothing really valuable. Just little stuff Chloe could sell easily for cash.

Although her heart pounded wildly, she walked to the front door as though she were an expected visitor. No one watching would think otherwise. She fingered the keys in her purse, looked out on the street, checked the windows of the neighboring houses, and held her breath as she put the larger bronze key into the lock. It turned and it was only after she'd stepped into the hallway that she remembered there might be an alarm.

No shrill sound pierced the air. There was no sound at all, except for the ticking of the large hallway clock Chloe had noticed the first time she was there.

She'd been too stunned then, and in too much pain, to fully appreciate how lovely the house was. The walls were a soft rose beige, the molding and doors some kind of warm, richly grained wood. The floors were a lighter wood, accented with richly colored oriental rugs. A home that was both beautiful and inviting.

"Isn't this the most beautiful place you could ever imagine, Megan?" she asked her baby. "It's just like something out of the movies." Only better, because it felt, even to Chloe who didn't belong there at all, like home.

She had to stop staring and move quickly. Take something and get out before Diana returned. But take what? Maybe she should look for money. Anything else would be too much to carry.

She felt sick as she moved into the kitchen where Diana had tended to her injuries only a few days earlier.

No. She couldn't do it. No way could she go through with

her plan and take anything.

A clatter of footsteps rang on the stairs and then a muffled scream. Chloe turned to see a slender girl with straight blond hair, a girl about her own age, standing in the doorway. She pulled the iPod buds from her ears.

"Who are you?" the girl asked. She sounded more baffled than frightened.

Chloe froze. The girl hadn't been here before. "I'm sorry."

"What are you doing here?"

Chloe's mind began to work again. "The door was open. I thought I heard Diana say to come in."

"You're a friend of my mother's?"

"No. I mean, not *friend* really."

The girl looked puzzled. "Are you the new cleaning lady?"

Chloe considered going with the cleaning lady bit, but figured that would only dig her in deeper. She needed to get away as quickly as possible.

"She helped me out—"

"What, you're her new charity case?" The girl's laugh sounded nasty. "It's creepy having you skulking around my house when I didn't even know you were here. How many times did you ring the bell?"

Chloe cleared her throat. "I knocked."

"Ah, no wonder I didn't hear you, I was upstairs listening to music."

Chloe inched toward the hallway. "I guess I'd better get going."

"Mom will be back any minute. She went to get ice cream and stuff." The girl scowled at Chloe. "It's funny that the door would be open, though. My mom's a bear about making sure it's closed and locked. Of course, she's been kind of distracted lately."

More footsteps, from the back of the house. And then voices.

"Is that bag too heavy, Jeremy?" Chloe recognized Diana's voice, which followed more loudly with, "Emily, we're home."

"In here," the girl called.

The dog who'd set Chloe's whole fiasco with Diana in motion pranced into the room and came to sniff Chloe's feet. His tail wagged like she was an old friend.

And then Diana strode into the kitchen and stopped in her tracks.

"Chloe." She set her package on the counter. "What are you doing here?" She looked suddenly stricken. "Is there a problem? A medical issue, I mean?"

"No. I'm good. Well, I'm mending anyway."

Diana looked relieved. "That's great news."

Jeremy was studying her face. "It must hurt still," he said solemnly.

Chloe shrugged. "Sometimes, yeah. But I'll live."

"Jeremy plowed into her on his bike," Diana explained to the girl, Emily.

"But he didn't mean too," Chloe added hastily. "It was an accident."

"We are all lucky she wasn't hurt worse," Diana said, putting a few items away into the freezer, before turning back to Chloe. "Did you come for money to cover a doctor's visit? I told you I'm happy to pay for that."

Chloe had come for that very reason but she found herself now, suddenly, incapable of deceiving Diana. She shook her head. "I was in the neighborhood and thought I'd come by to thank you for taking care of me."

Diana smiled. "It was the least I could do."

Emily opened a package of oatmeal cookies her mother had bought and ate one without offering them to anyone else. "Enough with the feel-good crap," she said, then addressed Diana accusingly. "She said you left the door unlocked."

Chloe's heart stopped. The moment of reckoning had come. How could she possibly explain herself now?

Diana's forehead wrinkled. "No, I'm pretty sure I locked it. But I couldn't swear to it. I'm really not thinking straight these days."

"Her husband died a few days ago," Emily explained, reaching for another cookie. "He was shot in some stupid convenience store robbery. You might have heard about it. He was a DA and a really great guy. We're all kind of off balance right now."

"Died?" Chloe felt the air sucked from her lungs. She tried to breathe and for a moment was afraid she couldn't. "He died? Oh, no. I'm so sorry." Chloe's eyes filled with tears. She looked at Jeremy. "Oh, geez. How terrible."

Diana, who had been puttering around the kitchen putting away groceries, stopped and, looking a bit surprised at the outburst, said, "Thank you. It's been pretty rough. The funeral was yesterday. Now I'm trying to move on. We all are." She paused and her face crumpled. "It's harder than I ever thought it would be."

"Of course," Chloe said. "Of course it is."

Chloe's scalp felt tight. She heard the rush of her pulse in her ears. It was like a tidal wave crashing over her. The end of the world, a collision of galaxies, a black hole sucking her down. So much hurt. So much was wrong. And Chloe felt herself at the very center of it.

Chapter 21

Emily opened the fridge and studied the contents for a few moments before shutting the door again. "Is that girl some kind of nutcase?" she asked Diana.

"I don't think so, but the visit was a bit odd, I'll grant you that."

"She's weird, is what she is." Emily gave heavy emphasis to the word "weird." She reached for another cookie, apparently having found nothing she wanted in the fridge.

"I like her," Jeremy said defiantly. "She's nice."

"Fat lot you know," Emily shot back. "You just like her because she doesn't blame you for running over her."

"I didn't run *over* her."

"Okay, into her. But you knocked her over."

Her children continued to bicker but Diana tuned them out. She sat down at the kitchen table and pressed her fingers against her temples. Her nerves were frayed to the point of snapping. Diana hadn't decided how much of what she'd learned about Roy to tell her children, or what any of it meant. Nor was she sure what she should do. She wasn't sure of anything anymore. Only that this had been one of the worst days of her life.

Although she could have sworn she'd been awake all night, the sleeping pill she'd taken must have kicked in at some point because Diana had awoken this morning from a pleasantly deep slumber. And in the grogginess of early morning consciousness, she'd begun the ritual of easing herself into the day. She'd known the other side of the bed was empty, but in her sleep-induced daze, she'd imagined Roy was in the shower. She lay warm under the covers, expecting him at any moment to emerge from the bathroom and flip on the light in the closet.

And then she'd remembered.

First, that Roy was dead. The knowledge rocked her with the impact of a thunderous wave breaking overhead. And while she was struggling to catch her breath, another wave of recognition crashed into her.

Her husband was an imposter.

The agony of that dual loss was so great that for a time Diana had been unable to pull herself out of bed. She'd curled into a ball and buried her face in her pillow. Finally, intensity of the pain propelled her on. She had to move or be sucked into a blackness so deep she was afraid she'd never claw her way free.

Gradually her world had come into focus, and over coffee she'd found within herself a renewed sense of determination. She had her children to think of, a newspaper column she'd been neglecting, the estate to settle. The demands of everyday life and the minutiae of death. And, of course, the puzzle of the man who'd been her husband.

After she'd taken Jeremy to school, Diana had gone back into the den, sat at Roy's large, heavily worn oak desk, and begun pulling together the records and documents she'd need for the attorney handling the estate.

As with most married couples, she and Roy had divvied up responsibilities without making a conscious decision to do so. Diana paid household bills but Roy handled the bulk of their finances. Not because Diana couldn't—she'd managed fine for years as a divorced woman—but because she found it tedious. She was thankful now that Roy had always been good about keeping records.

She pulled out the recent checking account and credit card

statements, the pink slips to their cars, which were both in Roy's name—again a matter of convenience—Roy's life insurance policy, and a photocopy of the deed to the house. She'd get the original from the safe deposit box when it became necessary.

But she couldn't find paperwork on the certificates of deposit she knew Roy kept in the file with the bank statements. There were two CDs, their rainy day funds, they called them. They sometimes joked that maybe the sky was gray enough to cash one or the other of them out and take a trip around the world, but of course they hadn't really considered it. Roy's temperament matched Diana's in that regard—financially conservative and risk averse.

After looking further and thinking maybe the CDs had been misfiled, she'd called the bank.

"No, ma'am," the bank officer told her. "Our records show that both those accounts have been closed."

"What? When?"

"The larger one, in June when it matured."

That couldn't be, Diana thought. She and Roy had agreed to let it roll over.

"The smaller one," the officer continued, "was closed out two months ago. There was a penalty assessed on that because the funds were withdrawn before the maturity date."

Diana's head swam. It didn't make sense that Roy would close the accounts, especially not if he had to pay a penalty.

She checked the bank statements to see if Roy had deposited the money into their meager savings account. He hadn't.

What he'd probably done was invest the money in a stock fund for a better rate of return, and simply forgotten to tell her. Or maybe he had told her and she had forgotten.

Rather than scour the brokerage statements, which she found complex and confusing, she called their broker directly. He was a man who'd had a daughter in Emily's class in high school. Someone Diana had met but rarely had dealings with.

"I was very sorry to hear about Roy," the broker told her. "It's a damn shame."

"Yes, it is." Diana paused, unsure how to begin. "That's what prompted my call. I'm trying to get our finances in order and I have such trouble making sense of the statements. I was wondering if Roy had made any investments recently."

"No, just the opposite."

"What do you mean?"

The broker seemed to hesitate. "He sold off quite a bit."

Stunned, she said, "How much?"

"Oh, off the top of my head, I'd say forty thousand. Roughly half your portfolio. I figured maybe the two of you were doing a big home remodel job or something."

Diana lost her breath. Both CDs and now a significant portion of their stock portfolio. She felt ill.

"Thank you," she said, attempting to cover her dismay. "I really have no head for financial matters."

"Any time. Please let me know if I can be of help."

She'd received similar news from Roy's life insurance company. He'd borrowed against the policy to the extent the payout would be minimal. By that point, she hadn't been surprised by the response so much as numbed.

Roy had always been responsible financially, as in every other way. The two of them paid their credit cards off each month, budgeted for vacations, bought their cars with cash. They owed nothing except the mortgage on the house. And they lived, if not frugally, well within their means. Yes, Roy bought nice suits, but usually on sale. And he wore easy-care shirts that didn't have to be sent to the laundry. He wasn't cheap. They ate out, took vacations, and didn't always chase a deal, but he was as solid and responsible as they came.

How could he have cashed out their CDs and sold off half of their investments without telling her? And what had he done with the money? The questions, like dark and ominous clouds, had shadowed her throughout the day.

Now, as she continued to rub her temples, Diana's head once again flooded with possible answers, none of them reassuring. A mistress? Another family? Gambling debts? Drugs?

Not Roy. Surely not Roy. But then, well, Roy wasn't really Roy, was he?

"Mom," Emily said with impatience, "I asked you when dinner was."

Diana looked up. "Sorry, I didn't hear you."

"Duh. I asked twice and you tuned me out. You're as weird as that girl."

Diana sighed. "Okay, I'm weird, but cut me a little slack here. I've just buried my husband."

Emily rolled her eyes. "It's not all about you, you know."

"I never said it was."

"But that's the way you act. Your husband, your loss, poor you."

Diana turned in a flash of anger. "I'm not—"

"Other people miss him, too," Emily said, her voice breaking and her eyes tearing up.

Diana felt instantly ashamed. What kind of awful mother was she, anyway? Jeremy had lost a father, and Emily, the closest thing to a father she'd ever known. Diana had paid lip service to their loss—no, more than that, she understood that they were grieving too, and she desperately wanted to be a source of strength for them—but she'd been so wrapped up Roy's deceptions and her own sense of loss, she'd tuned out their pain.

"You're right, honey. It's not all about me at all. Not by a long shot. This is devastating for you and Jeremy, too."

Jeremy, who'd been quietly petting Digger, didn't look up.

Emily glanced away.

Diana gave them each a hug. Jeremy returned the hug, his small body folding into hers like an animal burrowing into its nest. Emily remained rigid. She hugged Diana briefly and then pulled away.

"It was wrong of me to be so preoccupied. Please try to forgive me. I promise to be better going forward."

"That wouldn't be hard," Emily muttered.

Diana took a breath, then continued brightly, "How about we order pizza for dinner? I don't feel like cooking and I think we could all use a treat."

"Can I have a Coke?" Jeremy asked uncertainly.

"Sure." What was one night without milk?

Emily met Diana's eyes and lifted her chin. "Can I have a beer?"

Classic Emily, always pushing the boundaries. But for the moment, Diana wasn't about to push back. "Sure, if that's what you want. Now what kind of pizza shall we order?"

Stupid. Totally stupid. What had she been thinking?

Chloe huddled in a seat near the rear of the bus and pressed her head against the window. How could she have stooped so low?

To break into someone's home, to plop yourself smack in the middle of their tragedy, and under false pretenses, too. She placed both palms on her belly to shield the baby from her shame.

Roy Walker's death troubled Chloe in ways that didn't make sense. The store clerk, Hector, had died, and while Chloe felt truly terrible about it, there was a sense that it didn't involve her. Hearing about it on the TV and seeing his mother's tears as she spoke to reporters, Chloe had been choked by sadness, but this was different.

Diana had been so kind to her. She'd treated Chloe's wounds, driven her home, and even offered to pay for a visit to the doctor. And Jeremy—Chloe had seen the look in his eyes when he talked about his father. Roy Walker's death was something else. Chloe felt it as sharply as she'd felt anything in her life. And to know she was part of it, even an unwitting part, made her feel small and dirty and unworthy.

"Oh, Lizzie," she said with a hand on her belly. "How did this happen?"

She shivered even though it was warm and stuffy inside the bus. She'd made a mess of her life already and she was barely eighteen. And she didn't see any way to make things better. Nothing would bring back Roy Walker or the dead clerk. Nothing short of several thousand dollars would convince Weasel-face and his two friends to lay off Trace. And now that the lawyer had died, the police would ramp up the hunt for his killer. She had been naive to think she and Trace could do anything but run and hide. She'd go to the bank first thing in the morning, cash her paycheck, and then they'd take off. At least they had each other, and that's what counted most, wasn't it?

The bus lurched to a stop at a corner four blocks from the apartment and Chloe got off, thanking the driver as she did every time. She didn't always get a pleasant response, but she liked to think she was making an effort, however small, to make the world a happier place.

Two helicopters circled overhead and traffic was jammed. As she approached her own street, she saw it was cordoned off. Five or six police cars, as well as a number of news vans, were parked nearby.

She ran to a group of bystanders near the yellow tape. "What's going on?"

"There were shots fired," a man said.

164

"Shots?" Her mind fixed instantly on Weasel-face and his two friends. Had they come for Trace so soon? "Was anyone hurt?"

"I think there's an officer down," someone else chimed in, a boy about Chloe's age, madly working his iPhone. "Wait, here's a stream of the news."

He held the iPhone at arm's length so those around him could view the screen. Chloe pushed in closer so she could hear what was being said over the drone of the helicopter.

The anchor announced "breaking news" of a police-involved shooting. The picture cut to a shot of a male reporter just as Chloe spotted him and his camera crew in real life, standing near a uniformed officer to the left of the crowd.

"Thanks, Dan," the reporter said on screen. "Here's what we know at this point. Police were serving an arrest warrant when the suspect fired shots and then fled on foot. An officer was injured, and is now being treated at the medical center. The search for the suspect continues."

An arrest warrant.

Trace? Had they come to arrest Trace?

No, Chloe told herself. Their crummy neighborhood was home to probably dozens of suspects. The warrant could have been for anyone.

Quickly, Chloe punched Trace's number into her cell phone. It went straight to voicemail.

That proved nothing, she told herself. There were plenty of reasons he might not answer.

She pushed her way to the uniformed officer closest to the yellow tape. "What's happening?" she asked.

"Stand back, ma'am."

"But I live on this street."

"Sorry. You can't go in there, it's too dangerous. We've got a gunman on the loose."

"Gunman? On the news, they said a suspect."

"Right. A suspect fleeing from police. The area has been evacuated. We're not letting anyone back in until it's safe."

Chloe reached for her phone to try Trace one more time. Before she had a chance to hit redial, shots rang out. Four or five of them in rapid succession.

There was a flurry of police movement toward the yard of the house two doors down. The officer's radio crackled. "We got him. We need an ambulance down here right away."

Another voice over the radio. "Roger. On our way."

An ambulance, which had been idling at the curb maybe fifty feet away, slowly moved forward, easing through the crowd.

Chloe punched her phone frantically but her call to Trace went unanswered.

Chloe's knees felt weak. Her head swam. "Dear God, not Trace. Please."

Even as she prayed, she knew in her heart it was too late.

CHAPTER 22

Over dinner—if pizza eaten straight out of the Round Table box could legitimately be called dinner—Diana made an effort to concentrate on her children rather than dwelling on questions about Roy. Or worries about money. It had begun to dawn on her that Roy's deception might not be the most pressing problem she faced. With roughly half their financial holdings unaccounted for, Diana needed to give serious thought to how she'd support her family.

Despite the earlier outburst, when Emily had accused Diana of thinking only about herself, neither Emily nor Jeremy had much to say about Roy. Or about anything else. They sat at the table, silently eating the pizza as if performing a duty. Diana tried to draw them out, and then, finally, to simply fill the conversational void.

As dinner wound down, Emily began tearing off tiny pieces of her napkin and stacking them on her plate. "I should probably get back to school soon," she said without looking up. "It's hard to catch up if you miss too many lectures."

"Of course." Diana nibbled a piece of crust from Jeremy's plate. He'd already polished off two pieces of pizza, sans the outer crust, and gone off to watch TV.

"If you wanted," Emily added, "I could stay longer. I'm sure they'd grant me a leave of absence if I asked."

Diana shook her head so vigorously she almost choked on the bite of crust. "No, absolutely not. You shouldn't put your life on hold. College is where you belong right now."

If Diana couldn't work out the finances, it might be the last semester Emily got. But more than that, Diana knew that if Emily stayed at home, they'd be at each other's throats within a week.

Then she remembered her resolve to be a better mother. "Of course, you can stay as long as you like, Em, if you don't want to go back just yet."

"It's just that I feel bad leaving you—"

"I'll be fine." Diana squeezed her daughter's hand. "We all will be, even though it may not seem that way right now." The platitudes rolled easily off her tongue, but they rang hollow in her own ear. She felt certain that though she might carry on, she'd never really feel whole again. *Fine* was in the past. "It's going to be hard, honey, there's no denying that. Hard for all of us. But we can't simply stop living."

"I guess."

"And you'll be coming home soon for Thanksgiving. And then Christmas break."

Emily took a small sip of her beer. After making her stand, she'd barely touched the bottle. Diana noted this fact with a private smile. Her daughter sometimes pushed limits simply for the sake of pushing. Like the time she was thirteen and had fought tooth and nail for months to be allowed to take BART into San Francisco by herself. When she'd finally been granted permission, she made one very quick round trip and never raised the subject again.

"My father died when I was your age," Diana continued. "Well, a few years younger than you. I know how difficult it can be."

"Roy wasn't my father." Emily's voice grew wistful. "I wish he had been. I wish you'd married better the first time around."

Diana nodded. "Me, too."

Garrick hadn't been much of a father to Emily even before the divorce, but afterward, he pretty much severed ties altogether. That is, until he married for a second time when Emily was ten. His new wife had two children of her own, and ever competitive, Garrick suddenly discovered the need for a daughter. He began calling Emily regularly, sending her birthday and Christmas presents, and little gifts for no reason at all. He invited her to spend that first summer on Martha's Vineyard with him and his new family, and then regularly sent her plane tickets for visits to their North Carolina home.

Emily could barely tolerate her stepmother but she adored having her dad's attention. At long last, a father. And something of a fantasy life while she was with him. Garrick had money—and horses, and boats, and every electronic toy imaginable. Garrick didn't have to deal with homework or discipline or teacher conferences or making sure Emily got to school on time. For four years, Emily's semiannual trips east were the highlight of her life.

When she started high school, Emily announced she wanted to live with her dad fulltime. Although Diana was heartbroken at the prospect, she knew Emily was having a rough time fitting in at school, so she relented. Garrick was not so amenable to the idea of having a daughter day in and day out. Neither, Diana suspected, was his wife. So Emily remained with her mother, and the plane tickets, presents, and invitations to come visit dried up.

Diana had tried to be evenhanded about the divorce, but for deserting Emily a second time, she could never, ever forgive the man.

"He doesn't even return my phone calls anymore," Emily said, brushing the table with her thumb. She didn't look at Diana.

"Honey, it's not about you. It's him."

"But I'm his only real kid. You'd think he'd care just a little."

"Your dad is so self-centered he can't see beyond the end of his nose."

Emily looked up. "Then why did you marry him?"

Diana considered her answer. She wanted to be honest, but she also hoped Emily would learn from her mistakes. "Because I wasn't very smart. I was young and your father was my first real boyfriend. I was seduced by the idea of being in love. There was a lot I didn't see, or didn't want to see, and I think I believed he would change."

"And then I came along and made everything worse."

Diana sat up. "Absolutely not. Don't ever think that. Nothing that happened between your dad and me is your fault."

"But if might have been different if I wasn't there."

"Different as in empty." She touched Emily's cheek and brushed the hair from her face. "I can't imagine my life without you. It pains me to think of it."

"Dad has no problem with it." Emily picked at the label on her bottle. "Did he ever love me?"

Diana's heart ached for Emily. "He loves you still, honey. It's just that love isn't high on his list of priorities."

"That's true of most guys, isn't it." A statement rather than a question.

"No, most guys are not like that. Especially the ones who've had some time to mature. Don't let your dad sour you on the male species. There are lots of good, trustworthy guys out there."

"Like Roy."

Diana didn't hesitate. "Like Roy," she agreed. But she almost gagged on the words. If Roy was such a good, trustworthy person, why had he hidden so much from her?

"I guess some people get lucky." Emily sounded wistful again.

"You're young, Em. There will be plenty—"

But Emily had already pushed her chair back from the table

and was sprinting upstairs. Diana was weighing whether or not to go after her when the doorbell rang.

Digger raced to the front door, barking loudly. Diana rose from the table and went to the door after him. Through the glass pane she saw Inspector Knowles on the porch, rocking back and forth, heel to toe. He looked tired and a bit unkempt.

Diana tensed. Had the police discovered Roy's bogus identity? Or did the visit have something to do with the money missing from their accounts. A scandal involving bribes or some illegal activity. Her throat tight, Diana opened the door and ushered the detective in.

"I hope I'm not disturbing anything," he said.

"No, we've finished eating. Can I get you some coffee?" Were you supposed to offer coffee, Diana wondered, or was that just on TV? In any case, it would give her something to do, something to counter her nervousness.

Knowles shook his head. "Maybe some water, though."

"With ice or from the tap?"

"Tap's fine." The detective took a moment to look around the hallway, causing Diana a moment of panic. Was there something a trained eye might find significant? Finally, he followed her into the kitchen.

"I came to tell you we got the man we believe shot your husband. It will be all over the news soon and I wanted you to know first."

Diana's heartbeat quickened. She'd wanted answers and now maybe she'd get them.

Drugs? A woman? Something involving the missing money?

She braced herself, sure the black cloud she'd been under all day was about to open up in a deluge. Roy's dark side would be revealed.

Filling a glass with water from the faucet, she handed it to Knowles with a trembling hand. "Who is he, this man?"

Knowles drained his glass in a few long swallows, then set it on the counter. "Some punk kid from Oakland by the name of Trace Rodriguez. He's had a few run-ins with the law before, but nothing major. There doesn't appear to be any previous connection between Rodriguez and your husband. Way it looks, your husband was simply in the wrong place at the wrong time."

"Totally random, in other words?" Diana felt shaken. It wasn't what she'd expected, not with all she'd uncovered about Roy since his death.

"I don't know if that makes it better for you, or worse. Either way, it doesn't bring your husband back."

That Roy was gone, really gone, forever, was something that hit Diana anew every time she thought about it. But she refused to let her mind go there now. "How'd you find him?"

"We got a tip. I told you that was probably how it would go. The kid undoubtedly bragged to his buddies and one of them turned him in."

Was she supposed to feel relief? Some sense of satisfaction that Roy's killer would pay for his crime? Mostly what Diana felt was confused. "You're sure you've got the right man? What does he say happened?"

Knowles kneaded the back of his neck. "The suspect was killed resisting arrest."

"You mean he's dead? The person who shot Roy is dead?"

"He tried to run. Opened fire on one of the Oakland cops. We don't have the final ballistics reports yet, but preliminary indications are that his gun is a match for the weapon that killed your husband and the clerk. And his car matches the description of the car seen leaving the convenience store. It's got stolen plates. He switched them out with another car."

A murder that had nothing to do with who Roy was or what he was hiding. A chance encounter with fate. Like being hit by lightning or struck by a falling tree limb. Diana should have found the explanation, in some perverse way, reassuring, but she didn't. It left wide open the Pandora's box of unanswered, and unsettling, questions.

"What was Roy doing in the Bayview district?" she asked. "Do you have any idea why he stopped at the convenience store?"

Knowles shook his dead. "We'll probably never know. There's nothing to indicate that he was involved with the holdup."

Diana had been angry when the inspector first suggested that, so it should have made her happy to hear him admit he'd been wrong. But there were too many things that still made no sense.

Diana's mind raced. Nothing would bring Roy back, but she couldn't simply let this be the end of it. Jumbled fragments of information swirled in her head. Part of her wanted to tell Knowles about Roy's assumed identity. About the money missing from their accounts. She wanted to pound her fists and shout at the detective, "There's more to this than you think!"

But what if Roy's death really was a fluke? She wasn't eager to drag his reputation through the mud. She needed to consider carefully before she said anything to anyone.

"It's too bad," she said, gingerly testing the waters, "that the suspect died before he could tell you why he did it."

The detective sucked on his lower lip and regarded her with a warm but slightly disdainful and aloof expression that reminded Diana of her old journalism professor.

"Mrs. Walker, I understand you want an explanation that makes sense. Believe me, I do. But even if the suspect was alive and we had a full-blown trial, chances are you wouldn't have gotten that. Creeps like the guy who shot your husband don't live by the same rules of reason the rest of us do. They steal, they kill, they threaten and maim, to get whatever they want at the moment, whether it's money for drugs, recognition from a gang, or the satisfaction of following a spur-of-the-moment whim. This kid not only killed your husband and the store clerk, he resisted arrest and shot a police officer. I'm not the least bit troubled by the fact he's dead. It will save us the trouble and expense of a trial." Knowles paused and looked Diana in the eye before continuing. "And you, the agony of hearing the defense try to besmirch your husband."

Knowles's final comment put Diana instantly on alert. "Roy was a good man," she insisted. "And a victim. How could anyone denigrate a man like that?"

"I'm not saying they'd succeed, but you'd be surprised what defense attorneys will try."

And what, in this instance, they might have discovered. She ought to feel grateful the killer was dead. "In any case," she said, "I'm glad you found the man who shot Roy. It would be so much worse if I thought he'd gotten away with it."

"If anything new comes out of our investigation, I'll be in touch. Like I said, the story will be all over the news soon. You'll probably be contacted by the media. Whether you talk to them or not, is up to you."

Diana walked the detective to the door and then stood staring out into the night after he was gone. The search for Roy's killer was over, but her own questions about Roy weren't going away.

CHAPTER 23

As Skeet Birnbaum had predicted, the discovery of Miranda Saxton's remains attracted national attention. Journalists from the nation's networks, newspapers, and tabloids swept into Littleton, fighting for interviews with Chief Holt and anyone else who'd lived in town twenty years ago. And because Joel Richards had talked to most of these folks first, managing somehow to get just a bit more out of each source than the out-of-town reporters, Joel himself was courted as someone with inside information.

But the interest was short-lived. Last week, five days after the media had descended on Littleton, a famous actor was charged with the murder of his pregnant girlfriend. Two days later, a prominent U.S. senator became entangled in a prostitution scandal involving underage girls. Interest in a twenty-year-old murder simply didn't have staying power.

"Don't let it get you down, kid," Skeet told Joel between bites of an oversized glazed donut. He reached for the cup of coffee on his desk. "Keep your ears open while you continue working on other stories. As soon as Holt gets a lead on Brian Riley—"

"Or comes up with some new suspect," Joel added.

"You don't buy the theory that the medallion was Brian's?"

"Just trying to keep an open mind is all." A silver sun medallion on a braided leather cord had been found with Miranda's remains. Rumor had it that Brian Riley had worn a similar

175

medallion. The evidence further cemented the chief's belief that their original suspect was the right suspect.

"As soon as something happens," Skeet said, "the locusts from the big cities will be back. And you'll be several steps ahead of them. In any case, you've had that weeklong series that could be a good start on an article in some high profile magazine down the road."

"Thanks to you." With Skeet's help, Joel had enjoyed one full week of front-page stories and his own byline. It was a heady feeling, and Joel was disappointed to learn that the paper was pulling back on the coverage now that there wasn't much to report.

"I only made the assignment," Skeet told him. "You did the work. Damn fine work it was, too. And you're still building the backstory, right?"

Joel nodded. He'd interviewed Miranda Saxton's sister, a couple of local guys who'd known Brian Riley, and the woman who ran the household for Walter St. John's summer compound. He'd found a number of other people who'd known Miranda, but far fewer who'd known Brian, although most of the old-timers in town had heard of him. Joel had managed to track down a neighbor of the family, now living in a retirement home in Florida, and a high school classmate of Brian's who claimed she'd been the target of unpleasant and unwanted romantic overtures from him during their last year of high school. Joel found her stories so outlandish that he was inclined to dismiss them.

Some of what Joel learned had been incorporated into his newspaper reports this last week, but more of it had ended up in his files. If and when the story grew legs again, Joel would be ready. Miranda Saxton's disappearance was something that had caught Joel's interest the way reporting on city council meetings and falling school tests scores hadn't.

It wasn't just the crime itself, although that was certainly a big part of what intrigued him. As he'd dug deeper into the story, Joel had come to feel he'd known Miranda and Brian and the other key players personally. They lived in his mind, like imaginary companions, even while he slept. That last part wasn't such a good thing because Joel was sometimes exhausted by morning, but the details and anecdotes he'd collected made the events of twenty years ago as vivid to Joel as parts of his own life.

"Good," Skeet was saying now. "Keep on digging. But for the present, I want you to concentrate on that supposed drug thing at the junior high. What's with kids these days? And where the hell do twelve-year-olds get pot to sell?"

"All good questions," Joel said. He'd been as incredulous as Skeet when he first heard about it.

"Anyway," Skeet concluded, "I want something about this on my desk by the end of the day."

"You'll have it."

Five minutes later Joel was out the door on his way to talk to the school principal, who, as luck would have it, had been a math teacher at the junior high when Joel himself was a student there. He'd only gotten a C in the class—due in large part to the fact he'd sat next to Jane Beaumont, who had flaxen hair and dimpled cheeks and the sort of girl-witchery that made paying attention to anything else all but impossible. Still, Joel and the teacher had gotten along just fine.

At four-thirty, Joel made the final edits to his drug article and put it on Skeet's desk. He decided to call it a day and head home to spend some time with his father. The past ten days had been long ones, all of them crazy with phone calls and research and deadlines. Joel had hardly talked to his dad except to pat his knee or kiss the top of his head on his way in and out of the house.

Not that Joel ever did much of the actual work involved in caring for his father. That task fell to Mrs. Albert, the latest of a string of caretakers he'd hired when it became obvious Joel couldn't leave his father alone. Mrs. Albert's predecessors had been as careless and unreliable as his father, and none of them had lasted very long, but Mrs. Albert was a gem. She'd been with them for two years now and Joel constantly worried she'd leave them for a better position.

He'd called Mrs. Albert and told her to take the night off—no need to have dinner ready, he'd handle that as well. Joel enjoyed these evenings with his father. They'd eat a simple meal, then sit in front of the television until his father started nodding off, which was fairly early these days. There wasn't a lot of conversation, but in its place was a companionable silence Joel found comforting. It was the sort of evening he'd wished he'd had with his family growing up. The kind of evening his friends had taken for granted. But a fisherman's work never ended, and his father had spent most nights out in the shop repairing nets or cleaning equipment.

"What'll it be?" Joel asked his father as he scanned the contents of the refrigerator. "Fried pork chops or an omelet?"

"That's good," said his father, buttoning the old brown cardigan across his chest in a mismatched fashion. "I'm so hungry I could eat a horse."

Joel decided on the omelet and began chopping green onions and mushrooms.

"Is Julia coming for dinner?" his father asked.

"No, Dad. Just the two of us tonight." Julia had been last year, and Joel had only brought her home for dinner once. But she'd made an impression, probably because Joel's life had previously been devoid of female company. As it was now, again.

Julia had moved on to bigger and better things, and richer men.

"Why don't you call her?" his father asked. "Tell her to come on over."

"We broke up, Dad. Remember? It was a while ago."

"That's a danged shame. You need a girl. Someone like your mother. She's one of a kind, she is."

Joel ignored the use of the present tense. His mother had been dead for almost ten years.

"Too bad she couldn't be with us tonight."

"Yes, it is," Joel agreed as he cracked the eggs into a bowl. He wasn't sure if his dad was referring to his mother or Julia.

"But I know she's in a good place." His father rocked gently back and forth in his chair causing it to squeak. "Probably settled in real nice by now."

"And where would that place be?" Joel asked, willing to go along with wherever his father's mind had taken him.

His father looked at Joel with a scowl, the same scowl with which he greeted all stupid questions. "Why heaven, of course. Where else? Your mother was one of the kindest people who ever walked this earth."

Joel nodded and blotted the corner of his eye with the back of his hand. It was the onions, he told himself. "I know that, Dad."

That was the funny thing about dementia. You could be in la-la land one minute and back here on earth the next. Joel wondered if it wasn't something like being in a dream, where things made perfect sense even when you knew they didn't.

As difficult as it was to watch a parent slowly lose his mind, Joel found that he'd come to know his father through the candor of dementia far better than he had before. His father had been a distant and emotionally reserved man while Joel was growing up. To have asked what his father *felt* about something would have struck Joel as being impolite. But in the last couple of years, Joel had been able to catch glimpses of the man inside. The man who loved and cried and laughed. The man who was, at the core, his father.

"You still with the newspaper?" his father asked.

"Yep." Joel set aside the bowl of whisked eggs and showed his father the paper from Monday. "Front page," he said.

"That's you?" He squinted at the byline. "Doggone. Good work, son."

"I've been following the Miranda Saxton story. She was—"

His dad brushed the air with his hand. "I know who she was. I lived through the whole thing, remember? You were only a kid then."

In all his research, Joel had never thought to ask his father about Miranda. "Did you ever see her? Around town, I mean?"

"More than that." His father settled back in his chair, a smile on his face. "She spent a day on my boat once. St. John chartered us for the day. He and the senator and a bunch of the other self-important clowns who vacationed out at the compound. They brought that poor girl along, although it was clear she didn't want to be there. She was sick as a dog until she got her sea legs."

"What was she like?"

"Pretty. Not in-your-face stunning, but she had a lightning smile and an animated way of talking. You'd think hanging out there at the compound with all those fancy-pants she'd be impressed with herself and kind of stuck-up. But she wasn't. She was real down-to-earth."

Joel was sautéing the onions and he had to strain to hear over the sizzle of the pan. "Did she happen to mention Brian Riley?"

"Why would she do that?"

"There was talk they were seeing each other. That he killed her."

His father shook his head. "Hogwash. I knew the boy's father.

He killed himself, you know. I used to think he was a pretty decent man but I fault him for that."

"For taking his own life? I gather he was embarrassed when suspicion settled on his son." Joel wasn't sure where the conversation was headed but he wanted to keep his dad talking.

"The boy was never charged. That tells you something, doesn't it?"

Joel nodded, although in truth, it told him little.

His father took the nod as agreement. "I figured there was a lot of pressure from those high-and-mighties out at the compound to pin it on someone, and young Riley was an easy target."

"I take it you didn't think much of the crowd that hung out over at St. John's place."

"You take that right." His father chuckled. "They'd swoop in here every summer like a flock of magpies, using the town as their plaything and turning up their pointy noses at those of us who lived here."

Joel knew his father wasn't the only one in town who thought that way. "I don't suppose you ever met Brian Riley?"

"Can't say as I did. But your cousin Max was in school with him, if I recall."

The son of his mother's older sister, Max now living up north somewhere. Chicago, Joel thought. Maybe he'd give Max a call.

"Are those pork chops almost ready?" his father asked.

"Just about."

Joel could only hope that by the time the omelet was done, his dad would assume he'd been waiting for eggs and not chops. Or even, God forbid, a horse.

CHAPTER 24

"But I *have* to watch a network station," Chloe wailed.

The sales clerk at Best Buy gave her an exasperated look. "Which television set were you interested in seeing?"

Chloe pointed to a midsize model, picking it at random. She wasn't interested in the Discovery Channel or high definition football, which the clerk assured her were better programs for gauging the quality of the picture. "A local channel," she added.

The clerk sighed and went to a panel on the wall to switch feeds. Chloe's heart was racing. She had to know what had happened, but she knew it wouldn't be good.

She'd remained with the small crowd of bystanders on the street outside her building until it had grown dark and the last of them drifted off to the comfort of their own homes. Chloe hadn't known what to do next. She'd never in her life felt so lost.

The police had been screening the residents of the apartment building before letting them inside. Chloe didn't think they'd let her back into her unit even if she made it past the cop at the bottom of the stairs. She didn't really want to be in the empty apartment she'd shared with Trace, anyway.

What she wanted was Trace. She'd called the three local hospitals but none of them would tell her anything. Wiping the tears from her eyes, she'd tried to think what to do. She was growing cold and hungry and desperate for news. Finally, she'd remembered the big Best Buy store across the mall parking lot from the Craft Connection.

"Any channel in particular?" the clerk asked her.

"One showing local news."

"There isn't local news at this hour," he said impatiently. "You'd have to wait until ten and we'll be closed then."

Panic swelled in Chloe's chest. "No, you don't understand. I have to—"

"Yeah, you told me. If you want the news so bad, why don't you try the Internet? We've got a few computers that are hooked up."

Chloe practically ran to the other side of the store and clicked onto a news link.

The police didn't identify Trace by name, only as a prime suspect in the recent shooting of Alameda County DA Roy Walker. And they confirmed her worst fear—that the suspect had been shot and killed while fleeing from police.

"Taken to Highland Hospital where he was pronounced dead" were the exact words of the official police statement.

Fighting the rise of choking sobs, Chloe raced to the privacy of the restroom. There she locked herself in a stall and cried until she had no more tears left. She thought she'd been alone in the past, but it was never like this. There'd been social workers and foster parents and Rose at the group home, and then Trace. Now there was nobody. Just her and her baby.

She rubbed her belly, mentally messaging the tiny limbs of the child inside her. "Lisa," she told her daughter, "I'm all you have, and you are all I have." And that set her off on another round of tears.

By the time the store announced it would be closing in ten minutes, Chloe had come up with a plan for the night. She'd stay in the restroom until everyone had gone, and then she'd have the store to herself. She'd once read a library book about a girl who lived almost a whole week inside a Walmart. Best Buy didn't offer quite the same variety of goods as Walmart—no food or sleeping bags—but Chloe was sure the employee rest area would have a snack machine, maybe even a cot. If not, she could curl up in the big black recliner she'd seen positioned in the high-end electronics section. For tonight she'd be warm and secure. She'd figure out later what to do after that.

Just when she decided it was safe to venture from the restroom, she thought of something. Wouldn't a store like Best Buy have security cameras and motion detectors and alarms? Maybe even a night watchman? If she went out into the store, she'd have the cops down on her in no time.

Chloe felt faint. She grabbed the sink to steady herself. Why hadn't she thought of this earlier? Now it was too late. She was trapped inside the stupid bathroom for the rest of the night. Why didn't she ever think things through from the beginning?

She caught sight of her reflection in the mirror—her eyes red and puffy, her nose raw from the wads of toilet paper she'd used for tissue. She remembered how Rose used to stand girls who'd screwed up in front of a mirror and give them sixty seconds to verbally beat themselves up. Then she'd remind them that what was done, was done. "There's no point looking back when where you're headed is forward," Rose would tell them. And then she'd ask, "Which direction do you want to go?"

Chloe didn't have the energy for sixty seconds of recrimination but she knew she needed to go forward. With a gnawing ache in the pit of her stomach, she lowered herself onto the hard tile floor, pulled her knees to her chest, and began counting the hours until morning.

Chloe was almost half an hour late for work. Which was pretty ironic considering she'd been awake since six and had only needed to walk across the street to get to the Craft Connection. She'd overlooked the fact that Best Buy didn't open until ten o'clock, half an hour after she was supposed to be at work.

Mr. Black glared at her when she signed in. "You'd better have a good excuse."

"I'm sorry," Chloe said. "I really couldn't help it." She didn't elaborate. There was no way she could tell the truth, and she was too tired and too scared to fabricate a lie.

"I expect you to work through lunch to make up the time. We've got a new shipment of scrapbooking supplies that need to be shelved."

"That's fine with me."

"For now, give Velma a hand at the register."

Chloe pinned on her name badge and walked stiffly to the front of the store. Her neck had a crick in it from sleeping upright, and her butt was sore from the hard tile floor of the public bathroom where she'd spent the night.

"You doing okay?" Velma asked Chloe as she slid behind the next register.

"Just a little tired is all."

There was a long line of shoppers, most clutching the coupon that had run in yesterday's newspaper, and for the next half an hour Chloe and Velma didn't have time for conversation.

When there was a break from the steady flow of customers, Velma said, "You feel like talking about it?"

Chloe looked up. "About what?"

Velma raised her eyebrows the way Rose used to when a girl played dumb. "The young man the police killed last night, that was your boyfriend, wasn't it?"

"How'd you know?"

"Just putting two and two together from things you've said before." Velma came over right there in the store and put her arms around Chloe. "I'm so sorry, honey. I know I've said bad things about him before, about how he treated you and all, but that doesn't mean I don't feel bad for you now."

Chloe felt tears spring to her eyes. "I can't believe it's real. That Trace is actually gone. Dead."

"I know, I know." Velma rubbed Chloe's back before releasing her. "You've got a bit of rough road ahead of you."

Chloe nodded. Velma had no idea how rough.

"You talked to the police yet?"

"Why would I do that?"

"They want to talk to you, I know that much. They said so on the news last night."

Chloe's heart leapt with alarm. She looked around the store, hoping the manager wasn't watching. "Why me? What did they say?"

"Just routine stuff, I imagine. They said the cops wanted to talk to his 'live-in girlfriend.' They didn't mention you by name."

"I can't. I—"

"What do you mean, you can't? You didn't do anything wrong, did you?"

Chloe thought she might be sick. "Oh, Velma. My whole life is wrong."

Velma stepped back and looked at her sternly. "You didn't kill anyone, did you?"

"No."

"Did you rob anyone? Beat them up?"

"No."

"I bet you've never lifted a single item from the shelves here, have you?"

Chloe looked insulted. "Of course not."

"Then you listen up, girl. Go see the cops. Don't you go talking about your life being wrong and confessing every stupid little mistake you ever made. Just answer their questions as simply as possible. Be cooperative. Bat your eyelashes if you want—you're young enough and cute enough to get away with it."

Chloe had never thought of herself as cute. She wondered if Velma was putting her on.

"But don't you ever tell them you've done anything wrong. They can't have anything on you or they would have talked to you before this."

"It's not that simple," Chloe wailed.

" 'Course it is. Whatever you've done, or think you've done, spending time in prison won't change it." Velma nodded in the direction of the manager's booth at the back. "If you want to go now, just tell The Great One you're not feeling well. I can handle the register by myself."

"Thanks. I'm not ready just yet, but I'll think about it."

"Don't think too long."

Chloe waited until the end of her shift before calling the police. She hoped it would be a short phone conversation, but the person she needed to speak to wasn't even available right then.

"Where can you be reached tonight?" the woman at the police station asked.

Chloe gave the woman her phone number.

"How about a physical location?"

"Can I go back to the apartment?" Chloe asked.

"Let me check." It took the woman a moment to get an answer. "It's all yours. The investigation there has wrapped up."

Chloe should have been grateful to be home, but the apartment didn't feel like home anymore. It felt empty and depressing and unfamiliar. Chloe knew where the bedroom was, and which cupboard held the bread and the plates, but nothing about it felt *right*. Without Trace, it was nothing but a few ugly rooms with stained brown carpeting and pocked walls. She could tell the place had been searched by the police. She was glad she'd packed up most of their personal items last night and stashed the suitcase and gym bag in the basement. At least there hadn't been strangers pawing through her underwear.

She didn't know what she was going to do about a place to live. She couldn't afford the rent here by herself, even if she'd wanted to stay. But she didn't. What she wanted was a sunny yellow apartment with wood floors, a bay window, and a flower garden. A *home*. And she knew she'd never have it.

An officer showed up at her door a little past seven. He didn't bother calling first. Nor did he ask if he could come in. He just plowed past Chloe like he owned the place.

"I understand you're the live-in girlfriend of Trace Rodriguez."

The way he said "live-in girlfriend" made her sound trashy, but Chloe nodded.

"How long have you known Trace?"

She did a quick calculation in her head. "About seven months."

"You have any ID?" the cop asked. He was an older man with deep-set eyes and heavy jowls. What little hair he had left was buzzed close to his head.

Chloe handed over her driver's license.

"Barely eighteen." He raised his eyes to look at her and shook his head. Then he silently copied her license number and birth date into a notebook. "What do your parents think about this arrangement? Or do they even know?"

"They don't care," Chloe said with a shrug. A full answer would be way too complicated.

The cop handed Chloe's license back to her. "Your boyfriend was a piece of work, wasn't he?"

"What do you mean?"

"Among other things, he shot a police officer last night. A buddy of mine, in fact."

Chloe clenched her hands in front of her. "Is your friend go-

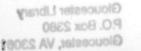

ing to be okay?"

"Better than the two men your boyfriend killed at the Quick-Stop a couple of weeks ago."

Chloe willed herself to be still. She felt a tornado raging inside her, making her dizzy. She wanted to bury her face in her hands and blurt out the truth—that she was there and saw what happened. To drop to her knees and say how sorry she was. To bare her soul and be done with it. Instead, she looked at the officer blankly.

"You don't know anything about that?" he asked with heavy sarcasm.

Chloe shook her head.

"He never said a word to you? Never acted like he was hiding something?"

"No."

"There was blood at the scene," the cop continued. "Besides the victims', that is. Blood type matches your boyfriend's. You didn't see he'd been hurt?"

Chloe's throat closed down tight. She could hardly breath. "He told me he got into a fight with a friend," she said. Velma would be proud of her but Chloe could feel the fires of hell lapping at her feet.

"Why were you with a creep like him anyway? Huh, can you tell me that?" He paused but not long enough for Chloe to respond. "Yeah, I know, you *loved* him." More sarcasm. "I've got a daughter your age. I don't know what's with girls today. You're all stupid as pig shit."

The cop rubbed his hands on his pants. "Okay, where were you a week ago last Sunday?"

Chloe shook her head and lied. "I don't remember."

"Yeah, sure. I bet you were with your boyfriend. You hang out with him when you can, don't you?"

"Not all the time."

The cop gestured toward the bedroom with his elbow. "How come the closets are empty? Where's all your stuff?"

"We, uh, don't have a lot."

"You got more than one change of clothes, don't you?"

How could she explain the suitcase in the basement? She couldn't. "I took stuff to the Laundromat."

"Yeah, sure. Looks to me like you and your no-good lover boy were getting ready to run from the law."

"No," Chloe said. "That's not true." They were running from thugs not the law. But she could hardly announce that.

"Do you have a job?" the cop asked.

"At the Craft Connection."

More scribbling in the officer's notebook. "Your boyfriend quit his job a couple of days after the robbery. Did he tell you that?"

"He was looking for something better," Chloe explained, even though she knew the response made no sense. Who quit a perfectly good job for no reason before they had another one lined up?

"And you bought that line?" the cop asked with another exaggerated shake of his head. "So what do you think now? Are you surprised to learn your boyfriend was involved in an armed robbery? That he killed two men?"

Chloe was slowly getting the hang of breathing again. "Do you mind telling me . . . what makes you think it was him?"

"We don't just think it. We know it." His icy glare was a challenge but Chloe said nothing.

"A number of things," the policeman said finally. "Blood type, ballistics on his gun, the car he was driving . . . It had stolen plates. You don't know anything about that either?"

Chloe's stomach knotted. She should confess the truth now, before he caught her in a lie she couldn't back away from. The cops probably had her prints from the plates and were just waiting to trip her up. She opened her mouth but the words wouldn't come.

The cop squinted his eyes at her. "Whether you want to believe it or not, your boyfriend was pond scum. And what's worse, he must have bragged about it. That's what tripped him up."

"What do you mean?"

"We got an anonymous tip telling us to look at your boyfriend for the robbery and shooting. And guess what? The more we looked, the better he looked. It would be nice to think the tipster turned him in because it was the right thing to do, but more likely it was payback. I don't suppose you'd have any thoughts about that, either?"

Chloe shook her head. But she knew with sudden clarity that it must have been Weasel-face or one of his two buddies.

She knew, too, that they'd come back looking for her.

She couldn't stay in the apartment even through the end of the month. She wondered if she dared stay working at the Craft Connection. She wondered if she should just tell the truth and take what came.

And then she thought of her baby. What would happen to Isabella if Chloe went to prison?

CHAPTER 25

Diana was emptying the dishwasher when Emily, still in her pajamas, padded into the kitchen Wednesday morning and popped two pieces of bread into the toaster. She leaned against the counter and traced the grout line in the floor tile with her left foot.

"You sure it's okay if I head back to school?" Emily asked.

Diana handed her a plate, still warm from the dishwasher. "We've been over this, honey. Not only is it okay, I think it's the right thing for you to do." In fact, Emily was scheduled for a flight to San Diego that afternoon.

"I guess that makes sense."

"You sound uncertain."

Emily shrugged. "It feels disrespectful somehow."

This from a daughter Diana sometimes felt didn't know the meaning of respect. "It's not, believe me. It's what Roy would have wanted." Diana smoothed the hair from Emily's face. "But if it makes you feel uncomfortable to go back so soon, we can put it off a bit."

"No." Emily sighed, "I'll never catch up with all the work if I wait any longer." She broke a slice of toast in half, then ignored both pieces. "Is that the man who shot Roy?" She gestured to the front-page story and photo in that morning's newspaper.

Diana nodded. She'd spent half an hour earlier, before the children were up, studying the news account and accompanying photo, hoping to understand. Waiting for a sense of closure.

192

Trace Rodriguez had a thin, clean-shaven face and dark hair, cropped close to the scalp on the sides. His eyes were dark also, and without expression. Diana thought she detected a bit of a sneer in his smile, but there was nothing overtly menacing about his appearance. And she found nothing the least bit settling about finally stamping a name and face on what had happened to Roy. If anything, the questions tormented her more.

She wondered if Roy had walked in on the robbery or if the gunman, this Trace Rodriquez, had brazenly entered the store knowing there was a customer inside. What went on in the mind of someone like that? What made him decide to rob a store in the first place? Money, of course, but that wasn't really an answer. Drugs? Greed? Or maybe a simple afternoon's diversion.

But mostly Diana had questions about Roy. Why had he been in a San Francisco convenience store that Sunday afternoon? Was he, as Inspector Knowles initially suggested, somehow involved in what happened? What had he done with the money he'd taken from their accounts? Who was he really, and why had he hidden his true identity from her and everyone else?

She wondered if there was someone who knew more than she did.

"I don't understand how somebody could shoot people for no reason," Emily said. "It's just so sick."

"I don't understand either, but it happens."

"I'm glad he's dead but that seems almost too good for him. We suffer and he doesn't. It's not fair."

"No, it isn't." Diana shared Emily's feelings of injustice, but her outrage was tempered slightly by Detective Knowles's cautionary words about the pitfalls of a trial. She shuddered when she thought what might have come out about Roy, had Rodriguez stood trial. She had no desire to see Roy's reputation tarnished, even now when she questioned everything she thought she'd known about her husband.

"Maybe it's better this way," she told Emily. "It's over."

Except Diana knew it wasn't really over. It wouldn't be over until she had answers, and she was afraid that might never happen.

Later that morning, after she'd taken Jeremy to school and failed to engage Emily in further conversation, Diana settled in front of her computer. She'd started this column three times, discarding each effort halfway through. Only the fact that she was already past deadline kept her from hitting delete and starting yet again. The pressing questions about Roy occupied her mind, and her attempts at light, frothy commentary on everyday events fell flat. She finally settled on the pleasures and pains of fall weather. How boring was that? But at least she'd make her word count.

When her phone rang, she knew instinctively it was her editor, Jack Saffire.

"Hi, Jack. I know I'm late but I'm putting the finishing touches on the piece as we speak."

"I need it by noon, Diana or I'll have to find something else to fill the space. I know you're going through a lot right now and I wish I could cut you a little slack, but I've got a deadline."

"You'll have my column within half an hour, I promise."

"Good girl. I knew I could count on you."

Diana smiled at the "girl." She knew women who would have taken offense, but Diana had never been one of them. "I'm not sure that I can continue writing this column," she added. "I might need to get a job. One that pays better."

"Are you asking for a raise?" He laughed. "I might be able to squeeze—"

"No," Diana said emphatically. "I meant a job that will support my family. Without Roy, well . . . finances are going to be tight."

"I'm sorry to hear that." Jack was quiet a minute. "Got any prospects?"

"I haven't even started looking. I know it won't be easy. But I wanted to give you fair warning."

Another short stretch of silence. "Gwen is leaving," Jack said after a moment. "She just gave notice yesterday. Her husband is being transferred to San Antonio."

"Poor Gwen."

"Poor me. I'm losing people right and left." He paused again, while Diana made sympathetic noises. Then he asked. "I don't suppose you'd be interested in taking over for her? It's not a lot of money but it's more than you take home now. And you'd have flexibility in terms of hours. As well as full benefits."

Gwen Smith handled the paper's advertising accounts and its classified section. Not a glamorous job, nor one that required creativity. But Diana would have a regular paycheck and, as Jack had pointed out, flexibility. With Jeremy to consider, that was important.

"I might be," Diana replied. "Do you need an answer right away?"

"Next couple of days. Gwen's not leaving for two weeks, but I'd like to get somebody on board by next week so there's some overlap."

Not Diana's dream job by a long shot, but it was steady work. Only thing was, Diana hadn't expected to start quite so soon. What would she do about Jeremy? She'd have to make arrangements for a housekeeper, too. So many logistical details to be worked out . . . but it *was* an attractive offer in many ways.

"Let me think about it and get back to you," she told him.

She gave the column one last read-through before emailing it to Jack. After he saw her lackluster effort, he might rescind the job offer and the decision would be made for her.

Diana printed out a copy of the column for her file and in the process of reaching for it, sent Roy's cell phone clattering to the floor. She'd set it on the desk when the police had returned it to her, and hadn't touched it since.

Her throat grew tight as she experienced one of those terrible moments when Roy's death hit her anew. It was always something little that touched off this sense of free-falling into the abyss. The pair of Roy's socks that had ended up in the dryer with her things. The notice from the library that the book Roy wanted had come in. The scent of the wintergreen Life Savers he favored, the sight of the apple tree in the backyard he had planted their third day in the house. The baseball mitt he'd picked out for Jeremy's birthday. A memory, triggered by something as random as a billboard for a Hawaiian vacation.

And now, Roy's cell phone. Unlike so many lawyers and busy executives, Roy stuck with what was simple. Diana had encouraged him to upgrade if only so she'd have something to buy him for their anniversary, but he hadn't been interested. She held the phone to her cheek, thinking about all the times he'd called her on it, mostly to convey a simple message about logistics or timing, but sometimes simply to tell her he loved her. She had always experienced a pleasant rush hearing his voice in the middle of the day.

She turned the phone on to check its battery power. It began vibrating in her hand. Three new messages.

The first, left the Monday after Roy was shot, was from a colleague who obviously hadn't heard the news about the shooting. The second, also left that Monday, was from a man who said only, "Roy? Hey man, call me. Enough of this shit, okay?" His voice was gravelly and he sounded angry. Diana checked the caller ID. No name or number. She punched the button to return the call, but all she got was a ringing phone. She let it ring ten times before hanging up.

The third message had been left last Wednesday from an area code Diana didn't recognize. A man who identified himself only as Bernie was checking to see if Roy had received the package he'd sent. "Nothing more on any evidence found with the body," Bernie reported in his message. "Just that leather cord and charm necklace I told you about. I'm kind of at a dead end here until you give me further direction."

Diana assumed Bernie was an investigator Roy was using on a case. She took a deep breath and punched in his number. She needed to tell him about Roy's death. So many loose ends, but Diana would have thought Roy's secretary, Jan, would have notified people by now.

The phone was answered on the second ring. "About time," a man said. "I thought you'd dropped off the face of the earth."

"Is this Bernie?" Diana asked.

There was a moment's pause. "Bernie Fusco." Dogs barked in the background. "Who are you?"

"Diana Walker. Roy Walker's wife. You probably haven't heard. Roy passed away ten days ago."

"What?" Bernie shouted at the dogs to be quiet. "You mean he's dead?"

"I'm afraid so."

"What happened? He wasn't sick, was he?"

"He was in a convenience store during a strong-arm robbery, and was shot."

"Oh, boy." Bernie took a couple of audible breaths. "I don't know what to say. How terrible. You have my condolences."

"Thank you. I know you left a message for him about some crime. You should probably call his office to make sure the right person gets the information. I can give you that number."

"Uh, thanks, but that won't be necessary." Bernie hesitated. "This was something Roy wanted himself. Personally."

Diana had been about to say that made no sense. But then, nothing about Roy made sense to her any more. "Maybe if I knew what the crime was I could help you."

"I guess there's no harm. It's been in the news. At least here in Georgia. Miranda Saxton, daughter of the Senator—she was missing for a number of years. Her remains were discovered recently."

Diana had seen the headlines but hadn't paid a lot of attention. She'd had more pressing concerns than a long-ago disappearance on the other side of the country. But she remembered now that Roy *had* followed the story, both in the paper and on the news.

"Why was Roy was interested in that case?" she asked.

"He's had feelers out about the Miranda Saxton disappearance for a number of years. I kept him apprised, but mostly there was nothing to report until the bones were discovered."

"Are you with the police?"

Bernie laughed. "Ex. Now I'm private. Much better arrangement for everyone."

Diana was gripping the phone so tightly her hand was beginning to hurt. She switched to her other hand. "What did Roy want to know?"

"What was happening with the investigation. Some people get a bee in their bonnet about an old crime and they can't let go."

But for that to happen, there was usually some connection. "You said something about a necklace."

"Right. The remains, well there wasn't much but bones and a skull. Some clothing fragments and a silver sun charm on a braided leather cord. That hasn't been made public, but I've got a friend on the inside. I told Roy and he asked me to send him a picture of it, so I did."

"Was it Miranda's?"

"Her father swears not. The police believe it might have belonged to her killer."

"The picture you sent Roy—was it to his office or home?"

"A post office box. I've got it somewhere." Bernie shuffled a few papers and then read off a number in Oakland. He cleared his throat. "I also sent along an invoice."

Was this what Roy had done with their savings? Diana couldn't imagine a private detective would cost that much, but what did she know?

"I'll look into it," she told him. "If you could give me some idea of the amount."

"Just under five hundred. I wasn't really able to do much for your husband until recently. And even that was pretty limited."

So the money hadn't gone to Bernie Fusco. Where then? And what was Roy's interest in Miranda Saxton? Diana tried to recall what she knew about the disappearance of the senator's daughter, and found it wasn't much. She'd been a sophomore at San Jose State at the time, and while she'd been aware of the disappearance, Georgia seemed a long way away.

Turning back to her computer, she began an Internet search. She'd just started reading a newspaper account of the discovery of Miranda's remains when Emily wandered up behind her.

"Mom, I don't want to miss my plane."

Diana quickly clicked to minimize the screen, but not before her eyes caught the phrase, "known to family and friends as Mia."

Diana's heart jumped and then skipped several beats. Mia! The name Roy had murmured in his semiconscious state at the hospital.

"Mom!"

"You won't miss it," Diana said. "Give me a few more minutes."

"You said we needed to leave by one and it's already one-fifteen."

Where had the time gone? Reluctantly, Diana pushed back her chair. The news account would have to wait. "Okay, let's hit the road."

"What were you doing? Looking at porn?"

"Of course not!"

"You sure acted guilty, clicking off the screen like that." Emily leaned over and brought the screen back up. "It's a newspaper article." She seemed disappointed.

"Something for work," Diana explained.

"Too bad. I thought for a minute there I had you."

Porn might have been easier to explain than the truth, Diana thought.

The traffic was light and Diana hit most of the lights right, so they made the airport in record time.

"You can just drop me off at the terminal," Emily said as they approached the airport.

"I'll walk in with you and see you off."

"Mom, I'm eighteen years old! I don't need you to walk me in. You can't go past security anyway."

"Well, okay. Take a twenty out of my purse for the cab ride to campus."

"A friend's picking me up."

"One of your roommates?"

"A guy I've been seeing."

Diana's head swiveled to look at Emily and she almost hit the car that changed lanes abruptly ahead of her. "You're seeing someone? As in, dating?"

"Why is that so unbelievable?"

"I didn't say it was."

"You sure acted like it. Like 'dull Emily, who'd date her?' "

"That's not what I meant at all. It's just that I would have expected you to say something before this."

"I came home for Roy's funeral. It didn't seem like the right time to bring it up."

Diana's head exploded with a thousand questions. How serious was it? What year was he? Where was he from? What was his major? What was his name? But she knew better than to ask.

"Nice guy?" she asked instead.

"I think so."

"That's wonderful, honey."

"Can I take the twenty anyway? I could treat Dog to dinner as a thank-you for picking me up."

"Dog?"

"That's his name. Well it's actually something else, but everyone calls him Dog."

Diana was afraid to ask why.

CHAPTER 26

Diana was pleased that Emily had a boyfriend—her first, as far as Diana knew—but she also felt a bit apprehensive. What kind of young man went by the name of Dog?

A nice guy, according to Emily, which wasn't all that reassuring from Diana's point of view. Hadn't she thought the same thing about Emily's father at one time? But if Emily liked this boy, Diana wasn't about to voice criticism. Not yet, anyway.

As Diana slid into the elementary school parking lot to pick up Jeremy, it was Miranda Saxton's murder that occupied her thoughts.

"I need to make a poster," Jeremy said as he climbed into the car, tossing his backpack on the floor.

"A poster for what?"

"For school. About the solar system. I need it by tomorrow. Most kids have already brought theirs in."

Diana winced. With so many things on her mind, she'd forgotten about the assignment Jeremy's teacher had sent home with students a week earlier. The last thing she wanted to do right now was tackle a time-consuming homework project.

"We'll make it tonight," Diana said. "Do you know what you want it to look like?"

"Big," Jeremy said. "Really big. With lots of glitter. And sequins for the stars."

Diana sighed silently. A big, glittery solar system with sequins would entail a trip to the crafts store, fifteen minutes away. The poster was going to be a *very* time-consuming project.

But it would have to wait. What couldn't wait was Diana's curiosity about Miranda Saxton's murder.

When she'd fed Jeremy a snack and sent him outside to play with Digger, Diana called up the Google search she'd started earlier. The discovery of Miranda Saxton's remains had been covered by most of the major media sources, but the stories were frustratingly similar, and short on details about her disappearance. A local paper, the *Littleton Post*, provided the most comprehensive coverage, but its online search function left much to be desired.

Finally, Diana managed to piece together the basics of Miranda's disappearance twenty years earlier. The girl had been a few months shy of eighteen when she disappeared the Saturday of Labor Day weekend. She'd gone to an end-of-the-season bonfire at the shore near a private estate where her family was vacationing. Diana got the impression that the party was mostly college-aged kids who'd been working at the town's resorts for the summer. The group had partied well into the night. When Miranda failed to return to her room by the next morning, the police were called in. No one at the party recalled seeing her leave, but that wasn't surprising, they said, because kids had been coming and going throughout the evening, either down to the water or back up to the parking lot to replenish food and drink supplies. Several of the kids admitted the partying had gotten fairly boisterous as the evening progressed, but they weren't aware of any party crashers or fights or other disturbances. It was, by all accounts, just a group of two dozen or so kids having a good time.

Diana found a photo of Miranda—a high school graduation photo from the looks of it—that had been circulated at the time of her disappearance. She had a heart-shaped face and long, straight hair, parted down the middle. She was pretty in a generic sort of way, but there was a sparkle to her eyes and a freshness about her that set her apart from many other, equally attractive young girls.

Although Diana had been only a year older than Miranda at the time, she'd been three thousand miles away in California and only vaguely aware of the news about her disappearance. What she did know was largely because her mother had used the occasion to lecture Diana about the dangers that could befall young women who failed to use "good judgment."

Now that she was older, she could easily understand how Miranda's disappearance would have rocked Littleton, and because she was a senator's daughter, the nation. It was the sort of tragedy that struck at the hearts of parents everywhere, prompting them to confront their worst fears.

But what interest would Roy have had in the case? Especially now, twenty years after the fact? Diana did a quick mental calculation. Roy would have been wandering through Europe around that time—his lost years, as he called them. Would he even have known that Miranda was missing? This was before the Internet and the emergence of twenty-four-seven news.

Maybe his interest was Saxton himself, and not the daughter? The senator's name had been floated at the last election as a possible presidential candidate, and there were those who thought he might actively seek the nomination in two years.

Roy wasn't involved in politics, even at the local level, but he might have been interested in a specific bill the senator had been instrumental in supporting. A search for Senator Saxton's name brought up so many links, Diana was overwhelmed. And most of the recent links brought her full circle back to the discovery of Miranda's remains.

Jeremy tromped into the room. "When can we make my poster?"

"Pretty soon. I'm just finishing up." In the back of her mind, Diana wondered how she would ever manage to work full-time and be available for Jeremy.

She printed out a couple of news articles on Miranda's disappearance and was ready to close out the search when her eye caught a photo of the young man police had suspected of being involved with Miranda's disappearance, and were now seeking for further questioning. When she clicked on the photo to enlarge it, her heart did a quick two-step and then stopped. She put her hand to her chest to assure herself it hadn't stopped permanently.

"Mom," Jeremy whined. "Can't you do that later?"

"Go give Digger some fresh water. I'll be right there."

Diana turned back to the photo, then hit print.

Nine years ago when she'd met Roy, before she'd met him face to face, in fact, and had only seen him in passing at the DA's office, the thing she noticed first was his smile. It came slowly, almost intimately, even when he was addressing a group of people. It tugged playfully at the corners of his mouth, lit up his eyes, and transformed his lean, angular face like the wave of a magic wand. His smile made Diana's knees weak in the early days of their dating, and it was the memory of that smile she hung onto, tucked neatly inside, next to her heart.

The same smile was on her computer screen now—on nineteen-year-old Brian Riley.

It had to be a coincidence. Surely Roy wasn't the only man with a magical smile.

Maybe the strain of Roy's death was playing tricks with her mind. Hadn't she caught fleeting glimpses of Roy everywhere lately? A driver in a passing car. A father with his son in the vegetable aisle at the grocery. For a moment she'd even seen Roy in the man pruning trees near the park.

But this wasn't simply a passing resemblance. The closer Diana looked, the more young Brian reminded her of Roy. They had the same deep-set eyes, the same angular face and slightly cleft chin. Could he have had a brother? Or a cousin? That would account for Roy's interest in the case.

Yes, Diana decided, a relative. Or even—and it took Diana a good sixty seconds to concede the obvious—Roy himself.

A sour taste rose in her throat. She was afraid she might be sick. Could her husband really have been Brian Riley, the murder suspect? It would explain why he'd adopted a new identity.

Jeremy appeared at the door. "Please, can we work on my poster now?" he asked with a touch of impatience.

"Just a minute, honey."

"But I need to start now!"

"I said in a minute," Diana snapped.

"I wish Daddy was here. He'd help me." Jeremy's chin quivered and Diana immediately felt guilty.

"I wish he was, too." She pulled Jeremy toward her and held him tight for a moment, clinging to the memory of the Roy she'd known, not the Roy whose shadow flitted at the edges of her mind. She kissed Jeremy's forehead. "I'm going to help you with the poster, honey. But we have to go to the store first to get the supplies we'll need. Get your jacket and I'll be there in a minute."

Jeremy raced off and Diana turned back to the computer.

It can't be, she thought. *It simply can't.* Her head was spinning and she was having trouble thinking rationally. Or maybe she simply didn't want to, because so many pieces fit. Roy using a false identity. Retaining Bernie Fusco. Miranda Saxton's nickname, Mia, rolling so easily off his lips. The money missing from their accounts.

What would she have done if Roy had admitted to her that he was a suspect in a long-ago case of foul play? Could she honestly say she wouldn't have thought any less of him? As far as she knew, Brian Riley hadn't been indicted; he was merely a suspect. But would she knowingly have exposed her daughter, and then a new baby, to a man who had, conceivably, murdered a seventeen-year-old girl?

Diana felt angry and sick. Angry at Roy for leaving her with so many doubts. Angry at herself for having those doubts. And sick about losing—both literally and figuratively—the man she'd loved and trusted.

Chloe was working the register while Velma helped a customer in the beading section near the front of the store. The customer—a pinched-faced woman in a turquoise blue pants outfit—had been at it forever, selecting an array of cheap glass beads as carefully as though she were selecting gemstones. She held each bead up to the light, put it in her tray, then took it out again as she reconsidered. Chloe was glad to have been spared the task of waiting on her. She was sure she'd have barked at the woman by now.

While she counted the small change the previous customer had unceremoniously dumped on the counter, Chloe glanced at the clock near the door. An hour and half until the end of her shift, and once again she didn't know where she would be spending the night. She was afraid to go back to the apartment. The chances that Weasel-face and his buddies would come after her so soon were slim, but she couldn't take the chance.

She knew Velma would let her stay for a couple of nights, even though Velma's apartment was smaller than Chloe's and she shared it with her sister. But Chloe didn't want to impose on her only friend, and she didn't want to face the barrage of questions Velma was sure to direct her way. So far, though, it was the only option she could come up with besides the ladies' room at Best Buy, and she wasn't going to do that again.

All day Chloe had been feeling agitated and angry and scared, torn in so many directions she was surprised she was still standing. She knew it was wrong to be mad at someone who was dead, but she was. She was angrier with Trace than she had been since he'd gotten them into this whole mess. She still loved him, of course, and she missed him desperately, but if he'd appeared in front of her right then she would have hauled off and socked him hard.

"This picture frame is on sale, right?" Another customer had stepped up to the register and was shoving a frame in Chloe's face.

Chloe checked the tag and nodded, then rang up the purchase and waited while the customer dug around in her oversized purse for her checkbook. Chloe never understood why people waited until the sale was complete to search for their checkbook. It usually didn't bother her much when she was working the register—a few minutes rest was a nice break—but when she was behind people like that in the grocery line it drove her nuts.

When Chloe happened to look to her left, toward the door, she stared for a moment then did her best to turn away.

Diana Walker and her son, Jeremy, had come through the entrance.

Did Diana now realize that Chloe had broken into her house the other day? Or maybe the cops had told her Chloe was the girlfriend of the man who killed her husband. Chloe wanted to die of shame and guilt.

She tried to signal to Velma, but Velma had her head down, counting beads.

Trapped, Chloe couldn't walk away from the register. She couldn't even turn her back to the door because another customer was waiting to be rung up.

Maybe Diana wouldn't see her. Or recognize her. Who studied the clerks when they entered a store anyway? People's minds were usually on the items they came to buy.

But not, clearly, a young boy's. Chloe saw Jeremy tug at Diana's sleeve and then point in Chloe's direction. Diana pushed his hand down to his side. She must have told him not to point, because Jeremy looked contrite and lowered his head. Finally, Diana looked in Chloe's direction herself, and after a moment, started toward the register.

There'd been a steady stream of customers all afternoon, but now, as luck would have it, Chloe's customer had gone and her line was empty. There was no way to avoid the encounter.

"Chloe, what a surprise," Diana said.

"Yes," Chloe agreed.

"Do you work here? Of course you do. What a silly question." Diana seemed as flustered as Chloe.

Jeremy wasn't daunted in the least. "I'm making a solar system," he announced. "For school. We're going to get paint and glitter and sequins and all kinds of cool stuff."

"Wow," Chloe said. "That will be quite the solar system."

"The sun's at the center, you know. It's going to be a big yellow ball." He turned to his mother. "Let's cover it in cellophane. I want mine to be the best in the whole class."

"I'm sure it will be," Chloe told him. "It sounds fantastic."

"How nice," Diana said, "that you live so close to the store. You could hardly ask for a better commute."

Chloe frowned. "It's not bad, I guess."

Now Diana looked perplexed. "You live right across the street, don't you? I dropped you off at the apartment complex there when you were hurt."

The problem with a lie, Rose had often reminded the girls at the group home, was that it could always come back and bite you. Chloe had been telling so many lies lately, it wasn't surprising one had done just that.

"I don't live there anymore," Chloe explained. "My roommate moved out and I couldn't afford the rent by myself." Lie upon lie. Would she dig herself in so deep she'd forget which way was up?

"So where did you move to?"

"I'm, uh, kind of between places at the moment." Chloe was too nervous to think quickly.

Diana's expression sharpened, as though Chloe had jarred some thought in her mind. "Well," she said after a moment. "Good luck."

"Can you help us with the glitter?" Jeremy asked. "I bet you know which kind would be best."

"I'm sure we can figure it out ourselves," Diana told him, tugging at his arm.

"But Chloe works here. She'll know."

"I have to stay at the register," Chloe told him. "But get the stuff in the sprinkle bottles. It's much easier to use."

"Good idea," Diana said. "Easy is what we need."

"And get some purple," Chloe added. "I saw a picture of the planets once and I was surprised they looked so purple. We've got some great new frosted markers on aisle 4A."

"Frosted. Cool." Jeremy darted in the direction Chloe had pointed. Diana nodded a thanks, and followed him.

Chloe breathed a sigh of relief.

Velma, who had finally finished helping the bead woman, ambled back to the register, shaking her head. "Some people," she muttered.

Chloe laughed. "Better you than me."

"That woman and little boy are friends of yours?"

"Not really."

"He's a cute kid. I love the enthusiasm they have at that age."

"Yeah." Maybe in another life, one where she'd grown up in a normal family, Chloe could have been a teacher. She liked that idea. Working with kids all day would be a lot more fun than waiting on short-tempered customers.

Chloe asked Velma to take the register while she restocked the day's returns. Mostly she wanted to avoid another conversation with Diana when she checked out. But Diana sought Chloe out in the aisles after she'd made her purchase.

"This is probably a harebrained idea." Diana took a breath. "I don't know what kind of apartment you're looking for or what your work schedule is, but I'm going back to work full-time and I need someone to help with Jeremy. Mostly in the afternoons. Maybe some evenings. I can offer room and board and a small salary." The words had come in a rush and now Diana stopped, as though they'd taken the last of her breath.

No way, Chloe thought. Work for the family of the man Trace had murdered? It was an insane idea. A bad, bad idea.

She shook her head, backed away a step. She would have turned and run if she could.

"I can be flexible about most everything but Jeremy's schedule," Diana continued. "You wouldn't have to do heavy housecleaning or anything."

There were hundreds of reasons Chloe should say no. But she couldn't help recalling the safe, comfortable feel of Diana's house. The brief pleasure she'd felt walking the quiet streets of the neighborhood. The way Jeremy's enthusiasm had a way of rubbing off on her.

Besides, Chloe had no place else to go.

Diana gave a self-conscious laugh. "Like I said, an off-the-wall idea. But let me give you my phone number, just in case."

"You don't need to."

"Oh." Diana looked to be embarrassed. "I didn't mean to put you in an awkward situation. I have a bad habit of speaking before I think."

"I already have your number. What I meant was, yes. I'd like the job." Chloe didn't know she was going to accept until the words were out of her mouth.

Diana looked as stunned as Chloe felt. "When can you start?" she asked. "I'm going to need someone fairly quickly."

"Tonight?"

Chloe could hear Rose's voice in her head. *Think before you act. Impulsiveness leads to trouble.*

But Chloe was already in so much trouble, what did a little more matter?

CHAPTER 27

Diana tossed another pinch of oregano into the bubbling pot of tomato sauce, then dusted her hands on her apron. What had she done, inviting a stranger into her home like that? It had all happened so quickly. A crazy idea she should have known better than to voice. And amazingly Chloe had accepted. Right there on the spot. She'd even had a battered, old suitcase already packed and waiting in the back of the store.

Before Diana knew what had hit her, Chloe was in the car heading home with them, chatting away with Jeremy like they were old friends.

Was Chloe homeless? Is that why she'd had her suitcase with her? She certainly didn't look it. No truly homeless person was that clean and neat. Chloe had spun some tale about staying in a friend's apartment while she looked for a new place for herself, but that didn't really explain what she'd been doing with her bag already packed.

Diana hadn't pressed the issue. Perhaps she should have. She recalled Emily's asking if Chloe was some kind of nutcase. Diana had dismissed the question as typical Emily, pushing issues to the extreme. But what if her daughter had been right? What if Diana had made a terrible mistake? She hadn't even asked for references. She was entrusting the care of her son to a woman she barely knew.

The silver lining to this barrage of doubts was that they had temporarily driven all thoughts of Miranda Saxton and the investigator, Bernie Fusco, from Diana's mind. And, to be honest, she was relieved to have the question of childcare settled. At least in the short run. If she needed to hire someone else down the road, she'd take her time and do it right.

Chloe was right that moment seated next to Jeremy at the kitchen table, diligently, and with surprising creativity, helping him with his poster, showing far more patience than Diana would have. Diana knew she'd have hurried the project along, cutting corners and sometimes stepping in to do the work herself, simply to get it done.

Still, she was glad she had a week before she went to work full-time. She'd watch Chloe carefully. She wasn't, she reminded herself, locked into anything.

"What can I do to help?" Chloe asked, getting up from the table.

"Is the poster finished?"

"We have to wait for the glue to dry before we can go on."

A step Diana would have omitted. "You could set the table," she told Chloe. "I guess we'll eat in the dining room since the kitchen table's being used."

"I could clear it," Chloe offered quickly, as though Diana was finding fault.

"No, it's easier to leave things where they are." She showed Chloe where the placemats and napkins were.

"Your house is so nice," Chloe said, folding the napkins neatly before placing them carefully on the left edge of the placemats.

"It's not very large," Diana pointed out. She hadn't thought through logistics of where Chloe would sleep until they'd arrived home. The only available bedroom was Emily's, and Diana couldn't in good conscience turn it over to Chloe. "I'm afraid things might be a bit tight for you. Do you think the den will be roomy enough?"

"The den's great," Chloe said.

"The day bed isn't all that comfortable, I'm afraid."

"I've slept on worse."

Diana decided Chloe had to be Mary Poppins reincarnated. She was entirely too chipper and accommodating to be a normal eighteen-year-old.

When dinner was done and Chloe had helped Diana with the dishes, she and Jeremy again tackled the poster—which was shaping up to be both large and sparkly, just as Jeremy wanted. Watching him painstakingly place individual sequin stars under Chloe's guidance, Diana began to relax. About Chloe, at least.

But with that worry no longer front and center, Diana's mind churned with ever-growing questions about Roy. Bernie Fusco had mentioned a post office box. There was nothing Diana could do about that tonight. And nothing more she could learn about Miranda Saxton—unless . . .

Now that Diana had hired a nanny, so to speak, she might as well take advantage of the fact. She usually took Jeremy along when she visited Allison and Len, but tonight she was glad he wouldn't be within earshot.

She picked up the phone. "Would it be okay if I stopped by for a bit?" she asked Allison.

"Of course. Is something the matter?"

"I don't know." Diana tried a sardonic laugh, but it came out flat. "That's what I need you to tell me."

Allison had made coffee and set out plate of store-bought chocolate cookies on the kitchen table. "Where's Jeremy?" she asked.

"At home."

While Len pulled ice cream from the freezer and began dishing it out, with both Allison and Diana declining, Diana told them about her new job and about hiring Chloe.

"What?" Allison was aghast. "That's crazy. You don't know anything about this girl."

"Jeremy seems to like her."

"Jeremy is seven years old," Allison pointed out, pouring Diana a cup of coffee. "He doesn't exactly have the experience or judgment to be making a decision like that. What's the rush, anyway?"

"We're going to need money, and the job's available now."

"Can't you live off savings for a bit?" Len asked. "I should think Roy, of all people, would have put something away."

Diana didn't want to get into their depleted accounts. "Our investment portfolio has suffered a bit over the last year. And the opportunity at the paper was too good to pass up."

Allison looked skeptical but Diana didn't give her a chance to press the issue. She reached for her purse and withdrew the photo of Brian Riley she'd printed from the Internet. Her hand shook as she laid it on the table in front of Len and Diana.

"This boy looks like Roy, don't you think?" Diana asked.

Len shrugged. "Sort of, I guess."

"I can see something of a resemblance," Allison added. "Who is it?"

"Do you remember when Senator Saxton's daughter disappeared?"

Len took a bite of ice cream. "Sure. It was all over the news."

"My parents went crazy," Allison added. "My mom must have called me every night for a while, just to make sure I was okay. I was in Florida, for God's sake. Nowhere near where it happened. Didn't they recently find her body or something?"

"A skull and some bones, I think."

Allison pushed the plate of cookies in Diana's direction. "Why the sudden interest in Senator Saxton's daughter? Is it for a column?"

If only it were that simple. Diana pointed to the photo. "This is Brian Riley, the boy they considered a suspect."

Allison frowned. "What are you getting at? You think this Brian Riley was related to Roy?"

"Maybe." That was as far as Diana could bring herself to go at the moment.

"What difference does it make?" Allison looked perplexed. She put a hand on top of Diana's. "I know the funeral was only a few days ago and Roy's death is really hard for you, but why make it harder than it has to be? Roy never mentioned this Brian, did he?"

"No, he never did."

Len mouthed another spoonful of ice cream. "At best, the photo is an interesting coincidence, but I agree with Allison, so what? It's not important."

The important thing was that both Allison and Len had seen the resemblance. It wasn't all in Diana's head. Her skin prickled and the back of her neck felt hot and sticky. She was afraid she'd be sick to her stomach.

It might seem unimportant to them. But they didn't know that Roy had hired a detective to follow the Miranda Saxton investigation. They didn't know about the large amounts of cash he'd withdrawn from their accounts. They didn't know that Roy wasn't really Roy at all, that he'd stolen the identity from a dead teenager.

They didn't know what she knew and Diana was afraid to tell them.

Chloe tucked the fluffy down comforter under her chin and scrunched into the billowy nest it made around her body. She had never slept in a bed as soft as this or with sheets that felt so silky. Like floating on a cloud. Diana had been wrong about the bed; it wasn't uncomfortable at all.

She'd been right about the room, though. It was small and a

bit cramped, especially with the daybed made up. She'd promised to clear more space, but Chloe liked it as it was. The walls were a pale gray-green. Books about law and history filled the bookshelf, and framed family photos dotted the walls. Above the small end table was a plaque with a child's handprint cast in plaster. Chloe found the room cozy and reassuring, which was totally weird since everywhere she looked she was reminded of Diana's husband—the man Trace had killed.

She felt a prickle of uneasiness whenever she thought about that, so she tried not to. She'd learned that it was sometimes better to focus on where she was, not how she'd gotten there or where she'd been. For now, this was her room. And even if it was only for tonight, she was going to enjoy it.

Except she wasn't finding that easy to do. Everything about working for Diana and living here felt wrong. Or maybe it was simply that Chloe knew it should feel wrong, because on some level, being here felt really good. She liked Diana and Jeremy. She liked being part of a family, even if it was an illusion. She'd even liked making the poster with Jeremy and sharing his excitement about the project. Chloe had never been excited by anything when she was in school.

"You'll have fun in school, won't you, Emma?" she asked her baby. "And I'll have fun helping you with projects, and reading to you, and volunteering in the classroom." Chloe's mother had done none of those things, but Chloe would.

She turned onto her side and watched moonlit shadows of bare branches from outside the window dance across the walls. Deep down, she knew she was doing a terrible thing by letting Diana think she was someone she wasn't. But maybe, Chloe thought as she drifted off to sleep, if she was super nice and super helpful, she could in some small way make up for her part in the terrible thing she'd done to them.

CHAPTER 28

Joel had fully intended to call his cousin Max right away. He wasn't sure his dad's memory was to be trusted, but if there was any chance that Max had actually gone to school with Brian Riley, Joel wanted to follow up. With a series of deadlines at the newspaper, however, and an unexpected trip to the emergency room with his father, who'd hit his head when he'd taken a fall getting out of bed one morning, it was several days before Joel found the time to make the call.

He'd seen Max sporadically in recent years, although the two of them exchanged the obligatory Christmas cards filled with family updates and, in Max's case, family photos. Max ran a plumbing supply company owned by his father-in-law and was apparently doing quite well for himself, but Joel had never felt they had much in common. Max had gone off to college before Joel entered kindergarten, and he'd returned to Littleton over the years only for brief holiday visits. With Max's parents now living in Florida, the visits had stopped altogether.

Still, Max greeted him like an old school chum, eagerly filling Joel in on his children's most recent accomplishments and inquiring, finally, about the health of Joel's father.

"His mind comes and goes," Joel said, putting an optimistic spin on things. "Physically, he's doing fine. He fell the other day, but he's okay now."

"That's good to hear. I always liked your dad. The Alz-heimer's is a real shame."

Max talked on about an hour-long special on dementia research he'd seen recently, which then led to a rather lengthy account about his purchase of a large-screen television. Eventually Joel found an opportunity to ask about Brian Riley.

"Wasn't that something," Max said, "finding that poor girl's remains after all this time. I'd pretty much forgotten about her disappearance, but with it all over the news recently, I dug out some of the stuff I kept from back then to show the kids."

Joel didn't understand why having known a murder suspect was something a parent would share with his children, but he supposed it was his cousin's idea of a brush with fame. "Did you know Miranda?" he asked.

"Not really. At least not well. Brian and I hung out sometimes, especially that summer after high school. We both worked in the kitchen at a local restaurant. I never did understand why the rich college kids got the slick jobs like lifeguard and caddy, and the locals got stuck in the kitchen, but that's the way it worked in those days. I guess it was all in who you knew and who you could trade favors with. While we busted our butts, the rich kids saw summer jobs as a chance to party and get laid."

"I'm not sure it's changed all that much." Joel had worked for his father during the summers when he was in high school and college, but he'd heard the same complaint from friends over the years. "Tell me about Riley."

"He was an okay kid. Kind of moody, though he never tried to weasel his way out of working or anything. I doubt we'd have been friends if it wasn't for the job. I hardly knew him when were in school."

"Do you think he killed Miranda Saxton?"

"Back then, I didn't know what to think. He had the hots for her, and I think she liked him, too, although it wasn't all heavy and in-your-face like you see with kids today. I couldn't see Brian hurting her."

"Not even if he got angry? I've heard he had quite a temper."

"Yeah, he did. I never saw him get violent, but what did I know? The cops arrested him so they must have figured otherwise, even if they couldn't convince the DA. I'll tell you, it weirded me out, the idea that I might have worked alongside a killer all summer."

"And what do you think now? The police are looking for him, you know."

"Yeah, I read that. I don't know all the details, but I gather there's some new evidence. I guess they're pretty sure they can make the case stick this time. Say, I've got some photos that were taken the night she disappeared. You want me to send them to you? Ought to add a little pizzazz to your story." Max laughed. "Just be sure I get credit when it's published."

"Photos?" Joel looked up from his desk at the *Post*'s deadline calendar posted on the wall at the front of the room. The right photo could make a story.

"Like I said, I was going through old stuff, telling the kids about Miranda, and I found some photos I'd taken that night. There was a big party, a bonfire, at the beach. It was mostly the rich folks but Brian and me and a few of the other local guys, we were there, too."

Joel felt a jolt of excitement. Max was the first person he'd talked to who'd been at the party the night Miranda disappeared. The college kids had been impossible to track down after twenty years, and he hadn't found anyone local.

"How did Brian seem that night?" he asked.

"He was always a quiet one, but he seemed to be having fun. Dancing, joking around, drinking some. He spent most of the evening with Miranda, but it wasn't like they were a twosome. She was with other guys, as well."

"Any of the other guys give her a hard time?"

"Not that I saw. Everyone knew she wasn't a skank, and with

her father being a senator and all . . . I won't say we were all on our best behavior, but nobody got out of line, either."

"An older couple saw Brian and Miranda alone together later that night. On the beach away from the party. Did that surprise you?"

"Not really. Like I said, Brian was a quiet one. He was more comfortable one on one than in a crowd. And it was pretty obvious how he felt about Miranda."

"What about Miranda? Wouldn't she have been wary about going off alone with him?"

Max hooted loudly. "Geez, Joel, what planet do you live on? Miranda was a very pretty, red-blooded, seventeen-year-old girl and Brian was a decent-looking guy she'd known practically the whole summer."

Joel felt himself blush and he was glad Max wasn't able to see him. Joel's lack of experience with red-blooded teenage females was probably obvious to his cousin. Joel hadn't even kissed a girl until he'd been in college, and Julia had been his first, and only, relationship.

"I don't suppose you've heard from Brian?" Joel asked.

"Never saw him after that night. We weren't really friends, and with the cops all over him and everyone in town talking about him, I kept my distance. No point getting involved, you know? I went away to school and that was the end of it. I guess he was still around when I came home that Christmas, but I never talked to him. I'll scan the photos and email them to you. Just remember to spell my name right." Max finished the sentence with a hearty laugh.

When the conversation ended, Joel transcribed his chicken-scrawl notes onto the computer. He also jotted thoughts of his own, piecing together what he'd read elsewhere and fleshing out his vision of the evening Miranda Saxton disappeared, as though he were writing a book. The more he learned about Brian and

Miranda, the more real they became to Joel. He could envision the party on the shore that summer evening as though he'd been there himself.

He closed out the file and opened a new blank document. He knew he needed to get cracking on the article about the high school football coach, but he was having trouble coming up with a catchy opening, probably because his heart wasn't in it. *Well-liked coach in his sixth season in Littleton, worked his players hard, emphasized sportsmanship, more wins than losses this year (by two games)*— it wasn't much of a story. Still, an assignment was an assignment, and readers of the *Littleton Post* cared about stuff like high school football. Maybe more than they cared about a twenty-year-old murder. Which was why, Joel reminded himself, he wasn't going to spend the rest of his life writing for a small-town paper if he could help it.

But instead of getting down to work on the article, he took another look at the note that had arrived two days ago: a single sheet of computer paper printed with the name Roy Walker and the opening paragraphs of Joel's story on Miranda Saxton from last week. It was unsigned and there was no return address. Joel had ignored the note at first because of looming deadlines, and had then decided that it was a hoax of some sort. Joel had checked Walker out on the web. He was a DA in California who'd been killed recently—the victim of a convenience store robbery. Whoever sent the note had to have known that Walker had been shot, since it bore a San Francisco postmark. Joel couldn't very well talk to a man who was dead, so why send the note?

This morning's mail brought a second letter, again unsigned. Two black-and-white photos printed on a sheet of computer paper, along with the words "Notice the resemblance? Riley aged well." One photo was a file shot of Brian Riley from the *Littleton Post*, the other from the obituary of Roy Walker that had appeared in the *San Francisco Chronicle*.

The two men did look a little alike, but so what? Walker had grown up in the Midwest and attended California schools as an undergrad and for law school. Joel hadn't been able to find any connection to Georgia or the east at all.

Joel's conversation with Max must have stirred something in his mind, however, because when he looked at the photos now, he saw that the resemblance was really rather striking. But why had the notes come to him rather than the police? Or maybe similar notes *had* been sent to the police, and they'd already followed up and dismissed them. Still, he ought to double-check with the authorities since they were actively looking for Brian Riley.

Joel sighed, minimized the blank document page on his computer screen, and went to talk to Skeet in his office.

"Hey there, hot stuff," Skeet said by way of greeting. "You going to have that story on Coach Hanson for me anytime soon?"

"Yeah, it's mostly written. I just need an opening angle." Mostly written in his mind, anyway. Once he got the lead in, he could pound the rest of the story out in no time.

"Shit, Joel. You're not going for the Pulitzer prize, here. It's a simple sports story for the local paper."

"Yeah, I know."

Skeet scratched his neck, and scooted his chair closer to his desk. "What's up?"

Joel put the two notes on Skeet's desk. "I got this in the mail a few days ago." He tapped the page on the left. "This one came this morning," he added, pointing to the second note. "Roy Walker is a DA in Oakland, California. Or was. He was killed recently. Somebody seems to think he might have been Brian Riley."

Skeet leaned forward and studied the photos. "Could be," he

said after a moment. "Or not."

"It's probably nothing, but I think I should turn them over to Chief Holt, don't you?"

"Yeah, probably. On the other hand, there's no rush. Walker's not going anywhere."

"But—"

"If there is any truth to what our anonymous tipster is suggesting, it will be quite a story. Finish that piece on Coach Hanson, then take a few days off. You might even want to fly to California to check on things firsthand."

Joel started to protest. California, home to his fantasies of fame and fortune, was also a frightening proposition, and Joel had never been there. "A plane ticket costs a lot, especially last minute."

"The paper won't be able to cover the whole thing, but I think we could come up with something."

"There's my dad to think about. I can't just leave—"

"I guess I could send Monica, instead."

Monica Couch was a thorn in Joel's side. In the sides of most of the people at the paper. She took female assertiveness to a whole new level.

There was no way Joel was going to let her get her claws into *his* story. And then he realized what Skeet was offering him. A ticket in the biggest lottery of all—a chance to make a name for himself. He'd never get anywhere if he didn't take risks.

"I'll book a flight for tomorrow morning and I'll have that story on the coach on your desk in under an hour."

Joel mentally clicked his heels on his way out of the office. He was suddenly sure he was on to something big.

CHAPTER 29

Diana stared at the postal clerk in disbelief. "My husband is deceased," she repeated, in case the woman had simply misunderstood. "I have a copy of the death certificate."

The clerk, an angular woman with thin lips and a glinty stare, nodded. "I heard you the first time. But without a key or a court order, I can't let you have access."

Diana had searched Roy's drawers for the key and hadn't found it. "I'm his wife," Diana explained. She pulled out her driver's license. "See."

The clerk didn't bother to look. "Even if that's true"—her tone made it clear she wasn't taking the statement for fact—"that doesn't give you have the right to Mr. Walker's mail. Your name is not on the contract."

"It's a post office box, for God's sake," Diana said, losing patience, "not a safe deposit box."

The clerk remained stone-faced. "We respect our customers' privacy."

Sure, Diana thought. If privacy was so important why was her mail was repeatedly misdelivered into neighbors' boxes and theirs to hers? She'd once inadvertently opened a stranger's bank statement, assuming it was her own. The post office didn't have much of a track record when it came to protecting people's privacy.

But it clearly did with respect to following rules. The clerk looked over Diana's shoulder and called, "Next in line."

Exasperated, Diana stormed out of the post office. She'd have a hard time convincing Ted Morris, a friend of Roy's from his law school days and the executor of his will, that he needed to come in person to clean out Roy's post office box. She wasn't sure she even wanted Ted to know about it. Not until she figured out Roy's connection to Miranda Saxton's murder.

Still steaming, Diana leaned against the side of the post office building and called Bernie Fusco. She pressed her fingers against her ear to block the background noise of traffic on the street.

"I'm sorry," she said. "The idiot postal clerk won't let me pick up Roy's mail. Can you send another copy of your bill to my home? Along with anything else Roy, uh, requested."

"I'll resend the bill, but there wasn't anything else. Not at this point. I already sent him a police photo of the pendant they found with Miranda Saxton's body. I could send it again if you want."

"Yes, please."

"I appreciate your willingness to pay my bill. Lots of people wouldn't want to, given the circumstances."

Diana would have liked to claim some sort of moral high ground on the matter, but in truth, she was simply eager to get her hands on whatever could help her understand who Roy was.

"How long have you been a private investigator?" Diana asked after a moment.

"Almost fifteen years now. Made the switch when I got fed up with the politics of big-city police work."

"Can I ask you a hypothetical question?"

"Sure. Can't promise I'll have an answer though."

"How hard is it for a person to come up with a new identity? To disappear and start over, so to speak."

"Not hard at all. Unless, of course, you've got the Mafia after you or you top the fed's most wanted list. Even then, there've been a lot of people who've escaped detection for years. All you need is a birth certificate. You can build from there."

Is that what Roy had done? Taken the birth certificate of a dead boy and built himself a new identity? "When did Roy first contact you?" Diana asked.

"It must have been ten years ago, at least. But like I told you before, until the discovery of Miranda Saxton's remains, it was mostly a matter of keeping my eyes and ears open—whether there'd been any new leads as to what might have happened to her, any witnesses coming forward, that sort of thing. I sent him semiannual reports but they were mighty short. Wasn't much to communicate."

All of which made sense if Roy was really Brian Riley.

Diana gave Fusco her home address and he promised to keep her informed of any new developments. What those developments might be or how they might be of use to her were questions she wasn't ready to face just yet.

Nor, she realized as she headed for her car, was she eager to tackle what awaited her at home—the writing of her final, farewell column. *Hey, it's been a great gig but my life has changed and I have to earn a decent income, so adios, folks. It's been fun while it lasted.*

That didn't cut it. Especially because she was going to miss writing the column. She'd started it when Jeremy was a baby, after quitting her job with the DA's office. It was a perfect outlet for someone who wanted to spend time with her family but didn't want her mind to rot. Diana loved the act of writing, even when she was frustrated by deadlines. But she didn't want to get all maudlin about her change in circumstances, either. And writing what was in her heart was out of the question.

She was also reluctant to head home because Chloe was there. That was the point of having help, of course, but sharing her home with a stranger felt awkward. It wasn't anything about Chloe, who by all appearances was going to work out wonderfully. It was simply the fact that someone was there in *her* house. Could Diana sit for a minute and read the newspaper while Chloe worked? Could she make herself a cup of coffee without asking Chloe if she wanted one also? Diana was hopeful it would all work out over time, but for the moment, home wasn't quite the sanctuary it had been.

She'd taken Chloe with her this morning when she dropped Jeremy off at school and introduced her to Jeremy's teachers and some of the other mothers. She'd taken Chloe grocery shopping, pointing out favorite brands and preferences in fruits and produce. And then she'd taken Roy's Lexus, leaving her old Volvo wagon for Chloe, and driven off, wondering what in the hell she'd gotten herself in for.

Diana drummed her fingers on the car's steering wheel, checked her watch, and called Chloe. "How's it going?" she asked.

"Great. You have an awesome washing machine."

The machine was already a couple of years old, and Diana hadn't considered it anything but functional even when new. Then again, she hadn't been relying on a coin-operated Laundromat. "Glad you like it."

"Oh, there was call for you," Chloe said. "I let the machine pick it up but I couldn't help overhearing the message. It was from someone named Alec Thurston."

Alec was the senior Alameda County district attorney, and Roy's boss. She'd talked to him by phone several times after Roy was shot, and he'd attended Roy's funeral. There was no reason for him to be calling her now, unless they'd made the connection between Roy and Brian Riley.

Diana hadn't wanted to go to the authorities with her suspicions. Not yet, anyway. Roy had been her husband.

Jeremy's father. His memory was all she had left of him and she didn't want it dragged through the mud. But neither could she ignore the bone-deep apprehension that shadowed her.

Maybe it was better if the authorities had discovered Roy wasn't who he claimed to be. The matter would no longer be in her hands. Still, she was surprised to find she was shaking.

"Did he say what it was about?" she asked.

"No, just that he wanted you to call him as soon as possible."

"Can you play the message again and get his number for me?"

"I already wrote it down." Chloe read off the number. "I really didn't mean to listen. I was in the kitchen when the phone rang so I couldn't help but hear."

"Don't worry about it," Diana told her. But she made a mental note to silence the volume on her answering machine in the future.

Diana's pulse raced as she punched in the number.

"Diana," Alec bellowed, "thanks for getting back to me so quickly. How are you doing?"

"Hanging in there."

"It's got to be rough. Our thoughts are with you. We miss Roy here, too. He was an asset to the department in so many ways."

"Thank you." Diana braced herself for what was coming. But Alec's next question wasn't what she expected.

He cleared his throat. "I wanted to ask if Roy ever mentioned the name Jamal Harris."

"Not that I recall. Why?"

"Did he say anything about a suspect in a West Oakland drug case?"

"No. Roy rarely talked about individual cases."

"Did you notice anything unusual about his behavior in the last few weeks?"

Other than that he lied to me? Diana thought. "Not really," she said aloud. "What's this about? Please tell me, is this about his murder?"

"No, it's about some irregularities that have come to light."

"What kind of irregularities?"

Alec sighed. He'd clearly been hoping Diana would know more than she did. "This Harris kid claims Roy made a plea deal with him, promised him probation instead of time. There's nothing on file to that effect, but Roy did talk to Harris directly—we have the kid's cell phone records. That's a breach of ethics. Harris's public defender knows nothing about a plea, but he says Harris told him not to worry, that he had an in with the prosecutor."

"That doesn't sound like Roy," Diana said, rising to her husband's defense in spite of everything.

"No," Alec agreed, "it doesn't. But a key piece of evidence in the case is missing, and Roy was one of a handful of people who had access to it."

"That doesn't prove anything," Diana said hotly.

"I didn't say it did."

"But you implied as much. You're suggesting Roy was bought off. Why would he do that?"

"I'm not suggesting anything," Alec said tersely. "I'm simply trying to get some answers. I was hoping you might be able to help."

Suppose Harris had learned Roy was using a stolen identity. Would Roy have compromised a case to keep that information from becoming public? Not the man Diana thought she'd known. But the man she was discovering him to be? Perhaps.

"Where is this Harris kid from?" Diana asked.

"San Francisco born and raised. A product of the projects."

No connection to Georgia, then. How likely was it that a San Francisco street kid would know the truth about who Roy was?

Not likely at all. "If you want my opinion," Diana said, "the kid is blowing smoke."

"Yeah, that's what we thought at first. It's just that he also called Roy's office and left a message the day Roy was killed. Something to the effect of 'You'd better not be messing with me.' "

Diana felt a knot in her stomach. She recalled Roy's secretary telling her about the call. And hadn't Diana, herself, found a similar message on Roy's cell phone?

"I'm sorry to have had to expose you to this, Diana. But we need to get to the bottom of it. And if there's anything to it, you'd hear about it eventually."

"Yes, of course." Diana's voice was tight. How many ways were there she could she feel betrayed by the man she loved?

Chloe folded the clothes she'd taken from the dryer. Jeremy's mostly—jeans and tees and socks. Lots and lots of socks, almost none of them matching pairs. She set them in neat piles on Jeremy's bed. Later this afternoon when he was home from school, she'd get him to show her which drawers held what.

Jeremy's room was bright and colorful, and all boy. Sturdy wooden bunk beds set at right angles with built in storage underneath and topped with cheery blue and red plaid comforters. The walls were off-white, with a wide blue stripe of sports images running horizontally around the room. The ceiling was a darker blue, festooned with iridescent stars. In the corner, an upholstered chair of soft denim was home to a baseball cap and a motley collection of stuffed animals.

She ran a hand across the swell of her belly, which was getting bigger by the day. Danielle or Daniel? It wasn't so clear-cut anymore.

"Well, little one," she whispered, "whether you're a boy or a girl, I'm afraid life won't be this good for us. Not anywhere close."

She wasn't sure where they'd even find a place to live. Diana would hardly let her stay here after the baby came. She would have to tell Diana about the baby soon. She should have told her up front, but Chloe had been so grateful, she hadn't even thought about it. Now, though, it was one more way in which she was being dishonest with Diana, and it made her feel bad.

She'd gone with Diana to take Jeremy to school that morning, feeling oddly dismayed by the throngs of eager boys and girls, all with fresh faces and clean, crisp clothes. Well-dressed, well-fed kids with backpacks and lunch bags and shoes that looked practically brand new.

She knew too, that the supplies for Jeremy's science poster, which had turned out better than either of them expected, hadn't been cheap. How was she going to give her child all that? She hadn't really thought beyond the dewy softness of a baby in her arms. For the first time, she caught a glimpse what life might be like for her little one, and she felt a stab of something akin to guilt.

That same tremor of uncertainty pricked at her skin now, but she shook it off and went back to folding clothes. The family dog, Digger, picked up a sock Chloe had dropped and started running around the bedroom with it.

"No," Chloe said, "drop it."

Digger ran faster, first one direction and then the other. Chloe stood firm. "Drop it, Digger. Bad dog."

Digger ignored her. But when Chloe didn't join in the chase, he gave up running and instead stood at her feet and shook the sock with his teeth. Chloe had to laugh.

But in the pit of her stomach, there was a hollowness that frightened her. Why had she assumed that having a baby would turn her life into the storybook fantasy she dreamed of? Even if

Trace were alive, it wouldn't have happened.

Thinking of Trace only made the hollow feeling inside her worse. She was living in Diana's home because Trace had killed a man. Had killed a man Diana and Jeremy loved. She shouldn't be here. She needed to leave.

Instead, she walked to her room and took Roy Walker's gym bag from under her bed where she'd stashed it after sneaking it into the house in a large bag from the Craft Connection. With all the supplies for Jeremy's poster, her suitcase, and the commotion of moving in, the extra bag had gone unnoticed. Now she needed to get rid of it, and quickly.

CHAPTER 30

Chloe adjusted the Volvo's side mirrors, then slowly and carefully backed out of the garage, which was near the rear of the lot. There was a long driveway to be maneuvered in reverse. She hadn't been completely honest with Diana about a whole bunch of things, so she supposed that in the big picture, it didn't matter that Diana assumed Chloe was an experienced driver. Chloe had her license but that was about as far as it went.

Trace had babied his Camaro and hardly ever let her drive it. And before Trace, well, she'd lived at the group home, so where would she get a car?

To make matters worse, Diana's Volvo was a lot nicer than any car Chloe had ever driven before. Nicer, newer, and more expensive.

She was beyond nervous about driving it, but she figured she'd be okay as long as she was careful and stayed off the freeways.

She had to pick up Jeremy from school, but first she needed to get rid of Roy Walker's gym bag. She'd gone through the contents once again. A couple of photos, a set of five keys, two sticks of gum, a baseball cap, a T-shirt and a pair of khakis, and a stick of deodorant. She'd removed the photos and the keys—she didn't know what they were for but *not* having a key when you needed it could spell trouble. She intended to toss the rest of the stuff, as she'd done earlier with the gun, and she decided it would be safer not to put it all into one trash can. Which meant she had to make several stops, with several attempts at parking.

The trash can outside Safeway was fairly easy. She parked at the edge of the lot where there were plenty of parking spaces so it didn't matter if she pulled in a little over the white line. At her second stop, the post office, parking was a real problem because the lot was small and the parking spaces tight. But she pulled into the yellow drop-off zone, got out of the car, and dashed to the trash can. She cruised around a bit looking for a third spot. She saw several trash cans on the main drag of a congested business district, but that meant parallel parking. No way! The traffic was heavy and pedestrians darted across the street. She was terrified she'd hit one of them. Finally, she found a Dumpster at a construction site near Jeremy's school.

By the time she'd finished, her skin was damp and flushed. But she thought she'd managed to carry the disposal off without calling attention to herself.

She arrived at Jeremy's school five minutes ahead of schedule and walked to the front gate where a cluster of mothers and au pairs waited to for the younger students. One day, Chloe thought with wonderment, she'd be waiting to pick up her own little girl, or boy. She'd been so focused on the baby inside her, she hadn't thought much about the years that lay ahead. And it made her realize, with frightening clarity, that the road she headed down was a very long one indeed.

The bell rang out shrilly and students began wandering through the gate. Not the rush to escape that Chloe remembered from her days in high school, but an orderly, if exuberant, stream, mostly in twos and threes. Jeremy saw her and gave a small wave but he stayed close to his teacher until they reached Chloe.

"Hey kiddo," Chloe said. "How'd the presentation go?"

"Great." Jeremy grinned, bouncing with excitement. "Everyone said my poster was the best in the whole class. Didn't they, Ms. Johnson?"

The teacher, whom Chloe had met that morning, nodded. She was young, maybe only a couple of years out of school, and wore an engagement ring with a tiny diamond. Chloe felt a stab of envy for Ms. Johnson, with her cute reddish-brown bob and a classroom of kids who adored her. Even the smallness of her diamond appealed to Chloe. It spoke about true love rather than showiness. Trace had never even mentioned a ring.

"Jeremy tells me you helped him with his poster," Ms. Johnson said.

"Sort of," Chloe hedged. Was that a bad thing? Maybe the kids were supposed to do the project all by themselves. "It was all his idea," she added. "I just helped with the cutting and stuff like that."

Ms. Johnson laughed. "That's fine. We don't expect second graders to handle this on their own. But Jeremy's poster was one of the best I've seen. Very creative. And accurate, too."

Chloe felt like bouncing with excitement herself. She hardly ever got compliments.

"I don't know what your arrangement is with his family, but if you'd like to volunteer in the classroom, we'd love to have you. Many of the moms do it, and some of the au pairs, too."

"I'd like that. I'll ask Mrs. Walker if it would be okay." Chloe's fantasy of herself as a teacher blossomed in full color.

"I've changed my mind," Jeremy said to Chloe when he climbed into the car a few minutes later. "I'm going to be an astronaut. Ms. Johnson said I might have an ap . . . ap . . ."

"Aptitude?"

Jeremy nodded. "She said I might have an aptitude for it. That means I'd be good at it."

Chloe laughed. "Sounds wonderful. What did you want to be before?"

"A baseball player. Or maybe a drummer."

"Well those are good choices, too."

"I've got a while to decide," Jeremy said solemnly. "Can we get ice cream?"

"Does your mom let you have ice cream after school?" Diana hadn't said much about what was allowed and what wasn't.

"She won't mind. Especially because my poster was so good."

"Well then, sure," Chloe said. "Let's celebrate. Where shall we go?"

"Fenton's."

"Where's that?"

"I know how to get there. Just go where I tell you."

Jeremy did a fine job of getting her from the school to a four-way intersection in a bustling commercial district.

"Turn here," he said as they approached the light.

"Which direction?"

"Down."

Down wasn't much help. Chloe was in the left turn lane with cars on her right, so she turned left. "This way?" she asked.

"Yeah. It's here, down a bit."

Cars and pedestrians again. And trucks double-parked at the curb. And stop signs that weren't visible unless you were looking for them. Chloe was a nervous wreck. She was on the verge of telling Jeremy they couldn't stop for ice cream after all, when he called out, "There it is."

She slammed on the brake but they were already past the parking lot entrance. She made an abrupt U-turn without signaling.

Right in front of a police car.

The officer flashed his lights at her and followed her into the lot.

Oh my God! Diana would be really angry. She'd probably fire Chloe on the spot.

Then Chloe thought of something else. Had the police had discovered her involvement in the robbery where Roy was killed? What if they ran her driver's license and arrested her right there?

Thank God she'd gotten rid of the gym bag. She *had* gotten rid of it, hadn't she? In her moment of panic, she wasn't sure. Her throat closed up and she had trouble breathing.

When the officer approached, she forced a gulp of air into her lungs and rolled down the window. Her hand was shaking when she handed him her license, which still listed her address as the group home. He'd probably write her a ticket for not updating her license, on top of everything else.

He peered into the car's interior. "This your car?"

"No, but I have permission to drive it."

"That your son in the backseat?"

Chloe shook her head. "I work for his family. Kind of like an au pair. It's his mother's car."

"And we're going out for ice cream," Jeremy announced. "To celebrate because my poster of the solar system was the best in the whole class."

"Is that so?" the cop asked.

"And Ms. Johnson said I have an altitude for space."

"Aptitude," Chloe corrected.

"I see." The officer looked puzzled.

"Chloe helped me. The poster was my idea, but she helped with some of the hard stuff like cutting straight."

"Well," the cop said, giving Chloe the once over, "I guess it wouldn't be right to spoil a celebration." He frowned. "You know why I pulled you over?"

Because I'm an accessory to murder? "Because I didn't signal?"

"Because you made an illegal U-turn in a business district."

"Oh."

His steely gray eyes met hers. "I'll give you a warning this time. Don't do it again."

"No sir, I won't. I promise."

The cop handed Chloe her license. His expression softened. "Enjoy your ice cream."

Chloe rolled the window back up. She was still shaking like leaf in the wind.

"Gosh, what's your mom going to say?" she moaned.

"We don't have to tell her."

Chloe turned around to look Jeremy in the eye. "Yes, we do. Honesty is important." She hoped God didn't strike her dead for hypocrisy.

Fenton's turned out to be what Chloe imagined an old-fashioned ice cream parlor would look like, and a popular one by the looks of the crowd. She would never have guessed so many people ate ice cream in the middle of a weekday afternoon.

"My dad used to bring me here after soccer games," Jeremy said, taking a bite of chocolate fudge swirl.

"You must miss him terribly." Chloe found herself once again straddling the line between truth and dishonesty. The weight of her role in Roy Walker's death was growing heavier by the day.

Jeremy looked sad. "I wish I could have shown him my poster."

"He'd have been really proud of you," Chloe said.

"Yeah. He was the best dad ever. Emily thought so, too. She's my sister, although she has a different father. She's older than me."

"I met her," Chloe said before she remembered the circumstances of that meeting—the afternoon she'd broken into their house. "Only once," she added, but Jeremy wasn't interested.

"They found the guy who killed him," he continued solemnly. "But my mom doesn't think it's that simple."

"That simple?"

"That's what she said to Allison. They think maybe there was someone else, too."

A shiver ran down Chloe's spine. "Someone who was with this man when your dad was shot?"

"I don't know. Someone named Brian."

Not a girl, Chloe thought with relief. But who was Brian? One of Weasel-face's friends? She was glad she hadn't ordered ice cream for herself. Her stomach felt the way it did the time she rode the roller coaster at the Santa Cruz Boardwalk.

She handed Jeremy a napkin. "Better wipe around your mouth," she teased. "You look like a chocolate clown."

The phone rang as they walked through the door and into the house. Jeremy dropped his backpack and raced to pick it up.

"Just a minute," he said and handed the receiver to Chloe. "It's some man."

"Hello," Chloe said.

"Mrs. Walker?"

Chloe responded with the protocol she'd learned at the Craft Connection. "She's not available at the moment. May I take a message?"

"Uh, I really wanted to speak to her directly." The man paused. "Who am I talking to?"

"I might ask you the same thing."

"I'm a friend of her husband's from the old days. In Georgia. We, uh, went to high school together. Are you her daughter?"

"I'm the . . ." Au pair? Nanny? Babysitter? None sounded quite right. "I'm hired help," she said finally, though that sounded no better.

"So you knew Roy? I was wondering how long he'd been in California."

Chloe didn't want to appear rude to an old friend, but she knew better than to give out personal information. Even if she'd known the answer. "I really think you should ask Mrs. Walker.

Can I take your name and number?"

The man seemed to hesitate. "Not necessary," he said finally. "I'll give her a buzz later."

Chloe was determined to be so efficient Diana wouldn't let her go. If she could overlook the traffic stop, that is.

She checked caller ID on the phone and wrote down the man's telephone number.

CHAPTER 31

Diana's head was still spinning from her conversation with Alec Thurston. She rolled down the car's window and motioned to the driver behind her that she wasn't leaving her parking spot just yet. Not until she'd had a moment to collect her thoughts.

When people used to ask Roy why he'd chosen to become a prosecutor, he'd sometimes quip that it was his fallback once he realized the position of Superman wasn't available. The comment, delivered with Roy's customary dry humor, always got a laugh, but Diana suspected it was closer to the truth than he realized. Roy was passionate about seeking justice for victims and making sure wrongdoers paid for their crimes. While he wasn't so naive as to believe that life fell neatly into camps of black and white, his worldview was colored with very few shades of gray. Which was why Diana was having a hard time believing that Roy had made an off-the-record deal with this Jamal Harris, especially one that involved evidence tampering.

Then again, she was having a hard time believing much of what she'd learned about her husband of late. That he'd cleaned out a substantial portion of their savings. That he'd been a prime suspect in the murder of Miranda Saxton. That he'd lied to Diana about so many things, not the least of which was his own identity. As painful as it was, Diana needed to face facts—the man she'd loved was a charlatan and probably worse.

But he was also Jeremy's father, and more than anything, that caused Diana anguish.

Jeremy adored his father. Whether Roy was coaching him on the best grip for holding a bat or explaining the workings of the criminal court system (in more detail than Diana deemed necessary for a seven-year-old), Jeremy lapped up the time spent with his dad. Some days she'd watch them together—the small boy with a cowlick at his temple and a sprinkling of freckles across his nose, and the slender, dark-haired man with a gentle manner and a twinkle in his eyes—and she'd experience a hiccup of what could only be envy, although she was loathe to admit it. Fathers and sons spoke a language all their own. It was a bond as elemental and absolute as the morning sun.

How could Diana ever explain what Roy had done in a way that wouldn't destroy Jeremy's memory of his father?

Diana was suddenly relieved that she would no longer be writing her column. Light and funny weren't part of her vocabulary anymore. In fact, she was having trouble remembering that they ever had been.

But she did have that one final column to turn in, and an increasingly short window in which to get it done.

Diana rubbed the back of her neck and sighed. Chloe would have picked Jeremy up from school by now, but Diana could still get in a couple of hours at her computer, knock the damned thing out, and be done with it. The column was one of the few loose ends in her life she could actually wrap up. One of the few things over which she had some control.

"You had another phone call," Chloe told her when Diana walked into the house. "I would have let the machine pick it up, but Jeremy answered before I could stop him." She looked contrite. "I'm sorry."

Diana brushed Chloe's apology aside with a wave of her hand. There were enough important things to worry about. "Who was it?"

"A friend of your husband's. From the old days, he said."

Diana's heart skipped a beat. "Did he leave his name?"

Chloe shook her head. "He said he'd call back, but I wrote down the number for you from the caller ID."

She handed Diana a square of paper with a phone number on it. "Also," Chloe said, taking a breath and lowering her gaze to the floor, "I need to tell you I got stopped by a cop today."

Diana was only half listening. Her mind had frozen at the phone number Chloe had written down. One with the same area code as Fusco's—eastern Georgia. *A friend from the old days.*

"Were you speeding?" she asked absently.

"No," Chloe stammered, "I made an illegal U-turn. In a business district."

"We went to Fenton's to celebrate," Jeremy explained. "I had the best poster in the whole class."

"That's great, honey." Diana smiled, tried to convey an appropriate degree of enthusiasm. Her mind was focused on the mysterious caller.

"He let me off with a warning," Chloe continued, her gaze still on the floor. "I'm so sorry. I promise I'll be more careful in the future."

"The cops along that stretch are notorious. You were lucky to get off with warning." Diana turned the conversation back to the phone call. "What did the caller sound like? Male?"

"Yeah, it was a man. A southern accent, I think, but not too thick. He didn't say a whole lot, just that he'd call back later. Oh, and he asked if I knew how long your husband had lived in California."

Diana's shivered involuntarily. Someone besides Diana had made the connection between Roy and Brian Riley.

That didn't prove that Roy was Brian, she told herself. But the odds were certainly greater.

While Chloe straightened up the house and prepared dinner, Diana worked on her column. She'd decided to write about endings and beginnings. It wasn't the memorable, touching piece she'd imagined as her literary farewell, but it was a good column, something she wasn't embarrassed to put her name on.

She read it through one last time and then emailed it to Jack Saffire at the paper. Surprisingly, she didn't feel the sense of regret she'd expected to feel. She no longer had anything in common with the witty and sometimes clever columnist who'd found joy in the ironies, and lessons, of domestic life.

Downstairs, she was greeted by happy chatter and the warm, comfortable aromas of food cooking.

"I made pasta," Chloe announced. "And a salad. I bought butter lettuce like you said, but they were out of mixed greens so I got baby romaine instead."

"And I got to tear up the lettuce," Jeremy added.

Diana poured herself a glass of wine and sat at the table next to Jeremy. "Tell me about your science presentation," she said.

Dinner was a relaxed affair during which Chloe and Jeremy kept up a lively conversation, allowing Diana a little breathing room. Sometimes Jeremy's nonstop questions wore her out. Not the way Emily's sullenness had, but still, it was nice to have some of his comments directed elsewhere.

Jeremy scooted off after dinner to play a computer game, and while Chloe cleared the table, Diana remained seated and finished her wine. Out of the blue, Chloe gave a little cry, and put her hand to her belly.

"What is it?" Diana asked. Dear God, let it be nothing. She didn't need a nanny with appendicitis. Not now, on top of everything else.

"Nothing." Chloe steadied herself with a hand on the counter. Then a slow, secret smile of wonder lit up her face, and it spoke volumes to Diana.

"Are you pregnant?" Diana asked without thinking.

The smile vanished as quickly as it had appeared as Chloe bit her lower lip and looked at Diana in surprise. "How'd you guess?"

"Your expression."

The smile returned. "It was amazing, the first time I've felt the baby. Like butterfly wings. Like, she's actually real."

Diana sat back, stunned. "Good lord."

"I'm sorry. I should have told you. I didn't really mean to keep it a secret. It's just that everything happened so fast. You needed someone, and I needed a place, and . . ." Chloe gave a helpless shrug. "I'm really, really sorry."

So much for my well-ordered new start in life, Diana thought. An attack of appendicitis would have been far simpler to deal with.

"You must be so angry at me," Chloe continued. "I don't blame you. I wasn't intentionally trying to hide it from you."

"You merely neglected to tell me," Diana said tartly. "It's a pretty big thing to forget."

"Yeah, I know."

Diana got up from the table. The relaxing effects of the wine had given way to irritation. "How long were you going to wait before telling me? And don't you think it's unfair to take a job like this when you know you'll be leaving soon?"

"I'm so, so sorry," Chloe said. Her voice quivered. "I seem to be saying that a lot lately, don't I? I'm making one mistake after another."

She looked so miserable, Diana's anger softened. "We never really talked about long term. I probably should have pressed you a bit about your plans before offering you the job."

"No, it's my fault. I should have told you right away."

"So what *are* your plans? Where is the baby's father? Is he someone you're involved with still?" Diana realized she didn't even know if Chloe was married, although she suspected that was not the case.

Chloe hesitated. "He died."

Diana's anger softened further. "How terrible. What happened?"

A shadow crossed Chloe's face. She opened her mouth and then closed it again, disguising her hesitation with a small cough. "He was in the army," she said finally. "Iraq."

"That's so sad. What about his family? Are you close to them?"

She shook her head. "He didn't have any, not that I know about anyway."

"Not someone you knew from high school, then?"

"No. We met at the movies, through, uh, friends."

The way she said it made Diana wonder how well she'd known the boy. And how little Diana knew about Chloe and her background.

"Are you keeping the baby," Diana asked, "or putting it up for adoption?"

Chloe's eyes widened. "I'm keeping it," she said, in a tone that implied the answer should have been obvious.

"Have you thought this through? It's not going to be easy."

"I'm a hard worker."

And so naive, Diana thought sadly. "How old are you, Chloe?"

"Eighteen."

The same age as Emily, Diana realized with a start. She was suddenly glad that whatever else Emily was, she wasn't pregnant at eighteen. Then Diana remembered Dog, the boy Emily had mentioned in the fleeting moments of their ride to the airport, and was hit with a wave of anxiety.

"What about your own family? Did you grow up around here?"

"Vacaville," Chloe said. "I never knew my dad. My mom, she was killed in auto accident when I was thirteen."

"You've had a rough time of it."

"I guess."

"Where'd you live after your mom died?"

"Foster care. Mostly in a group home." Chloe gripped the back of the chair she stood behind. "I really need this job," she said. "I really like this job, too. I know I messed up, but if you give me another chance, I promise I'll work hard for you."

And when the baby arrives, Diana thought. What then? But it felt wrong to push the question right now. Besides, Diana *did* need someone to help with Jeremy, and aside from being pregnant, Chloe seemed a perfect fit for the job.

"You've seen a doctor, right?"

Chloe shook her head. "I guess I should."

"Absolutely." Diana sighed and tried to ignore the knot of tension in her chest. "I'm not going to let you go for being pregnant," she said, "but I hope you'll be more up-front with me from now on. There are going to be a lot of things we'll have to work out. When's the baby due?"

"March. Five months from now."

Five months, Diana thought. It gave her some time, and a lot could change between now and March.

CHAPTER 32

Despite the brisk fall temperature, Joel's hands were sweating when he rang the bell to Diana Walker's big, Tudor-style house. And his brain had gone into freeze mode. The idea of meeting with her face-to-face, which had made so much sense back in Littleton, made no sense to him now.

At least it appeared that he'd arrived before the cops, which was some relief.

Joel had been on the brink of calling Diana Walker a second time when Skeet had phoned him.

"Have you spoken with her yet?" Skeet had asked without preliminaries.

"No. I called her this afternoon as soon as I checked into the hotel, but she was out."

"Better get your butt over there ASAP. The cops are probably on their way as we speak."

Joel had been stunned by the announcement. "What? Why?"

"Monica figured you were up to something and started snooping around. She must have checked your web history because she came across the searches you did on Roy Walker. And then, a copy of that first note you got."

Disbelief, and then anger, exploded in Joel's chest. "What was Monica Couch doing on my computer?"

"Technically, it's the paper's computer. But let's deal with that another time. She's apparently been in touch with the local cops out there in California."

"What the hell did she do that for?"

"Monica's not about to let you get one up on her. She's like a shark that smells blood."

She was a shark, period. "But I flew all the way out here—"

"Go on then," Skeet urged, "get moving."

And Joel had. Without taking the time to comb his hair or change out of the jeans and sweatshirt he'd worn on the plane, he'd charged out the door of his hotel room, grateful that he'd driven past the house earlier so he knew the way. Fueled as much by his resentment of Monica as his determination to get the story, Joel's single-minded focus had been to get to Diana Walker.

But now that he was here, on her doorstep, he wasn't so sure.

The door was opened by a fair-skinned girl in her late teens or maybe early twenties. She was six inches or so shorter than his own five-ten, and cute enough to leave Joel tongue-tied.

She waited for him to speak, and after a stretch of silence said, "Can I help you?" When he still stood there mutely, she shook her head in defeat. "I don't know ESP." She started to close the door.

"No, wait," Joel said. "I'm here to see Mrs. Walker. Is she available?"

"Oh." The girl smiled. "It's you. You're the guy who called here this afternoon."

"I am?"

"Aren't you?"

"Yes, but how did you—"

"Your accent," she said, and then her smile broadened. As an afterthought, she added, "I kinda like it."

"Thank you," Joel mumbled, troubled both at the "kinda," which was not a wholehearted endorsement, and because she'd noticed at all. He'd worked hard to rid himself of the accent.

Joel heard someone coming down the stairs behind the girl. "Who is it, Chloe?"

Chloe. The name fit the girl. She had a spirited, infectious warmth about her.

"It's that man who called earlier," Chloe called back. "The one whose number I gave you."

The woman who appeared at the door behind Chloe was attractive in a stylishly middle-aged sort of way. She had what his father used to refer to as "apple cheeks," and brown hair with coppery highlights that fell in waves around her face.

"I'm Diana Walker," she said. "You wanted to talk to me?"

Joel held out his hand. "Joel Richards."

"You knew my husband, is that what you said? An old friend?" She looked skeptical.

"In a manner of speaking. May I come in? I'd like to talk with you and it's not the sort of conversation for the doorstep."

Diana Walker hesitated, and Joel thought for sure she was going to close the door in his face. Then she stepped back, inviting Joel in, but with hesitation and bafflement. "Chloe, why don't you check on Jeremy. Make sure he's brushed his teeth and washed his face."

She led Joel to a living room with a TV, sofa, and matching loveseat off the main hallway. "How did you know Roy?" she asked. Unspoken, but apparent in her tone, was a hefty dose of suspicion. Joel didn't know how much Diana Walker knew about her husband's background, but he could tell from her attitude that something wasn't sitting right with her.

"I'm not really an old friend," Joel said.

"I didn't think so. You're much too young, for one thing." She pointed him to the sofa and seated herself on the loveseat.

"I'm sorry," Joel said. "It just seemed easier to say that than try to explain over the phone."

"Explain what?"

Even before meeting Diana Walker, Joel had decided to ditch the ploy he'd initially come up with to get her talking about her husband. He'd wanted to go slow and lead up to the question of Roy's identity. But with the local cops on the trail, there wasn't time for that. Besides, Joel had never been very good at pretense. Now that he'd met Diana, he knew he could never have made much headway following that path, anyway.

"Who are you?" she asked.

"I'm a reporter. With the *Littleton Post* in Georgia."

Joel picked up a flash of recognition in her eyes when he mentioned Littleton.

She crossed her arms over her chest. "I have nothing to say to you."

"Hear me out. Please."

When she didn't protest, he continued. "First, I'm sorry about your husband. I know it must be very hard for you. Losing someone you love is always hard, but to lose him to murder, out of the blue . . . well, it must be just awful."

She nodded but said nothing.

He looked around the room. It was done in muted earth tones, comfortable and homey. "Mr. Walker had an outstanding reputation as DA. I know that much from reading about him and talking to others, but I was hoping you could tell me something about childhood, his family growing up."

Diana had been sitting motionless throughout his speech, and she continued to sit there now, looking at him, her brow furrowed.

"His childhood?" she asked finally.

Joel sighed. "I'm not doing so well, am I? I never do at this sort of thing." He sighed again, spread his hands and leaned forward. "To be honest, there was a murder about twenty years ago, Senator Saxton's daughter. You may have read about it in the papers. Her body was recently discovered in an area that was being developed."

"Yes," Diana uncrossed her arms and leaned forward slightly. "I read about that."

"There was a suspect at the time, a young man by the name of Brian Riley. But without a body, the DA didn't want to go forward and Riley was never charged." Joel paused for a breath. "Your husband looks quite a bit like that man."

"My husband grew up in North Dakota," Diana said.

"That's what I read in his bio, but here, take a look." Joel pulled a handful of photos from his briefcase and handed them to Diana. "These are Brian Riley twenty years ago. And this"—he handed her one other photograph—"is an age-progressed photo of Brian. Don't you think he looks a lot like your husband?"

She was silent, but her hand holding the photos shook. Finally, she said, "There's some similarity, yes. They both have dark hair and dark eyes, but so do a lot of men."

"And they have the same angular face and cleft chin."

Diana shrugged, but her body had tensed and her expression looked strained.

"The suspect, Brian Riley, had a birthmark on his lower back, left side. Did your husband have a similar birthmark?"

Diana regarded Joel blankly for a moment, and then her face crumpled. "Oh, my God." She pressed the knuckles of her left hand to her mouth. With the other arm, she clutched her middle and folded forward in her chair as though she might be sick.

Joel got to his feet. "Are you all right?" He felt terrible about what he'd done. A story was one thing, but seeing this poor woman's distress reminded him he was dealing with people's lives. "Can I get you something? A glass of water? Should I call Chloe?"

Diana shook her head, gasped for breath. "I'll be fine. Just give me a minute."

"I'm sorry," he said. "You don't need this on top of everything else."

Amazingly, she managed a wry smile. "You're right about that."

"Did you know?"

"Not for sure, not until this moment. After Roy died, I started to suspect . . . well, a few things didn't add up. But I hoped I was wrong."

"The police will be contacting you soon," Joel said, sitting again.

"The police?"

He held up his hands. "I had nothing to do with that. I simply wanted to hear your story, see your reaction, find out how he'd managed to reinvent himself as Roy Walker. I wanted to get a feel for the human side before the whole thing exploded in the news."

"You wanted a scoop," Diana said, sounding both weary and accusatory.

Joel nodded. "I guess so. I got interested in the story when Miranda Saxton's body was discovered. I grew up in Littleton. My father knew Brian's father. He'd met Miranda, in fact. And the story sort of sucked me in. I spoke with people who'd known Brian, people who were at the party the night Miranda disappeared. It went way beyond the scope of my assignment at the paper."

"If you'd known my husband," Diana said, "you'd know he could never have killed anyone. He was the most honorable, caring, righteous man you'd ever meet. He was a great lawyer, a fantastic dad and a . . . a wonderful husband."

She stumbled on that last bit, but Joel supposed that was to be expected given what she'd just learned about him. "A lot of people thought the same thing about Brian Riley," Joel said. "They still do. Not the dad part, obviously, but that he was a good guy. Not someone who would have or could have killed Miranda Saxton. But the evidence says something different."

Diana's shoulders sagged. "I read the news stories online. Brian was the last known person to have seen her alive. And he had no alibi for the hours after the party. But—"

"There's the silver charm Brian wore. It was found with Miranda's remains."

Diana's face froze. "A sun charm on a braided leather cord?"

"Yes. Do you know it?"

"It was Brian's?"

"He had one like it."

She looked even more dismayed. "I knew it had been found with Miranda's remains. I didn't know it belonged to Brian."

"My cousin went to high school with him," Joel said, striving to make amends for the bad news he'd thrown her way. "He thought Brian was a good guy. In fact, he's going to send me some photos he took the night of the party. I'll make you copies."

Chloe and a boy about seven wearing blue dinosaur pajamas appeared at the doorway. The boy hesitated, and then sidled up to Diana. "Are you going to tuck me in?"

"Yes, honey, in a bit. Ask Chloe to read you a story first, okay?"

"I want you to read me one."

"I will, after Chloe's done. That way you'll get *two* stories."

The boy looked at Joel, and Joel felt a trickle of sour saliva pool in his mouth. He'd been feeling bad enough about breaking the news to Diana, and now it dawned on him that the ripples went even farther. He wasn't going to get much of a story out of it, either, since the news would break soon anyway.

The doorbell rang, and the boy ran to the window to look out. "Cops," he announced.

Diana paled and turned abruptly. "Chloe, call Allison and

Len for me, would you? That's the number I left by the phone for emergencies. Ask them to come over. Right now. And then take Jeremy upstairs." She gave the boy a hug. "Mommy needs to talk to the police about Daddy. Legal stuff. You go with Chloe and I'll be up as soon as I can."

Jeremy left reluctantly, looking back over his shoulder at Diana, who was rising to go to the door.

"Chloe, if Allison is out, tell Len I need him anyway. His cell is in my Rolodex under Phillips."

"Len Phillips?" Joel blurted out.

Diana gave him an odd look. "You know Len?"

The doorbell rang again as Joel said, "I recognize the name. He was one of the college kids at the party the night Miranda Saxton disappeared. He and Brian Riley worked at the same resort."

"What? Are you sure?"

"Yes, it's in my notes. Stuff I got from the detectives who worked the case."

Diana opened her mouth to respond, then shut it. She called to Chloe to forget about making the phone call, and then she went to answer the door.

CHAPTER 33

Diana awoke the next morning with a pounding headache, a dry mouth, and a fevered need to speak to Len. She hadn't expected to be able to sleep at all, but sometime around midnight she'd fallen into a deep, dreamless slumber.

The police officer who'd questioned her last night, a heavyset man in his fifties named Simms, had apologized profusely for bothering her with what he'd referred to as "a crackpot request" from an out-of-town police department. Could Diana shed any light on the possibility that Roy had lived in Littleton, Georgia, twenty years ago? Did he have any relatives there? Did *she* know anyone living in that area?

She had faltered for only a moment before deciding to cooperate with the police. Doing anything else, she decided, would only complicate matters and, in the long run, change nothing. She answered the detective's questions honestly and then recounted her brief conversation with the mother of the deceased Roy Walker from North Dakota. Diana didn't mention their depleted savings accounts, but since Simms hadn't asked, she saw no need to voluntarily damage her husband's reputation further.

Simms had clearly been surprised, and then unabashedly electrified, to discover that his routine crank-call follow-up was anything but routine. Nonetheless, his manner remained courteous and sympathetic, and he promised to do his best to keep the discovery from the press until the department had confirmed

Roy's true identity—something he expected would happen rather quickly with the help of fingerprints.

Since the press had already gotten wind of the story, Diana didn't see that an official "no comment" was going to have a lot of impact.

Joel Richards had left not long after Simms arrived, but Diana had asked him to drop by later this morning. She had questions—personal questions—and at the moment, he was her best bet for getting answers. Joel and, eventually, Len.

She hadn't wanted to confront Len last night when she was still reeling from Joel's revelation and feeling so hurt and angry she could barely breathe, but that was her first priority today. Talk to Len, find out what he knew about Brian Riley—then beat him to a bloody pulp for lying to her when she'd asked if he'd known Brian twenty years ago.

Len first, then Joel. It was bound to be an interesting day.

With that thought, Diana woke Jeremy, then brushed her teeth and showered. By the time she made it downstairs, Chloe was already in the kitchen, humming softly under her breath.

"Good morning," she said. "I made coffee. And I'm making Jeremy's lunch but I can't remember if you said apple slices or apple quarters."

"Quarters are fine." Diana poured herself a cup of coffee and opened the newspaper Chloe had already picked up from the driveway. She scanned the two front sections. Not a word about Roy or the murder of Miranda Saxton. Thank God. She wasn't ready to be publicly humiliated just yet.

But the ramifications closer to home couldn't be avoided.

"You're probably wondering what last night was all about," Diana ventured, although she felt sure Chloe had overheard enough to figure it out.

"Your husband," Chloe said. "His murder, I mean."

"It's actually more complicated than that." Diana found she

couldn't bring herself to tell Chloe that Roy wasn't who he claimed to be, and that he was wanted for murder. It felt too personal. "I'll explain another time, but if any reporters come around, don't speak them, okay? Don't let them in, and don't let them near Jeremy."

"No, of course not. I'm sorry about that man yesterday, I didn't know he was a reporter."

"That's okay. I meant other reporters. I'm expecting Joel Richards later this morning." Diana hesitated, then added, "His father might have known my husband's father."

If Chloe was confused, she kept her questions to herself, confirming Diana's suspicions that Chloe had heard much of what was said last night. Not that it mattered. Soon the whole town would know. The whole nation.

Jeremy hopped down the stairs with Digger at his heels and looked around. "Is the cop gone?" he asked.

"Long gone," Diana said.

"What'd he want?"

Diana brushed the hair from Jeremy's face with her hand. "Just some stuff about Daddy. They want to make sure they have the right information."

"Oh." Jeremy's expression clouded. Seven-year-olds were blessedly resilient but it didn't take much to bring sadness to the fore. Diana felt terrible for starting his day off with a reminder about his father.

"Hey, Mr. Sunshine," Chloe said brightly. "How about French toast for breakfast?"

"Yeah." Jeremy grinned. "I love French toast."

Once again, Diana was grateful for Chloe's presence.

Later that morning, Diana sat across from Len at a table she'd staked out in a quiet corner of a Starbucks in Berkeley—a location she'd suggested because she was sure neither of them would run into anyone they knew. She wanted a conversation without interruptions, and without friends eavesdropping.

"What's this about?" Len asked, handing her the tall cappuccino she'd ordered. "It feels a bit cloak and dagger, if you want to know the truth." He smiled, and Diana felt grateful. She knew he was trying to break the ice. Meeting for coffee—just the two of them—wasn't something they'd ever done before. Neither was heavy conversation.

She licked the foam from the top of her cup. Best to get right to the point. "Remember when I told you I thought Roy looked like the guy who was the main suspect in Miranda Saxton's disappearance?"

Len nodded.

"Well it looks like he probably *was* that guy. The cops somehow got wind of the fact that Roy resembled him. They're trying to make a final determination as we speak. Roy Walker isn't his real name."

Len rocked back in his chair. "Jesus. Are you kidding me?" He let out a whoosh of breath. "Wow. I don't know what to say."

"That's not all," Diana told him tersely.

Len raised an eyebrow and gave her a quizzical look.

"You were in Littleton the summer Miranda Saxton disappeared, weren't you?"

Len had been ready to take his first sip of coffee, but now he set the cup down, untouched. His broad face grew pale but his expression remained carefully casual.

"In fact," Diana continued, her tone hardening, "you knew Brian Riley, the young man whose photo I showed you. You worked with him."

The muscle in Len's jaw twitched. For a moment he didn't move, then he spread his hands on the table and stared at them before looking at her. "What do you want me to say?"

"I want to know the truth. How could you have kept this from me? How could you have lied to me!" Diana realized her voice had risen. She lowered it again. "You and Allison are my closest friends. I count on you. I trusted you."

"I'm not the bad guy, here, Diana. Don't yell at me."

"I'm not yelling."

"You were."

It was easier to be mad at Len than at Roy, but that wasn't fair. "Just answer me," she said. "Were you friends with Brian Riley?"

There was a stretch of silence, then Len said, "I worked at a resort in Littleton. It was the summer after my sophomore year at Yale. I'd met Brian but we weren't friends by a long shot."

"Why didn't you tell me when I showed you his picture? You implied you knew about Brian Riley only because of what you saw on the news."

"Tell you what? And to what end? You and Allison are friends. I like you. I wanted to spare your feelings."

"But you acted like I was way off base."

"As far as I was concerned, you were. So what if Roy looked like Brian? I couldn't say for sure that's who he was. And Roy is dead. Why would I want to rub salt in your wounds?"

"But at some point, you must have suspected Roy was Brian."

"Why? Like I told you, I didn't know Brian well. We worked at the same resort but I was a lifeguard, one of the college crowd who partied as hard as we worked." Len paused with a self-effacing roll of his eyes. Diana had always liked that about Len. He was never too full of himself.

"Brian was a townie," Len continued. "He bused tables. Our paths hardly ever crossed. When Miranda disappeared and the cops zeroed in on him, he was big news. Everyone had a story then, but if that hadn't happened, he'd never have been a blip on anyone's radar."

"You'd met him, though. You could at least have told me that." Diana knew she sounded peevish, but she was angry she'd been misled, even though she supposed she could understand Len's reluctance to speak up.

"I'm sorry," Len said. He leaned across the table. "Maybe I should have told you then that I'd known Brian, but what difference would it have made? I'm still not sure I believe they were the same guy."

"They were."

"You're certain?"

Diana nodded.

"Jesus. Who'd have thought?" Len settled wearily back against his chair. "What made you think I knew Brian in the first place?" he asked after a moment.

"A reporter from Littleton who's been covering the Miranda Saxton story recognized your name. You really never thought Roy looked like Brian before I said something the other day?"

"When Allison first introduced us, I thought Roy looked a little familiar, but I've met a lot of people over the years, and a number of them look like someone else I remember, so no, I never thought much about it. Besides, I knew him as Roy. It never dawned on me that might not be his real name."

"And you never asked Roy if he'd been to Littleton? Never pushed him just a little?"

Len held his cup with both hands and looked at Diana. "Once. He'd said something that made me think he was familiar with the coastal area of Georgia. I asked him about it, and he passed it off as a coincidence."

He eyed her earnestly. "I was out to make nice, Diana, not create problems. It was Allison I was focused on. You were her best friend. I was hardly going to win her over by making trouble with your husband. Besides, Brian Riley was never charged with anything. He wasn't a fugitive. Even if I'd been sure that's who

Roy was, what would have been the point in saying anything?"

She wouldn't have believed Len, Diana thought. She would have dismissed him as a wacko, leading to tensions in her relationship with Allison. Len was right. Speaking up earlier would have caused trouble. But once Roy was gone and Diana had raised the possibility, she thought Len ought to have been honest with her.

"I went to you and Allison with my suspicions," she said. "It wasn't easy to open myself up like that. And then you went out of your way to lie to me."

"I'm sorry, Diana. Truly I am. I did what I thought was right."

"Did you tell Allison you'd known Brian?" Diana couldn't bear it if Allison had known and kept quiet about it as well.

"No. If I was going to tell Allison, I'd have told you first." Len's voice was low and sincere. "Maybe I'm a coward at heart. It was easier to stick my head in the sand and say nothing."

"Do you think Roy recognized you?"

"I doubt it. Why would he? If Brian hadn't been a suspect in Miranda's disappearance, I'm sure I'd never have remembered him, either."

"Maybe he sensed something, though. You two never really hit it off. Maybe that's why."

"Could be, I guess." Len didn't sound particularly interested one way or another. "More likely it's simply because we were different sorts of people."

"What was he like?" Diana asked. "Brian Riley, I mean. Tell me about him."

Len ran his fingers through his thick mop of sandy brown hair. "It's not important, Diana. Roy is who's important. He and I may not have been best buddies, but he was a good man, and a loving husband and father. Whatever might have happened before he met you doesn't matter."

"Please," Diana insisted. "I really want to know." When Len

still seemed to hesitate, she pushed harder. "You've no idea what it's like to discover the man you've been married to is someone you didn't know at all. This isn't just something that happened in his past—I understand we all did things when we were young that make us cringe now—it's about how little he trusted me, how much of himself he kept private. It's like I didn't know him at all. So, please, tell me what he was like when you knew him."

Len rubbed his temples. "Okay, it's your call. But I have to warn you, I don't have a lot good to say about Brian. My impression was he had a chip on his shoulder and a bit of a temper. His father was the sheriff and I can see now that's got to be tough for a kid who courted trouble."

Diana swallowed against the knot in her throat. "Brian did that?"

"Yeah, he did."

"What kind of trouble?"

"I know he got into a couple of fights that summer. One of the guys he tussled with had to have stitches. And he didn't like to follow rules. The hired help weren't supposed to use the resort facilities, but Brian did anyway. He got tossed out of the pool area a couple of times. And there was some brouhaha when one of the guests' wallet was stolen from her purse while she was in the restaurant. They never figured out who took it, but I know Brian was questioned."

Diana's chest was growing tighter with each passing moment. The young man Len was describing was so unlike Roy, and yet she herself had caught glimpses of a quiet fury in him that always made her uneasy.

"Do you think he killed Miranda Saxton?" she asked.

"Back then we didn't know she'd been murdered. There were all kinds of rumors about what might have happened to her, but most people figured there was foul play involved. And did I think Brian had something to do with it? You bet. It was pretty obvious he had the hots for her. That's why he'd sneak into the pool area, so he could watch her in her bikini. And one of the fights I told you about, the guy he beat up, was a guy Miranda was hanging with that afternoon. Brian was a hothead, and I suspect he lost it one night and killed her. Maybe accidentally. Probably accidentally, but he didn't come forward."

Len's words stung even though Diana had asked him, had practically begged him, to tell her the truth. Devastated by the picture Len painted, she reminded herself that Roy had turned his life around. He'd been a successful and respected attorney. A good father and husband.

"The fact of the matter is," Len continued, "until Miranda Saxton's body was discovered a couple of weeks ago, I'd basically put that whole summer out of my mind. It seemed so unreal to me."

"And when you heard the news about her remains, you still didn't say anything to Roy?"

Len laughed in a humorless way. "Roy was the do-gooder, not me. I don't go looking for trouble."

That, Diana thought, was one of the basic differences between the two men. Roy could be almost preachy at times, while Len was much more laid back—unwilling, in Roy's estimation, to go out on a limb for anything. A man without a core, he'd told her more than once. She'd seen that as the reason they never got along.

But Diana wondered now if there wasn't more to it.

CHAPTER 34

Chloe was vacuuming the stairway when Digger suddenly went charging past her to the front door, barking.

"Mrs. Walker isn't here," Chloe told Joel Richards, "but she should be back any minute. She called to say she was running a bit late and that I wasn't to let you leave, no matter what." Those were Diana's exact words, but now that Chloe had parroted them back to Joel, they sounded almost flirtatious. She felt herself blush.

He reached down and scratched Digger's ears. The dog quieted immediately. "Shall I wait in the car? I don't want to get in your way."

"Oh, no. No problem. I'm just vacuuming. I'm happy for a break. Come on in." She led him back to the large family kitchen, which seemed a better choice than the more formal living room. "Would you like a cup of coffee?"

"No thanks. I never developed a taste for it, really. Probably the only newsman in the nation who doesn't drink coffee." He laughed.

"Me either," Chloe said. "Developed a taste for coffee, that is. I like the smell of it though. When it's fresh," she added, remembering the cold cups half full of old coffee Trace used to leave around the apartment. Sometimes he'd stick cigarette butts in the cups, or chewed-up gum. Totally disgusting.

"Yeah. Fresh-ground coffee has an enticing smell. I'm also good with coffee ice cream." He sat on one of the high counter stools and smiled at her.

"How about hot chocolate?"

"I'm good with that, too."

"I meant, would you like a cup? Now?" Chloe opened the refrigerator and reached for the milk before Joel could answer. She'd never talked to a reporter before and it made her nervous. Or maybe it was Joel. He was a bit older than Trace, a little taller, his hair shorter and lighter. But Chloe found him attractive.

"Sure," he said. "That would be great."

Digger had followed them into the kitchen, carrying his rope toy in his mouth. He dropped it at Joel's feet. "What do you like, boy? You want to play tug-of-war?"

"He loves it," Chloe answered. "But I can put him upstairs if he's a bother."

"No, I like dogs." Joel picked up the toy and dangled it for Digger. "How long have you worked for the Walkers?"

"Not long." Chloe spooned cocoa powder into two cups. She figured the less she said, the better.

"What was the husband like?"

"I never met him." She felt a flush of guilt when she remembered the dying man Trace had shot, his blood pooling around him. Her hand shook as she poured heated milk into the cups. "I didn't start here until after he died."

"That's too bad." Joel seemed disappointed, and it took her a minute to understand why. Joel was after a story, a story about a man who was wanted for murder.

She hadn't meant to listen in last night. Well, not at first. But the whole evening was pretty weird, with Joel and the cops showing up and Diana asking her to call Len and Allison and then changing her mind right away. Chloe knew something big was happening, so she'd listened enough to get the gist of it. Knowing about Roy made her feel a little less awful about what had happened to him. If he was a bad man, a murderer who'd run from the law, then it wasn't like Trace had killed an innocent person.

Why did everything have to be so complicated? Rose always told the girls at the group home there was right and wrong, and what tripped people up was forgetting that. She made it sound so simple. But it wasn't.

"So what's Mrs. Walker like?" Joel asked, taking the cup of cocoa Chloe handed him.

"She's wonderful. I've never met anyone quite like her."

"In what way?"

Chloe struggled to explain. "You know, genuinely nice. She treats me like a real person."

"A real person?"

"Like I'm somebody."

Joel cocked his head and smiled. "Interesting."

Chloe didn't know what he meant and she worried she'd given something away. "Tell me about being a reporter," she said. "It must be exciting."

Joel laughed. "It can be, but what I do mostly isn't. I'm hoping someday I'll get hired by one of the major papers where I can cover big stories, maybe even do some investigative reporting. Littleton is a small town. It's a popular summer tourist destination, but not much of interest happens there. Except for the discovery of Miranda Saxton's remains."

"She's the girl who was killed?" Chloe tried to fill in the gaps. She hadn't understood everything she'd learned last night.

Joel nodded. "It was twenty years ago but she was a senator's daughter so it's still hot news." He paused, sipped his cocoa, and studied her. "And the really hot story is that Roy Walker might be the person who killed her."

Joel was a reporter, she reminded herself, and she was part of his story. The thought made her uncomfortable.

"I sort of figured as much," she said finally, "from all that went on last night."

"And here he was, a DA no less, living under an assumed identity. Pretty amazing, isn't it? But maybe Roy didn't kill her," Joel continued, no longer looking directly at Chloe. "Some of the people who knew him twenty years ago think the cops acted too quickly, wanting to get the case solved. It's a mystery. That's part of why I find the story so intriguing."

"And that's what you're doing here? Trying to figure it out?"

"Don't I wish. That would be a *real* story." He looked wistful, like someone talking about a dream vacation he'd never be able to afford. "But I did come up with the angle that Roy Walker was Brian Riley."

She was impressed. "You must be really good to have figured that out."

"Actually, I got a tip." He sounded discouraged. "And now I can't even run very far with an exclusive because this woman I work with jumped the gun on me."

"That's mean."

"It's the way things work. Mostly what I'm doing now is fleshing things out, talking to people who knew Roy back when he was someone named Brian Riley, and to people who knew him as a DA, a husband and a father. People like news stories that are more than hard fact. They like the human interest stuff, too. They want to know why and how, not just what happened."

"That's why you were hoping I'd met him."

"Yeah. Too bad he was killed. Now we'll never know what really happened."

Joel probably hoped she'd jump in with something he could use in his story—a comment about Roy, even if it wasn't directly about the girl's murder. She pressed her lips together to keep from blurting out the truth about Roy's death.

"Tell me about Len Phillips," Joel said, changing the subject.

"I've only met him once. He and Allison are good friends of Diana's."

"Allison is his wife?"

"Girlfriend, I think. But he lives with her."

"What's her last name?"

Chloe realized she was probably saying too much. "I don't remember," she said.

"He hasn't returned my phone calls. I'd really like to talk to him. I don't suppose you know where he works?"

Chloe shook her head.

"Or where they live?"

"Sorry."

He gave Chloe a wan smile. "Loyal and discreet—you're a tough source to crack. I promise I won't say where I'd got the information." He paused. "Guess that will have to wait for a follow-up story, then."

Joel's hangdog expression might have persuaded Chloe to relent, but she heard Diana's car pull into the garage. "There's Mrs. Walker now," she said with relief. "I'll tell her you're here."

Chloe was still thinking about Joel Richards when she went to pick Jeremy up from school. She arrived fifteen minutes early, before any of the mothers or other au pairs had begun to gather. She'd wanted to allow extra time so she didn't make any stupid driving mistakes and wind up with a ticket. Plus, she knew Diana would rather talk to Joel in private.

He was so different from Trace. Different from any of the guys she'd known before. He was older, of course, and more educated. And really cute, she added, acknowledging the tingle she felt when she thought about him. Which she shouldn't be doing. What was wrong with her anyway?

Being a reporter sounded interesting, even if Joel said it wasn't. Maybe Chloe could be a reporter some day. She'd like that. She was good at talking to people and interested in learning about what was going on. There were all kinds of stories she could write.

She caught herself mid-fantasy. Reality check. She wasn't going to be a reporter anymore than she was going to be a teacher. She hadn't even finished high school. And with a baby to take care of, she never would.

Lost in thought, she hadn't realized the bell had rung and the children were already gathering for pickup. She got out of the car quickly and headed toward the school. She'd gone only about a dozen steps when a man in a blue sweatshirt bumped against her. She turned, expecting some sort of apology, and instead found that he'd grabbed her arm.

"You're doing real good without Trace, aren't you?"

Chloe's heart jumped when she recognized Weasel-face.

"You got a nice place to live," he said, "nice car to drive. It's a pretty cushy job—if you like taking care of little brats. You ought to be able to get your hands on some cash real easy. Maybe some fancy jewelry, too."

Chloe shook her head, too scared to speak.

"Sure you could. The Missus wouldn't even know it was gone. Or you get us a key and the code to the alarm. There's all kinds of ways you can make good on Trace's debt."

"I can't," she whispered.

"Sure you can. You wouldn't want the Missus to learn that you were a party to her husband's murder, now would you? Might not sit too well with her. Or with the cops."

"Please," Chloe begged. "I had nothing to do with the money you say Trace owed you. I didn't even know about it."

"That's not really the point," Weasel-face said. "Point is, you can make it right."

Jeremy had spotted Chloe and was skipping toward her, backpack bouncing with each step. She pulled her arm free and stepped protectively between Weasel-face and Jeremy.

"Your choice," Weasel-face said, lowering his voice. "You can get us out of your hair for good, or not. We could always take the kid instead, but it would be easier to skip the ransom route."

Chloe snapped her head his direction. "Don't you dare."

"Hey, kid," Weasel-face said, giving Jeremy a high-five. "You have a good day in school?"

Jeremy, uncharacteristically subdued, nodded.

"That's good." Weasel-face turned to Chloe. "You've got forty-eight hours to decide. I'll be in touch."

Chloe grabbed Jeremy's hand and, gripping it tightly, practically dragged him to the car.

"Is that your boyfriend?" Jeremy asked.

"Hardly," she said. "He's not a nice man. If you ever see him again, run the other way."

The back of her neck was damp with sweat and she felt light-headed. She thought she might throw up.

"Run away and tell an adult, right?" Jeremy said.

"Right."

Maybe she should follow the same advice. But where would she run, and how could she possibly tell Diana she'd been there when Roy was killed?

CHAPTER 35

"Chocolate or wine?" Allison asked. She set the brown paper bag she was carrying on Diana's kitchen counter and gave Diana a hug. "On second thought," she added, stepping back, "you probably need both."

"It's the middle of the afternoon," Diana pointed out. "A bit early for wine."

"Says who? Besides, think of the medicinal effects." Allison pulled a pink bakery box from the bag and set about opening the wine.

"Okay," Diana said with a laugh, "you've convinced me." She felt less despondent already. A good friend was truly an elixir.

"Len told me everything," Allison said simply. She'd come straight from teaching and was still wearing what she referred to as her "proper" clothing—in this case, black wool slacks with an amber sweater and darker toned jacket. "I'm so sorry, Diana. What you must be going through. I still can't believe it's true. Roy must have changed a lot from his younger days, because I never knew him to be anything but a sweet and wonderful man."

"He was, wasn't he?" Diana's voice broke. The emotional roller coaster of recent events had pushed her to the verge of tears. "Most of the time, anyway," she added with a stab at levity that only brought the tears closer to the surface.

Allison poured them each a glass of wine and divided four tiny éclairs onto two plates. "Tell me why you're so certain Roy was this Brian Riley guy."

Diana told her about the birthmark Joel had mentioned. "That's what clinched it for me, but that's on top of the fact that Roy was using a false identity and had hired a detective to keep an ear to the ground regarding Miranda Saxton, not to mention the physical resemblance between the two men." Diana swallowed hard. "It all adds up. After a while denial is no longer an option."

"Len insists he didn't know," Allison said with a huff, "but I think he's being a bit disingenuous. He didn't *want* to know because he didn't want to have to deal with it. He can be so irritating in that way."

"I was pretty angry at him, myself. But after listening to his side, I can understand why he didn't speak up."

"Still, I think he ought to have been more truthful, especially after Roy died." Allison slipped off her jacket and draped it over the back of her chair. "Len's been in such a bad mood recently that I didn't want to jump on him. But my gosh, he totally misled you."

"I appreciate your outrage, but it doesn't really change the facts. I'm sure Len realized that, too." Diana took a tiny sip of wine. Given her mood, she could easily have downed the entire glass.

Allison shrugged. "He should have been more honest."

"He didn't want to stir up trouble. He cares about you so he wanted to be nice to me."

"Sometimes I wonder how much he really cares."

Diana remembered Allison's comments to the same effect the day of Roy's funeral. Diana had been so wrapped up in her own troubles the past few days, she'd forgotten that Allison had worries of her own. "What do you mean?"

"I think he may be starting to have cold feet about this commitment thing."

"About marriage, you mean?"

"Whenever I bring the subject up lately, he closes down. And then he usually finds some reason to be irritated with me."

Len had been married twice before, so Diana could understand his reluctance to make a mistake a third time. It was also the reason she'd cautioned Allison to go more slowly. Not that there was anything inherently wrong with a man who'd had two failed marriages, but it did make Diana wonder what part he'd played in the breakups. Having spoken her mind to Allison about this so many times in the past, however, Diana wasn't sure what she could add now. Still, she tried. "Things have moved pretty quickly between you two. Maybe he's reacting to that."

"I know you think I've rushed into this. I do listen to you. But I'm so tired of being alone. I *want* to be married again."

"Len's good for you," Diana told her. "And it's clear he does care about you, even if he's been snippy of late. But marriage is a big deal. I think he's probably feeling a little nervous."

"He's changed," Allison said wistfully. Then she sighed and brushed the air with her hand. "Enough about me and Len. What are the police going to do about Roy and the Saxton murder. Since they can't arrest Roy or have a trial, they just drop it?"

Diana took a bite of éclair. It was creamy and sweet, but she had trouble swallowing it. All those popular fad diets that never worked—maybe despair was the answer to losing weight.

"Joel Richards, the reporter from Littleton, thinks the police will probably close the case. He says they'll be happy to put it behind them, and he seems to know the players fairly well."

"Makes sense."

"Joel seems less willing to see it wrapped up, though. He's young and eager for a big story. Plus, his father knew Brian and Miranda. I think that connection resonates with him."

"You mean he's not sure Brian killed the girl?"

Diana's conversation with Joel earlier that day hadn't provided the kind of answers she was hoping for, but it had given her a different perspective on Brian and the events leading up to Miranda Saxton's murder.

"There's no solid evidence that ties Brian to the murder, just lots of circumstantial stuff. I guess if Roy were alive and the case went to trial, it would be up to a jury to decide. A good defense attorney might shake things up."

"Len told me the only reason Brian didn't stand trial before was that there wasn't a body. The cops were sure he was involved. I guess now—" Allison stopped abruptly and put her hand on Diana's. "I'm sorry, I'm not trying to rub it in. We can stop talking about this if you want."

"No, talking is good for me. Besides, Joel said pretty much the same thing. Brian was the last person known to have been with her. A vacationing couple saw them on the beach around midnight. They were having a rather heated argument about something. Brian didn't return home until after six the next morning. And now there's a charm of Brian's that was discovered with her remains."

"The theory was that she rejected his advances," Allison said, "and Brian got angry. That's what Len remembers."

"Something like that, although Joel seems to think Miranda was as interested in Brian as he was in her. Of course, Joel wasn't there that summer." It felt odd to be talking about Brian, a young man from twenty years ago, rather than Roy, her husband. But it was also less personal.

"There was a big beach bonfire the night Miranda disappeared," Diana continued. "Mostly college kids who'd been working at the resorts that summer, but Brian was there, too. And Miranda, who was vacationing with her parents at some private retreat. Joel's cousin was there and told him a scuffle broke out around midnight. Some jerk was taunting Brian because of the silver charm. It had been his mother's. Some of the other guys joined in. Brian took a couple of swings, bloodied a few noses and the like."

"They thought he was a sissy or something?"

"Joel didn't know the details, but you know how kids can be. When they decide to pick on someone, the reason doesn't really matter."

"Still, none of it sounds like Roy."

"He was younger then," Diana reminded her. "And in some ways, it does sound like Roy. He had a pretty quick temper when it came to bullies."

When Jeremy was five a couple of the bigger boys on his T-ball team had started heckling him whenever he missed the ball. Roy came down on them so hard Diana had had to physically step between Roy and the boys. And he'd been equally hard on Jeremy the time Jeremy called one of his classmates "a big fat poop."

"Did Roy talk much about his mother?" Allison asked.

"He told me both his parents were dead, which is actually true. His father—Brian's father—was the sheriff in town. He committed suicide after Brian was arrested."

"God, how terrible. Talk about being weighted by guilt. Len told me Brian was a bit of a hothead—actually, he insinuated it was worse than that—but still, can you imagine how you would feel in that situation?"

"It must have been terrible for him," Diana agreed. Instinctively, she found herself defending Roy.

"That reminds me," she said. "The reporter wants to talk to Len. Do you think he'd be willing?"

"I don't see why not, now that it's out in the open. He no longer has an excuse for being a wimp and not speaking out." Allison was obviously more than a bit irked by what she saw as Len's duplicity.

The phone rang and Diana checked caller ID, thinking it might be Chloe. It wasn't. "It's Alec Thurston, the DA," she told Allison. "Mind if I take this?"

"No, go right ahead. I'll clean up."

Diana moved into the family room, receiver in hand. "Hello, Alec."

"How are you doing, Diana?"

"Fine." She knew he wasn't calling to inquire about her well-being, and she found herself on edge, waiting expectantly.

"I'm sorry to always be the bearer of bad news." Thurston hesitated a moment. "It's about Jamal Harris, the kid who claimed he had an *in* with Roy."

"Right, I remember."

"I'm afraid it doesn't look good. He now claims Roy hired him to kill someone."

"What? That's absurd."

"That was my initial reaction, also. I figured he was desperate to come up with some story that would give him bargaining leverage. He said he was going to meet Roy the Sunday Roy was shot, in the city. That would explain why Roy was there and why he didn't tell you he was going."

Why was Thurston giving this creep any credence at all? "Jamal Harris could have read about the shooting," she said hotly. "It was all over the news. He put two and two together and came up with a good story, and Roy isn't around to refute it."

"Don't forget the calls I told you about," Thurston said. "One from Harris's phone to Roy's cell. And then later that same afternoon, he called Roy's office."

The phone message: *Where are you man? You'd better not be messing with me.* She felt weak in the knees.

"It's going to come out," Thurston said, "whether Harris's claim eventually proves to be true or not. His attorney is going to go the publicity route if we don't agree to cut a deal."

"But it makes no sense," Diana insisted. "Who did Roy supposedly want killed?"

"Harris didn't know. They were going to cover that on Sunday."

With a sinking sense of dread, Diana thought of the money missing from their savings accounts. Was this what Roy had done with their hard-earned savings? Hired a hit man? "How much did Roy pay him?"

"Nothing yet. Harris claims the bargained rate was five grand up front, ten more when the job was done. That might account for the five thousand Roy had on him when he was killed."

Fifteen thousand to hire a killer. Only a fraction of what Roy had withdrawn.

But maybe this wasn't the first time Roy had hired someone to commit murder.

Diana couldn't believe what she was thinking. It wasn't possible. But nothing she'd learned about Roy in the last few weeks was possible.

"Was Roy supposed to meet Jamal Harris at the convenience store?"

"According to Harris, Roy was supposed to get the address of the meeting place from the store clerk, who was a friend of Harris's. Harris didn't want Roy to know the location of the meet ahead of time because he was worried Roy would set him up for some sort of sting. He didn't want anyone but Roy showing up. There's a good chance Harris is blowing smoke, but I wanted to warn you before you heard it on the news."

"On the news?"

"I'm sorry, Diana. Like I said, Harris's attorney feels the publicity will give him leverage."

These horrible accusations were going to be made public. It wasn't fair. Diana gripped the back of a chair to steady herself.

"The guy who shot Roy and the clerk, Trace Rodriquez, was he in on it?"

"Harris says no, and there's nothing we've come up with on Rodriquez that would tie him to it. He was a lowlife, but not big-time. I think he happened to hold up the store where Harris's friend worked." Thurston paused. "It's ironic, because if Harris had told Roy straight out that he'd meet him at Dewey Park, Roy would never have gone to the store and been shot."

"Dewey Park?"

"It's a scrappy piece of city-owned property across from Harris's sister's place."

"Near Bayo Vista?"

"Yeah, why?"

"Oh, my God," Diana said. "My God." She held onto the back of the chair to steady herself.

"I know it sounds bad," Thurston said, "but as I told you, it's going to be a hard story to prove. Impossible, frankly. And it flies in the face of what people knew about Roy. There's bound to be some publicity, but—"

"No," Diana mumbled. "No, you don't understand. I think Harris's story might be true."

"Look it's—"

"I found a slip of paper in Roy's car when I picked it up from impound, a handwritten address on Bayo Vista. Eleven hundred something. Across from Dewey Park." The apartment building where Diana had met Brenda Harris, the woman who'd complained about a brother in trouble with the law. Her brother was Jamal Harris.

Thurston said, "Well, that does put things in a different light. Let me get back to you, okay?"

Thurston didn't wait for a response. The line went dead.

"What is it?" Allison asked, having heard Diana's anguished cry from in the kitchen.

Diana couldn't speak. As devastated as she was by what Thurston had told her, she was more devastated by what she'd told him.

Hadn't she just confirmed everyone's worst suspicions about Roy? What kind of wife didn't try to protect her husband, no matter what?

She needed to be alone. She needed space to think.

"God, Allison. It just gets worse and worse. I want to dig a hole and crawl in."

CHAPTER 36

Chloe was scared. More scared than she'd ever been in her whole life, and she'd been plenty scared before. She wasn't frightened in the heart-pounding, rapid-breathing way people were when they heard a strange noise late at night. Hers was the wrenching terror of finding herself cornered and knowing there was no way out.

She didn't want to steal from Diana, not even a few dollars, although she knew Diana would never notice. And she absolutely couldn't let anything happen to Jeremy.

There *was* a third option, though—tell the truth and suffer the consequences. That idea was plenty scary in itself. And if Chloe went to prison, what would happen to her baby? She couldn't be sure that telling the truth would stop Weasel-face and his friends from going after Jeremy, but it was the only solution she could come up with.

But every time she thought about confessing to Diana, Chloe broke into a nervous sweat and her voice deserted her.

Today probably wasn't the best day, anyway. Diana had been acting weird ever since Chloe returned home with Jeremy half an hour ago. Allison had been here and they both seemed on edge. Diana had explained that she wasn't feeling well, but Chloe could see that there was more to it than that. And she didn't think it had anything to do with the two wine glasses she saw sitting next to the sink, either.

"Jeremy is coming home with me," Allison announced, with a

283

meaningful glance in Diana's direction. She turned to Jeremy, "We'll have a grand time. I've got a new DVD I think you'll like."

Jeremy looked quickly in Chloe's direction, and then at his mother. "Do I have to?"

Diana nodded. "I'm sorry, sweetie. Just for tonight."

"Why? I want to stay here."

"I'm happy to watch him," Chloe offered. Wasn't that what her job was all about?

"No," Diana said sharply. "I need quiet."

It sounded like a reprimand, and while Chloe was sure it was directed at her, she felt bad for Jeremy. He liked Allison but he must have been picking up on some of the same strange vibes Chloe was. Diana, who was normally a good mother, was not herself. "We'll be very—"

"Don't argue," Diana snapped. "I need time to myself. I want to be alone."

Jeremy sidled up next to Chloe and she put an arm around his shoulder. She could feel his little body quivering.

Diana looked suddenly appalled by her short outburst. She reached out for Jeremy and hugged him. "I'm sorry, sweetie. I shouldn't have yelled like that."

"Are you leaving me?" he cried. "Are you going away?"

"No, I'm not leaving you. I'd never do that. I've got a headache is all. And maybe a touch of the flu or something. I'm not going anywhere and nothing bad is going to happen to me. I just need to rest."

Diana turned to Chloe. "Why don't you do something fun tonight. Take a twenty from the drawer under the phone and go to a movie with some friends or something."

Diana ought to have realized that Chloe didn't have any friends, but Chloe got the message. She wasn't welcome. "Thanks, I'll do that."

"Come on," Allison said, taking Jeremy by the hand. "We'll make sundaes for dessert. With real whipped cream."

After Allison and Jeremy had gone, Diana went upstairs to take a bath. Chloe washed the wine glasses and the few dishes on the counter, being very quiet so as not to disturb Diana, even though there was no way she could have been heard over the hum of the bath fan.

To her shame, Chloe found herself looking around the house with an eye as to what she could steal, assuming she was going to steal anything, which she wasn't. It wouldn't be hard, really. Diana was very trusting. Like telling Chloe to take twenty dollars from the stash of bills in the kitchen. Diana didn't even lock up her jewelry.

Chloe forced herself to think about Thanksgiving, only a couple of weeks away.

Last Thanksgiving she'd still been living in the group home. There'd been only four girls for dinner. The other five had been invited elsewhere. Rose made a big deal out of the holiday and made them watch a movie about an abused and half-starved stray dog who collapsed at the back door of a poor, also half-starving family, on Thanksgiving Day. The family took the dog in and fed it even though they were short of food themselves. A few nights later, the dog saved the little boy from a house fire and after that life was good. Maureen and Ashley complained that it was a silly kids' movie and Naomi slept through most of it. But Chloe thought the movie was good and she liked the happy ending, although she never did understand why everyone looked well-fed and well-dressed just because the dog saved the boy's life.

They'd had turkey slices and mashed potatoes for dinner that night, a big step up from what they usually had. And one of the ladies from the auxiliary brought them homemade pumpkin pie. It was the best Thanksgiving Chloe could remember.

This year would be different. Trace was dead and Chloe would probably be in jail.

It was the week after Thanksgiving last year that Chloe had met Trace. They hadn't even made it to their one-year anniversary.

Somewhere Chloe's life had taken a bad turn. Several bad turns, in fact. Some people might say Trace was one of those turns for the worse, but Chloe knew he'd been one of the few bright spots in her life, too. He made her feel special and cared for. Maybe not all the time, but he'd chosen Chloe, picked her out of all the girls he could have had. And he hadn't dumped her when he learned about the baby.

"Poor baby," Chloe whispered, her hand reflexively resting on her belly. A dead father and a mother in jail. What kind of life was that for a kid?

Even without the jail part, how could Chloe possibly raise a child? Diana had asked about her plans for the future, and Chloe had been too embarrassed to admit she didn't have any. Planning wasn't something she'd done much of, ever. Mostly it was a struggle just to get from one day to the next. How had she ever thought she'd be a good mother?

"Oh, Hannah," she told her baby. "You deserve a good home. A mom and a dad who can give you so much more than I can."

As she finished straightening the kitchen, Chloe opened the drawer where Diana kept the envelope of money and counted it. Three hundred dollars. She wondered if Diana even knew exactly how much was there.

Chloe removed the twenty that Diana had offered, and then, because even that felt wrong, quickly replaced it. She shut the drawer, grabbed an apple from the fridge, and left the house.

Joel had spent the afternoon talking to Roy Walker's coworkers—to the extent any of them would talk to him. They all seemed to have heard that Roy might have been using an assumed identity and was a suspect in a long ago murder, though none would comment directly. Joel couldn't tell whether that was the nature of attorneys or if word had come down from above that they were to remain closed-mouthed. No one he talked to had come forth with anything other than "great guy, hard worker, we're saddened by his death." And nothing Joel managed to dig up on his background had indicated so much as a speeding ticket. No affairs, no hints of scandal, not even nasty comments from the defense attorneys he'd beaten in court.

Discouraged, Joel decided to watch the Walker house in the hopes he'd find *something* enticing to write about. His dreams for a big story were rapidly fading.

He'd been parked down the street from the house for less than an hour when a Volvo wagon backed out of the garage with Chloe behind the wheel.

While Joel's intention had been to learn something more of Diana's activities, it struck him that Chloe might be a better source of information. He followed her through city streets and into the parking lot of a large strip mall. She parked in front of a store called the Craft Connection.

Joel gave Chloe a minute's head start, and then followed her into the store. He spotted her at a register near the front, talking to an older black woman she seemed to be acquainted with.

"I just had my break, honey," the woman was saying while giving Chloe a hug. "Dang it all, I wish I'd known you were coming."

"I didn't know it myself," Chloe said.

"How's the new job working out?"

"Good." Chloe nodded when she spoke, but even from where Joel was standing some thirty feet away, he could tell she had reservations about it.

The black woman apparently picked up on that, too. "I don't

think you burned any bridges here. You want your old job back, I bet you could get it."

"No, that's not why I came. I was hoping maybe we could talk. What time are you off?"

"I close tonight, honey. And then I got to get home to my boy." She looked in the direction of a woman with a full cart who was in line, glaring. Then she turned back to Chloe. "You call me and we'll set up a time. I would just love to catch up."

"I'll do that."

The two women exchanged another quick hug, and Chloe turned to leave. Joel started to wander in her direction, eyes scanning the shelves like he was looking for something. When he sensed she was close, he looked straight, pretending to be surprised. "Hey," he said, "fancy meeting you here."

Chloe looked confused and Joel realized she might not recognize him. "Joel Richards," he prompted. "I'm a reporter. I was at—"

"Yes, I know who you are, but why are you here?"

"I needed some . . . some new pens."

"Pens?"

"Yeah. For my article."

Chloe looked even more confused. "You don't use a computer?"

Joel dodged the question with one of his own. "What are you doing here?"

"I used to work here."

"Oh, I see. You must miss it." Joel knew he sounded nuts.

Chloe laughed. "Hardly. I came by to visit a friend, see if she had time for a quick something to eat."

"Did she?"

"No."

"So you're eating alone?" He didn't wait for a response. "Mind if I join you?" The words were out of Joel's mouth before he knew it. He wasn't sure where they'd come from.

Chloe shrugged. "If you want. I was just going to Billie's Burgers."

"You *like* Billie Burgers?"

"Yeah, I do. And it's cheap."

They'd started walking and were already to the parking lot. "Dinner is my treat," Joel said. "I get tired of eating alone when I'm on assignment." He'd heard that line once in a movie and thought it sounded very cosmopolitan. "What's your favorite local restaurant?"

Joel's phone rang before Chloe could answer. "Are you near a TV?" Skeet asked.

"No. Why?"

"Get to one. Quickly. You've got ten minutes until news time there. Word is there's a breaking story about Walker. He may have been a dirty DA."

"What?" Joel hadn't caught a glimmer of dishonesty from anyone he'd talked to.

"That's all I know. We won't get the local feed here, so call me as soon as you know more."

Joel turned to Chloe. "About dinner, can we stop by my motel first?"

"No way." She spun around and glared at him. "What do you think I—"

"I didn't mean that the way it came out." Joel could feel himself blushing. He knew his face must be bright red. "That was my editor on the phone. I need to get to a TV right away. There's a breaking news story about Roy Walker."

Chloe appeared to be weighing his words. "Follow me," she said finally. "There's a Best Buy across the lot."

CHAPTER 37

Diana was grateful to have time alone. It would have been impossible to keep up the pretense that she was fine when she was anything but. She felt raw and shaky and physically sick, as though she'd been pounded to a pulp. She wasn't sure she had the strength to watch the upcoming news, but neither could she tear herself away from the television. Thurston had warned her there'd be coverage and she had to hear for herself.

Diana crossed one leg and then the other, trying to get comfortable. Even the sofa no longer felt familiar. Nothing in her life did.

And then the news anchor announced a breaking story and the screen switched to a perky blond reporting from the courthouse steps in Oakland. She looked straight into the camera, and with a sad shake of her head announced, "More surprising revelations about the prominent district attorney who was murdered two weeks ago in a convenience store robbery."

She brushed a loose strand of hair from her face before continuing. "Earlier today we reported that assistant DA Roy Walker was wanted for questioning in connection with the twenty-year-old murder of Miranda Saxton in Georgia. And just this afternoon we have learned that there is also an investigation under way into allegations that Walker tampered with evidence in a case before the courts, and that he struck a deal with a defendant to commit a murder." Here the reporter paused and again shook her head in disbelief. "The district attorney's office has so far refused to comment on these allegations. This is a breaking story. We hope to have more on our next newscast tonight at ten."

Diana flipped off the TV. Anger and disbelief churned inside her. The allegations couldn't be true. They couldn't. Roy wasn't a monster. He was gentle and conscientious and honest.

And, she thought with an ache in her heart, an imposter. He'd certainly had her fooled.

She didn't want to believe Jamal Harris any more than Thurston had, but what choice did she have? It was clear that Roy had been planning to meet him.

Moving from the couch to Roy's rust-colored leather chair, sinking into its buttery softness, she felt momentarily embraced by pleasant memories. She could recall the nights the two of them spent talking or reading or watching television. She could picture Jeremy in Roy's lap, first as a toddler and then as a young boy, their heads bent over a book while Roy read aloud— progressing over the years from *Dr. Seuss* to *Little House on the Prairie*—his softly resonant voice filling Diana with a sense of well being. Often Emily would join them, lying on the floor at Roy's feet with Digger at her side. All of the people Diana loved most in the world together in one place. Sometimes she couldn't believe she'd gotten so lucky.

She closed her eyes and felt a tear trickle down her cheek. *How could you have done this, Roy? How could you have?*

She wiped away the tears and looked around the room. In the aftermath of Roy's death, she'd moved his magazines and books from the side table, but the sense of his presence in the room remained strong. The watercolor on the far wall was his gift to her one Christmas. At first glance it looked to be a winter scene—a barren birch with a dusting of snow on its branches. On closer inspection, the first buds of spring were obvious, and on a low hanging branch, a robin with almost piercing eyes.

Diana had loved the painting from the first moment she'd seen it. She treasured it even more when Roy explained that robins had special meaning for him because his mother used to tell him, "Wherever there is a robin, there is hope. His song heralds the day with joy and the promise of life." And later, when Roy's mother knew she was dying, she told him to remember that whenever he saw a robin, he'd know she was there watching over him, and that she loved him. "Loved me very much," Roy had repeated to Diana that day with a catch in his voice. He explained that the sight of a robin still caused his heart to stir.

It was one of the few times he'd spoken of his mother, and Diana realized now, with a jolt, that he'd been talking about his real mother, Brian Riley's mother, who'd died of cancer when Brian was fourteen. The mother who'd given Brian the charm found with Miranda Saxton's remains—evidence that had further linked Brian to her murder.

If only Diana could sit down across from Roy and talk to him, let him explain.

If only he'd been the man she believed him to be.

If only, Diana thought with a bitter laugh, she could stick her head in the sand and make it all go away. But she couldn't. And first among the things she needed to deal with was bringing Emily up to date before she was broadsided by hearing about Roy from someone else.

Surprisingly, Emily answered the phone instead of letting it go to voicemail.

"Hi, Mom," she said, sounding not at all put out that Diana had called. A further surprise.

"Hi, honey. Are you somewhere where you can talk?"

"Sure. I'm studying with Dog."

"At the library?"

"No, in his room."

His room? Diana didn't like the sound of that but she bit her tongue. "Emily, I have to talk to you. It's going to be upsetting. Why don't you give me a call when you're alone?"

"Now's fine." Emily covered the receiver and mumbled something, presumably to Dog.

Maybe, Diana thought, it would be better that Emily had someone there when she learned about Roy, even if that someone was Dog.

"There's been more news about Roy," Diana said. "And it's not good."

"You mean about why he was killed?"

"No." Diana took a breath. "Roy Walker wasn't his real name. It was Brian Riley."

"Both are pretty bad, if you ask me." Roy's name had been the source of friendly joshing between Emily and her stepdad. Emily insisted "Roy" sounded old-fashioned and dull.

"That's not the issue," Diana said brusquely. "Twenty years ago Brian was a suspect in the disappearance of an eighteen-year-old girl. He was arrested but then released for lack of evidence."

"They thought Roy kidnapped her?"

"Kidnapped or . . . or something. Only he was going by his real name, Brian, at the time. My guess is that he changed his name to get a fresh start." *Changed his name* sounded better than *stole someone's identity.*

"But he didn't do anything wrong, right?" Emily's voice had risen a few decibels.

"I'm afraid he may have. The girl's remains were recently discovered, and there's evidence suggesting he was the one who killed her."

"What kind of evidence? DNA or something?"

"A charm he always wore. It was found with the girl's remains."

"No way. They say he killed her? As in murdered?" Emily's voice had grown almost shrill.

"I'm sorry to have to tell you this, but I didn't want you to learn about it from someone else. It's going to be in the news. There's bound to be coverage down there."

"Oh, God. The news?"

"And it gets worse."

"How could it?"

Diana explained about the allegations of misconduct, leaving out the bit about solicitation of murder. She figured Emily had heard enough as it was.

"Do you want to come home for a bit?" Diana asked. "I know it's a lot to deal with. You can use my credit card to book a flight. I think we should be together as a family."

"Let me think. I have an exam tomorrow morning I can't miss. But after that, yeah. I'll look at the flight schedule and let you know. How's Jeremy taking it?"

"I haven't told him yet."

"Poor kid." Emily paused. "And poor you. You didn't know about any of this before, did you?"

"No, I didn't. I'm still in shock, in fact. It doesn't sound like Roy."

"Maybe there's a mistake."

"I don't think so. We'll talk more when you get home, okay. I love you, Em."

"Love you, too." Emily spoke the words quickly and quietly, but it was better than her usual silent response.

Could it be that her daughter was finally growing up?

Emily called back minutes later. "I don't need a ticket," she said. "Dog is going to give me a ride. We should be there by seven or eight tomorrow evening, but don't hold dinner. We'll stop for a bite on the way."

Diana didn't want Dog there. She didn't want a stranger underfoot, much less her daughter's new boyfriend. And what about sleeping arrangements?

"We don't have room for him here," Diana explained. "Don't forget Chloe is staying in the den."

"Mom, we'll work it out. Don't worry. See you tomorrow."

Work it out. Diana cringed. She was *not* going to allow Emily to share her bed with a boy right there under her mom's nose. How could Emily suggest such a thing?

Allison called as soon as Diana hung up the phone. "I guess you saw the news? I didn't think they'd get it out there so soon. How are you doing?"

"I'm holding it together." Diana knew her voice suggested otherwise. "How's Jeremy?"

"He and Len are playing some computer game. We're making sure he doesn't watch TV."

"Thanks, Allison. I don't know what I'd do without you two."

"I just wish there was more we could do."

Diana set the receiver back in its cradle and forced herself to breath deeply.

And then she started throwing things.

She took one of Roy's prized CDs from the shelf and threw it across the room. And then another and another. Books were next. The thick, hardbound histories that Roy loved to read. His leather-bound atlas. The potboiler he'd been halfway through. They landed, pages askew, with satisfying thunks.

She picked up his boots from the front hallway and sailed them across the floor. His reading glasses, the stupid golfing magazines he refused to get rid of, even the pillows from his side of the couch.

"Damn you, Roy! Damn you!"

★ ★ ★ ★ ★

"Holy shit," said Joel, his gaze still glued to the TV at Best Buy. Then he looked over at Chloe, embarrassed. "Sorry, it kinda slipped out."

"No problem," she told him. No one had ever before apologized to Chloe for using what Rose called "inappropriate language." In truth, she found Joel's words quite apt under the circumstances.

The man next to them was talking to the Best Buy salesman about the pros and cons of plasma televisions. He gave Joel a sharp, disapproving glance.

"I never heard a murmur of anything about this," Joel said, lowering his voice. "Did you?"

Chloe shook her head. Poor Diana, no wonder she'd been in such a bad mood that evening.

"Wow." Joel turned his attention back to the TV. "I'm not going to be able to stick around for dinner, after all. I've got to get on this story. How about a rain check on the dinner?"

"That's not necessary. I understand you've got a job to do." Chloe was surprised to discover she felt genuinely disappointed.

"I mean it. I'm really sorry to cut out."

"I get it. Don't worry."

Joel looked at his feet. "No, really. Aside from the stuff with Roy Walker, I was looking forward to spending time with you."

"You were?"

"Yeah."

She was on the verge of asking why, but found herself giggling instead. "Okay already. You've got a rain check for dinner. Now get going."

He trotted off, then returned seconds later. "Hey, I forgot." He pulled an envelope from his jacket pocket. "These are some photos my cousin emailed me. He took them at the bonfire the night Miranda Saxton disappeared. I printed copies for Mrs. Walker. I thought she might want them. Although now, maybe not."

Chloe didn't feel much like eating and she certainly didn't feel like going to a movie. She picked up a hamburger and fries at a fast-food window, sat in her dark car in the parking lot, and nibbled at her dinner. Through the lighted window of the restaurant, she could see children running around and laughing in the play area. She'd once imagined herself and Trace and their two little ones (by then they'd have had a second baby) in this sort of setting. She and Trace would be smiling at each other over burgers as their children played.

It probably wouldn't have happened, Chloe realized. Trace didn't have the patience to be a good father. He was more interested in himself than anyone, and there were times he wasn't even nice. He'd even shot two people for no reason at all. But sometimes Chloe really, really missed him. How pathetic was that?

And what was she doing feeling happy because Joel Richards had been looking forward to having dinner with her? If she missed Trace so much, how come she wanted to see Joel again?

Too bad she'd never get that dinner. She'd be in jail soon. What would Joel think of her then?

Finally, when it was almost eight, Chloe returned to the Walkers'. A couple of news vans were out front, and a woman reporter in a red parka stood in the floodlight of a camera with a microphone in her hand.

Chloe ducked past the camera and ran to the front door. She entered the house quietly in case Diana was sleeping. One light shone in the darkened living room and it took Chloe a minute to make out Diana, sitting on the sofa. Around her, the floor was a mess, like someone had broken in and tossed the place.

"What happened?" Chloe asked. "Are you okay?"

Diana looked at her but didn't say anything.

"Shall I call the police? An ambulance?"

"I'm fine," Diana said. "Nothing happened. I just got a little angry and upset."

Chloe looked around the room. "You did this?" she asked in surprise.

"You must think I'm a nutcase."

"No, not at all." Chloe wasn't sure how much Diana wanted her to know, but with the reporters out front it was obvious something was going on. "I saw the news," she said.

"I'm sorry I brought you into all this. If you want to quit, I'll understand."

"No, I don't want to quit. Not at all." Chloe wasn't sure if she should be friendly and supportive, or say as little as possible. This was a situation that Rose, despite her lectures about good behavior and treating others well, hadn't covered.

"Can I do anything for you?" Chloe asked.

Diana shook her head. "I'm in shock, I think. Making this mess was stupid, but I was angry, and hurt. It was like I couldn't stop myself."

"I can understand that."

"It's just so awful. So unbelievable." Diana's voice sounded oddly disembodied, like someone talking in their sleep.

"First off, I learn that my husband had been using a stolen identity. For years. Then I learned that he's a murder suspect. And now they're saying he was a corrupt DA. That he tampered with evidence and tried to hire a hit man."

Diana smoothed the couch cushion with the flat of her hand. "I'm having trouble accepting it. I thought Roy was as honest as they come. Honest and honorable."

Chloe started picking books up off the floor.

"He wouldn't take gifts from anyone he did business with,"

Diana continued. "Wouldn't let others pay for lunch. As a DA he had to be above suspicion, he'd tell me."

"He must have been a good father," Chloe said. "I can tell from the way Jeremy talks about him. And he had to have been a good man for you to marry him."

"You'd think so, wouldn't you?" Diana stood. "Leave the mess. I'll clean it in the morning. What movie did you see?"

"I didn't. I went to visit a friend instead. And then ran into that reporter, Joel Richards."

"Ran into him?"

Chloe wondered if she'd done something wrong. "I think he was following me."

"Better him than the sharks out front, I guess. Are they still there?"

"There are a couple of vans. You sure you don't want me to pick up in here?"

"I'm sure. I'm going to head upstairs."

"Okay." Chloe started for her room, then turned. "Oh, I almost forget. Joel gave me an envelope to give to you. Some photos his cousin took, from the party the night that girl was killed. You know, a long time ago."

"The night my husband murdered her, you mean." Diana sounded weary. "There's no point tiptoeing around the truth."

"I'm sorry for all that's happened. You don't deserve this."

"Thank you. Unfortunately, life isn't always fair."

That was what Rose used to say, too. But Chloe had learned that lesson all on her own.

CHAPTER 38

Diana lay awake most of the night, tossing and turning and, above all, fretting. She was, in turns, sad, worried, angry, and confused. She tried to shut her mind down but that proved impossible. She tried counting backward from one hundred, only to find herself again dissecting every aspect of Roy's betrayal while the numbers faded into oblivion. Deep, cleansing breaths caused her mind to race faster, not slow down. And she could no more systematically relax muscle groups than she could fly to the moon. There was simply no quieting the torment that held her hostage.

From somewhere in the tangled web of dark thoughts sprang the darkest thought of all—that if Roy had hired a hit man, then she herself might have been the intended victim.

Oh, God. Had he been planning to kill her?

She sat up with a start, her heart pounding wildly.

No, not possible.

The very idea was unthinkable.

But there it was and it wouldn't go away.

Killing her made no sense. She and Roy had a good marriage, a child they both adored. Diana had no money of her own, so there was certainly no financial benefit to having her dead.

Or was there?

Her breath caught. Hadn't they purchased a life insurance policy for her when she was pregnant with Jeremy? It would help cover the expense of full-time help in the event anything happened to her. Diana had forgotten about the policy. She wasn't sure Roy had even kept up with the premiums, but he'd never mentioned canceling the policy either.

He'd already gone through a large part of their savings and borrowed against his own policy.

A wave of nausea rose up in Diana's throat. God, no. It wasn't possible.

Or was it?

She glanced at the bedside clock. The numerals glowed green in the dark, like the eyes of some alien beast: 3:19. In another few hours it would be time to get up. Surely with the light of day she'd see the flaw in her thinking, but for now, the pieces fell so solidly into place that she couldn't imagine any other explanation.

Shivering, she inched farther away from Roy's side of the bed. She remembered the nights she'd lain beside him, finding solace and strength in his soft breathing and the amorphous shape of his body under the covers. When she tried to call up that sense of calm now, she could only envision a monster's face—eyes hollow and mocking, mouth twisted in a cruel sneer. It was silly to let her imagination run away from her, but the image so frightened her she didn't dare put her hand out to prove to herself there was nothing in the bed next to her but a cold pillow.

Finally, Diana leapt out of bed and turned on the light. The image of the monster vanished, but not the unsettled feeling in her chest.

She grabbed her fleece robe from the back of the chair and slipped it on, then went to the window. The reporters were gone, but they'd be back. How long before one of them would come to the same conclusion she had?

She filled the tub with hot water, slipped off her robe and

nightgown, and stepped in. It had been ages since she'd taken the time for a soak, but she'd always found baths calming. And God knew, she was in need of calming. She swirled the water with her hand, then leaned back, closed her eyes, and tried to envision herself floating on a cloud high above the earth.

When she opened her eyes again, the water was tepid and the sky was no longer dark. She jumped out of the tub and dried herself off. Had she actually fallen asleep? She checked the time. She must have.

She was lucky she hadn't drowned.

Allison called a little after eight. Diana was in the basement looking for a plunger.

"I didn't wake you, did I?"

"I'd have to have actually slept in order for that to happen." Diana didn't mention her nap in the full tub. Allison would certainly have lectured her and might even have called adult protective services. That was all Diana needed at this point. The loony lady who was having a nervous breakdown.

"Things will get better, Diana. You have to remember that."

"It would be hard for them to get worse."

"So what have you been doing instead of sleeping?" Allison asked, trying for levity.

"Right now I'm trying to unclog a drain." Diana's relaxing bath had become this morning's headache. The drain had been slow for months, but Diana used the tub so infrequently that fixing it hadn't been a priority. This morning it hadn't drained at all. She wished now she'd called a plumber when she first noticed the problem.

"Leave it for Len."

"I can't ask him to do that."

"Why not? He likes to feel useful. He'll fix it when he drops Jeremy off. I've got a meeting this morning—an out-of-town guest is speaking at the school. It's a must-attend function I simply can't get out of. The department chair would have my hide if I tried."

"I can come get Jeremy. Len doesn't have to bring him here."

"But that won't fix your drain. Really, he won't mind. He should be there in about ten or fifteen minutes."

"Thanks. I appreciate that."

She felt uncomfortable, having Len deal with her cold bath water, but she doubted she'd be able to fix it herself. Minor plumbing problems had been Roy's job.

Roy had taken such good care of her, gone out of his way to please her. Could he actually have wanted to kill her?

When Diana got downstairs, Chloe was already cleaning up the wreckage from the night before.

"You don't need to do that," she said. It was embarrassing enough that Chloe had witnessed the mess. Diana still couldn't believe she'd lost it so totally.

"I'm happy to. And then, when you have time, there's something I need to talk to you about."

Diana's whole body tensed. Did Chloe want to quit, after all?

Diana couldn't blame her. Who wanted to live in the harsh glare of the media spotlight and rampant speculation? And Diana's acting like a lunatic couldn't have helped. But Diana's new job started on Monday. And she had too much on her mind already. She simply couldn't deal with finding someone new right now.

"Is it urgent?"

Chloe appeared to hesitate. "Not urgent, no. But I need to talk to you soon."

"This afternoon then. In the meantime, I have some errands I'd like you to run."

"Of course!"

They were legitimate errands, all of them, but Diana also wanted some time alone with Jeremy to explain about his dad. It wasn't going to be easy. She had no intention of spelling out every last sordid detail, but she had to prepare him for what he might hear from other kids.

Diana wrote out a list for Chloe, then set out the fixings for French toast and bacon, a meal she knew would please Jeremy. She set a place for Len, as well.

Jeremy arrived home clutching a large teddy bear in a 49ers jersey and helmet. "Len gave it to me," Jeremy said, grinning.

"The distributor is one of my clients," Len explained.

"Did you say thank you, Jeremy?"

"He sure did." Len patted Jeremy on the head. "We had a good time, didn't we, sport?" He turned to Diana. "Allison tells me you've got a clogged drain. Let me take a look."

"The upstairs tub. I hate to have you—"

"Don't be silly. It shouldn't take more than a few minutes."

"I was just about to fix Jeremy French toast, would you like some?"

"Sure. We didn't get much breakfast since Allison had to get to work."

Jeremy followed Len upstairs and Diana began frying the bacon. She didn't want to start the French toast until everyone was ready to eat. While the bacon sizzled, she picked up the envelope Chloe had handed her last night. The photographs from Joel's cousin he'd told her about.

It was kind of him to remember, but at the moment she was more interested in what Roy had been up to in the weeks before his death than what he'd done twenty years ago. Still, she took a quick look.

There were probably a couple dozen photos of college-age kids partying up a storm. Some were posed shots of small groups mugging for the camera, while others were candids, a number of them blurry and unfocused. As Diana flipped through them, she found one of Roy, or Brian as he was known then, sitting by himself on a log with a sour expression on his face. She couldn't tell if he was objecting to having his picture taken, as he often did, or if he was in a lousy mood. Diana recognized Miranda Saxton in a couple of the photos, including one where Diana was also able to pick Roy out of the group. So he hadn't been off sulking the entire night.

Kids laughing. Kids eating and drinking. Kids smoking. Photos that would be interesting to the people who'd been there that night, but not to anyone else. She was about to set them aside when she flipped to a photo of three bare-chested, grinning guys, their eyes glazed from too much to drink.

She did a double-take. Len? She held the photo under a light and looked more closely. Yes, definitely Len. She would have recognized him from the broad sweep of his forehead even if she hadn't previously seen photos of him as a younger man.

Len had been at the bonfire? Anger sparked in her chest. He hadn't said a word to her about being there despite their clearing of the air the other day over coffee.

She'd begged him to tell her the truth about Brian and she'd thought he had. He certainly hadn't painted the most flattering picture. Why hold back the fact that he'd seen Brian at the bonfire?

She turned off the burner under the bacon, and examined the photo again. Len was holding something out for the camera—a string or necklace of some sort. She grabbed her reading glasses for a closer look. It appeared to be a metal medallion about the size of a nickel strung on a leather cord.

The significance took a moment to register, and then she felt her pulse pound in her ear. She phoned Joel. He answered sleepily.

"I know it's early," Diana said by way of apology. "I'm sorry to bother you."

"No, that's fine. I thought you'd be avoiding the press right now."

"Chloe gave me the photos," she said, ignoring his comment. "I wasn't sure if you'd still want to see them."

"Tell me again what your cousin said about a scuffle that night. Something about some of the guys teasing Brian."

"Right. They tried to get him riled by teasing him about being a mama's boy and wearing some charm that was hers. They kept grabbing for it. I wasn't there, of course, but I can imagine the kind of comments they'd make." Joel paused. "And I can understand how Brian would feel upset."

Diana caught a hint of emotion in Joel's voice. She wondered if he'd been subjected to similar teasing at one time. "None of the other guys wore medallions or charms?" she asked. It seemed to her that kids today, of both sexes, wore all kinds of jewelry.

"I'd have to ask my cousin, but I'd guess not or they wouldn't have made such a big deal of it."

If Len had taken the medallion, if Brian no longer had it when he and Miranda left the party . . .

Behind her, Diana heard Len and Jeremy coming down the stairs. She thanked Joel and hung up abruptly. Her hands were trembling.

"All fixed," Len said, then caught the expression on Diana's face. "Is something the matter? You look upset."

"Why didn't you tell me you were at the bonfire the night Miranda Saxton disappeared?"

Len stopped short. "What are you talking about?"

"You were there, weren't you?"

"You're really coming out of left field here, Diana."

She knew she should shut up, but she was too angry. "You

and your buddies. You were teasing Brian, weren't you?"

"It was a party, for Christ's sake," Len growled. "We were having some good-natured fun. Not that Brian understood fun. He was a straight arrow even then."

"So you teased and taunted him?"

Len went to the sink and ran himself a glass of water. "You keep pushing me for the lowdown on what he was like," Len said, turning to face her. "I've tried to spare your feelings, but the truth is, he was a pain. Pranced about with a stupid charm around his neck like he was some hot-shit Indian chieftain or something. Oh, so special. And Miranda, she was all gaga over a fucking townie. He was screwing a senator's daughter, acting like he belonged. Like he was one of the crowd. Sure we razzed him a little. He deserved it."

Diana glanced at Jeremy, who was watching, bewildered. She was glad he didn't know they were talking about his father. "That charm," she said. "When you were teasing Brian, did you take it from him?"

Len looked uncomfortable. "That was a long time ago, Diana. What does it matter?"

"It's important."

"What are you getting at?"

"The police found it," she said hotly. "With Miranda Saxton's remains."

Confusion flickered across Len's face. "What? Who told you that? Roy? I thought you didn't even know Roy was Brian until after he died."

"It doesn't matter how I found out," Diana said. "It's a fact. The charm and leather cord were found with her remains."

The muscle in Len's cheek tensed. "If it's true, it's strong evidence he killed her."

"Except Roy didn't have the charm by the end of the night. You did." She wanted to hear him admit it.

Len set his glass on the counter, untouched. There was a darkness to his expression she'd not seen before. A steeliness in his eyes that unnerved her.

"Like I told Roy," Len said, "it was going to be his word against mine. Now that he's gone, it's my word, period."

Diana's heart slammed against her ribs. "You admit it then? You took Brian's charm?"

"Wherever you're going with this, Diana, you need to drop it."

She shook her head, stepped back a pace. "I can't. Don't you see what—"

Len laughed coldly and started pacing around the room, flinging his arms in the air. "God, you're as stubborn as he is. He wanted me to turn myself in, if you can believe it. Came to me a couple of weeks ago with an ultimatum. Like he was in any position to tell *me* to do the right thing. Mr. Rising Star DA with a stolen identity who's also the prime suspect in a murder. You think anyone was going to believe him? His whole career would have been down the tubes. The only sensible option was for him to keep his mouth shut."

Despite the coolness of the morning Diana felt flushed. Perspiration layered the skin at the back of her neck and under her arms. She had always been fond of Len, had stood up for him when Roy was dismissive. Now, finally, she understood what Roy had seen.

"But Roy didn't kill her, you did. You're not going to get away with this."

Len raised an eyebrow. A slow sneer spread over his face. "In fact," he said smugly, "it looks like I am."

Rage swelled inside her, hot and sharp. "It's not just Roy's word against yours."

Len laughed. "What? You think your accusations are going to amount to anything?"

Diana shook the handful of photos. "I have a picture of you with the charm. It was taken the night Miranda Saxton was murdered."

The color drained from Len's face. He grabbed the photos from Diana and started shuffling through them. "Where'd you get these? Did Roy have them?"

Diana moved closer to Jeremy. "Go out back," she told him. "Check on Digger."

Jeremy didn't move.

"Answer me!" Len yelled, his face inches from Diana's. "Where did these photos come from?"

"Go on," she urged Jeremy, giving him a gentle shove. "Get outside."

Len stepped between them, grabbed Diana by the shoulders and shook her, knocking the bottle of syrup to the floor in the process. "Who else has copies?"

Jeremy tugged ferociously at Len's belt. "Leave my mom alone."

Len shook him off. "Stay out of this, kid."

Diana tried to pull free but Len's grip tightened. She could feel his fingers digging deep into her flesh. He was half a foot taller than she and many pounds heavier. The more she struggled, the more he clamped down.

Jeremy came at him again, pounding his fists against Len's leg. "Let go," he yelled. "Stop hurting her."

Diana's fury raged. When Len eased his hold of her to fend off Jeremy, Diana made a grab for the phone. Len knocked it from her hand.

"You can't get away with this," she screamed. "I won't let you."

"Shut up, Diana. Just shut the fuck up."

Len shoved her hard. She hit the granite countertop square

on her spine with such force it took a moment to catch her breath.

Jeremy came at Len again, arms flying. Len smacked Jeremy hard across the face and Jeremy fell, his face bloodied, his breathing labored.

Diana shrieked.

Len slapped her. "Keep your mouth shut, you stupid bitch."

Diana's face stung and her eyes teared up. But it was seeing Jeremy, his face smeared with blood and his eyes full of fear, that sent her over the edge. She began biting and scratching. She barely drew blood. Len was bigger and stronger. She tried to knee him in the groin, but missed.

Out of the blue, his fist came at her head from the side, and connected. A solid punch the likes of which Diana had never imagined. Her vision blurred and she lost her balance. She tried holding onto the counter, but Len hit her again. And then again. One eye was already swollen shut and she tasted blood. It was like being pummeled by ocean waves, one after the other. She didn't even have a chance to grab a breath.

Len came down on the top of her head with both fists. Diana fell, striking her head on the granite as she went down.

She felt a sharp pain, and then nothing.

CHAPTER 39

Chloe pushed her grocery cart down one of the many aisles of produce at the Berkeley Bowl market, overwhelmed by the choices around her. She'd never seen a market like this. So big, with so many different kinds of fruits and vegetables.

Diana had been very specific about the kind of apples she wanted—six Fuji and three Pink Lady. Good thing, since there must have been thirty types of apples to choose from. Maybe more. And she wanted a pineapple, but there, she hadn't been more specific. Chloe counted nine different types of pineapple. How was she supposed to know which one to get? She'd always thought a pineapple was a pineapple, just like a lemon was a lemon, although glancing over now at the bins of lemons, Chloe realized she'd been wrong about lemons, too

She wondered fleetingly if this errand was some sort of test. It was certainly a change from Diana's previous "get milk and bread and whatever cheese looks good" sort of list.

And she had sent Chloe all over town to a handful of specific markets, which she'd not done before. The list reminded Chloe of the time she'd been on a scavenger hunt, at Abigail Tilson's twelfth birthday party.

She didn't mind chasing all over town for Diana, but she suspected Diana's real motivation was to get Chloe out of the house. She wished Diana had been more up-front about it and simply told her to skedaddle. That's what Chloe's mother used to do. "I'm expecting company," her mother would say when she wanted time alone with one of her men. "So skedaddle. Make yourself scarce."

Usually Chloe never made it farther than the tool shed in the backyard or the curb at the end of the block. Where was she supposed to go? It wasn't like they ever stayed any place long enough for Chloe to make friends. They moved so often she'd lost count of the places they'd lived. Four months here, six months there. Each time things were fine until her mother got behind on the rent, and then they'd move again.

And now she wondered if she might be on the verge of doing the same thing to her own child. What kind of fantasy world had she been in to think she'd be a good parent? She was a hard worker, but at minimum wage even hard work wouldn't get her very far. And if she was at work all day, who'd care for her baby?

Assuming they even let her keep the baby when she got out of jail.

If she got out.

She absolutely had to tell Diana about her role in Roy's murder. If she didn't, Weasel-face would, and he might hurt Jeremy first. Still, Chloe's stomach turned somersaults every time she thought about what she had to do.

She had been afraid to make her confession last night once she saw that Diana was already falling apart. Afraid, but relieved to have an excuse to put it off until morning. She was going to have to do it this afternoon, though. No matter what. Weasel-face's deadline was just about up.

Chloe again turned her attention back to the pineapples. Hawaiian Gold, Terra Gold from Costa Rica, or a Mexican Coastal—what did it matter? Diana wasn't going to forgive Chloe for what she'd done, no matter *which* pineapple Chloe selected.

★ ★ ★ ★ ★

With her list of errands completed and the car full of her purchases, Chloe pulled into the driveway. The news crews were gone, which was good. She'd hated having to walk past them, each time desperately afraid that one of the reporters would recognize her as Roy's killer. She hit the garage door opener to pull in, but nothing happened. She punched it again, muttered under her breath. The stupid thing probably needed new batteries. She'd have to haul all the bags up the front steps.

And then Chloe laughed at herself. She sounded like a spoiled teenager. Until coming to work for Diana she'd never even had use of a car, much less a garage and an automatic door opener.

She carried the bags to the top of the stairs and then into the kitchen. It took her five trips. All the while Digger was barking like crazy at the back door, wanting in. There was no sign of Diana or Jeremy. No note either, which was odd. And the kitchen was a real mess. Eggs had splashed on counter and dried, and an open bottle of syrup lay on the floor along with a fork. The loaf of bread was out on the counter, along with the carton of orange juice.

Was this a test also? Fine. She let Digger in, put away the groceries, and set about cleaning up the kitchen. She'd get it so clean and sparkling, Diana would tell Chloe she'd never seen it look so good.

All the while Chloe was aware of a low hum, like an engine or a car idling. She would have assumed it was from the news vans but they were gone. Maybe a delivery truck or a work crew? She looked out the window, at the street, but didn't see any unusual vehicles. So she went back to scrubbing syrup off the floor, which was harder than it should have been because Digger wouldn't leave her alone. He kept nudging her, sitting at attention, and then whimpering.

"I don't have time to play with you right now," she told him.

Where *was* everybody? Had there been an emergency? Maybe Jeremy had fallen and cut himself.

Or, Chloe thought with alarm, what if Weasel-face had come by? He said he'd give her until tomorrow to get the money, but maybe he'd become impatient. Her knees felt weak. She should have told Diana right away. Warned her that Jeremy might be in danger.

She couldn't stand the uncertainty. Where had they gone?

Finally, she decided to check the garage to see if the car was still there.

She went out the back door and through the open breezeway to the garage.

The minute she opened the side door, she was engulfed in a cloud of dark smoke. She choked and stepped back into the fresh air. Almost instantly, flames erupted near the rear of Diana's Lexus, which was still idling in the closed up garage. The source of the engine noise Chloe had noticed earlier.

Chloe hit the automated garage door opener on the wall but nothing happened. The problem had to be with the door itself rather than the remote. The only light filtering into the garage, and the only fresh air, came from the narrow garden door she'd opened. With the smoke so thick, it was hard to see. Holding her breath, she felt her way to the driver's side and tried the door. Locked. She tried the back door, then the passenger door. All locked. Through the windows she could make out Diana's form slumped in the driver's seat and a dark heap she assumed was Jeremy sprawled in the back.

Chloe pounded on the window, screamed their names.

The fresh air had fanned the flames and the fire was bigger now. Her lungs hurt and her eyes stung. She felt along the wall until found something heavy, a shovel from the feel of it. She took a swing at the passenger side window. The shovel bounced of the glass. She swung again, harder. With the same result.

She turned, ran inside, and frantically punched 9-1-1 into the phone. She gave the address first, she'd learned that much in eighth-grade safety class. And she remembered saying the words *fire, engine running,* and *two people locked in a car.* She thought she made a point to say that one of them was a child. It seemed like that was important and might get help there faster.

Chloe knew she sounded hysterical. She *was* hysterical, although she was trying hard to remain calm enough to answer the dispatcher's question. All the time in the back of her mind she was praying. *Please let them be alive. Please let them be okay.* And imagining the engine exploding, blowing the car and its occupants to smithereens.

The dispatcher was still talking, urging Chloe to stay calm. How could she stay calm? She had to do something. She dropped the phone and ran back outside. Neighbors had shown up. They were gathered in cluster, except for a man who'd unreeled the garden hose. "Where's the fire?" he asked.

"In the garage," Chloe screamed. "There are people inside. In the car."

The man dropped the hose and tugged on the garage door. Another man came to help him, and they managed to lift the door.

Chloe started to dart forward. Maybe she could find a hammer.

The widow from next door held her back. "You can't go in there," she said. "It's too dangerous."

Chloe was struggling to get past her when she heard the wail of sirens. She was so relieved she turned to the older woman and fell into her arms, sobbing like a crazy person.

She suddenly understood why Diana had wanted her out of the house for so long.

So she could kill herself and take Jeremy with her.

CHAPTER 40

Joel was in the rental car heading to the Alameda County district attorney's office when his cell phone rang. He knew it was illegal in California to answer it while driving, but what was he supposed to do, miss a hot tip on a breaking news story?

"Joel Richards," he said by way of greeting, and then felt a tingle of pleasure when he recognized Chloe's voice on the other end. But his initial delight gave way to confusion, and then dismay. Chloe was babbling. She sounded hysterical. She kept apologizing for calling him, saying she didn't know who else to call, and that it was terrible, whatever "it" was.

"Calm down," Joel told her. "Take a deep breath and start at the beginning."

He heard a shallow intake of air and then more sobbing. "They were in the car. Diana and Jeremy. I tried, I really did, but I'm afraid they might die."

"There was an accident?" Joel wasn't following.

"A fire," Chloe said.

"The car caught on fire?"

"Not the car. The garage."

Joel gave up. "Where are you?"

"At the hospital."

He breathed a sigh of relief. At least she'd managed to summon help. "Which hospital?"

"Summit."

"Are you hurt?"

"Not me." She sounded angry that he didn't get it. "Diana and Jeremy."

The conversation was going nowhere. "Hang on," he said. "I'll be right there."

He pulled over to the curb to Google directions to the hospital. He might push the limits of the law a little by talking on his cell phone while driving, but he wasn't stupid enough to search the web, too.

Joel found Chloe in the waiting room near emergency intake. Her clothes were smudged and grimy, her hair disheveled. Her right hand was swathed in a cotton bandage. When she spotted him, she ran into his arms like it was something she did every day. Joel was surprised at how right it felt.

"Tell me what happened," he said after a moment.

She stepped back, and began talking before she'd even taken a breath. "Diana sent me off to do errands and when I got home, no one was around. I went to the garage to see if the car was gone. There was smoke everywhere. I couldn't see. I couldn't breathe. The car's engine was running. The air smelled like exhaust and horrible burning stuff." She started crying again. "I couldn't get them out."

"They're alive, though. Right?" Joel was guessing, but they'd been brought to the hospital, which was better than the morgue.

Chloe sniffled and nodded. "There's some lung damage, though. At least I think that's what the doctor said. And I don't know what else. Allison is talking to him now."

"What started the fire? And why were they in the car?" Joel's instinct as a reporter was to get a clear sense of the event, and he was having a hard time understanding the bigger picture.

"I think," Chloe said, her voice so soft it was barely more than a whisper, "that Diana tried to kill herself."

"Good God, how terrible. Why? She wasn't the one who did

wrong, it was her husband." But hadn't Brian's dad killed himself out of shame for something his son had done? The tragic parallel wasn't lost on Joel.

"She was upset. Crazy upset. Or maybe . . . if she didn't try to kill herself . . ." Chloe looked at Joel with anguish. "I've done something really, really horrible."

A plump, middle-aged woman with light brown hair came over to them. Chloe turned to her. "Allison, how are they? What did the doctor say?"

"He wouldn't commit one way or the other. Lung damage, brain damage—he threw out a lot of words without saying much. Good thing you found them when you did, though." She paused and regarded Chloe with narrowed eyes. "Diana has abrasions on her face that have the doctor puzzled. They didn't come from the fire or the carbon monoxide. Did you and she have a fight this morning?"

"What? No. Of course not. You think—"

"Just asking. I'm sure the police will want to ask you, also."

"Why would I want to hurt Diana? I tried to save them!"

The woman, Allison, held up a hand, but her expression remained skeptical. "It's an obvious question, Chloe. Don't take it so personally."

Joel felt himself bristle on Chloe's behalf. How could anyone not take such a comment personally? But instead of standing up for herself, Chloe seemed to shrink.

"Anyway," Allison said, "we can pray that they'll both be fine. I'm going to head home for a bit, but I'll be back later to see how they're faring. And the doctor has my number. I take it you've already given a statement to the police at the scene?"

Chloe nodded. "And again to someone else at the hospital."

"Good. I left a message for Len. I don't know why he's not picking up. But he called me after he dropped Jeremy off at home and everything seemed fine then."

So that's who Allison was, Joel realized. Len Phillips's fiancée. Joel was dying to ask her a whole host of questions, but he knew this was not the time.

After Allison had left, Joel put his hand on Chloe's shoulder. "There's nothing you can do here right now. Why don't I take you home so you can get cleaned up, and then we'll get some lunch."

She looked down at her sooty jeans and shirt and seemed surprised to find that they were, in fact, dirty. "Yeah, I guess I'd better get some clean clothes. But no lunch. There's something the police need to know."

CHAPTER 41

Chloe's stomach was in knots and she felt queasy. She wished now that she'd listened to Joel and eaten lunch. But she'd wanted to talk to the police and get her confession over with before she lost her nerve. She'd thought it would go quickly—she'd tell them about her role in Roy's murder and about Weasel-face's threats, and they'd cart her off to jail. Her stomach might still hurt, but at least the confession would be behind her.

Instead, she and Joel had been hanging around the station now for almost an hour, waiting to talk to someone.

"Can't you ask them to call you?" he asked.

"No, I need to do it in person."

Finally, the uniformed officer at reception told her that Sergeant Crandall would see her, and directed her to a room down the hall. Joel came with her, without being asked. She was happy to have moral support, although she knew he'd be disgusted with her when he heard what she had to say.

Sergeant Crandall was a middle-aged black man with a frosting of gray in his closely cropped hair. Chloe thought she recognized him as one of the officers who'd responded to the fire, but she couldn't be sure. She remembered very little but the smell of smoke and the choking panic she'd felt.

He half stood as she entered the room and beckoned her over with a wave, although his was the only one of the half a dozen desks occupied. "Chloe Henderson? I've been trying to track you down."

Her heart jumped into overdrive. They'd been looking for her?

"Diana might not have tried to kill herself and Jeremy," Chloe said quickly, wanting to get the words out before they started interrogating her. "What I—"

"We don't think so, either," Crandall said.

Chloe's throat closed up. Allison was right, the cops thought she'd hurt Diana. "You think I did it?"

Crandall gave her a funny look. "That wasn't what I meant."

It had to have been Weasel-face. Chloe had trouble breathing. No matter how you looked at it, what happened was still her fault.

"I think I know who tried to kill them," she continued. "Not his name, but I can give you a description. And I can take you to him, or I will be able to. Tomorrow."

Crandall's brow furrowed. "You know where to find Len Phillips?"

"Len? No, why?"

"Jeremy Walker told the doctor something about—"

"Jeremy's able to talk? He's okay?" Relief flood Chloe's chest.

"I'm not a doctor, but that's my impression. He's asking for you. The hospital has been trying to reach you." Crandall eyed her critically. "Now, what's this about leading us to Len?"

"Not Len. A man I call Weasel-face. He was a friend of my ex-boyfriend. I think he might be responsible for what happened to Diana and Jeremy."

Crandall shook his head. "No, it was Len Phillips. The boy, Jeremy, told the doctor that Len hurt them, but won't say more without you there. He's too upset to talk. That's why we've all been trying to track you down."

"Len? But why?"

"That's what we'd like to find out. Apparently, Len tried to grab some photographs from the boy's mother, and then he hit her."

Joel spoke up for the first time. "Photos? The ones my cousin sent me?"

"Probably," Chloe said. "I gave her the envelope last night but she was too upset to look at them."

"Oh, shit." Joel looked white as a sheet. "That must be what she was talking about."

Crandall frowned. "You two want to tell me—"

"I should have seen it," Joel said, slapping his forehead with his open palm. "Damn, how stupid of me." He pulled his cell phone from his pocket and began scrolling the screen, then he handed it to Chloe. "Do you recognize Len in any of these pictures?"

They were snapshots of kids partying at the beach. She thought she recognized Len as one of three bare-chested guys hamming it up for the camera.

"This one," she said. "I'm pretty sure that's Len."

"What's this about?" Crandall demanded. He hadn't moved from behind his desk, but he was standing and looking agitated.

"The Miranda Saxton murder," Joel said. "If I'm right, it wasn't Roy who killed her, but Len. Diana asked me about the medallion. Look, Len's got it. I should have seen that myself."

"You want to start at the beginning?" Crandall said impatiently.

"You're familiar with the murder that took place in Georgia some twenty years ago, and that the main suspect, a boy named Brian Riley, was passing himself off as Roy Walker?"

"Yes. His identity hasn't been confirmed but I know that's the working theory."

"After Miranda Saxton's remains were discovered and Brian's medallion was with them, the case heated up again, but nobody knew where to find Brian. I got an anonymous letter a couple of weeks ago pointing me to Roy Walker. That's why I've come here from Georgia."

"You're a cop?"

"A reporter."

"Fantastic." Crandall rolled his eyes.

"I don't know about any of this dirty DA stuff that's just come out," Joel continued, "but I'm betting Roy didn't kill Miranda."

Crandall crossed his arms. "Why should I trust you?"

"I'm from Littleton. The police chief knows me. Give him a call."

"Explain to me why you think it was Len Phillips who killed the girl."

"I gave Diana printouts of pictures my cousin emailed me. He was at the party the night Miranda disappeared. Diana called me this morning, asking about the kids at the party and about the medallion. She must have seen what I should have. Except I've never laid eyes on Len before."

"Jeremy spent last night with Len and Allison," Chloe added. "I bet Diana confronted Len when he brought Jeremy home."

Crandall frowned. "Ever since hearing the kid's story about Len hurting them, we've tried to reach him. He's not answering his cell. His wife claims she doesn't know where he is either."

"Allison isn't his wife," Chloe said. "They just live together."

Crandall gave an exasperated sigh. "Whatever. Let's go talk to the kid. You want to ride with me or meet me at the hospital?"

"Chloe and I will meet you there," Joel said.

Jeremy was propped up in a big hospital bed. He had a swollen eye, scratches on his cheek, clear plastic tubing running under his nose, and an IV in one arm, but he was eating an orange popsicle and managed a smile when he saw Chloe.

"Hi, kiddo." Chloe hesitated, then kissed his forehead.

Jeremy's bottom lip began to tremble. "Where's my mom? Why isn't she here?"

"She's in her own room. She's going to be fine, but she's not as strong as you are so it's going to take her a bit longer to feel good."

This was a sanitized version of what the doctor had said, but he'd told Chloe the odds were that Diana would eventually be fine.

Chloe brushed Jeremy's hair from his forehead. "How do you feel?"

"I threw up. And my throat hurts. And also where Len kicked me."

"He kicked you?" Her voice rose in anger.

Crandall shot Chloe a look that she interpreted to mean *calm down*. She took a breath and let him take over with the questions.

"Can you tell us what happened?" Crandall said.

"Len brought me home from spending the night," Jeremy said with a glance at Chloe, "and we fixed a stuck drain in the upstairs tub."

"About him hurting you and your mom," Crandall prompted.

"They were in the kitchen. Len was yelling. His face was all red and he was making loud breathing noises. Then he hit my mom. I tried to stop him and he hit me, too."

Besides Crandall and Chloe and Joel, there was a second cop in the hospital room, and a doctor. A lot of people in a small space. Even Chloe felt intimidated. She wondered if Jeremy would clam up, but he seemed fine talking as long as she stayed by his side.

She felt sick. Len was a friend. How could he hurt Diana? How could anyone hurt an innocent kid?

Joel stood behind her. When Jeremy started talking about Len putting a smelly rag over his mouth, Joel gave Chloe's shoulder a reassuring squeeze. She was glad he was there.

"I think that's enough for now," the doctor said, stepping forward. "Jeremy needs to rest."

"Will you come back?" Jeremy asked Chloe.

"Absolutely." She couldn't tell her story to the police yet. Not until Diana was well enough to look after Jeremy. But she only had another day before Weasel-face's deadline. She'd have to talk to them soon, whether she wanted to or not.

Joel dragged her to the hospital cafeteria, saying they had to eat and, anyway, he was starving. When Chloe showed no interest in ordering, he sat her at a table, and went off to stand in line, returning with two sandwiches and two sodas.

"I hope you're not a vegetarian," he said.

Chloe shook her head. At the moment she wasn't interested in food, period.

"This is amazing stuff." Joel peeled the paper wrapper from a straw. "Len, who was what, like Roy's best friend? And it turns out he's the one who killed Miranda Saxton. If that's really the way it plays out. And what he did to Diana and Jeremy . . . wow. Like something in a movie."

"Len wasn't Roy's best friend. I don't think Roy even liked him much. It's Allison and Diana who are friends." At this point she didn't really care much who murdered some girl twenty years ago. She was worried about Jeremy and Diana.

"I wonder if Roy suspected Len." Joel picked up his sandwich, then put it down again with taking so much as a nibble. "Wait a minute, Diana said the private investigator Roy hired told her about the medallion being found with Miranda Saxton's remains. That means Roy probably knew too, right?"

Chloe nodded. She liked Joel, she really did, but he seemed in high gear, like something *good* was going on. All she saw was hurt and unhappiness.

"So he would have known that his friend, or whatever Len was, had killed her and let Roy take the heat for it."

"I guess."

Joel seemed to realize she didn't share his enthusiasm for unraveling the murder. He reached across the table and put his hand over hers. It was warm and comforting, and brought tears to her eyes. "Diana and Jeremy are going to be fine," he said. "You heard the doctor and you saw Jeremy. The kid's amazing. Everybody is going to be okay, thanks to you."

"Except for Roy."

"Yeah." That seemed to slow Joel down a bit. "That's a damn shame." He patted her hand and returned to his sandwich, finally managing to take a bite. "You aren't eating," he noted, when he'd swallowed.

"I've been so stupid, Joel. Not just stupid, bad. I've done something really, really bad. I'm going to turn myself in."

"Whoa, what are you talking about? You saved two people's lives today."

Chloe fixing her gaze on the speckled gray Formica table top. "I was there when Roy was shot. My boyfriend was the one who shot him. And I didn't do anything to stop him. I didn't even call the cops." She looked up. Her mouth was dry and her throat so tight she was having trouble forming words. "I drove him away from the store where it happened. He was hurt and I helped him escape."

Chloe sensed Joel pull away from her. He set his sandwich back on his plate. "And then you came around to flaunt what you did in Diana's face?"

Chloe could hear the revulsion in his voice. "It looks that way, doesn't it? But that's not how it happened. I was supposed to break into their house, get some money so we could run away. But when I was standing outside, Jeremy ran into me on his bike and Diana fell all over herself helping me. She was so sweet." Tears poured down Chloe's cheeks. "She's been nothing but good to me."

"Wait. Go back. Why did your boyfriend kill Roy?"

"I don't know. I mean, I only know what he said. He needed money to pay off some guys." Chloe wiped the tears with the back of her hand. "Trace set the robbery up with the clerk at the store. They were going to split the money. I don't think anyone was *supposed* to get hurt."

"But the clerk was shot too, wasn't he?"

She raised her eyes to look at Joel. "Trace wasn't very smart. Or very nice."

Chloe realized that on some level she'd probably always known that, but it suddenly seemed so clear she was surprised it had taken her this long to admit it.

Joel looked appalled. "What were you doing with a jerk like that?"

She made a stab at humor. "It seemed like a good idea at the time."

Joel simply stared at her. She could imagine what he must be thinking. She'd done terrible things and she deserved his contempt. But it still hurt.

"No, seriously," Joel said. "What could you have seen in a guy like that?"

"I thought he loved me." Chloe's tears turned to sobs. She couldn't help it. "I never had anyone love me before."

"You think someone who loved you would involve you in murder?"

"I said I was stupid. What's worse, I'm pregnant. With his baby."

Joel's eyes widened and he looked at her like she might be contagious.

"You see why I need to go to police and turn myself in." She reached for a napkin and blew her nose.

Joel pushed his plate away and tapped the edge of the table with his fingers. The muscles in his face were taut, his mouth grim. He didn't speak for so long, she expected him to get up and leave.

"You didn't know your boyfriend was going to shoot anyone, is that right?" he said at last.

"No. I didn't even know he had a gun. I was angry, really angry with him for all of it." Chloe knew it was more complicated than that, but she was certain of one thing—she'd never have gone along with a plan to rob a store or carry a gun.

"I tried to get him to turn himself in. But I never went to the cops myself. I'm an accessory or whatever. Trace told me that. He said I was as guilty as him, and we'd both be sent away. Maybe to death row. But I have to tell them now. There's this guy . . ."

She told Joel about Weasel-face and how he said he'd hurt Jeremy if she didn't steal from Diana. "At first I thought he was the one who set the fire."

"That's the guy you were going to lead the cops to?"

"Yeah. Tomorrow is the deadline." She put her hands over her face. Inside she was weeping rivers, drowning in sorrow, but her eyes had cried themselves out.

"I've made such a mess of my life," she said.

"It could be better," Joel agreed solemnly.

"I want to see Jeremy again, and then I need to talk to the police."

Joel looked at her hard. "Not without an attorney."

"Why? It won't change anything that happened."

"Chloe, you were an involuntary accessory. I don't know the law, but an attorney can explain things the right way."

"I know what I did."

"You've made stupid mistakes in the past. Don't compound them by making another one. Trust me on this."

Joel sounded like a little boy begging for a special treat. "Where am I supposed to find this attorney?" she asked.

"Let me make a few calls. I have a story to write for the newspaper, too. Just promise me you won't do anything right away. I'll meet you back here in a couple of hours, okay?"

"Okay." That would give her time to spend with Jeremy, and maybe to explain everything to Diana before she turned herself in to the authorities.

When Joel had finished eating and gone off to take care of what he needed to do, Chloe made her way slowly to Diana's hospital room. She couldn't remember ever feeling so sick and ashamed, and yet she needed to tell Diana the truth.

CHAPTER 42

It was the painkillers, Diana thought. That's why she was having such trouble sorting things out. Her mind, her heart, her moods—everything was a jumble. She'd thought now that she was out of the hospital and home again, the fog might lift.

So far, it hadn't.

Jeremy was safe. She was safe. That was what was important above all else.

And Chloe had saved them. That was important, too.

Diana looked at the clock on the bedside table. Late afternoon already. She'd been home from the hospital for several hours now. She must have fallen asleep because it seemed like she'd only just come upstairs to lie down and rest for a moment. That had to be the work of the painkillers. She never napped.

She closed her eyes again and ran her tongue over the jagged edge of her broken tooth. At least that didn't hurt. Every other part of her body did.

Her mind drifted back to Chloe's startling confession at the hospital yesterday afternoon. If Diana hadn't been floating on pain medication, hadn't come through so much, hadn't been so grateful to be alive and to know that Jeremy was safe, she might have reacted differently. But while she'd taken in Chloe's words and the grim details of Roy's last moments, what had spoken loudest to Diana was the anguish in Chloe's voice. And she remembered thinking that Chloe was a victim, too.

Allison said she should turn Chloe out. Said that Chloe had "used and abused her." Allison had become almost hysterical when Diana tried to explain she didn't see it that way. But Allison wasn't thinking straight about a lot of things right now, particularly things that involved Len and Diana. She refused to believe that he intended to hurt her and Jeremy. Or that he'd blackmailed Roy, even though the police had matched the dates and amounts of Roy's withdrawals with deposits made by Len into his own account, one Allison knew nothing about.

Diana wondered if their friendship was strong enough to survive.

Diana opened her eyes when she heard a knock on the door.

"Mom? Are you awake?" Emily poked her head in and then came to stand beside Diana. "How are you feeling?"

"I hurt all over but otherwise, I'm doing okay." She twisted her head toward the door. "Where's Dog?"

"Jeremy's showing him something."

Another surprise that had emerged from the ether of her stay in the hospital. Emily had come to her room last evening with a handsome, all-American boy who appeared a bit preppy for what Diana assumed would be her daughter's taste.

"Dog's a nickname," he explained when Emily introduced him. "It's my sister's fault."

"She wanted a dog and got a baby brother instead?"

"That, and it's my initials." He looked a bit abashed. "Short for Douglas Oswald Gainsworth."

"The third," Emily added. "As in the Gainsworth hotel chain."

Diana had already made the connection herself.

"Pleased to meet you," Dog said. "I'm sorry about the circumstances, though."

"I'm happy to meet you, too," Diana managed. "I'm sorry I won't be much of a hostess, but make yourself at home. Emily can show you around." Who slept where no longer seemed important. Her brush with death had given her a whole new perspective on life.

"Thanks, but I'm staying with my aunt in Berkeley."

"Berserkly?" That had been the medication talking, and Diana was instantly mortified. She and Roy might have laughed about some of the politics that came out of Berkeley, but she also had friends in Berkeley. She shopped there, for heaven's sake. She hadn't meant to sound critical.

But Dog laughed. "A rebel aunt," he explained. And Diana had liked him immediately.

Now, with just Emily by her side, Diana patted Emily's hand. "He seems like a nice boy."

Emily smiled and her eyes sparkled. "He is." Then she grew serious. "I'm so glad you're okay. I don't know what I would have done if something happened to you or Jeremy. I guess I never thought about that before."

"Nothing did. Nothing permanent anyway."

"But it made me realize. I don't appreciate you enough sometimes."

Diana hoped she remembered this conversation when the painkillers wore off. Assuming she wasn't imagining the whole thing. Emily was being so . . . so sweet.

"Dog and I are going out for a bit if that's okay," she continued.

"It's fine. Chloe's here, isn't she?"

Emily nodded. "I was wrong about her being a flake, wasn't I?"

"People are complicated, Emily. I think we're all a little flaky at times." Diana hadn't told Emily the whole story about Chloe, though she might, in time.

"Like me, is that what you mean?" Only Emily said it with a laugh, not the nasty accusatory tone of the past.

"And like me."

Emily kissed Diana's cheek. "Can I bring you anything before I go?"

"No thanks. I'm getting up now."

It was almost dark when Diana opened her eyes to another knock on her bedroom door. So much for getting up.

"I brought you some soup," Chloe said, setting a tray on the dresser. "You haven't eaten anything since you've been home."

"I can't seem to stay awake long enough to get out of bed. How's Jeremy?"

"He's fine. He and Emily's boyfriend seemed to really hit it off."

An older male paying attention to him would please Jeremy no end.

Chloe took a plastic bag from the tray she'd brought. "I have something for you," she said. "I know you must hate me—"

"I think maybe I should, but I don't. I hate that Roy's dead, that Trace shot him for no reason, that you would be with someone like that. But I don't hate you."

"I hate myself."

"You saved my life and Jeremy's, Chloe. Don't forget that."

Chloe bowed her head. "I should have saved your husband's. Or tried, at least. I'll never, ever forgive myself."

Diana was still sorting out her feelings, but when all was said and done, the anger she felt was directed at Trace and the senselessness of it all, not at Chloe.

"I took your husband's gym bag the day he was shot." Chloe continued. "We thought he might have had money in it."

Diana could see the pain and shame in her face.

"There was a gun. I threw it in a Dumpster to get rid of it. And some clothes that I threw away, too. But also, these things."

She handed Diana the bag. Inside was a set of keys, a photo

of a younger Roy with a slender, regal-looking woman she assumed was Roy's mother, and a second photo, of Len, Allison, Roy, and herself.

"I'm so sorry," Chloe said. "For everything."

Diana studied the photo of Roy, or Brian as he would have been known then, and the woman whose features he'd clearly inherited.

"I talked to my attorney again," Chloe continued. "He doesn't think the district attorney wants to 'go for blood,' as he put it. It turns out they'd like to resolve things as quietly as possible, but he says they'll want to check with you first."

Would they expect her to demand retribution? To insist that justice be done. Diana didn't see how sending Chloe to prison resolved anything. "I'm glad they're being reasonable."

Diana turned her attention to the keys Chloe had handed her. There were five in all. Four she recognized as house, office and car keys. She fingered a small, flat key she didn't recognize. The number imprinted on the face was the number of Roy's post office box. She experienced a rush of adrenaline.

"Chloe," Diana said. "I'd like you to do me a favor."

CHAPTER 43

Diana held the ordinary white envelope in her hands. Roy's handwriting, addressed to himself and postmarked the morning of his murder. It was among the letters Chloe had brought her from Roy's post office box.

She wanted to read it, and at the same time she was afraid to read it. Her memories of Roy were all she had. She didn't want them poisoned any more than they already were.

Finally, she took a deep breath and slipped her finger under the envelope's flap.

I have no reason to doubt Jamal Harris, but you never know about people, especially ones who end up in the justice system. And he's not going to like what I tell him. If things go bad, I want the record set straight—for Diana and Jeremy more than anything. And because I can't let evil triumph.

For the past nineteen years I have built a life as Roy Walker. A wonderful life. Much better than anything I ever dreamed possible. And it's because of this—because of the family I adore and professional achievements I'm proud of, that it's so hard to do what I have to do.

My real name is Brian Riley. I was born and raised in Littleton, Georgia, where the golden summer of my eighteenth year turned my life inside out.

I worked that summer as a busboy at one of the local resorts catering to rich and powerfully connected summer folks. Senator

Saxton was a guest at a nearby compound, along with his wife and his daughter Mia. To make a long story short, I fell head over heels in love with Mia (it seemed like love at the time, although I suspect it was little more than youthful passion that would have faded by winter). She professed to feel the same about me. She was funny and smart and beautiful, but there was a reckless abandon about her, too, an eagerness to throw off the confines of her privileged life and embark on adventure. She'd start Yale, her father's alma mater, in the fall, and she worried that she was being sucked even more deeply into a life she sometimes found suffocating.

Labor Day weekend, the last big fling of summer, there was a party on a private section of beach owned by the resort. Mostly it was the stuck-up college kids who summered in Littleton and called being a lifeguard a "job." A couple of them had been giving me a hard time all summer, calling me a townie and a redneck (although I think they meant "blue collar") and constantly pointing out that they were Ivy League while I wasn't even headed for college. One of them, Len Phillips, was especially nasty. He'd be a junior at Yale and had the hots for Mia. It stuck in his craw that she preferred me to him.

Everyone was drinking the night of the beach party, but those guys were really pouring them back. They were loud and obnoxious, and seemed intent on ramping up their efforts to belittle me, maybe because they saw it as their last chance. They would intentionally bump into me, spill their beer on my shirt, burp in my face. I'm sure you get the picture. And then Len started in about the silver sun pendant I wore on a leather cord around my neck. It had belonged to my mother, who died of cancer my freshman year in high school, and wearing it was my way of keeping her close. Len called it "sissified" and "dorky." He kept saying stuff like "Little townie misses his mama." I took a punch at him and missed. He grabbed the pendant and yanked it from my neck, then dangled it in front of me with a shit-eating grin on his face.

Mia told me not to let it get to me, that those guys, especially Len, were stupid and juvenile. Still, it was humiliating. And the fact that Mia felt she needed to stand up for me made me feel even weaker. Finally, she suggested we take a walk along the beach. It was a beautiful, warm evening. I should have been in seventh heaven, but the teasing from earlier in the evening kept getting under my skin.

We walked and talked and messed around until almost midnight. I thought we should go back, but Mia kept saying no, this was her last night as a "free soul," and she wanted it to go on forever. I guess that irritated me, too, because anyone as beautiful and rich as she was, anyone who had as many con-nections as she did, was freer than I'd ever be.

"But I'm not free," she insisted. "My whole life is rules and expectations." She held her hands to the stars and said, "Like I've never made love on the sand under the open sky. Let's do it."

And maybe to be contrary, or maybe because I had the sense I was being used, I told her no. She got mad, we exchanged heated words, and I left her there alone, which I should never have done. But I was angry and hurt, humiliated by the guys at the party, and to tell the truth, a little drunk. I spent the night in a boathouse near one of the docks, feeling sorry for myself and wondering if I should tie weights to my legs and drown myself.

That was the last I saw of Mia. Her father reported her miss-ing the next morning. As you can imagine, there was a huge search for her—and all sorts of speculation. Had she been swept out to sea? Had she run away, which was, to my mind, not inconceivable given her eagerness to experience life. Or had she met with foul play? And since I was the last person known to have been with her, suspicion quickly turned to me. Mia's body never turned up, but I was questioned, and eventually arrested, although I was never charged, much to the anger of the power elite in Washington and most of the local townspeople, my dad included.

He was the sheriff in Littleton at the time, and although he'd excused himself from the active investigation, he bent over backward to show that he wasn't covering up for his son. We'd never had a warm or close relationship, but his lack of support stung. He assumed I was guilty and accused me of disgracing him and blackening his reputation. He said he couldn't hold his head up anymore because of me. The next January, he shot himself.

That's when I left town. I drove away one afternoon and never looked back. I traveled, working odd jobs along the way, and eventually found myself in California, where I decided to make a clean break from my past. I adopted a new name (not legally, I'm ashamed to admit now) and enrolled in community college. I worked hard, I studied hard, and to my amazement, I did well. Well enough to earn scholarships that helped pay for my subsequent education. I graduated from law school and took a job with the DA's office.

Life was good to me. My career was on track, I had a wife I adored, a lovely stepdaughter, and then a son of my own. I couldn't have asked for anything more. But I realize now, it was a life on borrowed time.

A year ago my wife's best friend, Allison Miller, introduced us to a guy she'd begun dating. I recognized Len Phillips right away, and I could tell from the smirk on his face that he not only recognized me too, but that he'd sought me out, a fact he later confirmed. He'd seen my photo in a law journal he happened to read because a customer at the car dealership where he'd taken his car for service had left it behind.

He saw a gravy train. It didn't start out as blackmail, although we both understood that's what it was. He agreed to keep quiet about my past—no point making things hard for you and your wife, he said—but he started hitting me up for money. At first, he offered excuses like he was a little short until the end of the month. And then he wanted to "borrow" money for a birthday present for Allison (which I noticed she never received). If I dragged my feet, he'd remind me that he had the power to bring me down.

To my shame, I paid up. Every time. It was a little like being the frog in a pot of boiling water—the heat got turned up slowly. The amounts he asked for were small at first, and it wasn't hard for me to find the money. But he raised the temperature little by little until he was asking for amounts that I couldn't easily come by. Before I knew it, I was in over my head.

So many times I came close to telling Diana the truth. I told myself I'd come clean and take what came. But I loved Diana. I loved Jeremy. I loved my job. I loved the life I'd built. I didn't want to throw it all away.

And then Miranda Saxton's remains were found. I knew the investigation would heat up again, and authorities would begin looking for me. Len recognized that as well, and he began demanding more and more money.

Years ago I'd hired a private investigator to follow developments in Mia's disappearance. The guy kept his ear to the ground. He learned of a charm found with Mia's remains and sent me a photo, which he'd obtained from a buddy of his on the force. He'd been told it was evidence that a man by the name of Brian Riley had killed her.

Once I saw the pendant, I knew what had happened. I flew into a quiet rage. All the time Len had been milking me for money, he'd known that I was innocent because he was the one who killed Mia.

I confronted him and he laughed in my face. Said nobody would believe me even if I was stupid enough to come forward with some "cockamamie" story that put the blame on him rather than me. We both knew who had my pendant that night, but there was no proof. And he doubted anyone who'd been there would remember, even if they'd noticed at the time.

He insisted I had nothing to gain and much to lose by speaking out. Sadly, he was right.

I am a rational man, a man who believes in the law, but what Len did was so grievous, so evil, I began to fantasize about revenge.

I knew Jamal Harris from his previous brushes with the law. He'd cooperated with us in the past by pointing the finger at gang leaders, but now he was facing serious time himself. In one of our conversations (yes, technically they are interrogations, but as a DA you can build an odd sense of rapport with repeat offenders), I mentioned some guy who had done me wrong. Jamal said he'd get rid of him for me. Just like that. I thought he was kidding but he was serious. One thing I've learned about guys like Jamal, they rarely joke.

We're going to meet this afternoon and I'm supposed to give him Len's name. He'll "do the deed," as he puts it, and in return, I'll hand over some cash and his freedom—from the current charge at any rate. I've made it clear I can't promise help in the future.

But in the last forty-eight hours I've discovered that Diana is right when she says my world lacks shades of gray. Killing someone is wrong, even if I'm not the one pulling the trigger, and even if that person is as despicable as Len. As much as I detest him, I can't be a party to murder.

I'm going to meet Jamal and explain my change of heart in person—I owe him that much. I will tell him our deal is off. I'll do what I can for him with regard to the current charge, but the evidence I made go away is coming back. And then I'm going to tell Diana the truth. Diana and the authorities. I doubt they'll arrest Len—it's his word against mine, after all—but I'm hoping for the best. I'll be disbarred and God know what else. Diana may leave me, although I pray that's not the case. It's not a good solution, but I think it's the only one I can live with.

I think, but I'm still not sure.

What does it say that I am sending this letter to myself? It shows, even to me, that I lack the strength of my convictions. Should I, at the last minute, decide to give Jamal Len's name, I can simply retrieve this note from my postal box and burn it. No one will be the wiser.

Will I do that? I hope not. I don't think so. But you never know.

Diana's eyes were wet by the time she came to the end. Roy may have doubted his resolve to do the right thing, but she didn't. He'd have told Jamal the deal was off.

Later today, she'd call Alec and maybe even the press. She wanted the truth known. But first, she needed to explain to her children and Chloe. Yes, Chloe.

A breeze stirred the bare branches outside Diana's window. She saw a robin sitting on the top branch with his head cocked her direction. He seemed to be staring back at her. When she walked to the window, he chirped several times, then flew past the window and off into the blue sky.

Whenever you see a robin, you'll know I'm there, and that I love you.

"I love you too, Roy," she said quietly. "And I miss you so much."

CHAPTER 44

Eighteen months later

A gentle breeze blew through the classroom window, ruffling pages of the children's picture book Chloe read to the assembled three-year-olds sitting at her feet.

"Oh, dear," Chloe said, holding the book face out. "What should the little bunny do?"

"Run," the class shouted. "The wolf is trying to trick him."

Chloe loved her job as a nursery school assistant. And she loved the classes she was taking toward her degree. It would take years to finish, but she didn't mind. Every day was a blessing.

When story time ended and the children had gone home, she took a moment to reread the letter from Diana. She mostly kept in touch by email, but when Jeremy wrote Chloe letters, Diana usually added a few words.

Jeremy had drawn her a picture of Digger and written in large, block letters: I MISS YOU. PLEASE COME FOR SPRING BREAK.

Diana had echoed the invitation in her own note.

Chloe would try to make the trip, at least for a few days. She'd have a chance to see Velma, too, the only person aside from Diana and Jeremy she missed from her old life.

She couldn't believe how much had changed in one year. She'd spent last spring working in a soup kitchen, serving dinners to the poor—part of the community service she'd been ordered to do for her involvement in the robbery that ended Roy Walker's life. She still felt she deserved stiffer punishment, but Diana had not only spoken out in her behalf, she'd convinced Chloe that living a good life and helping others was a better way to make things right.

She'd helped Chloe see a lot of things more clearly, in fact.

Chloe's phone rang as she was packing up her things.

"How about dinner tonight?" Joel asked.

Chloe hesitated. "I should study."

"You can't study all the time."

"There's so much I don't know."

"But so much you do know."

"You're sweet." They usually saw each other on weekends, except for the one weekend a month Joel went back to Georgia to see his dad. Chloe understood he'd asked her out tonight because he was worried she'd be feeling sad.

Her baby girl was one year old today, but Chloe wouldn't be the mom clicking pictures and cooing, "I love you." She'd given her daughter up for adoption to a wonderful couple who could provide for her and give her the sort of life every child deserved. It was the hardest thing Chloe had ever done, but she knew that for once in her life, she'd made the right decision.

"If I'm so sweet," Joel said, "how come you won't have dinner with me?"

"Did I say I wouldn't?"

Joel laughed. "Good. I'll pick you up about six. How's that sound?"

"Perfect."

Chloe wasn't living with Joel, she'd had enough of that. But she had moved to Los Angeles when he landed a job with the *Times* following his award-winning series on Roy Walker and the Miranda Saxton murder. She liked Joel a lot. She thought she was probably even in love with him, but she enjoyed her independence. She shared a small student apartment with another girl and was slowly making friends from her classes. There was a lot of life Chloe wanted to experience before she settled down. And when she did settle, she was going to do it right. Someday, if she was lucky, she might even end up with a nice house in a nice neighborhood with trees and birds and a grassy yard for her kids to play in.

Diana was at her office desk, having just responded to Emily's latest email, when Jack Saffire stopped by, something he did several times a day. He'd lost his wife to cancer three years earlier so he understood some of what she was going through. Diana had always found him easy to work for, and when she'd started at the paper full-time, it had been an easy transition from boss to friend.

Emily teased her about Jack, claiming she could see a romance brewing. Emily was wrong, of course. Jack was a dear friend, nothing more, but Diana looked forward to their occasional dinners together, as well as their conversations in the office.

"What do you hear from Emily these days?" he asked.

"She just emailed me. She made the women's JV volleyball team."

"Hey, that's great."

It *was* good. Many things about Emily were good these days—better than they had been in years past, at any rate. Emily was still seeing Dog, but not exclusively. Her grades were decent, she had friends, and while she still took offense easily, she usually apologized once she calmed down. Baby steps maybe, but they were steps in the right direction.

Jack sat on the edge of Diana's desk. "We've been getting

good reader feedback on that foster care article you wrote last week."

"I'm glad." It had been Chloe who had opened her eyes to the realities of foster care. In fact, Chloe had given her a new take on many things. Theirs was a convoluted relationship—one Diana had trouble explaining to others. Sometimes, even to herself. But it felt right, and that's what mattered.

"You think maybe you could do a follow-up piece?" Jack asked.

"Absolutely." She enjoyed the administrative side of newspaper work more than she'd expected, but she'd leapt at the chance to start writing again. That felt right, too. She'd only done four stories so far, but she was pleased that Jack was receptive to having her do more.

"I don't suppose you'd be interested in taking on an assignment covering Len Phillips's trial?"

"No," Diana said emphatically. "Absolutely not."

"I didn't think so. Still, it would be a great angle."

But not one Diana had any interest in providing. Len had managed to evade authorities for almost five months before being picked up in Arizona. A motion for extradition to Georgia was pending, although it was unclear if there was enough evidence to convict him of killing Miranda Saxton. And he was about to stand trial in California for the attempted murder of Diana and Jeremy.

He admitted to fighting with Diana, but claimed to have stomped off after their argument, having done nothing more than strike her. Someone had tried to kill Diana and her son, he said, but it wasn't him. And since Diana could remember nothing that happened after their fight in the kitchen, it was Jeremy's testimony that would make the case. Len had hired one of the area's best defense lawyers, no doubt with money he'd coerced from Roy, and Diana had been warned they were likely to go after Jeremy with everything they could muster.

Thurston told her not to worry, that Jeremy would make an excellent witness. "We'll get a conviction," he assured her, but Diana got livid every time she thought about it.

The only silver lining, she supposed, was that Allison was finally able to see Len for what he was. Their friendship had suffered, and Diana missed the easy spontaneity of their earlier relationship. But they still talked, and things were getting better between them.

Jack looked at his watch. "Hey, it's almost lunchtime. How about we grab a bite to eat?"

"Sorry. Today's a short school day and I promised Jeremy ice cream at Fenton's."

"Another time, then," Jack said, clearly disappointed.

"You're welcome to come along," Diana added.

He smiled. "I'd like that. It's been years since I've eaten ice cream for lunch."

ABOUT THE AUTHOR

Jonnie Jacobs is the best-selling author of thirteen previous mystery and suspense novels. A former practicing attorney and the mother of two grown sons, she lives in northern California with her husband. Email her at jonnie@jonniejacobs.com or visit her on the web at http://www.jonniejacobs.com.